TENDER TOUCH

Jack took hold of Emily and carefully turned her to face him. The sight of her tearstained face unstrung his emotions. "Emily, what you've said is not true."

"It is," she argued with a weary resignation. "It's what Neil thinks. It's what those men thought. No white man will ever respect me, knowing what I've been through. And no man is ever going to want a woman like me."

"I do."

He said that quietly as his hands came up to frame her face. And even as she began to shake her head in denial, he leaned forward to prove it was true. His mouth touched to hers and pressed gently until the fit was perfect and complete. Then he angled his head slightly to cause an exquisite friction. Emily made a soft sound of wonder, and as he pulled back, she was gazing up at him with such longing that his will caved in around his heart. His fingertips caressed her damp cheeks tenderly.

"I know what it's like to be shut out by circumstance, Emily. I know how much it hurts when those you love don't love you back. But you can't give in; you can't give up. It'll get better. You have to give it time."

"I want to believe you, Jack," she said, in a fragile voice.

"You have to believe me, 'cause it's true."

"Then prove it to me again, Jack. Please make me a believer."

She reached up to lace her hands behind his head, drawing him down to where ̄ ̄ ̄ ̄ waited.

DANA RANSOM

TEXAS DESTINY

ZEBRA BOOKS
KENSINGTON PUBLISHING CORP.

ZEBRA BOOKS are published by

Kensington Publishing Corp.
850 Third Avenue
New York, NY 10022

Zebra, the Z logo Reg. U.S. Pat. & TM Off. The Lovegram
logo is a trademark of Kensington Publishing Corp.

First Printing: August, 1994

Printed in the United States of America

For the Love Designers Writers Group,
who unfailingly inspire me
at their Autumn Authors Affair,
and who have introduced me to some
wonderful people

One

The screaming went on for hours. He'd had no idea they could keep a man alive that long once such a level of suffering had been attained. He'd heard of it, of course. But he'd never been forced to listen while it was being done.

He was a Texas Ranger. That, in itself, said much more about his character than he ever would. He was brave, though not necessarily conscious of his own courage, any more than he was aware of fear, or of the danger of his own situation. He'd been ranging since he was sixteen and had been in the thick of it probably twenty times during each of the following four years. He'd faced down rustlers, outlaws, hostiles, and Mexicans with a cool head and an unswerving sense of right. He never considered the odds, and he always rode into battle as if he was invincible. All the rangers thought of themselves that way. They had to, or they wouldn't be able to look death in the eye with a calm indifference. He wasn't a man who admitted to being afraid of anything, but up until this point in his young, necessarily hard life, he'd never had to lie helpless in the broiling West Texas sun with two Apache arrows protruding from his thigh while Indians committed nameless atrocities on his partner.

Jack Bass wasn't going to let them do the same to him. They'd stumbled upon the camp by accident, he and Fos-

ter Richards. They hadn't been looking for trouble, but it
was quick to find them. They'd ridden hell-bent with better
than a dozen braves in pursuit over the rocky countryside.
He'd taken the arrows to the leg in rapid succession: if an
Apache had the opportunity to hit a man once, more were
sure to follow. They were that good with the bow, that fast.
He'd tried to hang on, but woozy with pain and the shock
of it, had fallen hard as they'd rounded a sharp bend in the
rutted canyon. His horse had taken a shaft in the hindquar-
ters and, mad with pain, run on without him, which was
why the Apache must have thought he'd gotten away.

Seeing his comrade go down, Foster had reined in, meaning to come back for him. A ranger never left one of his
own behind. They'd shot him off his saddle and swarmed
before he could get his feet under him. The spiny ocotillo
that broke Jack's fall also concealed him as he lay too
stunned to move to his partner's aid. By the time his senses
returned to him, the Apache had taken Foster back to their
campsite, and then the screams started up.

Jack was too far away to see what they were doing. He
wasn't sure he wanted to know. Just imagining was bad
enough, when it came to the torturing of a man he'd shared
his chuck with for over two years. The arrows were deep
in his right leg. He couldn't pull them out, nor could he
stand. Otherwise, he would have somehow managed to get
close enough to end it with a well-placed shot. There were
too many braves for him to fight and it was the only thing
he could have done for his friend. But he couldn't get up.
He could do no more than weep in silent frustration as
those agonizing cries continued. That, and wonder how long
it would take before they came looking for him.

He lost track of how long he'd been lying there, his face
toward the cloudless sky. It was so hot, the sweat had been

cooked right out of him. He couldn't have cried another tear over the fate of his friend if he'd wanted to. He was too sick with fever and grief even to care if he was slowly dying . . . until he heard the sound of movement close by. And he knew discovery was only a heartbeat or two away.

When he was a boy, he'd asked his uncle why the Apache were so cruel. The answer had troubled him. He hadn't understood it then. He was told that in order to survive in the harshness of West Texas, the Apache needed to draw spirit power from all the things around them. A man's power was the strongest of all, and it was at its peak at the point of crossing over into the world of shadows. The longer he was kept at that threshold, the more those around him could absorb from him. That, and the more simple pleasure of revenge, were why the Apache tortured their captives to death. And suddenly, in his fevered state, Jack was furious. The thought of a passel of murderers gathered around whittled away at him. No way was he going to allow it. He wanted his mama to have something she'd recognize when it came time to bury him.

He heard the sounds again, footsteps coming closer, and he knew he had just seconds left.

"God forgive me," he whispered hoarsely, as he dragged up his Colt revolver. Conjuring the faces of his family, he jammed the barrel against the roof of his mouth before he had time to do much thinking about it, scenting acrid powder, tasting gun oil, squeezing his eyes shut as he squeezed the trigger back.

Click.

No . . .

Frantically, he tried again and again, but each time there was the impotent snap of the hammer upon an empty chamber. He let the pistol fall to his rapidly jerking chest. Oh, God, what was he going to do?

He and the Apache sighted one another at the same moment. He heard a startled gasp as he brought his pistol up to bear in a defensive move.

"Don't make a sound or I'll blow your head off," he rasped out, not knowing if the other spoke English, but certain the meaning was clear.

"Don't shoot, Ranger. I can help you."

A woman's voice. In perfectly accented Texan English. He blinked, not trusting the clarity of his mind. A white woman? Though his vision was cloudy, he could make out the traditional squaw dress upon a nicely shaped form, dark hair, darkly tanned skin. His gun hand began to wobble in his weakness and confusion. With surprising speed, she kicked at it and the revolver went flying. He let his hand drop to the dust and his eyes sagged closed. There was no use pretending he was a threat to anyone.

"Wasn't loaded anyway," he muttered faintly. He waited, breathing harshly, waiting for her to yell out an alarm or to run back to the camp and return with warriors eager for his hide. He wasn't prepared for the sudden cool chill of water against his brow, upon his temples, over his eyes, and finally against his cracked lips. He sucked at the cloth greedily, drawing moisture to ease his parched throat. He moaned in protest when she took it away.

"That's enough for now. Rest easy. I'll get you some more."

He looked up into eyes of a startling green. The rest of her features were obscured by the blinding halo of sunlight framing her. All he could manage was a weak, "Thank you." Then he heard her begin to rise up, and his hand shot out to snag her wrist. "Where are you going?"

Her palm slid over the back of his, rubbing the fierce tension from his grip. "It's all right. I'll be right back. You can trust me."

"Why? Why are you doing this?"

She was silent for a moment, as if she wasn't quite sure, herself. "Because you have a nice face."

He gave a wobbly laugh. That was a helluva reason, but he wasn't going to discount it if it saved his life. "An' I'm a nice man, too." He nodded toward the distant camp. "Too nice for what they got in mind for me."

She smiled briefly, grimly. "On that, we're in agreement." She moved his hand from its imprisoning circle, coaxing it down to rest upon his chest. "I'll be back."

Jack had no choice but to believe her. Something in her beautiful eyes and that faint smile said he could.

Time faded in and out, his perception of it growing weaker, just as his comrade's cries for mercy were growing weaker. A white woman with the Apache. His mind was too hazy to hold to the curiosity. When was she coming back? Would she be alone? He'd just about given up on her, then he heard the shush of moccasins and felt the gentle touch of her hand upon his brow. He struggled to focus on her somber expression. Her voice was hushed and urgent.

"I've got a horse and some water. I'm going to have to cut those arrows out so you can travel. If they're not taken care of, the heat of your body is going to dissolve the sinew that holds the arrowheads on the shafts. Then it might cost you your leg."

No need to think on it. "Cut them out."

She had a knife, a long-bladed, wicked-looking thing, and she held it like she knew how to use it. "What's your name?" she asked, as she ripped through the denim of his jeans.

"Jack." She bumped one of the arrows and he gasped. Her hand was instantly over his mouth.

"Shh!" Then her hand eased off, stroking along one sweat-dappled cheek. "I'm sorry, Jack. There's no easy way to do this."

"I didn't mean to yell out," he mumbled. "I won't do it again."

"Well, Jack, just in case you aren't as brave as you'd like to be." She wet his bandana with the water from the pouch she carried, wadded it up, and wedged it into his mouth. "Bite down."

And she went right in to cutting.

His leg jerked violently. She had to sit on it to hold him still. His other heel dug furrows in the hard-packed ground and his head tossed frantically from side to side. But he was quiet. The first arrow was imbedded in the meaty swell of his outer thigh. With a little careful wiggling and a cautious tug, it came free in one piece. The second was higher up, closer to the hip, and it went deeper, scraping bone. She dug until his face completely drained of color, and his eyes rolled back white. It was too deep and she hadn't the proper tools for removal. Too much more prodding and poking and she ran the risk of severing something vital. She was going to leave it, but her hand moved along the hard contour of his thigh in appreciation. What a shame it would be to lose such a finely made limb.

Jack was panting around the wadding of cloth, but his gaze was aware. He saw her hesitate and he nodded for her to go on.

"Hang on, Ranger. I'll get it this time."

And she began her probing. She'd reached bone when she felt him abruptly slacken. Then it was easier to do what she had to. No sooner had she drawn the arrow from his leg than the wicked triangular tip dropped off, falling free of the shaft.

"That was close, Jack," she sighed, and she began to bind up the wounds with a quick efficiency. By the time she'd tied the last binding, he started to come around. She took the wadding from his mouth and allowed a small trickle of water to replace it. He swallowed and lifted up for more. With her hand behind his neck for support, she let him drink his fill, then settled him back onto the hard Texas soil. There was no time to allow him a proper recovery period.

"Can you ride?"

He nodded.

"Where are you out of?"

"Ysleta."

Her lips pinched together. That was a long haul for a fit man. But that wasn't her problem. She was saving his life. He couldn't ask more of her than that. He couldn't expect her to risk more just because her skin was white. She was only helping him because she had no heart for the savagery of her adopted people. That was why she'd been out walking alone in the tangled Texas brush, trying to block out that poor man's screams. If Jack was found, they would do the same to him as they had to his partner, and to save him from that, she was willing to go only so far. She had more than just herself to think of.

"Be much obliged if we could hurry."

"Grab on, Ranger."

Jack looped his arm around her shoulders and she straightened with surprising strength, dragging him up until he could get his sound leg under him. The change from horizontal to vertical emptied his head of blood, and for a moment, it was all he could do just to lean into her, clinging to consciousness by the fingernails. His legs were shaking, and fever had the landscape swooping like an eagle in full flight. But he held to enough presence of mind to mutter, "Sorry to be such a bother to you, ma'am. Be all right in a second."

She hoped so. Every second of delay was a second closer to discovery. She had to get him on the horse and safely away. "Come on, Ranger. Walk with me. Walk with me."

He tried. His wounded leg was useless, and the other as uncertain as a foal's. She could feel the effort in the way his breathing chugged, gusting along the curve of her throat as he clung to her for balance. But he made no complaints about the pain he had to be feeling as they moved awkwardly toward the scrubby little buckskin that stood cropping dry grass at the end of its tether. She hadn't had the time to rig the animal up with more than just a crude Apache bridle, and she wished she had when it came to getting the ranger mounted. He simply lacked the power to pull himself up. After he made several futile attempts, she finally cupped the taut seat of his Levis and pushed while he went up over the horse's back on his belly. He hung there, breathing hard, unable to move again, so she took the initiative, gripping his bad knee and dragging it over the animal's rump so he was straddling the horse. Slowly he straightened, gathering the single rein up in bloodstained hands. And he turned the horse toward the camp.

"What are you doing? Not that way!" she hissed at him.

"Have to go back for my pard."

"No."

"Can't leave without him."

She grabbed the braided rein and jerked the horse to a standstill. He sat on the animal with all the strength of a rag doll, but there was an unwavering determination in his pale-eyed stare. It was as if he actually thought he had a prayer of rescuing his friend. Or as if he didn't care as long as the effort was made.

"They'll kill you," she stated flatly.

"Don't matter." He was tottering, forced to grip a handful of mane to keep from going over. But he was still yanking the rein in the direction of the Apache stronghold.

"Jack, listen to me. You have to listen. Your friend, he wouldn't want you to save him. He wouldn't want to live . . . the way he is now."

Understanding dawned and the ranger gave a low, moaning cry. He sagged against the horse's tawny-colored neck, his eyes closing, his features drawn with anguish. The truth he spoke was awful.

"He came back for me."

Aching for the tortured loyalty in his voice, she put her hand on his shoulder, pressing firmly. "Then don't let his sacrifice be for nothing. You have to save yourself. Do it for him."

He didn't move for a long minute, clearly struggling with sobs of remorse, but then he nodded, once in feeble resignation, then again with conviction. When he didn't sit up, she began leading the horse in the direction of Ysleta, trying not to wonder how the wounded man would stay aboard all the way to that old Spanish mission. It wasn't her concern. Once he rode out, she was free of obligation.

But he wasn't riding. He was sprawled along the animal's neck, bobbing lower with every stride until he started to slide toward her. She caught him by the shoulder and levered him back up. His unfocused eyes opened, fixing on her in a dazed fashion. He licked at his cracked lips.

"Thank you, ma'am. I can take it from here." He reached

down for the braided rein with fumbling fingers and just kept right on reaching; hand leading, shoulder following, head dipping all in the same downward plunge. She wedged herself under him and shoved him back onto the buckskin. But she could no longer fool herself into thinking he could stay there on his own. He wouldn't go twenty feet without biting Texas dirt.

It was a two-day ride to Ysleta pushing hard. She knew right then he would never make it. She might tell herself she was saving his life, but the truth was, if she let him ride out on his own, she was doing no better than turning him over to torture. He'd be dead of thirst and exposure by the end of the first day. Not knowing which fate was more cruel, she hesitated, torn between conscience and her own loyalties. It would be more merciful just to cut his throat.

"I can't go with you," she said out loud, and he blinked slowly, as if surprised that she would think he'd ask it.

"You done enough, ma'am. I'll be fine."

"No, you won't," she argued angrily. Then, before she could rationalize what she was about to do, she gripped a handful of mane and swung lithely up behind him. Steadying him within the circle of her arms, she kicked back with her heels. The buckskin jumped forward, carrying them quickly and purposefully away from the Apache camp.

She pushed until well after the midnight hour, allowed by the three-quarter moon to continue as the air cooled and shadows thickened into darkness. It wouldn't take them long to discover her gone. She wouldn't worry about it, having already decided that she would say she'd been taken prisoner by the wounded ranger and that it had taken her awhile to effect an escape. The thought of returning to the white civilization with him never crossed her mind. There was nothing for her there, and she had every reason to return to the Apache. She still hadn't figured out just why she'd been willing to risk so much for this stranger. Perhaps because he was a link to what she'd been. Or simply because she couldn't walk away from anyone helpless and in need.

She stopped to let the horse rest because she was too tired to hold the ranger up any longer. He'd been unconscious or close to it for several hours. Without her support, he sagged to the ground with a silent bonelessness and lay unmoving while she saw to the hobbling and cross-tying of the horse. Only then did she come to kneel beside him to check his wounds and give him water. He swallowed it down without opening his eyes or betraying any kind of awareness. She guessed the grueling travel had pushed him beyond the limits of his endurance.

But he was alive.

Theirs was a necessarily cold camp, without light, without food, without blankets. Huddled down over her updrawn knees, she fought off the night chill while studying the wounded ranger. She hadn't seen a white man up close for over five years, and the sight intrigued her. She'd grown used to the broad, flat features of the Apache men. They had a certain majestic strength about them, but she'd never thought of them as handsome. Not like this ranger. Take away the dirt, the film of sweat, the bristle of beard, and the bruising of pain and she imagined he would be quite attractive to the female eye. He had the long, lean toughness of a Texas man. They were like a breed of longhorn, all sinew and stubbornness, as worn as bootheels, as weathered as leather, and as impervious to outside influence as the hard-packed soil. He had the tight-muscled thighs of a man who lived out of the saddle. She'd noticed that when tending him. And his hands, so work-roughened, were backed with a crisp, dark hair that fascinated her. Apache men despised body hair and went to great lengths to keep their skin smooth.

His face was turned toward her, a nice face with rugged, angular lines and a contrarily soft mouth. But it was the kindness she'd seen in his eyes that appealed to her so strongly, that and his capacity for compassion that prompted her into such a rash act to save him. She didn't know anything about him but she knew he was worth saving.

His head began a restless tossing, and when his eyes opened, they fixed on her in confusion then with a spark of recognition. She came to crouch beside him.

"How do you feel?"

"Fine, ma'am," he lied. His forehead was burning beneath her palm, and pain had scored deep grooves at the corners of his eyes and mouth. He must have figured complaining was useless when there was nothing she could do to give him ease. Typical stoic Texan.

"We're going to rest for a while, then I'll get you into Ysleta tomorrow. If we leave before dawn, we should be able to make it."

He nodded then was taken by a series of hard tremors. His features clenched up tight, but when she said his name worriedly, he managed a mild smile. "Just a chill, ma'am. Nothing to worry on." At least, not until those shivers had his teeth clattering noisily.

"I don't have any blankets," she told him apologetically.

"Th-that's all right. I'll m-make do without." And his teeth continued to rattle.

"We can't risk a fire."

He nodded, understanding her reasoning.

"I suppose I could lie next to you."

His eyes went momentarily round and he was quick to stammer. "N-no need, ma'am. I'm f-fine."

"But I'm cold."

"Oh. You can have my jacket."

"No, I think I'll just tuck in beside you."

He swallowed convulsively and vowed, "I won't try nothing improper," with such sincerity she had to smile. As if she feared he was capable of anything improper.

She stretched out on the hard ground, aware that he'd gone rigid as a felled tree trunk. His warmth drew her in closer until they were flush from shoulder to toe.

"Better?"

"Yes, ma'am," he whispered hoarsely.

She rolled onto her side. She'd shared the last ten years with two different husbands, so lying with a man was nothing new to her. And she was cold and he was hurt, in need of the shared heat. She heard him suck in a startled breath when her arm slipped around his middle.

"Can I borrow your shoulder, Jack?"

"Sure." His arm made a cautious circle about her as she settled in against him. By the time her head nudged in beneath his chin, he was scarcely breathing.

"Jack?"

"Ma'am?"

"I won't try anything improper, either."

His soft laughter made a pleasant vibration. The unnatural stiffness ebbed into a companionable welcome. She rose and fell with his lengthy sigh of weariness, and it was shamefully easy to feel right at home within his embrace.

By daybreak, he was too sick to know her.

Hoping it was fever, rather than the more fatal effects of

blood poisoning, she gave him water and checked his wound. It looked clean of any festering but was hot to the touch. He moaned when she applied the slightest pressure, so she just redid the wrapping and left it alone. She didn't know that much about such things, only that she'd done what she could, and if he was meant to survive, he would. All she could do was get him back where he belonged so the rangers could take over his care—or take care of his burying.

She hoisted him up on the little buckskin, letting him drape belly-down in front of her. He couldn't sit and she couldn't support him. It couldn't have been a comfortable ride, but it allowed them to make much better time. She held the rein in one hand and the back of his britches in the other as the horse loped across the arid ground.

It was almost nightfall by the time she made out the low adobe features of the Ysleta Mission where the rangers quartered next to the border town of El Paso. She drew up outside the perimeter of light and sound and stared toward the evidence of the life she'd once led, a life she couldn't return to. She had to go back to the Apache. She never even considered taking him into the town or remaining there herself. This was as far as her responsibility extended.

"Jack?" She shook his shoulder until he roused with a rumbling moan. "Jack, your camp's just up ahead. Can you make it that far?"

"Sure," he muttered thickly. She had the feeling he would have said that had she asked if he could fly.

"I can't take you in any farther."

"This is fine, ma'am." And he wiggled off the animal's back to prove it. And sank right down to his knees. She tried not to feel dismayed as she looked down upon him. He'd be all right. He would.

"After I'm gone, you just yell out and someone's bound to hear and come get you."

He nodded, not looking up. He was on all fours, weaving weakly.

"Jack?"

"Ma'am?"

"Oh, hell."

She slid off and dragged him back up on the horse's back, balancing him there as she kicked the buckskin up into a jarring canter. He was no longer moving.

She didn't approach the ranger barracks, instead singling out a humble adobe dwelling on the outskirts of activity. She rode right up under the eaves and kicked at the string-latched door. When it opened to reveal a wary Mexican couple, she gave Jack a push. He crumpled soundlessly on the front stoop.

"This man's a ranger. He needs help."

As the couple bent over him, she wheeled the horse around and headed out into the night.

And she never once looked back.

Two

For three days, he didn't know where or who he was. He thrashed weakly in his fever bed, hearing screams and weeping helplessly. He heard voices, but didn't understand them. He saw faces, but didn't recognize them. It was like being lost to madness. On the fourth day, his eyes opened to the sight of familiar ceiling beams stuck in adobe, and the first thing he did was reach for his right leg.

Still there.

Noting the movement, the ranger's surgeon leaned in close to feel his brow. "How ya doing, Sergeant? Fixin' to wake up, are ya?"

Jack scrubbed his tongue across dry lips and tried to speak. No sound came out. Frustrated, he tried again and issued a croaking request. "Captain . . . make my report."

The doctor held a cup of water to his mouth and he gulped greedily until it was taken away. Then he was eased back down on his pillows. "Reports can wait until you're stronger. I want you to just rest—"

Jack caught the man's sleeve in a firm grasp. "Captain Marcus—now. Please."

"All right. Doan go gettin' yourself all riled up. I'll see he's fetched if you'll lie back. Lie back, now. Fair enough? He's been by right regular, anyway. You had us pretty worried for a while."

Jack's hand dropped away. The small movement had effectively sapped his strength. He heard the doctor yell for someone to get the ranger captain. Then the dressing was peeled back on his thigh.

"Sergeant, you don't know how lucky you are to still be toting this particular part of you. Cut those arrows out yourself, did you?"

Jack shook his head. His mind was foggy. Someone did. Who?

"It'll all come back to you. Last few days been pretty hard on the body. If those barbs hadn't been taken out, we'd have been burying you about now." He pressed against the torn muscle and Jack's foot began a fierce spasming. "That hurt?"

"It's . . . fine."

Observing the fresh sweat of pain that popped out along the ranger's brow, the doctor smiled wryly. "Sure it is. Doan rush it, or I might be getting my saws out after all."

"You'd best be saving 'em for someone else," came a deep, authoritative voice from behind him. The doctor moved aside so the tall ranger captain could assume his place. He took up his friend's slack hand in one of his and placed his other on Jack's shoulder. Relief was obvious in his expression. "Good to see you with your eyes open, Sergeant. Had me fretting for a while that I'd have to start looking for a replacement."

Jack wet his lips. "No, sir. I'm fine, Cap'n. Be up and around tomorrow."

"Two weeks," the doctor amended sternly.

"Tomorrow," Jack restated. He didn't argue the point, he just stated it plain. The surgeon made a disbelieving noise and moved away from the two men.

Neil Marcus smiled down at his young second-in-com-

mand. Unlike the doctor, he had no doubts that Jack would
be up on his feet in the morning. He'd found in the soft-
spoken, unassuming Jack Bass everything that made Texas
Rangers a force to be reckoned with. Even when a raw
recruit of sixteen—he'd lied and said he was eighteen—he'd
had the right stuff for the job. Jack Bass was quiet and
deliberate, with a dislike of violence, though he never hesitated when called upon. He was fair and fearless and would
ride straight up to death when duty demanded it. In the four
years they'd served together, Neil Marcus was proud to
command him and call him friend. There was no one he
trusted more or could depend upon as completely.

"What happened out there, son?"

With admirable brevity, Jack laid out the events leading
up to their run-in with the Mescalero band as his captain
grew grim.

"Foster?" Marcus asked finally.

Jack tucked his head, answering in a voice raw with guilt
and grief. "I had to leave him, Cap'n." That said everything.
He offered no excuses. In his mind, there were none. He'd
left a comrade behind to die. There was no greater shame
for a ranger to bear. He looked up through eyes swimming
with regret when Marcus pressed his shoulder.

"Foster was a good man," the captain concluded. "A
good ranger and a good friend. He'll be missed. Now, put
it behind you, Jack. He'd be the last one holding you to
blame and you know it."

"Yes, sir." Knowing it didn't change anything. "I'd like
to lead a party out after his murderers."

"Come see me about it as soon as you're fit."

"Thank you, Cap'n." Revenge wouldn't bring his partner
back, but it would make him rest easier in the Hereafter.

And it would appease some of the sorrow weighting Jack's heart.

Suddenly, he gave a start of recall and tried to sit up. Marcus caught him by the shoulders, restraining him with a gentle, "Easy now, son. What's wrong?"

"The woman who brought me in, where is she?"

"What woman?" He eased Jack back down on the pillows, frowning to himself, fearing the delirium had returned. "A couple of Mexicans delivered you up. Said you'd been dumped off at their doorstep."

"No." He shook his head determinedly. "There was a woman."

"Easy, now. You saying an Apache squaw brought you here?" That was highly unlikely. Neil readied to call the doctor over when Jack persisted.

"She took care of my leg, got me a horse, brought me here."

"Jack—"

He waved off his friend's look of patience. "She was real. She saved my life, Neil. A woman from the Apache camp. A white woman."

Neil Marcus went very still.

"A white woman with green eyes."

"What was her name?" It was asked in a steely whisper.

"She never said. Why would she go back with them? Cap'n, we've got to go after her. If she'd been living with the Apache—"

"I'll take care of it, Sergeant," Marcus said softly.

"But if they find out she helped me—"

"I said, I'll see to it!"

Jack blinked in confusion. "Yes, sir."

The ranger captain stood, his expression unreadable. "Rest up, Jack. We'll talk later."

Only as he walked away did Jack wonder about his odd restraint. A white captive wasn't something a man of Texas overlooked easily. And as he sagged back on his healing bed, Jack Bass vowed to find the woman with the green eyes and bring her back where she belonged.

He owed her.

"Hey, Jack. How's the leg?"

"Sarge, good to see you up and around."

"Sorry to hear about Foster. Helluva feller."

Jack winced at that, but continued his laborious journey across the ranger compound. He was up and around, just barely. He felt as though a bear trap had him by the thigh. Each slow step brought pure agony, but he was determined to ignore it. He had obligations to tend, and he couldn't see to them flat on his back.

He was grateful to find the crude cabin he shared with five others empty. They'd be out on patrol and he was able to sink down on the edge of his bunk with a heartfelt groan of misery. Resisting the temptation of dropping down into his covers to seek a more comfortable oblivion, he stripped out of his soiled clothes, washed up, and put on fresh socks, jeans, and plain blue shirt. His pantleg was snug over the bandaging and caused an incessant ache. He'd endure it rather than ruin a pair of trousers by slitting the seam for ease. He was next to helpless with a needle and thread when it came to mending. And he felt next to helpless when he thought of Foster Richards. He sat on his bunk, his eyes closed, his heart breaking all over again as he remembered. He should have been able to do . . . something. Anything.

He was relieved from his morose thoughts by a light tap

on the door, and he smiled at the whiskered face that peered in.

"Hey, Pete."

"Hey, yourself, Jack. Kinda soon to be up and about, ain't it?"

"Got tired of lying around."

"Should have found yourself some willing skirt to make the time pass easier."

Jack gave the older man a closed-lipped smile and felt himself blush awkwardly at the teasing. He was well known for his reluctance to take up with the women who hung out around the ranger barracks. His compadres dubbed him "Gentleman Jack" for his modesty and shyness around females and for his annoying lack of vices. He didn't smoke, he didn't swear, he didn't drink to get drunk or gamble for anything but fun, and he stayed clear of the border whores. However, the men all liked him, so they forgave these faults. But that didn't stop them from ribbing him plenty.

If he'd been of a mind to explain himself, he could have said it wasn't because he didn't like women; he liked them a lot. It was just that from the very strong and very admirable women in his life, he'd learned a tremendous respect for female kind, and to use them selfishly sat poorly with him. He was hardly inexperienced. Since his sixteenth year, he'd formed mild attachments to several ladies in El Paso, but it was always the same; he'd be gone for a lengthy stretch of time out in the heat of West Texas, and when he returned, he'd find they'd struck up affections elsewhere. He'd never held any ill-will toward the women or toward the fellows who'd replaced him, and that was another reason he was so well thought of among his peers. They liked a man who didn't hold a grudge over something as trivial as bed partners.

"Jack, what's this I heared about some white woman living among the Mescalero?" Pete Myers settled himself before the cabin stove and helped himself to coffee. As he blew on the steaming brew, he listened to the young sergeant's story with a mounting suspicion. "An' what did the cap'n have to say about all this?"

Jack's brow furrowed. "That's the funny part, Pete—he didn't say much of anything. He got kinda snappish and said he'd see to it. Didn't know quite what to make of him."

The grizzled ranger took a sip of coffee and scowled into the tin. He'd been with the company a long time, had seen plenty and heard plenty, was usually to be trusted with what he'd learned, and believed in what he said. "Neil ever tell you about how he come to be a ranger?"

Jack shook his head. "Figured if it was any of my business, he'da told me."

"Going on five years ago, him and his wife and baby girl were coming across from Galveston when they was set on by Apache. He survived it, just barely, but there was no sign of the woman or child."

"Didn't he go looking?"

"Took him near three months to heal up, an' by then the trail was stone cold. Guessed if they were still alive, they'd been sold down below the border and there was next to no chance of him ever seeing them again. Took to ranging, 'cause he saw it as a way to strike back at them what stole his family."

Jack considered this, feeling the pain his captain must have experienced. He had family and knew the fear and panic of having them threatened. He thought a minute, then asked, "But what's that got to do—"

"Heard tell Mrs. Marcus was a right fetchin' woman with dark hair and pretty green eyes."

Jack looked up quick. "An' you think—?"

"Don't you?"

That the woman who saved him was his best friend's wife.

So why wasn't Neil Marcus chafing to go after her?

Jack chewed on that question all day as he hobbled about El Paso, seeing to the restocking of the gear he'd lost. He mourned the loss of his horse and took his time finding a new one. A ranger didn't keep a string of animals the way a cowboy did. He had one and it had to be good, with enough bottom to carry him every day for a month, if need be, and the endurance of a grass-fed mustang. He found a hard-looking sorrel of sixteen hands that seemed fit for the job, then bought a double-girted western saddle and a bridle with a severe bit inlaid with silver and the finest steel. He got a Navajo blanket for use under the saddle by day and over him by night, then saw to the replenishing of his personal arsenal. He traveled armed to the teeth because he found a man who went ready for anything seldom had to prove it. Carrying a Winchester repeater, a breech-loading shotgun, a Colt Hogleg revolver, two old single-shot Dragoon pistols, and a fine-honed Texas blade, he felt himself ready for any challenge as he rode back to Ysleta and tied up outside his captain's house.

Neil Marcus didn't seem surprised to see him, nor did he ask after his sergeant's health. He figured if the man was fit enough to be standing there, he was fit enough for the job. His orders were terse.

"Take fifteen men and enough mess for a ten-day scout. If you come up with nothing, I want you back here and that'll be an end to it."

"Yessir."

"And Jack . . . bring back Foster for burying, if possible.

I wired his folks over in San Antonio and they expressed the want to place him in their family plot."

Jack's features grew taut. "Yessir," he vowed, softly. Hopefully, if they found his partner, there wouldn't be enough left of him to tell how horribly he'd died. That wasn't something he'd want to send home to anyone's folks.

There was no mention of the white woman with green eyes, so Jack kept the rest of his plans to himself.

They rode out of Ysleta the next morning in quiet single file, each man toting a tin cup on his saddle and his own rations of flour, bacon, green coffee, sugar, beans, rice, and soda, sixty rounds of long-gun ammunition, and thirty for the pistols. On the trail, they'd hunt up their own game and sleep in their blankets under the stars. And not a one of them would have forgone the grueling ten-day forage to remain in the relative comfort of their camp. They were out for evens with those responsible for Foster Richards's death. And each of them respected his young sergeant's right to redeem himself through retribution.

While wrapped up in his Navajo blanket, trying to knead the ache out of his thigh, Jack stared up at the canopy of evening lights and tried to puzzle out his captain's attitude. There was a good chance his wife was still alive. Why wasn't he the one leading this expedition? A woman and child torn from his life for five long years . . . Jack couldn't fathom the man's indifference, not when longing for his own family was like a daily ritual. They'd parted badly from him and he hadn't been able to make himself return. And it was eating him up inside. While he'd give just about anything to have someone to belong to, here was his captain, willing to turn the other way. He couldn't understand it, but then, Neil Marcus hadn't confided any of his personal pain and the boundaries of their friendship wouldn't permit him to ask. So the best Jack could do was speculate and fill up on his own loneliness until sleep finally came.

They found Foster Richards late the second day out. The Apache had left him as a warning. His corpse was pinned to the ground with one of the twenty-inch iron stakes soldiers used to tether their horses. Jack left the ranks of his men long enough to throw up his lunch, then returned to soberly see to his friend's remains. The men left him alone, figuring it wasn't their place to interfere. Jack jerked the stake free and carefully bundled the body in a canvas he'd brought for that purpose. His were the only dry eyes. But then, he'd already cried his soul dry for his fallen comrade. Grimly, he sent a detail of four men back to Ysleta with the body and the rest of his hard-faced unit rode on with a mounting eagerness for confrontation.

None of them so much as blinked when it came to crossing the Rio Grande into Mexico, even though their jurisdiction ended at the Texas side of the broad river. Jack told them quietly, "I'm going on, but I can't ask the same of you." They all followed. The trail was fresh, and their blood was hot.

They spent days winding through Mexico in search of the elusive Apache band. The Indians moved light and quick and were harder than ghosts to track, but Jack knew something about tracking and was able to keep them on course. Knowing that both their allotted time and their rations were almost at an end put a sharper edge on the men's anticipation. To a man, they pushed, using every second of daylight in pursuit of their friend's killers.

What they stumbled upon wasn't the fight they expected, but a fight was a fight when it came to men with tensions stretched taut for an entire week; an enemy was an enemy. It didn't take long to decipher the ugly scene they happened upon late the eighth day. The Apache band had split, the warriors heading off to hunt. A number of their women had left the main band to harvest mescal. The fleshy green desert plant was their main food source, and the women, armed with hatchets and piñon sticks, had been busy digging the roots while under the guard of a small group of braves. It was a case of sheer strength in number when a detachment of Mexican soldiers came upon them. The Apache men were quickly slain and the Mexicans had set up their own camp to enjoy the women at their leisure before taking them to sell as slaves.

"We got no time for this, Jack," hissed one of the men crouched at his elbow. "T'ain't none of our business. We can't go tangling with the Mexicans on their home ground over a bunch of redskins."

But Jack was thinking of a certain green-eyed woman and he couldn't force himself away from the spot. "They're women," he argued softly.

"They're Injuns," the ranger countered, as if the one overruled the other. "This ain't what we're here to do."

But it was what Jack had come to do.

"One of them could be the woman who saved my life. Ride on, if you like. I'll take care of things here."

There were over thirty Mexicans—twice their number—but Jack hadn't bothered counting. Odds didn't matter much to him. He was scanning what women's faces he could see. They were too far away for him to tell if any of the bound females was his captain's wife.

"Dang it, Jack. You know we ain't gonna do that. How do you know she's even down there?"

"I aim to go look."

He borrowed a broad-brimmed Mexican hat from one of his men and slipped down the rocky embankment into the shadowy edges of the camp. Most of the men were at their meal, with a smaller number guarding the horses. The women were tethered like animals in a separate area, and that was where Jack headed. He searched their frightened faces, seeing terror in the uplifted dark eyes. But none of those eyes were green. He was about to give up when he saw a pair of small-sized bare feet protruding from the back of a wagon bed. Pale bare feet.

He wasn't a man to use profanity, but a low oath ripped out when he saw what they'd done to the woman. She'd been bound spread-eagled upon the bed of the wagon. Her soiled and bloodied clothes were torn open. He didn't waste his time looking or speculating but slid over the top of her, staying low so he wouldn't be spotted, to get a good look at her face.

The feel of his weight woke the slack figure to rebellion beneath him. His hand fastened over her mouth as it opened for a scream. He found himself staring down into frantic green eyes as he reached up with his knife to sever the ropes about her wrists. And he was totally unprepared for an attack at close range.

Her fingers curled around the hilt of his knife, wrenching it free, sending it snaking toward his throat before he could gather the wit to effect a defense. He felt the cut of the blade even as he grabbed her hand. She fought him. She was strong for a woman.

"Easy, ma'am. I'm a ranger. I don't mean you no harm. Remember me? You didn't save my life jus' to snatch it back, did you?"

"Jack?"

She said his name in a tremulous whisper. Then the fight was gone. Her arms were tight about his neck, and in one jolting moment of gratitude, she kissed him hard, right on the mouth.

For a second, every dazed fiber of him channeled into an acute awareness of those warm lips and the inviting feel of her spread beneath him and he was gravely shocked by the powerful punch of desire. This wasn't the time for it, he told himself brusquely, and if she was Mrs. Marcus, she wasn't the woman for it, either.

"Be real quiet, now. I've come for you."

She nodded, and he turned to cut her feet loose. Just as he was sliding out of the back of the buckboard and had reached up for her, a shout of alarm rose up in the camp. Gunfire erupted all around them. The Apache women started screaming in frightened unison.

Jack seized her by the waist and yanked her underneath the wagon as he pulled his own revolver. She crouched at his side, gripping his jacket. "Stay down, ma'am. Looks like we're caught in a crossfire. My boys will lay down some heavy cover and we can run for it."

She didn't appear to be listening. Her hold on him intensified. "Jack, promise me."

"What?"

"If you can't get me free, you won't let them have me again."

Startled by the request, he glanced at her and was held by the fierce urgency of her gaze.

"Promise me . . . please."

And very quietly, he said, "Yes, ma'am," and she sagged in relief, never doubting he would keep his word. He was a man of tremendous courage and conviction as well as compassion, and she trusted him.

"Here." He pressed his single-shot pistol into her hand. "Just in case I'm not alive to see it done."

She clung to the heavy Dragoon as if it offered up salvation, and he guessed in a way it did. She smiled so bravely it snagged at the heart of him and then she curled tight against him, glaring out at the enemy as if no longer afraid.

The pitched battle continued for some minutes. Firing from cover, the rangers had the advantage, and it didn't take the Mexicans long to figure that out. As more and more of their number fell, they began to edge toward the horses and thoughts of escape. More were shot down as they fled, but enough slipped away to provide an element of worry to the Texans.

"Jack, get the hell out of there!"

Jack paused for a moment to wiggle out of his jacket. He passed it to the woman at his side, thinking of her tattered state of dress.

"Put this on. I'll be right back for you."

Then he ducked out from beneath the wagon and trotted to where the Apache women were still bound and weeping. With a few quick pulls of his knife, he freed them, crying, "Go on, run," and they scattered toward the hills. As he turned, he saw his green-eyed savior crawl out from under the wagon and start running after them.

"No! Wait, ma'am!"

His leg wasn't healed enough to allow for a rapid pursuit, but he pushed it to the limit as he scrambled after the woman wrapped in his coat. He managed to snag the back of it and wrestled her down before she slipped out of it. Again she was fighting him, cursing him in Apache and Spanish. Jack was confused. She had to know he wasn't going to hurt her.

"No, ma'am. It's all right. It's all right. I'm taking you back with me."

"Let me go! You don't understand—I can't go with you. Please! Please, let me go!"

"Mrs. Marcus!"

She froze, going as stiff as if he'd struck her. He'd no doubt whatsoever that the name meant something to her. It meant that she was another man's wife.

"I'm taking you back to your husband."

Three

The detachment of rangers came swooping out of the rocks leading Jack's horse.

"Climb aboard, Sarge, before they figure out how few we are," called out the man who held his reins. "I'd hate to have my bacon caught on this side of the river."

Neil Marcus's wife had gone limp in his arms. Jack didn't know if she'd fainted from the news or the stress of the situation. Whichever, he was quick about loading her into his saddle and climbing up behind her.

"Let's make tracks, boys."

He wheeled his sorrel about and applied his heels smartly. They rode hard, well into the darkness, until they were splashing up the waters of the Rio Grande. Only when they were safely across did they pause to make their camp. They were disgruntled to have to break off their chase of the Apache, but all realized it was too dangerous to stay in Mexico. And they weren't returning empty-handed.

Jack knelt down awkwardly at the fire to pour a tin of coffee. His men were settling in for the night, talking softly among themselves. Those who weren't on guard were beginning to take to their blankets. He wasn't tired. He studied the solitary figure seated on the perimeter of their camp and slowly approached her. He couldn't miss the way she gave a fearful start when she heard his step. He couldn't blame her for being frightened in a camp of strange men who'd abducted her against her will, even if it was for her own good. He pitched his voice soft and calming.

"It's all right, ma'am. It's just me. I brought you some coffee."

He squatted down a nonthreatening arm's length away and extended the cup. She didn't look at it or him. Her face was turned toward the river, her expression stoic.

"I'd like to wash up," she said flatly. "I'm—dirty."

Jack glanced toward his men and along the riverbank. "I can walk you downstream a ways."

She looked at him then, and her tone was scathing. "You don't have to do that, Sergeant. I won't run away."

"It's for your protection, ma'am."

She made a disbelieving sound. "Are you sure you don't want to hobble and sideline me along with the horses?"

"Do I need to?"

His quiet sincerity made her chuckle. "No. I give you my word I won't try to escape."

"Good enough for me. But I'll walk you anyway. Be right back."

He went to fetch his carbine, blanket, and slicker, advising the sentries that he was leaving camp for a short while and not to be too quick about putting any bullets in him when he returned. If they wondered where he was off to with the ragged-looking white woman, they didn't ask.

Once out of range of the camp, where only a sliver of moonlight upon the still river waters lit the night, Jack paced off a section of the shoreline to make sure it was safe, then pronounced, "You can wash up here."

She took off his jacket. Apparently, she was unaware that there was little modesty left in the clothes she wore beneath it. Jack angled his eyes away.

"Ma'am," he muttered uncomfortably. "I thought you meant to just scrub up."

"I'm going to bathe, Sergeant. Look away, if it embarrasses you, but it's nothing you haven't already seen."

He could feel his face heat. "Them circumstances were a bit different."

But he couldn't tell that to the sensory memory he carried: the feel of her kiss, the feel of her softness, the sight of her pale nakedness burned eternally from that one brief glimpse.

"You go on and take care of what you have to," he growled. "I'll see you have your privacy. Just don't go out too far. I don't want to have to come in after you." He wasn't exactly warning her. After all, he'd taken her word. But it didn't hurt to emphasize his determination to hang onto her, now that he had her.

He heard her wade out into the water and tensed all over at the sound of her contented sigh. He paced for a moment until his leg got to paining so fiercely, he had to give it ease. Settling down on a rocky outcropping, he kept his attention focused away from where it longed to stray, and his senses tuned to the suggestive noises coming from the river. He could hear the trickling of the water, the quiet splashing, the soft murmurs of pleasure and discomfort she uttered alternately. She was in there for a long while, and each second added up to an additional notch of torture as he envisioned her in his vivid mind's eye. It wasn't a lustful musing. It was more like a tormented yearning he couldn't seem to push aside. He kept thinking of how brave she looked taking his single-shot pistol, of how determined she was when cutting out those arrows. How yielding she felt beneath him in that wagon bed. By the time she finally climbed out, he was sweat-drenched and trembling.

"I'd like to rinse out my clothes. Is there something I can put on while they dry?"

He forced a dry swallow. "Yes, ma'am. Just wrap up in my slicker there. It should give you plenty of cover and keep you warm."

"Thank you. And it's Emily."

"What?"

"My name. My name is Emily."

"Yes, ma'am."

He heard her chuckle softly, and then the sounds of her washing her ripped garments. Now he knew how a fence line felt just before it was stretched to the snapping point. That tautness vibrated when he heard her draw near.

"Oh, I feel much better. Now, how about you?"

"Ma'am?" It was almost a gasp.

"Your leg. How's your leg?"

"Fine—"

Before he could protest more vehemently, she crouched down at his side. His vision was possessed by the sight of her, with her damp hair streaming like heavy dark satin beyond her shoulders, his canvas slicker swimming over her nakedness. When her fingers touched gently to his thigh, he almost leapt out of his boots.

"You're bleeding."

"It's nothing, ma'am—Miz Emily."

"Drop your pants."

"What?"

"Take down your britches. I want to bind those wounds up tight. You've caused me too much trouble for me to let you bleed to death now."

"I can tend to it myself—"

"I've seen your bare skin before," she chided patiently. "When you come right down to it, Sergeant, we have few secrets between us. Your leg?"

"Yes, ma'am."

While he stood to wriggle out of his denims, Emily Marcus went down to the river's edge to soak her ruined doeskin blouse. From his ignominious position with pants pooled about his ankles, Jack ripped open the side seam of his long johns over the bulky bandage. That was all he planned to bare for her scrutiny. Then she was back and he went tense all over.

"This will be easier if you sit down, Sergeant. And stop looking as though I mean to geld you! I assure you, my motives are pure."

"Yes, ma'am." Even in the darkness she could see his face color up hotly. But he sat.

Then she settled on her knees beside him and began to carefully unwrap his saturated bandage. There was a lot of bleeding, he had to admit. Maybe it was best she tended to it now. When she was down to torn skin, he tensed and twitched as she sponged away the seepage. It wasn't that she was hurting his wounds. The misery stemmed from another source altogether, and he was mighty glad for his long shirt tails as she bent over his lap to bind the injuries tight. He would be mortified to death if she were to guess how her closeness and tender touch acted upon him. He was endlessly grateful when she began to speak, latching onto the topic as a means to cool his rapidly rising ardor.

"So Neil is alive."

"Yes, ma'am, Miz Marcus."

"Where is he?"

"In Ysleta, ma'am."

"You know him?"

"He's my captain. And my friend."

"Does he know about me?"

Jack hesitated. What could he answer, the truth? And have her wonder why her husband didn't ride to her rescue? He chose a more diplomatic course. "I didn't even know for sure that I'd seen you. Most of the boys were of the impression that I was out of my head. I don't think any of them believed for a minute that you were real."

"Is that too tight?"

He tested the binding by flexing at the knee. "It's fine." His thigh wasn't what felt too tight. "Thank you, ma'am."

"No, thank *you*, Jack."

She said that so poignantly, his throat got all choky-feeling. Her hand lingered along the length of his leg, pausing to rub absently over his kneecap. Restlessly, he slipped out from under her touch and jerked his jeans up, angling slightly away until he had them pieced together over the shameful proof of his arousal. What was he thinking? The woman was Neil Marcus's wife! It wasn't safe or smart for them to be loitering, off away from the others.

"We'd best be getting back into camp," he muttered gruffly.

"Please . . . can we stay here for a minute?"

He paused, puzzled by the sudden panic in her voice. Up until now, he'd been marveling over her control. Such strength and resilience wasn't natural after a violent trauma. She'd held herself together with a will as strong as baling wire. And he was quite frankly awed by her. After all she'd been through, to fuss over his leg like she had . . . Lord, the woman had grit. Or had she been pushing all the ugliness down, keeping the feelings submerged until it was safe to vent them with the proper horror? He wasn't sure until she asked very softly, "Jack, do you mind if I borrow your shoulder?"

"Sure."

He opened his arms and she filled them, stiffly at first, then trembling from top to toe as he folded her in close. Her face burrowed into the hollow above his heart, and her fingers curled up in the fabric of his shirt, twisting, wringing it in her restless hands. A terrible tenderness got ahold of him and wrenched at him just as plaintively. He found himself nudging his cheek against her damp hair, following that with the unconscious brush of his lips.

"It's all right, ma'am. You go on an' cry if you want. I don't mind."

Her reply was surprising. She sounded angry that he would suggest it. "I don't want to cry. They can't make me cry. Damn them, I won't cry."

His embrace deepened to absorb the spasms of weeping as her resistance finally gave way. It was a good, cleansing cry, expressing her shock and fright and fury. And Jack simply held her, providing her with the safe foundation.

After a time, his leg buckled and he sank down on the silty shoreline of the Rio Grande with Emily Marcus still cradled to his chest. She was too weary to pull away, and he was too weak of will to let her go.

"I'm sorry," she murmured at last, freeing one hand to scrub across her eyes.

"Don't be."

Her head returned to pillow on his shoulder, and instead of clutching, her palms began a subtle, disturbing shift over the swell of his upper arms. Her voice was low and inflectionless.

"They came at us without warning. I was so afraid that they would kill us all . . . and then I was afraid because I knew they wouldn't. They took me first when they found I was a white woman. I fought as hard as I could, but there were too many, and they were so much stronger. Oh, Jack—"

"Shhh," he whispered forcefully. "You've got nothing to be ashamed of, Emily, nothing at all."

Her silence doubted him.

It was then a particular anger overcame him. His palm eased under her chin, lifting it so they were eye to eye. He was scowling. "Don't you ever think you have to apologize. Not ever."

She stared at him with tears glimmering and smiled a small, sad smile. "You are such a good man," she told him simply.

And then she kissed him.

Unstrung by her vulnerability, by her awesome courage, Jack kissed her back. He hadn't meant to, but she tasted so sweet, and she had him so stirred up inside. It wasn't a passionate exchange. He could have placated his conscience by saying he was complying to comfort her. But that wouldn't explain why he couldn't seem to pull away. Or why his one hand cupped the back of her head while the other rode the gentle curve of her cheek as their mouths moved together in a slow, sliding harmony.

He didn't even breathe until she sat back, and then he found he was gasping. They looked at one another for a long, silent moment, then he said, "Ma'am, I'm—"

Her fingertips pressed to his just-kissed lips. "No. Please don't say that you're sorry. You've no idea how much I needed that just then."

"I'm not sorry. I just got a bit confused about things . . . I guess."

"Hey, Jack," came a quiet cry from the edge of the camp. "Everything all right?"

He swallowed hard so his answer wouldn't betray his state of discomposure. "Sure, Sandy. Everything's fine."

"We'd better go back," Emily said in a hushed tone. She stood, then reached down for Jack's elbows, helping him struggle to his feet. He stepped away rather purposefully, then snatched up his good Navajo blanket and wound it about her shoulders. She smiled faintly and preceded him back into the ranger circle. If it had been any man other than Jack Bass who'd come out of the darkness with a beautiful woman who was wearing nothing but his slicker and a blanket, talk would have carried tongues away. But each and every man knew and respected the sergeant and so they thought nothing of it.

Emily lay down in a vacant spot close to the fire, her face turned toward the flames to feel the welcoming heat. Her eyes closed almost immediately and she was fast asleep, but it was an uneasy rest. Within minutes, she jerked awake with a soft cry of alarm.

"Jack?" she whimpered.

"Right here, ma'am."

She rolled toward him anxiously and clutched the hand he slipped reassuringly over hers . . . clutched and wouldn't let go. Surrounding it with both of her own, she drew his palm up to rest near her frantically beating heart until the pace slowed and her breathing slowed and finally, her fingers slackened. But Jack didn't pull away.

Emily Marcus. Neil's wife. He couldn't allow himself to forget that. He couldn't.

She was awake, but it took her a long time to stir. It wasn't just the compilation of aches and pains that aggrieved her body. It was the torment to her mind.

Neil was alive.

She couldn't begin to comprehend what that would mean. It changed everything. She'd been gone for five years. She'd accepted the cruel fact of his death and had gone on to make the best life she could among the Apache. Now she was thrust back into the white world and she suffered the shock of adjustment all over again.

She listened to the rangers talk. After five years of hearing only the Athapascan language spoken, the rangers' words sounded strange, and that frightened her. Her own language sounded foreign. How was she going to fit back into a world that no longer seemed familiar, a world she wasn't even sure wanted to accept her back?

She was aware of the curious stares. They weren't pointed or rude, but they expressed what she was going to be up against every day. She'd been living with the Indians. What did that make her—victim? Or whore? The men of Texas weren't terribly free thinking when it came to other races of humanity. They considered themselves superior to all who walked upright, and the harsh lessons of the War hadn't changed that stiff thinking one degree. They weren't forgiving and they weren't accepting. So where did that leave her? The citizens of El Paso wouldn't be half so polite in their scrutiny as this group of rangers. How would she stand it? Did she want to?

Just when her doubts and anxieties were about to run off with her, Emily caught sight of the ranger sergeant. Immediately her worries eased. He noticed her attention and provided a small smile of greeting that warmed through her in a big way. The sensation of safety returned.

He didn't cross over to her right away. He was busy talking with his men, but his gaze seldom left her. His eyes were pale, an ice blue both piercing and passionate in intensity. He was hatless in the cool of early morning and his hair had cleaned up to a glossy deep-auburn color. And he was much better looking than she had first assumed.

She'd kissed him and she'd liked it. He was amazingly gentle for a man of action, and she'd needed that touch of tenderness to still the terrors of the previous day. She trusted him. There was no better way to explain the complexity of her feelings than with that simple truth. She'd depended upon men before for protection and security, but never had she given over the private aspects of herself the way she had to the ranger, Jack. And he'd known, somehow, he'd known instinctively just what to do. She'd never realized a man could have that kind of sensitivity. Most were outward thinking, not inward feeling. He'd let her weep in his arms and he'd said it would be all right. She believed him; she needed to believe him.

He paused at the fire to fill a plate, then came toward her, limping badly. She could tell each halting step was an effort, yet he betrayed no discomfort through his expression. Harder for him to conceal were the two fresh splotches discoloring the taut denim over his wounded thigh. He was bleeding again and she didn't like to think of how he was going to endure a day of hard and fast travel.

" 'Morning. Hungry?"

"Yes." She sat up and took the plate from him. Not much in the way of a meal, but far better than what she was used to. While she forked up the mound of rice and beans, she noticed how he absently massaged his leg, favoring it with an unequal distribution of his weight. "Sit down, Sergeant."

He smiled thinly. "No, thanks, ma'am. Don't think I could get back up." At least he was honest about his own infirmity. "Finish that up so we can get under way. Bet you're pretty eager to get home."

Home? She paused then set her fork down. Where was that?

"Ma'am?"

"No, Jack, I'm not," she admitted quietly. She looked up, seeing he was perplexed by her answer. How to explain? "I just found out I have a life to go back to. I need some time to get used to the idea. It's hard to think. I'm just so tired. If only there was someplace I could just rest, get my strength back, get my thoughts clear. I'm scared, Jack, scared of just dropping in on Neil after all these years. He's going to need time, too. But I guess time is a luxury we don't have. You and the men have to get back."

"They do, yes, ma'am. Supplies are low, and the horses are about worn through."

"Are you going to be able to make the trip?"

Again, the faint smile. "I did before."

"And it almost killed you," she pointed out.

He shrugged, as if it wasn't worth considering.

"I wish there was someplace the both of us could go to heal up for a few days." As she said that aloud, she surprised herself. And him. He colored up awkwardly and looked away. She concluded somberly, "But I guess that's just not possible, is it?"

She'd cleaned her plate and set it aside. It was then she took an interest in her appearance. She was still wearing his slicker. Her hair was loose, clean but tangled. She didn't want to consider how her face looked. Every inch of it hurt from the slaps she'd incurred from the Mexicans. It would be naive of her to believe she was unmarked by the abuse. She looked like a woman who'd gone through hell, and that much was true.

"I'd better get ready," she said dully. "I'd like to freshen up first."

"Ma'am. You can go on down by the river's edge and—here."

She looked curiously at the garments he extended. One was a man's chambray shirt and the other was her faded brown skirt. Only the violent rent up the front had been painstakingly sewn together with a collection of rough stitches. She stared at the crude seam through a pooling of emotion. Jack cleared his throat uncomfortably.

"Now, don't you go making fun of my needlework. I'd much rather stitch up a bullet hole than dally with such stuff. But I figured you'd be more comfortable wearing those." His voice trailed off in embarrassment.

"It's fine," she murmured huskily. "I'm much obliged to you for your thoughtfulness." She looked up at him and tried hard not to break down completely before the push of gratitude. He wouldn't meet her eyes.

"Figured if you could cut arrowheads outta my hide, the least I could do was your mending." He hadn't been able to sleep all night, anyway. But that, he didn't mention.

"Thank you." She reached out a hand to touch his cheek, but he shied from contact. And she was somewhat bemused by her sudden strong desire to put her arms around him and kiss him expressively. Instead, she allowed him his dignified retreat and carried the armload of clothing down to the river's edge, where she could change in private.

Doing what she could to restore some order to her hair by finger-combing and braiding it, Emily then washed in the cold waters before dressing. Jack's shirt—and she liked believing it was Jack's—fit her fairly well, though the cuffs required a few extra turns. She wore it tucked out over her patched skirt and used a strip woven from her doeskin blouse to belt it loosely at the waist. Her feet were bare, but they were toughened by the hard Texas earth, just as she'd been toughened by the hard life it allowed. Everything about Texas was unyielding . . . except Jack's small smile.

She returned to the camp and was surprised to discover all the rangers but Jack mounted and ready to ride. His horse was still cropping grass minus its tack. He was addressing his men in a low, firm voice, and she could just make out the last of his words.

"I consider the circumstances under which we found Mrs. Marcus no one's business but hers. And if I find out that any of you thought different and were loose of lip, I won't like it. I think she's been misused enough by unkind hands, and she doesn't deserve to be misused further by unkind words. Tell the captain I'll be bringing his wife home as soon as she's better suited to travel."

The rangers gathered up their reins without comment, each lifting his hat politely as Emily approached, before they turned as a unit and started for Ysleta. She looked to Jack for an explanation, blinking back the tears his beautiful words had brought. He didn't address her directly, but rather stole covert glances as he disassembled their camp.

"Got to thinking my leg could use a few days to heal, then we can take our time going back . . . as much time as you think you need."

Emily swallowed hard, unable to speak. He was doing it for her. He wasn't the kind of man who would take even a minute away from duty to see to his own state of health. And that made her marvel at him all the more.

She came aware that he was breaking camp and asked with a mild interest, "So where are we going?"

"Someplace I know of close by." With those cryptic words, he began to saddle his sorrel. His expression was locked down tight around a racing heart and mind. And he refused—absolutely refused—to believe he had made this choice just so he could spend a little extra time alone with Emily Marcus. He didn't like thinking of what that would make him: a man lusting after his friend's wife.

He climbed aboard the tall sorrel and freed a stirrup as he put down his hand. Emily took it and lithely swung up behind him. Her arms curled about his middle as she scooched up close, her thighs overlapping his, her soft breasts pressed to his rigid back. He'd meant to take it slow and easy that morning, but the agitation she quickened inside him prompted him to kick his horse up into a brisk canter. The sooner he got where they were going, the better.

It was a half day's ride from where they crossed the river. If Emily was tired or wished to stop, she never voiced it. She clung to him, moving in time with him, bumping against him until his nerves were about rubbed raw. Their conversation was as sparse as the countryside.

"Jack what?"

"What?"

"Jack, what's your last name?"

"Bass."

"Jack Bass."

He almost shivered from the caressing way she pronounced it. And he was very aware of the way her thighs were rubbing against his, of her hands resting easy at his belt buckle and the softness of her hair tickling his cheek and neck as she leaned over his shoulder to talk to him.

"Any relation to the ranger, the train robber, or the tracker?"

"The tracker's my Uncle Harmon. The ranger's Will, my—my mother's husband. The train robber's dead and buried and thankfully, no kin to me."

Emily mused over this information for a moment, then said, "Isn't Harmon Bass part Mescalero Apache?"

"Yes. So's my mother."

"Then—"

"So am I." He wasn't particularly ashamed of that heritage, but it wasn't something he bragged on, either. He just never brought it up in conversation. He supposed he didn't mind Emily knowing. It explained his easy acceptance of her situation. He couldn't condemn her being among those of whom he was a part. What he couldn't explain as easily was his reaction to her. It was as if he'd never been around a woman.

Then, with gratitude, he saw the small spread up ahead with its low adobe house and lazily turning windmill. He felt Emily straighten behind him in interest.

"Whose place is this?"

"My family's," he told her gruffly, as his gaze hungrily detailed the familiar landscape. "It's my home."

Four

"Jack!"

A black-haired girl launched herself off the front porch, grabbing him about the neck and nearly dragging him down from the saddle. He slid off and into her squeezing embrace. After kissing him wildly all over the face, after a four-year absence, the first thing she demanded was, "What did you bring me?"

Jack laughed and knocked the wetness of her kisses and his glad tears from his cheeks. "You haven't changed a bit, Sarah. I brought you a visitor."

The dark-eyed girl pouted as if that was small consolation, but she smiled prettily enough up at Emily. "Howdy, ma'am. Step on down." Then she looked between the two of them in wide-eyed wondering. "Oh, Jack! You haven't gone and gotten yourself married, have you?"

Jack flushed. "Don't you have any manners at all? No. This is Mrs. Marcus. Where's Mama?" As he asked, his chest tightened up in a flurry of anticipation.

"Over at Uncle Harm's. She's checking on Amanda. They're expecting again."

"Expecting what?"

"A baby, you dolt. Number three."

"Three?" Suddenly, it felt as if he'd been gone a lifetime. "Good to know he's found something to do with his idle time," Jack muttered. Sarah giggled naughtily, understanding much more than he would have liked. He turned and reached up for Emily, guiding her easily to the ground. He was aware of his sister's gauging attention and stepped quickly away from the other woman. "When's she going to be home?"

"Soon, I guess. She wouldn't trust me to start supper."

"Where's everyone else?"

"Daddy and the boys are out tallying the spring calves. Should be in by suppertime, too. Are they ever gonna be surprised! What's this?" She fingered the ranger star pinned on his coat.

"What's it look like, smarty-girl?"

"When'd you get to be a ranger?" She grinned provokingly. "They written any books about you yet? That'd get Uncle Harmon's goat but good. I think he kinda likes being the hero of the family." They'd grown up enjoying the exaggerated versions of their uncle's life as printed between the covers of a dime novel series. Of course, they'd never believed a word of it. Well, most of it, anyway.

"Haven't done anything worth canonizing," he muttered modestly, and looking at him, Emily doubted that was true. She imagined they could write up a whole encyclopedia on brave acts and sheer heart.

"Think Mama'd trust you to put on some coffee?" Jack started for the house, and about that time, his sister noticed his limp.

"Oh, Jack! You're hurt. You're bleeding! Why didn't you say something? Get inside and off your feet right this minute!" She ducked under his arm and her action insisted that he make it at least appear as though he was dependent upon her strength. He hobbled obediently up the steps, grinning down at her.

"What?" she demanded.

"You sure have gotten pretty."

Sarah Bass scowled at the compliment. "I don't want to be pretty. I want to learn how to track outlaws. Do you know what Uncle Harmon called me when I asked him to teach me?"

"What?"

"A girl!"

"You are a girl."

She sniffed. "It was the *way* he said it."

"Oh."

"You could talk to him, now that you're home. I bet you could get him to see reason. You're his favorite, after all."

"I don't think I can talk fast enough to convince him that you're not a female. He's got pretty good eyesight, and after siring three kids, I figure he knows how to tell the difference."

"Jack Bass, you can be such a—" She broke off and glanced over her shoulder with a sweet smile. "Are you coming in, Mrs. Marcus?"

Emily followed into the small, clean—clean for Texas—living quarters, where Sarah was busy fussing over her older brother. When the girl had him seated with a stool pushed under his bad leg, his hat and coat off, and his face about three shades of red, she scurried into the kitchen to start the coffee brewing. Jack looked up at the smiling woman and offered apologetically, "My sister, Sarah."

"She's going to be a beauty."

"She's going to be a hellraiser," he amended with a grin.

Just then, they heard someone at the door. Turning, still smiling wide, Jack saw his mother standing at the entrance, and he immediately erased the broad grin as he came to his feet. Too late. She was frozen in place, her eyes round and wide. Hers was an expression of terror.

What did she see when she looked at him?

"Mama, look who's here! What a great surprise, huh?"

The intrusion of Sarah's gleeful cry made Rebecca Bass blink. Then slowly the tension eased. A great surprise, indeed. One that jolted her almost beyond recovery. "Jack," she said softly, tone uncertain.

"Mama."

She came toward him then, her arms open, but he withdrew behind a narrow smile as she hugged him close. Her reception had stopped the joy cold within his heart just as the sight of him had stopped the blood cold in her veins. It was hard to just push aside something like that and pretend it didn't happen. Or that it hadn't happened before. Jack pulled away uneasily, unable to meet her teary eyes.

"Mama, if it's no bother, Mrs. Marcus and I would like to bunk over for a few days."

"Jack's hurt, Mama. And he's a ranger."

"Hurt? What happened?" She was instantly all maternal concern as her gaze flew over him, jerking up short at the bloodstains on his pant leg. "Gun shot?"

"Apache arrows. It's all right. They're healing. Mrs. Marcus, here, is the one who needs the rest. She's had kind of a bad time of it. Can you put us up? If you'd rather not—"

"Of course, we can. You sit down. Get off that leg. Sarah, fetch me something to use for bandaging. Mrs. Marcus, pleased to meet you. Jack, let me have a look—"

"Mama! I'll see to my own leg! I've had enough females hovering over me. Can't a man be spared a little pride?" He snatched the clean strips of linen from his sister and the basin of water. "I'm going to use the front bedroom, if that's all right with you." Then he stalked off in an indignant hobble, slamming the door behind him.

Rebecca Bass stared after him, her expression bewildered for just a moment. "He was only a boy when he left. I just can't start thinking of him as a grown man." Then she smiled a bit wistfully. "Would seem he's found a bit of my brother's arrogance, too." She sighed then looked at her guest. "Mrs. Marcus, what can I get you?"

After the whirlwind greeting, she wasn't sure what to say. "Nothing. I'm fine, really."

"You'd say no to a hot bath?"

"No. I wouldn't say no to a hot bath."

Rebecca smiled. "I'll put some water on. Make yourself at home."

Home. Emily hadn't been beneath a white man's roof for five years. The walls seemed close, the room, crowded. But the bath was pure luxury, once it was poured in Jack's parents' bedroom. She sank into it with a heavenly sigh, letting its heat soak up the bodily aches and the spiritual pains. It had been a long time since she'd bathed in anything but the chill of a stream. She worked a lather between her rough palms and marveled at the delicate scent and the silky feel. She'd forgotten the simple pleasures of being a woman. She'd been Apache for too long.

How did Jack Bass see her?

She was wondering when a soft tap came on the door.

"Mrs. Marcus?" Rebecca peered in. "I found you some things to put on." Her dark eyes assessed the fair skin appearing over the waterline, taking in the sundry scrapes and obvious bruising. She was all too familiar with the signs of abuse. But she said nothing as she laid the clothes out on the bed. "Take as long as you like."

The woman with her son had been brutalized.

That fact tormented Rebecca Bass. It made her think of other things, old things better forgotten, yet not quite laid to rest. So when Jack came out of the front room, she looked up into his familiar face, seeing not her son, but a remembered shadow of evil. And she heard herself say, "She's been beaten." She hadn't meant it, but the accusation was there, a sharp edge in her voice. Jack stopped and sucked a startled breath, recoiling in disbelief.

"What are you asking, Mama? Are you wondering if maybe I had a hand in it?"

It was the anguish in his voice that reached her. She forced herself to look beyond the pale eyes and the finely shaped mouth to the gentleness of the man she knew her son to be. And realizing how badly she'd hurt him, she reached out for his arm. He flinched away.

"No, Jack. Of course, I don't think that."

Of course, she did. But what he didn't know was why. What he'd never known was why—why she would be so quick to suspect him of such viciousness when he'd never in his life done a malicious or mean-spirited act. As if she was always on guard against the appearance of that bad blood his stepfather warned flowed through his veins. His reply was testy.

"She's been living with the Apache. The Mexicans took her and used her pretty badly. I'm taking her back to her husband as soon as she's fit. Jus' doing my job, Mama. Maybe it wasn't a good idea for me to stop off here."

"Jack." She put a hand on his arm to stay him as he tried to brush by her. That hand moved along his sleeve in a loving overture, soothing the tension, smoothing the rocky start they'd gotten. "I've missed you so much, so very much. It's good to have you home."

He surrendered himself up to her embrace, feeling her

kisses on his cheek, the warm affection of her hug; and his chest filled up with cautious emotion. Cautious because he could still see the look in her eyes when she first beheld him and could still hear the cut of her voice.

Then, over her shoulder, he saw Emily Marcus emerge from the bedroom and all those confused emotions clarified into one; into a longing so pure and achingly sweet he felt powerless in the face of it.

She was wearing one of his mother's dresses. It was of simple weave and practical style, but on Emily Marcus's tall and shapely figure, it was transformed by her lush beauty and poise. The fit wasn't good, but that made it all the more appealing. Fabric strained across the bodice and the hem brushed gracefully at bared mid-calf. She'd plaited her dark hair so that it fell in a heavy braid across her shoulder. And even with the shadowing of bruises, with the rings of weariness about her eyes, she was the most splendid-looking female Jack had ever seen.

Aware of the stillness that had come over her son, Rebecca looked between him and the lovely Mrs. Marcus. She realized in an instant that he had lost his heart to another man's wife and that someone would have to have a good long talk with him.

Soon.

"Daddy's here," Sarah cried, as she raced for the door. "I want to be the first to tell him you're home."

From the concealing cavern of the front door, Jack watched his half-sister dash across the yard, carelessly putting herself in the path of the buckboard that was turning in. At the reins was the man who'd raised him, Will Bass, onetime ranger legend in his own right. The big man levered his crutches around so he could ease down upon them as he slid from the seat. His expression was somber as he listened to Sarah's excited ramblings. Then he lifted his graying head and looked toward the house. There was no anticipation in that look.

A loud whoop and hollering rose from the two boys flanking the buckboard on horseback. They were dismounted and running for the house in a flash. How big they'd gotten, Jack mused with a bittersweet fondness. Sidney—somber, serious-minded Sidney—would be fourteen, and precocious Jeffrey, the baby of the family, all of twelve. They were both dark, like their mother, and eager to fling themselves into their long-absent brother's embrace.

By the time Will made his way to the house, the younger boys were winding down from their boisterous questions and Jack was able to clear them out of the way so he could greet his stepfather. "Hello, Will," he offered neutrally with his outstretched hand. *Will,* not *Papa.*

"So you're back."

Will Bass moved past him with that flat observation. And left with his hand empty, Jack lowered it slowly, scrubbing his palm restlessly upon his injured thigh.

"How long you staying?"

Jack followed him inside. "Couple of days, if that's all right."

"Imagine your mama's already told you it was."

So much for his welcome. After the way they'd parted, should he have expected any different? He supposed not. He made introductions to Emily all around, but he was noticing the way Will fingered the ranger badge pinned on his discarded coat. But being the prideful man he was, Will never mentioned it.

Dinner with the Basses was a crowded, noisy affair. Emily sat quietly and absorbed it all in. A family meal, her first in such a long, long time. Jack was the center of attention, and she enjoyed his modest blushes as he tried to sound casual about his accomplishments with the rangers. Will tried to remain stoic but was slowly drawn into the conversation when talk touched on familiar names and familiar deeds. Soon, the tension eased at the table, but not her curiosity. Just as their curiosity concerning her simmered.

Jack was diplomatic about heading off his family's questions. He told his younger siblings that he was escorting her to El Paso—end of discussion. She looked into their fresh, innocent faces and wanted to weep. For the secrets she carried. For the ache of longing she hid inside. By the time the meal ended, she was at an emotional and physical ebb. And as always, Jack was quick to perceive it.

"Mama, Mrs. Marcus looks as if she's ready to turn in. Where do you want her?"

"She can bunk with me," Sarah offered eagerly. She was intrigued by her brother's guest. They didn't see many visitors, and she was hungry for the chance to share a little lights-out gossip.

"Only if you promise not to keep her up with your gabbing," Rebecca ordered.

"Oh, Mama . . ."

"Sarah, Mrs. Marcus is tired. I won't have you pestering her."

"She won't be a bother, Mrs. Bass. Not at all." Emily followed that claim with a poignant smile. And seeing it, Jack was reminded of something he'd forgotten.

What had happened to Neil and Emily's daughter?

Something as simple as the touch of a hand sent Emily bolting from her blissful sleep into a world of remembered pain and panic. She lay for several tortured seconds with a scream wedged up in her throat before her thoughts cleared enough to permit time and place to intrude. Then she remembered: she was at Jack Bass's home. She was sharing a bed with young Sarah Bass, who'd nudged her shoulder in the process of rolling over. There was no threat here, no danger, yet she couldn't close her eyes. Her every nerve and fiber was acutely alive from the sudden push of alarm. And she knew it would be a long while before she was able to rest again.

Quietly she slipped from the bed, thinking a little crisp night air might take the edge off her restlessness. The main room of the Bass home was lit by firelight. That uneven flame cast the auburn head bent toward it in a warm blaze of copper. Jack was seated on the floor before the hearth, his leg stretched out in front of him, the strong, whipcord length of him clad only in a pair of faded long johns. Emily was aware of a different kind of restlessness as she approached him.

"Mind if I join you at your fire, Sergeant?"

He looked up in surprise, his pale blue eyes wide open and deep enough to drown in. His lips parted as he breathed an unconscious invitation. It was all she could do to resist sinking into the warmth of his stare, down to the luxury of his mouth. Then he blinked, remembering himself.

"Ma'am, I'm not exactly dressed for entertaining company."

She allowed her gaze to travel along the snug byways of cotton flannel. It was an exhilarating journey. "Neither am I," she murmured, plucking distractedly at Rebecca's linen nightgown. "So, shall we just cloak ourselves in our proper respectability?"

He smiled thinly. "Pull yourself up a piece of floor."

She sank down next to him, wrapping her arms about tented knees, and for a time, both of them studied the fire, each making a concentrated effort not to glance at the other. Finally, Jack couldn't stand the suspense.

"Miz Emily, can I ask you something?"

She looked to him with what was almost a playful smile. "Like I said, we don't have many secrets between us. Ask away."

"When you took me to Ysleta, why did you leave me outside camp, instead of coming in to safety with me?"

The gentle amusement was instantly gone from her face. She stared back into the flames. "I didn't know I had anything in Ysleta, but I had every reason to return to the Apache."

"Your daughter?"

She flashed him a quick look. "Yes. Cathy. I couldn't leave her and—I couldn't leave her."

"Is she all right?" His brow puckered in concern. "I mean, she wasn't with you when the Mexicans . . ."

She shook her head. "No. She was at the main camp with my husband's mother."

"Your . . . husband?"

Emily smiled wryly and sighed. "I'm afraid this is going to be complicated."

"Yes, ma'am. It sounds like it is."

"I thought Neil had been killed. I saw him fall, Jack. I couldn't believe he could survive it. I had Cathy, who was just an infant, and I had to protect her. I had no hope of being rescued and nothing to go back to. I did the only thing I could: I took an Apache husband."

"And he still has your daughter."

Emily nodded. "It was so simple before. My life was in the Apache camp. It was hard, but I had no reason to want to escape it. Cathy doesn't know any other kind of life, any other people. And after being among them for so long, I couldn't see returning to the white world to face its scorn. Can you understand?"

Oh, yes. He understood. There was little Indian blood in him. An eighth. No one would guess it, looking at him. But his uncle was clearly of crossed blood, and so was his mother, and he'd seen the narrow minds of Texas react to that mix of heritage. It was unfair and it was cruel, and he could see why Emily Marcus would choose not to submit to the prejudice of it.

"But now I find out Neil's alive," Emily continued, in a distraught tone. "Cathy is his child. I'm his legal wife. I can't just ignore that."

"So, what are you going to do?"

"The right thing, I hope." She glanced at him with a desperate sincerity. "I guess that would depend on Neil, on whether he'll take me back."

"He'd be crazy not to." Jack turned away bashfully when he realized he'd stated that aloud. "And your Apache husband, you think he'll just let you go?"

"The Apache are not romantics, Sergeant. They see marriage in terms of utility. I gave him what he wanted. I don't think he'll come after me."

She said that quietly, with so much emotion, Jack had to wonder over her meaning. And she looked so suddenly sad, he found himself foolishly saying, "If you were mine, I surely wouldn't be willing to give you up to any other man."

"That's very sweet," she told him, smiling as if to add, but very naive. "Unfortunately, most men tend to view their women like their horses, and use them until they're spent, then get new ones."

Feeling obligated to speak up in his own defense, he argued, "I would never do that."

"But you aren't like most men." And she realized then how true that was. Jack Bass was a notch above all she knew and understood about the male species. If she was his, he would come after her and nothing short of death would stop him. That knowledge played about her heart with an unsettling quiver. But she didn't belong to him. She was divided between two men, and she wasn't certain of either one's devotions.

"Neil will take you back, ma'am. I know him; he's a good man. I've ranged with him and have been proud to call him friend for four whole years. You got nothing to worry about."

She wished she could share his confidence.

They were both silent and pensive for several minutes. Then Jack asked, "What are you going to do about your daughter?"

She looked to him with teary eyes. "I don't know, Jack."

"I'll get her back for you, Emily."

He said it easily, as if it was just that simple. She was about to call him on his rather ill-thought-out ambitions when she happened to gaze into his eyes. And there she saw a deep, steely conviction. And she believed, if only for a moment.

With a tremendous sigh, she said, "Oh, Jack, I wish you could. But I don't know where the band is. After the run-in below the border, they're bound to head back into the mountains of the Bend. No one could find them if they're determined to hide."

Then Jack smiled at her as if she was the one being naive. "That's not quite true, ma'am. Happens I know the best tracker in all of West Texas. And could be he'd be willing to find your little girl for you."

His uncle was Harmon Bass, and no one could hunt a trail like he could. And no one could follow an Apache like an Apache.

"I'll get her back for you. I'll see you're a family again."

She didn't answer that. She couldn't. Because a certain sacrifice would have to be made in order for her to return to Neil Marcus, and it wasn't one she cared to discuss, even with the compassionate Jack Bass. That was something that would weigh upon her soul alone. And she wasn't sure she would be able to stand it.

Jack watched her. She was trying so hard to be brave, but he could see the tremors of distress shivering along her strong frame. She stared solemnly into the fire, but dampness had begun to bead along her lower lashes. No one should have to be as miserable and alone as she looked in that moment. So he opened his arm to her and patted his shoulder with his other hand. And she settled in without a word.

He told himself he was doing it because he felt sorry for all she'd been through. Or because she was the wife of his good friend. Or because he was just a decent human being. But the truth touched on none of those reasons. The truth was, he would have done anything in the world for Emily Marcus.

Because he'd fallen in love with her.

Five

It was a lonesomely situated frame house out in the middle of nothing. Set at the foot of the Chisos Mountains, with Blue Creek meandering through its side yard, his uncle's ranch was much as Jack remembered it. He'd helped erect the main house Amanda had ordered from the East and had paid a fortune to have it freighted from the last rail stop. It had come in boxes, each nicely labeled, and they'd put it together like a big jigsaw puzzle out in the hot bead of the West Texas sun, two whole stories of stately magnificence, with the upstairs full of bedrooms. Harmon had mused over the grand scale and asked if his wife was planning to rent it out like a hotel. She'd smiled back at him and said with a sultry sincerity that she meant for him to fill all those upstairs rooms for her. Apparently, he'd been working at it.

It was a scorcher of an afternoon, too hot to allow one even to have an active imagination. Taking advantage of the relative cool of the front porch, a man reclined on its swing, bare feet propped on one arm and head on the other, with a straw Stetson angled over his face. Resting in the curl of his arm was a blond-headed child of about three, and nestled beside him, another blond girl of five. All were contentedly snoozing as Jack tied up his horse, appearing the picture of lazy tranquillity.

He approached the porch quietly, but even as his boot lifted toward the bottom stair, a low drawl came from beneath the tipped Stetson.

"You could wake a dead man from his nap with those heavy feet of yours. Thought I taught you better than that."

"Thought you were sleeping."

"How's a man supposed to rest, with you making all that noise?"

Harmon Bass thumbed up the brim of his hat and there it was, that brief recoil when he first laid eyes upon his nephew. A recognition that had nothing to do with him. It was enough to make Jack hesitate on that bottom step.

"Hey, Uncle Harm."

"Hey, yourself. Hang on while I divest myself of these younguns." He rolled nimbly over the elder child and tucked the younger in next to her. Neither stirred in the languorous afternoon heat. He lingered for a second, looking down on the sleeping pair, then gently brushed the wisps of fair hair back from their brows to bestow light kisses. And Jack couldn't help smiling at this image of the infamous Harmon Bass, the relentless legendary tracker and tough dime novel hero completely humbled by the role of father.

Harm crossed the porch in his easy Apache glide. His expression was stoic. Jack couldn't read either welcome or objection in those bland half-Indian features, so he stood uncertain until his uncle took two steps down and took him up in a crushing embrace. And Jack was overcome by the feeling of unconditional acceptance.

"You've been gone too long," Harm told him simply, and that said everything. He'd been thought about and he'd been missed. And that was what he needed to hear. "When did you get so tall? Guess I'll have to start looking up to you now." Harm stepped back, keeping his hands resting easy upon the broad spread of his nephew's shoulders as his blue eyes detailed face and form with obvious affection.

"No," Jack murmured softly. "It'll always be the other way around, Uncle Harmon."

Harm pointed to the small splotches on the thigh of his denims. "Trouble with Apache?"

"How'd you know it wasn't outlaws?"

Harm snorted haughtily. "No white man can place that tight a pattern. Sit on down. Let's make some talk."

Jack sat down on the front steps with his uncle and enjoyed a feeling of easy camaraderie he'd never shared with another. Harm was his mother's brother, only ten years his senior. He'd ridden in and out of their lives throughout Jack's growing-up years, and he'd plainly thought the sun rose and set on his free-spirited uncle. While Will Bass taught him about responsibility and integrity, it was from Harm that he learned his lessons in life.

Harm was a shrewd survivalist. Behind his small stature and mild manner was as cunning and dangerous a man as ever had been bred in the sear of West Texas. Since joining up with the rangers, Jack had heard things about his uncle that shocked him half to death. But he couldn't disbelieve them. Harm was part Apache, and that was like breeding wolf into a family pet. The resulting animal might look like a dog and behave like a dog, but there was always that element of wolf that one had to watch out for. That unpredictable streak of viciousness ran through Harmon Bass, but ironically enough, it was Harmon who'd taught him about the value of family and the power of love found in belonging. On the front steps, with his girls slumbering peacefully a few feet away, Harm might look all lazy and domestic, but Jack wasn't fooled for a minute into thinking the wildness was no longer there. And that was what he was counting on.

"Exciting life you look to be leading these days, Uncle Harmon."

Harm gave him a bland smile, taking no offense. "Don't smirk until you've tried to keep up with a three- and a five-year-old."

"And Amanda," Jack added.

Harm chuckled. "Amanda *does* tend to keep life from getting boring." His expression softened as he considered the plucky eastern girl who'd stampeded right over his heart six years ago. "Know what she's started breeding?"

"Besides kids?"

Harm gave him an elbow. "Horses. Sitting out here, smack dab in the middle of Apache country, and she decides to raise horses. Like growing apples in the Garden of Eden. How's any self-respecting Indian supposed to look down on a fine batch of horseflesh without doing what comes naturally? She's torturing them, pure and simple."

Jack smiled. "So you spend half your time chasing 'em down and bringing 'em back?"

"Only had to do that once. Can't say we've come up with any missing since then."

He said that casually enough, but Jack understood. The Apache had tested him, and he'd taught them a harsh lesson. Only one was necessary for them to learn Harmon Bass wasn't someone you messed with.

"Felt so bad about it," Harm continued. "I took to keeping a few cows wandering around just so they'd have something to steal. Bad thing for a man to lose face in front of his family. Live and let live, I always figure. I drew the line at Ammy's pets, and as long as they don't cross over it, they make fine neighbors. And they keep an eye on Amanda and the girls on the occasion that I have to be gone."

Trusting the Apache to guard one's wife and children. Jack marveled at it, but apparently Harm didn't think it strange. Not when he'd been partially raised among the Mescalero. He spoke their language, he walked their paths, he respected their ways. They were family. To him, it was that simple. If everyone in the Bend was of the same open mind, Jack and the rangers would have had a lot less work to do over the past few years. Unfortunately, that wasn't the way things were.

"So," Jack began with a roundabout ease. "You still do much tracking?"

"Off and on, to shake off the scent of living tame, more than for the money. Amanda's got so much of that, she could buy half the state of Texas for a side yard flower garden, if she was of a mind to. I'm purely embarrassed by how much she's spent on some of those mares out back. Can't see the fuss over a bunch of critters made for riding, stealing, or eating, but she likes 'em." He had no interest in his wife's vast inheritance, and no matter how he might grumble, he let her spend it on anything she chose to, so long as it made her happy. And when Amanda was happy, he didn't need anything else. His wants and needs weren't terribly complicated; a family to love and be loved by, the pride of providing for them, the ability to protect them, that was all. Amanda Duncan had made his life a paradise, even if she did tend to talk his ear off at times. She more than made up for that in other, more pleasurable ways.

"What did you come to ask me?"

Taken off guard, Jack blinked at his sudden directness.

"Well? You've been dancing around something ever since you got here. What is it?"

"I wanted to come over for a visit."

"I been here for four years, and this is the first time you've thought to come calling. What's on your mind?"

Jack flushed, feeling guilty of neglect, but also desperate for his uncle's help. "I don't want you to think I stopped by only because I wanted something from you."

Harm put his hand to the back of his nephew's head, tapping it lightly. "Jack, I didn't think that for a minute. We're family. If there's something I can do for you, just ask it plain. But you'd better ask soon, otherwise I'll be obliged to ask you to stay for a meal, and I wouldn't wish Amanda's cooking on someone I care about."

"I heard that, Harmon Bass, and just wait until you see what turns up on your plate for supper!"

Amanda Bass came out onto the porch, a beautiful and very pregnant picture of indignation. She was a complementing contrast to her husband of six years: fair to his dark, tall to his slight, city-bred to his rugged rearing. She was a gurgling, reckless stream next to his still, deep waters, and they played upon each other in sparkling harmony— most of the time. Jack was wondering if this was one exception. She looked mighty cross.

Looking not in the least chagrined, Harmon leaned back on his elbows to gaze up at her. "I kinda had my eye on that bay mare. A little gravy and biscuits on the side. What do you think, Jack?"

"Think I'll stick to beans." He rose up awkwardly, favoring his leg. "Hello, Amanda."

She came up to hug him tight and plant a warm kiss upon his cheek. Though there were only three years separating their ages, she'd always treated him with a maternal tenderness. Her palm rubbed over his other cheek, rasping on morning stubble. "Look at you, Jack Bass. Last time I saw you, you weren't even shaving. Has it been that long? Shame on you, for not coming to see us sooner." Then she stopped her prattling and stared at him long and hard, beginning to frown. "Goodness, Harmon, isn't he getting to be the spitting image of—"

"Ammy," Harm interrupted smoothly, "Jack's come a ways and he's thirsty."

"Oh, I'm sorry. What can I get you, Jack?"

The truth would be nice, he wanted to say. The truth she'd been about to speak before his uncle had stepped in. But he smiled and said, "I'm fine. You don't need to wait on me. I know where the kitchen is."

"Isn't he polite, Harmon?" She canted a devilish glance at her husband. "Maybe he'll be a good influence on you."

She eased down onto the step between them, nudging in beside Harm with her arm looped through his. Jack was aware of a peculiar tension between his aunt and uncle, but he *was* too polite to make mention of it. But he did watch curiously as Amanda's hand began a subtle stroking up and down her husband's arm. It was a seductive movement, and instead of responding, Harm looked increasingly uneasy.

"So, Jack," she asked, never looking away from Harm's taut profile, "tell us what you've been doing."

And as he spoke a condensed version of his last four years, he followed the path of Amanda's bare toes as they rubbed over the darker brown of Harmon's foot. Harm edged his away. And when her palm began to circle down the top and up the inside of her husband's thigh, that's when his uncle stood in agitation.

"Ammy, Jack and I have some talking to do."

She stiffened at the obvious dismissal and rose up with a curt, "Excuse me. I didn't mean to bother you." That was aimed pointedly at Harm, and when he showed no reaction, she bent to give Jack another kiss on the brow. "Don't leave without saying goodbye." Then she marched into the house, mindful enough of the children to ease the door shut quietly.

Sometime later, Jack came in to say his goodbye. Amanda was in the kitchen, still stewing, but she warmed to him in an instant, hugging him tight.

"How long are you staying at your family's?"

"I don't know, Amanda."

"Well, you try real hard to get back over here. The girls would love to meet their Cousin Jack."

"They're beautiful girls, Amanda."

She simmered proudly, the way mothers do, and kissed his cheek. "So, when are you going to settle down and have some of your own? You're great husband and father material."

"Someday." He said that so elusively, she smiled.

"Someday soon, I hope. Don't you smirk. Someday some woman is going to chase you all over West Texas and you won't stand a chance."

"We'll see." He returned the kiss to her brow, and then he was gone.

Harm wandered into the kitchen a while later to see what she was banging upon the stove so viciously.

"I think that piece of meat is dead already," he commented mildly. She gave him a severing glance and went back to beating the roast with a tenderizing mallet.

"If you can't abide my dinners, you can always go out and turn over some rocks in search of your own."

"Ammy . . . *shijii,* you know I was only teasing. I'd eat just about anything without complaint."

"And that's supposed to be a compliment." She pushed him aside and stormed to the pantry to jerk out a bag of flour. "What did Jack want?"

Harm watched her through impassive eyes, feeling the smolder of her anger. Suffering for it. "He asked if I would help him find a six-year-old white girl running with a band of Mescalero."

Amanda paused briefly without turning. "And what did you tell him?"

"I didn't say yes or no."

"Why not?"

"I don't like leaving you this far along."

"Go," she told him tersely. "That would solve everything. Let's see, I should have this baby in about two months, will nurse it for at least a year. Why don't you come back then, when you're interested in treating me like a wife again?" When he touched her shoulders, she shrugged him off with a growl of, "Don't, Harmon. Don't start something you've no intention of finishing."

"Ammy, I love you."

"Really? When was the last time?" And she stomped into the dining room with a handful of plates. She began to smack them down on the tabletop, then stood with the last one clutched in her hands, breathing hard. She was being unreasonable, but she didn't care about reason. She was hot and tired and uncomfortable, and so hungry for her husband's affection, she couldn't look at him without wanting to take him down to the floor. And his damned Apache restraint was pushing her to the edge of desperation.

All those sacred centuries ago, who had decided that once a woman was carrying a man's child, she should no longer crave intimacy with him? If she knew, she'd have found a way to go back in time to disembowel him! It was her own fault. Harm had to do little more than think about making love to her and she'd find herself pregnant. And then she'd have to hide the truth from him until he literally bumped into it. Then his honorable retreat.

Who made Apache men so stubborn and self-righteous? She'd gut them out, too. Harm had explained it to her during those long, chaste months before Leisha's birth. A couple was expected to display continence during such times. If a man demanded a connection with his wife too soon, he was acting against his growing child. Maybe Apache women weren't interested in their men, once they were breeding. Then Harmon should have found himself an Apache wife, because that wasn't the case with her at all. A heightened feeling of sensuality accompanied each of her three pregnancies. The changes in her body made her feel voluptuous and ripe for the caresses of a man—her man. Some of that excitement was lost when she practically had to corner and force herself upon him, and then endure his repentant attitude afterward. With Becca, she'd tried to respect him for his beliefs. She'd been a good, modest wife, and if he wondered why she'd grown so fond of midnight baths in the chill of Blue Creek, he didn't ask. Probably figured it was safer that way. But this time, with this child, she was as edgy as a she-cat, and Harm shied away from her with a wary prudence. And she was ready to hang him up over her cook fire.

Amanda was pulled from her brooding by the sound of his light tread in the hall. She was immediately in a panic. "Harmon?" He waited for her to rush up to him, his expression carefully veiled. "Where are you going?"

"Out."

"Out where?"

"Just out."

He started for the door, away from her. And Amanda had a sudden recall of Rebecca telling her that sometimes

Apache men went out and were gone for months without word.

"Harmon—please don't go!"

She caught at his arm and he turned toward her. Seeing her fright and dismay, he couldn't hold to his bad temper. His arm moved easily about her shoulders in a gesture of comfort as she leaned upon his chest, clutching tightly.

"I would never leave you." He said that softly, caressingly.

"I'm sorry, Harmon. I don't mean to be so disagreeable."

"Shhh, *shijii*. I'm sorry, too."

He'd just begun to relax. Then she was nuzzling his throat, nibbling with impatient kisses.

"Ammy . . ."

"Oh, Harmon."

"Ammy, stop. You're making it hard—"

"I'm trying to," she purred, drawing his face toward her so she could kiss him. And she was met with his open-eyed, sealed-lipped response. Amanda gave him a shove and headed for the kitchen. "Never mind. If I have to work that hard to make you want me, I don't want you. Just go away."

"Ammy . . ."

She heard him follow and hurried faster. She felt stupid and unattractive enough without him seeing her face swell up with silly tears. "Go away! Go with Jack. Go to hell!"

Harm whipped his arms around her, hauling her back until she was wedged back to front against him. She struggled. She was seething and sobbing. Then his mouth moved along her temple and his hand circumscribed one plump breast, and she went still all over.

"Shhhh!" he whispered at her ear, before lowering to kiss the junction of her jaw and neck. She made a soft, liquid sound and arched her body as her head leaned back upon his shoulder. He continued to touch her and kiss her until she was moaning his name in a daze of desire. He cupped her chin, angling her so he could kiss her properly, with all the passion she could ever ask for. She turned in his arms, holding to him, loving him fiercely, answering the demand of his mouth with complete abandon. When he pulled away, it was only an inch or two, so that their faces were still close together and he could possess her with the intensity of his gaze.

"I love you."

"I know you do." She touched his cheek, his hair, with her fingertips, then touched his lips very gently with her own. "And I love you, too, Harmon. Too much sometimes."

"Never too much," he corrected. Then softly, "I'm going with Jack."

She didn't say anything. She only nodded.

"After I take you upstairs and lay you down."

"Oh, Harmon—"

"Mama? Daddy?"

Harm kissed Amanda quickly, then turned to his daughter Leisha with a smile. If he was annoyed by the interruption, he never once betrayed it. "How would you like your *sikis* Sarah to come stay with you for a while? I have to go away for a short time and your mama will need you to help Sarah take care of the house and the baby."

"I will, Daddy." She didn't ask where he was going. It was enough that he would trust her with a job of importance.

"Good. Then I won't worry. You can start now by watching your sister. I'm going to help your mama lie down."

"Isn't she feeling well?" The small brow crowded with concern.

"Your mama's fine. I'm going to help her feel better, is all."

That was good enough for a five-year-old.

And about twenty minutes later, Amanda was feeling better. In fact, she felt wonderful.

"You make it hard for a man to remember his honor," Harm scolded tenderly, as she cuddled up to him all soft and sated and smiling.

"I'm not in the least bit sorry," she replied, as she drew aimless patterns across his bare chest with her forefinger. Then she paused and glanced up. "Are you?"

"Ammy, you make me crazy." But then he was kissing her with a thoroughness that was an answer in itself, a very delightful answer. She nestled against his shoulder, pleased with everything in her world.

"Harmon, when does Jack want you to leave?"

"Right away."

The idle forays along his chest became more purposeful, as if she was storing up the feel of him. "Whose child are you looking for?"

"The daughter of his ranger captain. His wife rescued Jack from the Mescalero, and now he wants to free her child for her."

"Rescued him?"

"You would have heard all that if you hadn't been trying so hard to distract me down there on the porch."

"Did I?"

"What?"

"Distract you?"

"Only about as much as having you peel my skin off an inch at a time."

"I like your skin where it is." She backed that claim with a leisurely caress. "Be careful, Harmon."

"I will. I'm always careful. And I'm curious."

"About what?"

"This woman. The way Jack talks of her—"

Amanda came up on her elbows, all sudden interest. "What do you mean? How does he talk of her?"

"The way I used to talk about you. As if I wanted no part of you when I was ready to die from the want of you. The way a man talks about a woman he wants to bed."

"You think he's in love with her?"

Harm's features sobered. "I hope not." Then he clasped her face in both hands and kissed her hard. "I have to go." But when he tried to stand, she was hanging on him most distractfully. He reached for his shirt, slipping it on and starting up the buttons. Amanda's palms slid under his shirt tails.

"Are you sure you have to go right this minute?" Her touch was making it hard for him to remember having any honor at all.

"I think I'd better."

"Yes. You'd better."

And he sank down upon the bed with her, forgetting everything.

Harm rode into the Basses' front yard during the waning hours of afternoon. Emily studied him from her position on the porch as Jack went out to greet him. Harmon Bass. She'd heard of him. His skill was legendary among the Mescalero, and he was talked about around their fires even though his family ties to them had died out. He was considered one of them and he was spoken of with respect. She watched him swing down off his horse, familiar with the way he moved and not fooled by his small, wiry frame.

His grace was sure and lethal, and there was a directness to his stare that she admired. Here was a man who could help her. She recognized it at once and was grateful to Jack for bringing him to her.

Harm came up to the porch. He spoke to her in low Apache syllables, asking questions about the people she'd lived with, particulars about her daughter, anything he thought might aid him in his search. They conversed in a language that excluded Jack, because he was a ranger, because some of the questions might endanger the Apache if the answers were made known within ranger circles; not because they didn't trust Jack, but rather from an inbred caution. If Jack was hurt by their quiet foreign conversation, he didn't show it. He wasn't as interested in finding the renegade Apache as he was in restoring Emily Marcus's child. And Harm could do that. He had no doubts at all.

When they were done talking, Emily placed her hand upon Harm's shoulder in a light, thankful gesture, then, after sparing a small smile in Jack's direction, she went inside, leaving the two men alone.

"I appreciate this, Uncle Harmon."

Harm shrugged as if words weren't necessary. To his thinking, they weren't.

"How long do you think it'll take?"

"Depends on how far they've burrowed back into the mountains. I'll find them. Then what?"

"Come get me. Here or at Ysleta."

If he thought that a strange request, Harm didn't say so. He merely nodded. "I'd like Sarah to stay with Amanda while I'm gone."

Hearing the sudden quiet in his tone, Jack had to ask, "Are you sure you want to be doing this? I'd understand if you didn't want to leave her."

Harm's smile was small and wry. "It's better that I'm gone."

Jack grinned. "Serve you up something nasty for supper, did she?"

Harm responded to his nephew's ribbing with a smug look. "She dished out what I deserved."

Jack followed him back to where his horse was tethered. "Oh, speaking of Sarah, she tells me she wants you to teach her to be a tracker."

"She's a girl." That was said with the expected Apache indignation.

"She's a Bass."

Harm smiled blandly. "We'll see." He paused before mounting and gave his nephew a long look. "She is a brave woman, your Mrs. Marcus."

"Yes."

One word gave away everything.

"She is another man's woman."

"I know that, Uncle Harmon."

And Harm said nothing more. He put his hand to Jack's cheek in unspoken sympathy, then drew him up for a tight Apache embrace, one meant to show a wealth of feelings and affection.

"Take care, Uncle Harm," Jack murmured, pulling away at last.

"I will."

Then he swung onto his horse and headed toward the Chisos.

Jack stood out in the dusty yard, watching him disappear from sight. Then he looked back toward the house.

She is another man's woman.

He couldn't afford to forget that.

Six

The night air was hot and arid and served to dry the sweat of remembered fear clinging to Emily Marcus. How long would it take for an undisturbed sleep to return? How long before she could push away the panic and the pain and go on?

She was wiping at the dampness on her cheeks when she heard a soft step behind her. At first, she thought it was Jack. She hadn't seen him inside. The disappointment she felt then became a quickening anticipation now.

"Can't sleep?"

The question came from Rebecca Bass. Jack's mother came up beside her and stared up at the stars, away from the tracks of moisture on the other woman's face.

Emily wiped away her tears and sought an evasive answer, unsure of how much Jack had told his mother. "Just a lot on my mind."

"It'll take awhile, but you'll find yourself resting easy again."

Emily cast a startled glance her way, but Rebecca only smiled in sad understanding.

"A strong woman can endure anything, Mrs. Marcus. All she has to hold onto is the truth that what she is isn't what's been done to her."

"How—"

"How do I know? Oh, I know. My brother Harmon and I survived four days of sheer hell when we were little more than children. My situation was much the same as yours. For a time, I even hated him for keeping me alive. I didn't think I could live with the shame of it. But you know what I discovered?"

Emily shook her head.

"That shame was inside me. No one looking at me could see it. What had happened to me wasn't out in the open, where all the world would know of it. I was the only one keeping the guilt alive."

"How did you get rid of it?" That was asked quietly, hopefully.

Rebecca smiled out into the night. It was a fierce expression. She was a lot like her brother, Emily decided, strong and tough. And Emily found herself listening.

"By getting angry," was her unexpected advice. "By staying angry—not at myself, but at those responsible. And by finding the best kind of revenge, not the kind Harmon went after in Apache retribution, but a stronger vengeance. I refused to let them have power over me. I refused to let what they'd done destroy my life or steal my joy of living."

"That sounds too simple."

"A simple concept, a difficult practice. A daily practice, one that gets easier. You have the strength inside you, Emily. We both do. What makes it easier is the support of those who love you."

Emily was thinking of Jack when Rebecca's words cut through his image.

"Is your husband a strong man?"

Emily blinked, pushing aside the picture of Jack Bass in favor of Neil Marcus. It was hard, surprisingly hard, because she no longer had a clear visual of the man she'd wed and to whom she'd borne a child. The only stark impression she carried was the one of him falling from his horse, pierced by Apache arrows. She couldn't remember his smile or his touch or the sound of his voice. And that frightened her. It was like trying to evoke the memory of a stranger. But she did remember he was strong, and she said so.

"He might not be able to accept right away," Rebecca warned gently. "Be patient, Emily. A man doesn't have the same kind of strength a woman has. To them, strength is a physical thing, an aggression directed at others. They react to anger, to fear, to hurt as if it has to be controlled by force. A woman's strength is in her spiritual calm, in her ability to get beyond those same things without feeling obligated to act them out. Men are taught they have to be in charge of their emotions, of their situations. They're never taught that sometimes the better way is just to accept and go on. My brother is the strongest, hardest man I know, yet he struggled for years to overcome what I had found peace with. It took the gentleness of his wife to show him that acceptance wasn't surrender."

"What of your husband? He doesn't hold the past against you?"

Rebecca smiled. "Will gave me the courage I needed to look for strength inside. He's never once looked at me as if I'm stained by circumstance."

"You're lucky, Mrs. Bass."

"No, I'm a survivor. I have to be, for my own sake, for Jack's. You see, Will isn't Jack's father."

And that one statement clarified a whole world of questions. And opened up an entire realm of uncertainties to Emily. What if she was even now carrying the proof of what she'd been through? That was a notion too cruel to comprehend, but a very real possibility.

"And how did you survive that?"

"I love my son, Emily. I love all my children. I won't lie to you and tell you it's been easy, but I've never once regretted having him. Not once. I wish he and Will could have been closer, but he had Harmon to supply the love he needed, and Harmon thinks the world of him."

At that point, Rebecca was tempted to tell Emily Marcus she couldn't find a better confidant than her son. Jack would understand her doubts and could supply her with endless insights. But Rebecca didn't suggest it. Because she'd seen the longing in her son's eyes and she recognized the danger in that innocent desire. So instead, she left the woman with a mild warning.

"Jack has a pure heart, Mrs. Marcus, and a generous soul. Please don't take advantage of those things." Then, she placed a supportive hand on the other woman's arm and squeezed gently. "Goodnight."

Emily lingered on the porch, not knowing how to take comfort from Rebecca Bass's words. She didn't feel strong. She felt as if part of her dignity had been unfairly stripped away, never to be returned. Accept? She didn't know if she could. And if she couldn't, how could she expect anyone else to? What kind of man would take back a woman who'd slept with an Apache, who'd been used by her Mexican abductors? And she was afraid because she didn't know if Neil Marcus was that kind of man.

Maybe it would have been different if she'd been in love with her husband before she was taken from him.

She caught sight of movement out in the deep shadows of the yard, and eventually, she was able to discern the uneven footfalls. Jack. If she'd listened to anything Rebecca told her, she'd have gone back inside, quickly and quietly, before he saw her. But she couldn't. She waited with a building expectancy, knowing exactly when he saw her. He stopped, then he continued the laborious gait up to the steps.

" 'Evenin'."

Emily couldn't respond. She was too engrossed in the study of Jack Bass. He was hatless, and moonlight shone bronze upon his bared head. Because of the heat, he'd left his shirt open and untucked, the sleeves rolled and pushed up above his elbows. Every uncovered inch of him was firm and tanned and dark, with a masculine furring. A purely sensual reaction growled through her and she was shocked by the overwhelming want to put her hands on him, to feel that crisp matting and sleek musculature.

Mistaking her taut expression, Jack came up beside her, all soothing empathy. "He'll find her, don't you worry. You'll have your family back, I promise."

And because she hadn't been thinking about her family at all—and should have been—Emily's reply was brittle. "Happily ever after."

"I'd like to think so, ma'am."

She gave a heavy sigh. "Yes, so would I."

They stood there on the top step, elbow to elbow, her facing out and him in while the night sounds and the tension thickened about them.

"What about you, Jack?"

"Ma'am?"

"Where's your happily ever after? What are you looking for after the rangers? A family of your own? A farm? A ranch?"

His mouth tightened into a thin smile. "Haven't given it much thought," he muttered.

"Oh, yes you have," she argued provokingly. "You don't have the look of a man who shuns deep thought."

He just continued to smile, his lips clamped shut against

the answer he couldn't speak aloud. Her. He was looking for a woman like her. *Like* her, because unfortunately, she was already spoken for.

Seeing he wasn't going to reply, Emily altered the question slightly. "Why did you leave here to become a ranger? The excitement? The danger?"

"A tradition, more like. Will was a ranger up until he got shot. Harmon tracked for them. You might say I grew up surrounded by legends. Some awful big shoes to step into. I cut my teeth on stories and heroes, and the first time Uncle Harm let me ride out with him, I was sold on it. There was nothing else I ever wanted to do. I wanted the chance to—" He broke off, ducking his head with a bashful smile.

"You wanted to what?"

Her encouragement made his flush deepen. "It's kinda silly."

"What?" She put her hand on his forearm to nudge him and the contact shocked through both of them.

"I wanted the chance to do good. I wanted to make a difference, to make amends for—some of the bad things that happen for no cause."

Emily thought she understood. He wanted to compensate for the facts of his conception. But what she knew didn't go anywhere deep enough.

He'd wanted to be a ranger to erase the threat of Will's warnings. He needed to prove he wasn't like his unknown father, that he wasn't cursed with the same bad blood or prone to whatever evil that man had inflicted upon his family. There had to be some way to atone for it. Some way to apologize for scaring his mother half to death just by the fact of his very existence.

It hadn't gotten bad until he'd started growing to a man's

height, until his voice had lowered a rumbling octave. If he laughed a certain way or smiled a bit too widely, his mother recoiled in nameless horror. If he came up on her unexpectedly, she'd cringe as if he represented some terrible danger. Harm, too, though his uncle was quicker to recover. It had to do with his father, but no one would tell him the particulars. And by the time he was a young man, he was terrified of finding out.

What if they were right?

How was he supposed to tell a woman like Emily Marcus why he'd left home? How could he expect her to understand the events that began on his fourteenth summer and exploded when he was sixteen? He didn't understand, and he'd been there. He'd been helping Harm sink the well for their windmill. Jeffrey, who'd been a pesty and overactive six-year-old, hadn't listened to repeated warnings to stay away. When he nearly took a tumble down that hundred-foot shaft, it wasn't anger, it was fright that had Jack mercilessly shaking the boy, trying to impress upon him the seriousness of what had almost happened. His mother had come tearing out of the house, had yanked his brother away from him and struck him across the face hard enough to drop him to his knees. He'd never forget the glaze of panic and hatred in her eyes. Hurt and confused, he'd sought refuge at his uncle's, and Harm had taken him in without comment or question until Will had come to get him several days later. From that moment on, he was living under their suspicion, and the harder he worked to throw it off, the more wary they became.

The morning he'd left for good four years ago, he'd been laughing with Sidney over some stupid thing as he'd come out of the house. He bumped into their mother and reached out to catch hold of her when she lost her balance. She'd lunged away. He could still hear her awful shriek. *Don't you touch me! Don't you ever touch me!* He'd been in tears. He'd begged her to tell him what it was he'd done. What did she see when she looked at him? What had his father been, some kind of monster? Yes, she'd told him. A monster.

He was stuffing his belongings into a bag when Will demanded an explanation. He was going away, far away, he'd said. He couldn't stay where he wasn't wanted. Will had argued with him. What would he do at sixteen? What could he do, except get himself in trouble and end up . . . just like his father? That broke down the last of Jack's restraint. All the mean and terrible things he'd hidden away inside himself burst free. He'd yelled, he'd cursed, he'd screamed in his anger and frustration. And they'd had an ugly fight, concluding with Jack's parting words. He was tired of trying not to live down to everyone's expectations.

He hadn't gotten far, just as far as Harmon's front door. It was dark and he was cold and scared. Amanda made him up a bed, and in the morning, Harm sat him down for some serious talk. He didn't try to talk Jack out of leaving. He didn't say he was too young, too inexperienced, or too anything. He told him to be smart and sent him to his old friend Calvin Lowe, an ex-ranger who was sheriff in Terlingua. Jack liked Calvin and he took his uncle's advice. It was Calvin who hooked him up with the rangers and the way of life he'd been enjoying.

"Jack?"

"Ummm?" He glanced at Emily.

"You looked a million miles away."

Her hand moved slightly, coming to rest upon his flat middle. The way her fingertips stirred along that taut plain stirred plenty inside him. And suddenly, uncomfortably, he was reminded of the way Amanda had played upon his uncle's passions as they sat on their front steps. Was that what Emily Marcus was trying to do, seduce him? That thought alarmed and aroused him. Nervously he sought to defuse the situation. But he never thought to move her hand.

"I was thinking that Neil was probably my first good friend. He was the lieutenant when I joined up with the Frontier Battalion. I was sixteen and blind stupid brave. I could ride and track, but was about useless with a gun. He taught me how to shoot, how to take pride in myself, and how to stand behind my decisions without apology. I rode into the thick of it for the first time at his direction. He didn't say, "Go," he always went first and said, "Follow me." When he moved up in command, he asked for me to be brought up with him to serve as his sergeant. That was a helluva compliment for someone my age.

"I was remembering when I had to order my first man hung. They were hard times and we were few, too few to guard a prisoner. When we got the information we needed from him, we couldn't turn him loose to spread the alarm, so he had to be killed. 'Bout broke my heart to do it. I was all ready to turn in my star when Neil sat me down and told me that I was one of the few standing between the enemies of Texas and those I was sworn to protect. He told me always to be fair, to think of my men before myself, and to sleep well at night, and if I couldn't do those things, he told me to go home and become a farmer or a rancher without regret. He said not everyone had the stuff to be a ranger, and it was nothing to be ashamed of."

"And you stayed."

"Yes, ma'am. 'Cause of your husband."

About that time, her fingers were threading through the nap of his chest hairs, and his heart was banging so fast and frantic beneath her touch, he feared the pressure would

cause his ribs to crack wide open. He stood there, breathing
hard into the incredible longing, fighting it as if he were
fighting for his very life. Still, his hand rose up, coming
to rest on her hip, moving there with just a subtle shift of
material over her soft skin.

"Jack . . ."

Her voice sounded small and strained. And he was full
of panic and just as crazy with passion. In another minute
he was going to be making love to her, and he knew he
shouldn't. He knew he couldn't. But he wasn't sure how to
stop himself.

"Ma'am, please . . . I . . . ummmm . . . I don't think we
ought to be . . ."

Her hand dropped away, and she angled slightly so that
his did, too. "How's your leg?" she asked abruptly.

"My . . . leg? It's—it's—"

"Fine?" she supplied for him, with a faint smile. "Can
you ride?"

"Yes, ma'am."

"Then I think we ought to leave for Ysleta tomorrow
morning. I have a life to get back to, and I want to feel
comfortable in it before Cathy's returned. She's going to
have a hard time adjusting."

"I think that'd be best," he agreed hoarsely. He snatched
a glance at her, but she was looking outward, her expression
giving away nothing at all. "I'll see you in the morning."
And he made for the house, aghast at how close he'd come
to betraying everything he held dear.

Emily let her breath out in a gust when she heard the
door shut behind her. A wild trembling rose up through her.
Didn't she have enough problems without courting this po-
tentially dangerous liaison? She wasn't flirting with Jack
Bass, nor was she being playful or teasing. It was no game.

She was dead serious. She wanted him, and he responded in kind. She wanted everything about him: his kindness, his gentle touch, the sweetness of his kiss, the strength of his resolve, and especially, his acceptance of who she was and what she'd been through. Don't take advantage, she'd been warned. Was that what she was doing? Was she so desperately afraid of what she'd come from and where she was going that she'd use any means to prolong the safety of his company? It was wrong; he didn't deserve it. He wasn't the kind of man to take such a thing lightly. It would ruin his life. And was that any way for her to repay him for his kindness? Or Neil for the vows they'd taken?

No.

She waited several long minutes, long enough for him to have settled down on his fireside pallet. She went in, never looking in that direction.

"G'night, ma'am."

She didn't pause. "Goodnight, Jack." And she hurried to her room, knowing that if she hesitated for even a second, she'd be stretched out in his blankets with him.

When Jack announced his intention of leaving, his family rallied around expressions of regret; even his mother and stepfather. All had enjoyed the company and the break in sameness that came out in the West Texas wilds. And Jack was family. His mother saw they had plenty of rations and fussed over the condition of his leg. His brothers moaned and pleaded for an extended stay. Sarah gave him an extra sloppy kiss when he told her he'd spoken to Harmon and had received the elusive "We'll see." That was as good as a yes. And Will surprised them all by leading out a fine-limbed gray for Emily to ride, muttering that the boy could return it next time he was in the area. Meaning, "Come back soon." And that was enough to have him so tight-throated he could hardly get out the final goodbyes.

Then it was him and Emily, alone, on the long trail to Ysleta.

They made good time because neither of them dared linger over cook fire or conversation. They rode hard across the hard land, stopping only to spell the horses the first day. That night, Emily slept with Jack's carbine and he slept with one eye open, careful to keep it from resting on Mrs. Marcus. He forced himself to think of her as Mrs. Marcus. That made it easier for him to maintain his distance. But thinking of her as someone else's all day didn't stop him from dreaming of her as his own all night.

On the third day, Jack began to show signs of wear. His leg ached constantly, cramping up to the point where he was half doubled over it as he rode. If Emily asked, he'd say no, he didn't want to stop, so she took to watching him, waiting for him to rub at it. Then she'd say she was tired, and he never had an argument to that. That night, his leg wouldn't support his dismount or hold any weight at all. Without a word, Emily saw to their campfire and secured it for the night, making their supper and forbidding him to do anything except rest. He hated it, but he did it. And watching Emily Marcus take charge only made his admiration for her grow stronger.

The closer they got to Ysleta, the quieter Emily became. He figured she was worried about her impending reunion with Neil, but he didn't think he should be the one to offer up any comfort. That had gotten him into a world of trouble last time, and out in the desert flats, there'd be no interruptions to save him if things got carried away. He told himself what was between Emily and her husband was none of his affair. He'd drop her off and he'd get on with his own duties. As if she'd never kissed him. Or he'd kissed her back.

Then, after riding across hundreds of miles of gray desert, El Paso was a sudden surprise to the senses. The cool greenery of the city's gardens beckoned below sun-drenched peaks. Looking down on the valley of the Rio Grande, the eyes were delighted by the sprawling vista of acres under cultivation with grapes, apples, apricots, pear and peach orchards, watermelons, grain, wheat, and corn. Beneath the shading cottonwoods, Mexican girls from across the river in El Paso del Norte were selling their fruits and Jack bought up a handful for him and Emily so the sweet juices could cut through the desert dust as they started down the city's staggering streets.

El Paso was civilizing under the approach of the railroad as harbingers rushed in to set themselves up in vice. Every corner in the business district was occupied by a saloon, with at least three set in every block. In the past six months, close to sixty men and women had been killed in shootouts, stabbings, or beatings, and the town had shrugged it off with a hard border philosophy of "Anything goes and nobody really gives a damn." No one but those assigned to keep an uneasy peace between men so callous to the spilling of blood that not a one of them had a natural attitude about death.

As tired as she was by the long trek, Emily sat her saddle with a stiff anxiety. She was barely aware of the stares of the curious. Her thoughts were crowded with her dread of the approaching reunion with her husband. What would it be like? Good Lord, would she even recognize him? What if he didn't want her to stay? What if he did?

She was so agitated, she didn't even notice that Jack had turned the horses in until she felt the light touch of his hand upon her knee and heard the quiet call of her name. She glanced down at him in a daze.

His upturned face was so handsome, so familiar to her. For one mad minute, she was tempted to say, "Let's go, Jack. Let's just ride off for someplace far away." But of course, she didn't. He wouldn't have gone, for one thing. Then, as the moment stretched out and she stared down into the gentle blue of his eyes, she thought, yes, maybe he would.

"C'mon down, ma'am."

For the first time, Emily realized they were tied up before one of El Paso's store fronts. She came out of the saddle into the supporting reach of his arms and her fingers clenched tight into the swell of muscle, absorbing his strength, needing it badly. As much as she wanted to just linger there with her hands on his arms, his on her waist, she knew she shouldn't, and she stepped away.

"Why are we stopping here?"

Jack gave his small, endearing smile and looked unsettled. Then he glanced at the store and murmured, "Thought you might like to get yourself something pretty . . . you know."

Yes, she did know. She hadn't given it much thought, but now she was conscious of how she must look, coming in off the desert wearing Rebecca Bass's ill-fitting gown, her feet bare, her face bruised. That wasn't the way she wanted to greet her husband after a five-year separation. And she blessed Jack for thinking of it.

He followed her inside, looking for the world as if he would rather be having a tooth pulled, yet still staying close. For a moment, Emily was simply overwhelmed. She stood in the central aisle, trembling slightly, her eyes welling up with uncertain tears. It had been so long. She wasn't sure what to do. When the shopkeeper approached her, she shied away from him, backing into Jack, who stopped her retreat with the reassuring curl of his hands about her elbows.

"Help you folks?"

When Emily didn't reply, Jack spoke up awkwardly. "The lady needs some female fittings."

The store owner sized her up in a glance and grinned wide. "Jus' your luck, ma'am. The Overland stage jus' dropped off a pick of frilly things. You be needing them for work?"

Emily didn't catch his meaning right away, but Jack did. His hand flashed out, gripping the man by the forearm. His voice was still soft and polite, but the fellow was wriggling under the crush of his fingers.

"I said lady."

"Oh, I be beggin' your pardon: my mistake. Well, now, let's see what I have."

Jack released him and he scooted back nervously. "If you'll jus' follow me, ma'am, I think we can rig you out in something right fashionable."

She started forward and Jack hung back, muttering, "I'll be outside."

Her eyes widened in sudden panic. "No! Jack—"

" 'Less you want me to stay," he amended gently.

Please, her expression begged of him.

"I'll be right here, waitin'."

Emily went with the shopkeeper, but her gaze kept darting back to the young ranger loitering uncomfortably amid the dry goods and kitchen sundries. She scarcely noticed the gown she was shown, nodding absently that it would be fine. Putting it on was another thing. After wearing loose adaptations of white clothing while among the Mescalero, she was intimidated by all the wired underpinnings and mostly by the unfamiliar bustle. She struggled with it heroically, then finally surrendered.

"Jack?"

He responded to the wavery anguish in her voice, rushing to the back of the store, then pulling up short outside the small back room. "Ma'am?"

She explained her predicament briefly and, mortified beyond belief, Jack went to see what he could do about it. He approached a matronly lady shopping for tatting materials and cleared his throat.

"Ma'am, I was wondering . . . could you . . . I mean . . ."

"Yes?"

"Do you know how to put together one of them contraptions that plumps up a lady's skirts?"

The woman's eyes rounded as she took in the blushing, dusty young man accosting her with such a personal question. He was quick and awkward about relieving her shocked dismay.

"The lady with me, she's having a bit a trouble . . . if you could help out. Please." The last was practically a wail of distress.

"Oh, I see. Yes, of course." She patted his arm and he wished he could melt right down through the floorboards in humiliation.

With the woman's aid, Emily was able to manage the rigors of style. She came hesitantly out of the back room, clutching at the unfamiliar skirts, and waited anxiously for Jack to catch sight of her. Her breath was suspended, her heart racing, and then he glanced.

And then he stared.

The gown was of a patterned antique gold silk, with an overskirt of brown taffeta that swagged in the front and bunched up over the bustle in back to form a ripply waterfall. Twenty tiny buttons ran from a high neck to the edge of the bodice waist, creating a snug hourglass silhouette. Ivory gloves covered roughened hands and tucked in beneath turned-back three-quarter-length cuffs. And from beneath the narrow row of pleating at the hem peeped a pair of pointed-toed slippers. Jack felt as though he'd swallowed a handful of desert sand and suffered sunstroke all at once.

Uneasily, Emily waited for his reaction. When it didn't come, the elder lady prompted, "Well, sir? What do you think of her?"

"She looks right fine, ma'am," he croaked.

"Fine?" the older woman chided. "She looks lovely. And once you clean up, young man, you'll make a right handsome couple."

"But we're not . . . she's not . . ." Jack finally just shut his mouth.

Emily's green eyes captured his. She searched his gaze anxiously. "Is it really all right?"

"You could make a man's heart stop, Miz Emily."

She smiled at that.

"Here," the matron offered, dabbing some vanilla extract behind Emily's ears. "Perfect." She took one gloved hand and pressed it into Jack's, pleased by the picture they presented together. Then she bustled off to see to her lacemaking supplies.

Jack's fingers clutched about Emily's. He was grateful for her gloves. His hands were suddenly sweaty. It was more than the dress. It was the abrupt realization that this was who she was: a proper lady, properly wed to another, not just an Apache captive he'd rescued from the desert. He had got to feeling for all the world as if she belonged to him, but she didn't. And this would most likely be the last time they'd ever be alone together.

She must have been thinking the same thing, for suddenly she stepped forward, beginning to put her arms around him. He jumped back in alarm.

"Don't be huggin' on me, ma'am. I'll get you all dirty." That was the only excuse that came readily to mind. Not a good enough one.

"Do you think I care about that?" she scolded quietly. "Stand still."

He did so, freezing up inside and out as she leaned in close. The scent of vanilla teased him. The light touch of her fingertips upon his stubbly jaw tormented him. Then his eyes squeezed shut as he felt her soft kiss against his scratchy cheek, a kiss that brushed over highlight and hollow, then edged dangerously close to the corner of his mouth. He sucked a short breath. Quickly he ducked his head and sidled away. Then he gave her a tremulous smile.

"You're welcome, ma'am."

Then Emily drew in a fortifying breath, and she said, "I'm ready. Let's go."

And with Jack's palm cupping her elbow, they stepped out on the boardwalk together, leaving the opportunities and temptations of a lifetime behind.

Seven

Captain Neil Marcus was quartered in a small adobe at the end of the ranger barracks row. It was a stark dwelling, the home of a bachelor and a military man. That made it practical, but not particularly inviting. But Emily was used to utility more than luxury and hadn't been expecting more. However, Jack, who'd come from a good home with a strong female influence, saw immediately all that it was lacking and wished that his captain had done something to lessen the severity in the welcoming of his long-absent wife.

It would have been nice if he'd been at home.

When no answer came to his knock, Jack eased open the door and called inside. Then he looked back at Emily, chagrined.

"Not here. You'd might as well step in outta the heat, ma'am."

Emily moved past him, and he could see her stoically taking stock of her new residence. If she was dismayed by the simplicity, she didn't let on, but he felt obligated to point out all the positives.

"There's a woman who brings around meals, so you don't need to be worrying over what to fix. At least until you're ready to take over the kitchen. Put up some curtains to keep out the morning sun and lay 'em open at night to catch the breeze and it'll be right nice in the bedroo . . ." He let that trail off, suddenly tongue-tied and calling himself the biggest kind of fool. Bedroom. Say it. Think it. The bedroom she was going to share with Neil, her husband.

"It's fine," she remarked quietly. "I'll be very comfortable here. You don't need to stay, Sergeant. I'm sure you have things to attend to." Then she looked at him with a remote expression, as if they were nothing to one another. And that, he realized glumly, was how it should be.

"Yes, ma'am," he mumbled, reaffixing his hat upon his head. But as he turned toward the door, she said rather breathlessly, "Jack, thank you." He tipped his hat to her with an answering, "It's been my pleasure."

Just then, the door opened inward and Neil Marcus was regarding the two of them.

The second she saw him, remembrance flooded back over Emily. He hadn't changed a bit from the tall, unbending figure who'd brought news of her father's death back from the war. His dark hair was a bit sparser, maybe, and his beard a little fuller, but there was still the commanding presence that had always impressed and slightly intimidated her. She remembered that he liked lots of sugar in his coffee and that he slept without covers even on the coldest night. Didn't like to be hampered by them, he'd always told her. He put on his gun belt before he put on his boots and he ate breakfast with his revolver on the table beside his plate. He liked all his personal effects laid out in precise order at the ready for his convenience, and he liked his lovemaking the same way.

And for a brief instant, Emily almost grabbed onto Jack Bass to beg, "Please don't leave me here with this man!"

But of course, she didn't.

"Hello, Neil."

He looked at her through inscrutable dark eyes, then said brusquely, "You can put your things in there."

Smiling slightly, she touched her skirts. "This is all I have."

He gave her a nod, then turned to Jack. "How's the leg?"

"Fine, Cap'n." He looked between the two of them in ill-concealed confusion.

"You can bring me your report in the morning. The men have already filled me in on some of it. Get some grub and turn in. You look like hell, boy."

"Yessir, Cap'n." He headed for the door again, a terrible agitation churning through him. Then a quiet voice pierced him deeper than any Apache arrow could.

"Thank you, Sergeant. There's no way I can ever repay you for what you've done."

He glanced at her once, briefly, and away. "You already have, Miz Marcus. Cap'n." He nodded his goodbye and the door to the Marcuses' house shut behind him.

It was a long while before Jack could decipher the emotion that had him so unsettled. It gnawed on him all the way back to his cabin. It plagued him even as he was being greeted by his comrades and bunkmates. It had him so achy and turned-inside-out-feeling that for the first time in his life when his friends produced a bottle of whiskey, he didn't say no to a glass. Grinning, they poured him one, then several more, laughing good-naturedly as he wheezed and wiped at his watering eyes and matched them foolishly gulp for gulp. Until he fell off his chair.

He didn't remember his pards slinging him into his bunk. He watched the world whirl companionably for endless minutes. Then it came all at once, like a breath-stealing punch to the gut, why he was so unreasonably upset.

He was furious with Neil Marcus.

How dared he treat his wife with such indifference? He hadn't kissed her, he hadn't really even said hello. Lord above, if it had been his wife returned to him after five years, he'd have been down on his knees, weeping and wailing with gratitude. He'd have spent every penny he had to fix up the gloomy adobe into a cheery semblance of a home so that her first impression was one that would make her smile and feel welcome. And he wouldn't have wasted precious time discussing reports with his sergeant. He would have taken her into his arms and straight to bed.

But she wasn't his wife.

And that hurt so much in his drunken state, he couldn't begin to comprehend it.

The sound of coarse laughter distracted his fuzzy thoughts. Slowly he gained an awareness of his surroundings. His head was buzzing unpleasantly, and his mouth tasted like his socks had been lying in it. He needed coffee and he needed a meal, but he couldn't seem to move. So this was the state his fellow rangers were so eager to rush into every weekend night. He failed to see the attraction. In fact, he couldn't see much of anything. But he could hear just fine.

"A real looker, all cleaned up," one of the boys murmured in appreciation. "Never know where she'd been, to see her all gussied up like a lady."

A low whistle sounded, and Billy Cooper, one of the younger rangers, speculated, "Betcha we don't see the captain anytime tonight. I know what I'd be doing were I in his shoes."

"It ain't his shoes you'd like to be filling," came another ribald comment.

Cooper snorted at that. "If the man were smart, he wouldn't fill anything till he was sure someone hadn't beat him to it."

"Whatcha mean, Billy?"

"Only that if my woman had been spread beneath the Injuns and the Meskins, I sure as hell wouldn't want her to try to pass off any of their issue as mine."

Jack wasn't aware of making any conscious decision to move, but suddenly, he was up and at Billy Cooper's throat.

"Take it back."

"What'sa matter with you, Jack?" the young private sputtered.

"Take it back, you son of a bitch!"

The fact that Jack Bass snarled the savage oath startled his men almost more than the pistol he produced.

"Hey—!"

Jack wrestled the ranger off balance and flung him up against the rough board wall, grabbing a handful of his hair in one hand and jamming the barrel of his gun beneath the boy's chin with the other. He was panting hard, but there was a fearsome calm to his expression. His eyes gleamed like a freshly stropped blade, and his voice was low and razor-sharp.

"I said take it back, or I'll be blowing your brains right through that wall."

"Jeesus, Jack! What the hell—"

The others were on their feet, stunned and stupefied, all but one man, who held to the sense to run for their captain.

Billy Cooper was wide-eyed and trembling. He had no doubt that he was on his way to his Maker. He'd seen death before, and it was cut into every taut-muscled angle of Jack Bass's face. He could practically feel the air ventilating the back of his skull as the sergeant pressed in close enough for the seethe of his breath to scorch him.

"Don't you ever let me hear you talking about her that way. Not ever. Not ever! You hear?"

"I didn't mean nuthin' by it. Honest, I didn't. I was jus' talkin'." The boy was almost blubbering. No one dared move in his defense until a firm voice sounded behind them.

"Jack, surrender up that gun right now."

For a long second, Jack didn't move. Then his gaze cut slowly to his captain. His features were congealed into something frightful and coldly dangerous as he sized up Neil Marcus.

"Jack, now."

Marcus's hand stretched out impatiently, hanging empty for a timeless beat, then filled with the plain blue gun. The sound of relief gusted through the silence in the room.

"Now, someone want to tell me what the hell's going on in here?"

It was Billy Cooper who spoke up. He made his tone light, and he even managed to smile as he put his arm amiably around Jack's taut shoulders. "Nuthin', Cap'n. We was jus' horsing around. Right, Jack?"

But there was nothing playful or the least bit good-humored in Jack Bass's hair-trigger tension.

"Nuthin'?" Neil drawled sarcastically. "Sure looked like plenty of something to me. C'mon, Jack. Let's get you some air."

Neil had him by the back of the shirt collar like a misbehaving pup, swinging him about with a quick jerk and propelling him out the door with a forceful shove. The rest of the men settled down into an uneasy muttering, wondering what the hell *had* happened.

Jack staggered out into the yard. His leg buckled weakly and his head seemed to be spinning in great dizzying circles. If Neil hadn't caught his arm, he would have gone down to the dust bonelessly.

"Tell me I'm wrong, but you've the smell of a man who's made an intimate acquaintance with the bottle."

Jack didn't tell him anything. He was wildly upset—by what he'd done, by what he was yet feeling. He wanted to punch his captain. He wanted to wade into his friend with both fists flailing. He'd wanted to splatter a comrade's thinking parts with the blast of his .45. Over careless words. Over indecent thoughts.

"Jack, what's wrong with you? I ain't never knowed you to take a taste or cause a ruckus. And I don't know who that was in there with the look of killing all over him, but it sure as hell wasn't you."

No, Jack thought in a panic of anguish and fear. It was his father.

"I'm gonna be—"

Neil anticipated the rest and held him out at arm's length so he could indelicately heave up all the poisons from his system. And when Jack was trembling and white-faced, his captain dragged him over to the horse trough and pushed his head under. When a froth of anxious bubbles broke the surface, he hauled him out and dropped him on his rump, where he leaned back against the trough, shaking and gasping for breath.

"Talk to me, Jack."

Jack wiped his dripping face with unsteady hands. Talk to him? And say what? I went crazy? I want your wife so bad, I completely lost control of my mental faculties? I wanted to kill that man in there just for speaking ill of her, and I'd still like to kill you because you have what I want? Yessir, all those things would make a lot of sense, coming from Gentleman Jack Bass, who never caused trouble or harbored a mean thought. Or he could say, well, sir, it was only a matter of time before my bad blood showed itself. Couldn't hide what I really am forever.

He gripped his jaw tight and said nothing.

Neil Marcus stared down at him, angry and shaken himself. Of all the men in his command, this one was the last he'd expected such behavior from. Something had happened to make his trusted sergeant snap like the coil of a revolver. A big something, but no one was saying exactly what it was. He might have excused it as rowdy drunkenness that, as Billy Cooper said, was horseplay gone a bit too far. But not with Jack. And that bothered him no little amount.

His voice lowered to a caring rumble. "C'mon, Sergeant. Let's tuck you in for the night. You look to have had a bad time of it."

That touch of sympathy was all it took to unstring Jack's wired emotions. His unstable world focused on the face of his friend and mentor. Violence gave way to regret and confusion, and he was suddenly all moaning misery. "I'm sorry, Cap'n. I don't know what happened. My head and heart just went all wrong inside."

"Rye whiskey'll do that, son," Marcus advised tolerantly, not having any idea what it was his young sergeant was confessing to. He hoisted up his second-in-command and gave him the support of his arm, then ended up carrying him over his shoulder as Jack went limp as a sack of grain.

The mood in the ranger cabin was one of anxious speculation. When Neil toted the unconscious form inside, they looked to him in question, hoping for some explanation as to what had occurred.

"Too much to drink," Marcus concluded. "Shame on you boys for allowing such a thing. Make sure you all walk real quiet around him tomorrow, 'cause he's going to feel a whole stampede of hurt when he wakes up. You all right, Billy?"

"Yessir, Cap'n."

"No hard feelings?"

"None. I jus' don't understand—"

None of them did. Least of all Jack.

But when Neil Marcus returned to his quarters and gazed down upon his sleeping wife, he understood all too clearly. And he didn't like what he was thinking. Not that he thought anything improper of Jack Bass. Hell, the boy was the incarnation of what was decent. But it must have taken something out of the ordinary to set him off like a hot-tempered fool—something like the lovely woman slumbering in exhaustion alone in his bed.

Emily Marcus was enough to make any man lose control. But not him, not tonight. The last thing in the world he considered was crawling in bed beside her, after where she'd been.

He went into the other room, finding a bottle there and drinking deeply from it. Carrying it with him, he left his home and walked purposefully down the quiet street, past the barracks filled with snoring rangers to the squalid huts where the camp followers stayed. His knock was answered in an instant, and a sultry Mexican woman wound around him in a passionate answer to his problems, an answer he'd sought frequently over the last five years when the question was loneliness. He stepped inside and closed the door behind him.

The Apache must have attacked during the night, because his skull felt fairly split in two by an avenging war club.

Jack groaned mightily and dragged his covers up over his head.

"Don't look now, boys, but I think he's alive."

"Shhhh. Doan speak ill of the dying. Or the wishing they was dying."

Quiet laughter.

Jack moaned miserably and wished they'd all go away. Somehow, his heart had found its way up between his ears, and it was banging there like crazy. He thought about asking one of his pards to shoot him, but he didn't think they'd be of a mind to show him any mercy. They were having too much fun at his expense.

What had he done?

Whatever it was, he was never doing it again!

"Jack, got some coffee here, if you've a mind to join the living."

"I'm not," he mumbled.

"Want some advice? Doan make no sudden moves, and whatever you do, doan open your eyes."

More laughter.

Some friends. Mocking a man on his deathbed.

Bravely, he peeled down the covers and took a look. He regretted it immediately. It felt as though someone was cooking up his eyeballs in a hot skillet with a slab of fatback on the side.

"Tole you not to open 'em."

"Here you go, Sarge. Nice an' hot, an' made special for what ails you."

Jack made a tremendous effort and managed to crawl up into a seated position. His hands shook like those of a man who'd taken the ague as they wrapped around the tin. He hunched over it for a long, motionless minute, letting it steam open his thinking processes. Then he remembered everything and his eyes flew open wide in spite of the searing shock.

Good God, he'd been ready to kill Billy Cooper!

For a minute, he was afraid he was going to get sick again. Then that feeling of illness settled deep into his soul and no simple retching could drag it out.

The others had been watching him curiously, cautiously, and they knew exactly when the facts hit him hard. Discreetly, they gathered up their gear and started to amble outside to give him room to think. Only Billy Cooper lingered.

"Hey, Jack. Feelin' more yourself this morning?"

Jack looked up at the uncertain young ranger and his chest turned inside out. He tried to speak and found he couldn't. He grabbed for a couple of hurting breaths and managed to rasp, "Billy, I'm sorry. I—I—"

"No need to go on and on, Jack. Enough said." He put out his hand. "Both of us were outta line, and I want to get it behind us fast."

Jack reached out and took the proffered hand. Billy grinned and slapped him on the shoulder.

"Almost scared me into embarrassing myself," he admitted. "That I wouldn't have forgiven you for. See you later."

Get it behind him. How was he supposed to do that? Jack mused, as he sipped the rest of his coffee. Then he took his time washing up and dressing, because he knew he had to go find his captain and come up with some plausible excuse for the inexcusable. Because he couldn't tell him the truth.

He looked like a man who'd been dragged through Hell behind a fast horse when he finally hobbled out of his cabin into the blinding brightness of morning. He was all too aware of the speculative glances from his comrades, and as much as he wished he could shrink beneath them, he didn't. He held a position of respect and he couldn't jeopardize it. So he walked as tall as possible, tipped his hat low over his aching eyes, and pretended to ignore the whispers as he went to discover the whereabouts of Neil Marcus.

And when he found out, he wasn't pleased.

The son of a bitch had gone to spend the night with his whore!

If he hadn't gotten so angry all over again, he might have been shocked at thinking of his friend in such terms. But he was angry. Angry and disappointed and jealous all at once. How could a man with a woman like Emily Marcus at home be out rolling with a common tart? He stalked across the street, limping straight up to the woman's door without ever once stopping to consider what he was about to do. He was stepping into something that was none of his affair. But all he had to do was picture the hurt on Emily's face when she found her husband gone. And that was invitation enough to involve himself.

Juana Javier was well known and well used by the rangers in Ysleta. She was pretty in a carnal fashion, with her hot black eyes and pouty lips. She was well fleshed, but most of it was in the right place, so no one seemed to mind the excess, especially when it was squeezed into one of her bright dresses or bared for their boisterous handling. Jack Bass was the last man she ever expected to find on her front steps at any time of day or night, and she regretted having to inform the handsome ranger that she already had company.

Jack was too incensed even to blush at the whore's insinuation. But he remembered himself enough to remove his hat.

"I'm here for my captain, ma'am. Is he inside?"

"You want to come in and see?" she teased, with the slow draw of her fingertips down his chest. When that stroke dipped below his belt buckle, he shifted aside.

"Just go on and roust him for me, if you would."

"I already rousted him once this morning. I'm willing, but I don't know if he could go again. Maybe you would like to take his place with me, eh? I could show you—"

"Begging your pardon, ma'am, but I don't have the time for you to show me anything. Could you tell the cap'n that I'm waiting on him?"

"Tell him yourself." With that, she swayed away from the door, leaving him to follow awkwardly. His nostrils flared at the heavy scents of musky perfume, sour whiskey, and illicit acts. He didn't like being in such a place, and he didn't think his captain ought to be there, either.

Neil Marcus was sprawled naked across an unmade bed. His hand dangled off the side, fingertips brushing over one of two empty bottles. He was snoring determinedly. Without the slightest sympathy, Jack grabbed up the wash pitcher and upended it over his head. Sputtering wildly, Marcus sat up, then he glared blearily at his sergeant.

"Jack, what the hell are you doing here? Didn't know you were of the persuasion to visit such company."

"I came to take you home. Get dressed."

"Home?"

"To your wife," he hissed, in case the man needed a reminder. "Where you should be."

"You get the call to the pulpit, boy?"

"Let's just say I got the call to be your conscience, Neil. You got a woman waiting on you. You don't need to be here."

"Don't tell me what I need, Jack," he growled, in surly humor. But he'd begun to dress.

Jack glanced uneasily at the smirking harlot who lounged against the doorway. Her robe was gaping open to display an immodest amount of pale flesh. He looked away. When Neil was finally dressed, if haphazardly, and he started past her, she latched on around his neck and kissed him long and lavishly. He didn't try to pull away.

"I'll see you soon," she cooed huskily.

"No, you won't," Jack argued, as he pushed his captain ahead of him.

Juana laughed knowingly. "Then you come back, Ranger, with your pretty teeth and long legs. I'll show you how to do things with them that you never dreamed of."

"I don't doubt that, ma'am." He tipped his hat politely and shoved Neil outside.

The ranger captain walked with him in a sullen silence. Neil reeked of misspent pleasures and cheap woman. Hopefully, Emily wouldn't recognize the odors. Hopefully, she'd still be asleep and no wiser.

No such luck for either thing.

She was awake and standing at the open door when Jack brought her husband home. Neil strode right by her, heading for the coffeepot in the kitchen, leaving Jack to awkwardly doff his hat and struggle with an explanation.

"It's my fault, ma'am. Me and the cap'n got a bit too deep in the bottle last night, and it was morning before either of us knew it. I apologize for keeping him out all night. Won't happen again."

Emily Marcus gave him a long look and he knew without a doubt that she saw right through his lie. She gave him a small, stiff smile and said, "Thank you for seeing him home, Sergeant."

Then she closed the door in his face.

Eight

Emily was trying, she really was. In some ways, Neil's remoteness made it easier; in some it was worse. She was grateful that he didn't come to her at night or make any overtures of a personal nature. Her marriage to him, as with her Apache husband, was made of necessity. She'd never known any desire for his touch. And since the time she'd spent with her Mexican captors, she'd dreaded the day when he'd demand his husband's rights. She didn't mind that he kept his distance. However, had he greeted her at the door with a show of affection, it would have been easier for her to forget the one whose touch she did yearn for. But forget she must.

She threw herself into the role of Neil Marcus's wife. She took over the cooking for him and washed and mended his clothes. She bought what she could and laboriously sewed the rest to replenish her wardrobe so she would have the look of a lady instead of a white squaw. She added touches of hominess to the adobe, the suggested curtains first. She made it a point to be very visible in the camp, as if she had nothing to be ashamed of, and she learned every man's name so she might greet him warmly. It wasn't as bad as it might have been, but it was far from perfect.

Respect for Neil kept the rangers from gossip and had them calling her Mrs. Marcus with polite deference. But in

El Paso, opinion was harder to control. They knew who she was and where she'd been; they were aware that she'd been living with and probably sleeping with savages for five years. And they just plain didn't know if they were willing to accept her in their midst. She was met by stares and whispers, but no one dared accost her with their comments, mainly because she took to wearing a pistol belt when she went to town. Neil had given it to her without comment when she'd asked. Once, she'd heard someone sneer, "Apache whore," as she passed. She'd stopped and turned with tremendous dignity, her hand resting easily on the butt of her .45 as she asked with an icy civility, "Were you talking to me?" The speaker looked surprised, then quickly shook his head. Word traveled fast from that encounter, and she never heard another slander spoken loud enough for her to hear.

At least the good people of El Paso made no bones about how they felt. She wished she could say the same for her husband. Although she wanted to put it all behind her, pretending the past five years didn't exist wasn't the way. Neil refused to discuss it. And he never brought up the subject of their daughter. He acted as though she'd been late coming back from shopping, rather than like a man who'd missed his wife for five long years. The minute she stepped back under his roof, life went on as usual, except for its intimate aspects. He hadn't touched her, but he did watch her. He hadn't truly spoken to her, other than to express his preference for the evening meal or to tell her he was going out. He was a cool stranger who happened to sleep beside her. Sometimes. Other nights he went to his other woman. And she didn't begrudge him those nights.

What grieved her more than his distance was the sense of loneliness within the ranger camp. Even as an outsider while among the Apache, she'd sensed a feeling of community that drew her in as one of them. The women had worked together, each helping all. Even when she couldn't understand their chatter, she was cheered by the sound of happy voices. And there were the children. Here, her arms were so achingly empty. Ysleta offered nothing for the wife of a ranger. It was run by men, for the comfort and convenience of men, and they resented the encroachment of anything feminine or civilized. The women in town were mostly those of bad reputation, and the ladies wanted nothing to do with her. Her days were pockets of dreary isolation broken only by the return of her silent spouse, and just when she began to think she had nothing to look forward to, there was Jack Bass on her front steps with a handful of Texas bluebonnets and prairie verbena.

His smile was small and shy as he snatched off his hat. "Afternoon, ma'am. Don't mean to bother you. Jus' that I happened upon these and I remembered my mama saying that flowers always make a place homey and I didn't recollect you having any." He extended the slightly wilted bouquet in a clutched fist. His tone grew low and gravelly. "Welcome home, Miz Marcus."

It was all she could do not to break down in tears.

Emily took the bedraggled flowers with a faint, "I'll put them in water."

"They are kinda sorry looking. Maybe that'll perk 'em up some."

"They're beautiful, Sergeant, and I thank you."

He worried his hat brim for a moment, then muttered, "I'd best be going."

"No! I mean, can't you stay for a cup of coffee?"

"Better not. I'll be seeing you, ma'am."

She wanted to protest that she hadn't seen him for more

than a week, that she hadn't had a real conversation with anyone since he'd dropped her off at the door, that she was so sick of her own company she could scream. But she said nothing beyond a soft, "Thank you again for the flowers. It was very k-kind of you."

Emily turned away, but too late. He'd already caught the snag in her voice and had come to a stop.

"Ma'am?"

She swallowed hard. "Yes?"

"Coffee sounds right nice. If it's no bother."

The flowers were shivering in her hands, but she was smiling to herself as she replied, "No bother at all. Sit yourself down, Sergeant. I'll put some on." And she rushed into the kitchen.

Jack advanced cautiously into the little dwelling. It had a different look about it now. A woman was in residence. Details to that effect were scattered throughout the rooms. It was nice, comfortable. A place a man could return to after a long day and relax. How he envied his friend Neil Marcus that privilege.

"How's your leg?"

She came back carrying a vase. She'd actually made something attractive out of the scraggly wildflowers and displayed them proudly on the table. Then she looked up at him and he remembered the question.

"Fine, ma'am. Been getting lots of rest. Not much action the last few days. Almost looking forward to some to break the monotony of the days."

She nodded, understanding exactly what he meant. The rangers were active men. Sitting around bred restlessness and the inclination toward mischief. And she knew she was just dying for something a little different to alter the pattern of her days. Any distraction that would ease her worry.

"Sit down, Sergeant. It'll only take a minute for the coffee to brew."

He sat, but he seemed uncomfortable doing it. Was it because the two of them were alone in his friend's house, she wondered, or because he noticed how hungrily she was studying the appealing lines of his face and form? She couldn't help the first, and she didn't want to stop the second.

"I hear tell they're having some sort of doings in town tomorrow night," Jack offered up a bit awkwardly. "Dancing and such. You and Neil going?"

It was the first she'd heard of it. Perhaps her husband had plans to take another. Emily smiled narrowly. "I don't think so, Sergeant. I'm not much in the mood for dancing."

"But the music's always good and peppery, and you'd get the chance to talk to folks. I don't imagine you have much call for that cooped up in here."

How well he knew it.

"I'll talk to Neil," she promised. A dance did sound good. Music, laughter, activity. And one more very inviting quality. "Are you going to be there, Jack?"

"Haven't decided, but I probably will. I'll go most anywhere for free food." He smiled wide and dimples creased his lean, browned cheeks.

Before she could stop herself, Emily said, "You should smile like that more often."

Immediately, the engaging grin was gone. She wondered what she'd said to make him suddenly look so uneasy. Something beyond the simple statement, she was sure.

Just then the water started steaming in the kitchen.

"Things are starting to boil," he told her.

Oh, she thought, how she wished they would.

She returned with two cups, and when he took his, their

fingertips nudged over one another's. And it felt to Jack as if hers did just a little bit of eager caressing.

"Thank you, ma'am." For the coffee, for the unspoken encouragement.

They were silent for a time, steeping with awareness of each other. Then Jack said, "I haven't forgotten about your daughter. I should be hearing from my uncle sometime soon. I know what it's like to get to missing family, and you an' Neil must be all torn up with it."

She almost replied that she had no idea what Neil was feeling, but there was no sense in spilling that to his sergeant. Except that she so desperately wanted to talk to someone, to confide in someone. And Jack Bass was all she had. He was her only friend, the only one she trusted.

But even as she was thinking of unburdening her heart to him, she could see the way he was erecting a cautious barrier between them. As if being friendly was fine but getting close was out of bounds. And she couldn't blame him, not really. Why should he want to involve himself in her problems? He was her husband's friend, foremost, and she must remember that.

Tears welled up in her eyes before she could think to stop them. She hadn't planned to weep, nor did she care to, even in front of the sympathetic Jack Bass. But the sorrow inside her swelled so suddenly it was like trying to halt the tide. She turned away, hoping he wouldn't notice.

"Ma'am?"

She could hear the concern in his tone, and that touched an even deeper chord of misery. Why was this man the one to be so sensitive to her moods? She was blinking hard, struggling to control the upward surge of emotion. Through the blurry periphery of her vision, she saw him reach out for her hand, and she moved away with a jerk; a jerk that caused the coffee in her cup to slosh over its edge. The scald of hot liquid made her gasp and leap to her feet. Jack was instantly on his, taking the cup from her, cradling her injured hand within his. And through the haze of tears, through the sharp throb of pain, came the awareness of his gentle touch, of how warm and rough and tender it was.

"It's all right, ma'am. It's not much of a burn. Probably smarts though. You should put it under some cold wa—"

Her fingers had twined through his and she'd come a step closer. Too close for him to ignore the way she had his heart jerking in a startled rhythm. Or the way she was looking up at him through jewel-like eyes, her gaze all soft and shiny and suddenly expectant. Very slowly he lifted her hand. Very lightly he brushed his mouth over the sore, reddened skin. Her fingers opened, their tips moving along the lean stretch of his cheek, down the strong line of his jaw. As she settled in even closer, he had to force his desire-drugged mind to do some pretty fast thinking.

"Jack."

As she whispered his name, Emily raised her face, wanting his kiss. But his other hand cupped the back of her head, firmly directing it to his shoulder. She could feel the cords of tension inside him and knew he'd wanted to kiss her, too. Somehow, just knowing that was a comfort. And knowing how hard he had to fight that want served to raise the intensity level. She leaned into him, enjoying the now familiar contours, absorbing the indescribable comfort he offered with just the slightest show of caring. She shut her eyes and reveled in the soothing magic of his hand stroking through her hair. She couldn't remember ever wanting anything as badly as she wanted Jack Bass.

"Your husband should be the one doing this," he said quietly.

But he didn't stop.

"Yes, he should." But Neil wasn't. And he hadn't. "Oh, Jack, I've been feeling so sad and empty inside," she admitted, with a despairing candor.

But that wasn't quite so true now, not now that he had his arms around her.

"And you should be telling that to him, too."

"I've tried, but he doesn't want to listen."

"And I don't think I should be listening to this, Miz Marcus." He was pulling away from her, his sense of honor levering him back, making him force a distancing wedge.

Feeling it, Emily was suddenly deeply hurt and desolate. Her tone was gruff. "I didn't mean to embarrass you, Sergeant. Forgive me for making you feel uncomfortable with my confessions. I'm not usually so burdensome."

She tried to draw away, but suddenly his arms wouldn't allow it. She looked up in confusion and was lost in the incredible compassion she found in his gaze. He touched her face, smoothing away her tears.

"I'm sorry, Emily. I didn't mean it to sound that way. It's just that you and I—"

Just then the front door swung open. Jack took a hurried step back, bringing a proper distance between them as he turned to greet his captain.

"Jack, you looking for me?"

"No. That is, I just stopped over to see how Miz Marcus was getting along. I hope that's all right with you."

"Sure." Then he looked between them, eyes narrowing as if he was wondering if maybe it shouldn't be.

"Well, then I guess I'd best be going," Jack concluded awkwardly. He affixed his hat and tipped it to Emily. "Ma'am. Be seeing you tomorrow night."

"Thank you for stopping by, Sergeant. It was very thoughtful of you."

"Cap'n." As Jack strode by Neil on his way out, Emily couldn't help noticing with satisfaction how much better he moved. His limp was scarcely apparent. Maybe he'd be fit enough for some dancing.

"What's tomorrow night?" Neil asked, as he shut the door.

"A dance in town. I think I'd like to go." She said that casually while watching him for a reaction. There was none.

"If you like."

He walked into the adjoining room, shoving over the vase of flowers so he could put his hat on the table. The blossoms drooped listlessly and Emily realized with some regret that they wouldn't revive. It was too late.

Taking a fortifying breath, she said, "Sergeant Bass has his uncle looking for Cathy."

"I know."

"You know?"

"He told me."

"Then why didn't you tell me?"

"Tell you what?" He glanced at her impatiently, and suddenly, she couldn't bear the silence anymore.

"Why didn't you tell me you cared whether or not Cathy was returned?"

He was frowning. "Of course I care. Why wouldn't I? She's my daughter."

"And I'm your wife. But you don't seem to care about that very much."

"I don't know what you're talking about, Emily."

No, he probably didn't. So she would spell it out. "It's been five years, Neil. Don't you want to know—"

"No," he interrupted curtly. "I don't. I know that you're

alive. I know that you're here. I don't want to know any more than that. There's no point in it. Let it rest."

"Can you?"

He didn't answer, and when her questioning stare demanded one of him, he began to turn away.

"Neil." Her tone shook with desperation. When he looked her way, she put her arms around him and hugged tight. He went rigid. It wasn't the self-denying tension she'd felt in Jack Bass. It was a denial of her. She refused to recognize it, holding to him tighter. He was hard and lean. There was no comfort to be found anywhere along his unyielding frame. "Neil, I want us to be a family again."

"That's what I want, too." But even as he said those words, his hands rose to her shoulders, not to embrace her, but rather to push her away. "I've got some company business to attend to tonight, so I'll be late. Don't wait up for me."

Emily was no fool. She knew what kind of business he was attending to. Her voice was strained when she asked, "Do you want supper first?" as she stepped away from him.

"No. I'll grab something with the boys."

"Fine."

And she let him go, pretending everything was fine. Pretending there was a chance that they could be a family again. Pretending even as she wept in her empty bed that night up until the time her husband returned, smelling of that woman. He tossed the covers from his side of the mattress and lay down in his long underwear on his half of their passionless marital bed. And he started to snore as more of her tears rolled unnoticed to the pillow beside his.

The town dance was held in a clean-swept barn on the edge of El Paso. Fiddles were squealing energetically by the time Emily appeared, squired on her husband's arm. All the rangers except those on patrol were in residence, as was a good portion of the town's populace. Food and punch were in abundance and whiskey flowed discreetly out of sight of the ladies. As soon as they were aware of their captain's presence, his men came to pay their respects, bowing politely to his lovely wife. The one who showed her the greatest deference was handsome young Billy Cooper.

"Billy, I thought you were on duty."

"Still am, Cap'n, but Jack offered to stand my watch for a couple of hours so's I could get in a little dancing."

Emily was aware of a crushing sense of disappointment. Jack wasn't coming. She was careful to retain her smile.

"Enjoy the dancing, but keep clear of the liquor. I'd hate to see you shot for falling asleep while on guard."

The boy's features sobered. "Yessir. And Miz Marcus, might I say how nice you're looking this evenin'?"

She murmured a soft thank you and tried not to act as disheartened as she felt. Suddenly all the joy seemed sucked out of the evening she'd so anticipated. She couldn't fool herself any longer. She hadn't spent so much time on her appearance to impress the citizens of El Paso. It had been for Jack Bass. And it was for nothing.

She stayed by Neil because she knew no one else well enough to venture off for conversation. It wasn't a terribly unpleasant duty. Neil Marcus cut a striking figure, all oiled and spit polished. He was handsome in a hard way and was obviously well liked by his men, for all the regard they showed him. Those were reasons enough for her to hold to his arm proudly, as if the two of them were truly happy. She owed him that illusion before all his friends, and she was pleased by their acceptance. Their women were not so free with their favor. Emily felt their cautious scorn but was safe at her husband's side. He might not have paid her more than cursory attention, but he allowed her a place beside him, and that said enough to hold obvious gossip at bay.

She'd fallen into a rote habit of smiling and nodding, but the sounds and the sights never reached her. She felt a distancing numbness from all that went on around her, as if she knew and they knew she had no real right to be there among them. All she had was a good man's name to cling to. Without that, she would have been shunned for her past. All the hopes she'd held of fitting back in while the mood was light and the music gay faded as the night wore on. No one spoke more than a brief greeting to her, and Neil escorted her about as if she meant no more to him than the pistol riding on his other hip—an expected and casually toted accessory, ignored until there was a reason for its use.

And then all that changed when she happened to glance across the room to see Jack Bass standing elbow deep in conversation with his comrades-in-arms.

He looked wonderful. Emily couldn't tear her gaze away. He was dressed in ranger-fine, with a black Stetson shaped to stick to his head when on a spirited horse. It was a good piece of felt, made to carry drink from a stream, wave as a signal, and shade his eyes when he napped. His boots were shop made and expensive, snug to the leg and high of heel. His clothes were riding clothes: a cool, cotton shirt, blue jean trousers, a good-quality leather belt with a silver buckle—nothing to get in the way of his reach or the use of rope, knife, or gun. Even his dark-blue roundabout jacket was tailored for the job, fit close to his body and cropped short enough at the waist to leave his gun exposed. Even in his off hours, he looked ready for business, a look that belied his mild manners and amiable smile.

That smile seemed to freeze when he saw her, then he

reached up to touch his brim in greeting before returning his attention to his friends. Emily chafed, wanting to go to him but discouraged by his dismissal. She had to remind herself that he was a single and attractive man who might not enjoy being hampered by the company of a married woman. She had no right to intrude upon his spare time or his amusements. But she wanted to.

From that impersonal distance she watched him, restless and unreasonably jealous of any female who approached him. And many did. In each case, he was unfailingly polite, scooping off his hat, smiling that small, shy smile, speaking as if it pained him to put the words together, and uniformly refusing trips to the dance floor. Then he'd subtly maneuver the unattached lady over to one of his unattached friends to pair them up, looking relieved to be left on the sidelines. It was almost as if his affections were engaged elsewhere, and Emily frowned, wondering who the lucky woman might be, until he finally approached them to exchange howdies with Neil and he glanced down into her eyes. Then she knew who held his heart and was staggered by the knowledge.

"Miz Marcus," he murmured in his soft-syllabled drawl. "You surely are making your husband the envy of every man here tonight."

"Very pretty flattery, Sergeant. And well practiced, I'm sure."

"No, ma'am. It's not. Flattery, I mean." Or practiced, either. His heightened color said that plainly enough. He wasn't a man given to pretty sentiments, but he spoke the truth when he recognized it. There wasn't a male in residence who wouldn't have been proud to claim Emily Marcus as his own. She was a stunning female, all grace and poise. No question about her being a lady capable of rising above any circumstance. It was more than her looks, though those were eye-catching enough in a gown of midnight blue-and-silver striped silk. The dress managed, with its loose draping folds and modest neckline, to be both elegant and softly feminine. And the way her thick, dark hair was swept away from her face accentuated her perfect features. It was more than her beauty. There was a strength of character in her, a certain toughness set against vulnerability, that made a man's pulse tremble. And Jack's was quaking.

Neil was looking about then, his attention focused on a man across the room. He glanced at his wife's clutching hand and began to frown. Then he looked to his sergeant and saw the answer.

"Jack, I've got to make some serious talk with the sheriff for a couple of minutes. Think you could mind Emily for me? She seems to be comfortable with you."

Jack stared at him as if poleaxed. Then he muttered, "Sure, Cap'n. Be glad to."

Then his best friend placed his wife's small hand upon his arm, offering him everything he desired in that one innocent gesture.

They stood stiff and silent for a long moment, then Jack cleared his throat to ask if she was having a good time. Yes, she could say without hesitation. Now, she added to herself, with only the tiniest bit of guilt. And for the first time, she became aware of the music, her toes catching the tempo and her heart the gliding rhythm.

"Do you dance, Sergeant Bass?"

"When I have to, ma'am." And he smiled at her.

"I wasn't going to make it an order." She was smiling back.

"Do you want to give it a go 'round?" The thought of having Emily in his arms already had his senses reeling.

"Will your leg hold up for it?"

"Should."

"If it doesn't, I can hold you up."

"Yes, ma'am. You've proved it before."

And one hand settled lightly at her waist while the other engulfed hers in a warm, possessive clasp. She put her free hand on his shoulder and let him move her back into the flow of dancers.

He held his own. He wasn't terribly quick or graceful, but he had a good sense of timing. And she wouldn't have really cared if he was stomping all over her feet. It felt good to be near him, to be following his steady lead. He was the only man she trusted enough to let him guide her blindly.

He was in love with her.

She'd seen it in his eyes. But what was she going to do about it? What could she do? She was married, more than once. She could offer him no encouragement and could accept no proof of his affection. She was dismayed by the circumstance but overjoyed by the fact. She'd never had a man's love before. She'd borne their touch, their possession, and their children, but she'd never experienced their love. And even at this wrong time, it felt very right.

Because she had fallen in love with Jack Bass, too.

Nine

It was Heaven and Hell.

The woman in his arms was everything Jack desired. She was strong, brave, sweet spirited, and beautiful. Her touch made everything inside him all hot and fluid, like the spring waters at Boquillas. She was the kind of woman a man looked for all his life, and if he was lucky enough to find her, he was smart enough never to let her go. Most of his fellow rangers were happy with the solitary life. They were content to roll themselves in a blanket under the stars, eat their meals out of a tin, and wash when they started scaring game away. They had no dreams beyond the moment, and most didn't care if the future lasted fifty years or fifty minutes. But Jack wasn't like them. He'd come from a solid family background. He'd seen the love between his mother and Will, between his uncle and Amanda. He'd held his baby brothers and sister in his arms and had known right then that he wanted children of his own. He wanted the vision Harmon had given him years ago—looking out over land of his own, a wife and kids beside him, a table to sit at and the satisfaction of belonging. Heaven was finding the woman to make that dream come true.

Hell was having her belong to someone else.

He could look down into her eyes and see everything he wanted reflected back. He could touch her and feel the response a man longed for. But he couldn't have her. And knowing that was killing him.

He admired Neil Marcus more than any man alive, other than his uncle and his stepfather. Thinking of betraying him in thought, let alone deed, was breaking his heart. If only he was certain Emily was happy. But he knew she wasn't. Neil was stepping out on her and the whole camp knew it. What Jack didn't know was why. How could any red-blooded man look at a woman like Emily Marcus and not want her? Regardless of what she'd been through. How could he take her for granted as he saw Neil doing? If she was his woman . . .

But enough of that thinking. She wasn't and she wouldn't be. All he was doing was winding himself up tight over what he couldn't have. There was no point in it. But he couldn't seem to help himself. Holding her chastely, even as they danced, was better than bedding any other woman. And he knew there was something very wrong with that kind of thinking.

He was almost grateful when Pete Meyers came up to cut in. Emily hesitated, but Jack surrendered up her hand to the older ranger with a reassuring smile.

"He won't try nothin' improper, ma'am." Then his pale eyes impressed that upon the man with a fierce narrowing.

"Like she was my mama," Pete vowed. He winked at her playfully and Emily relaxed. Then Jack felt safe to leave her in his care.

His leg was paining more than he'd let on. He figured he'd find a chair somewhere alongside the old ladies and give it ease for a few minutes. Then he spotted Neil and changed his plans. His captain was standing alone, dipping indiscreetly into a silver pocket flask. Not a good sign.

"Hey, Neil."

"Have a taste?"

Jack shook his head and smiled wryly. "Got no taste for what comes after."

"Smart man." But that didn't stop him from taking another long drink. He was watching his wife move about in Pete Meyers' arms.

Following his moody stare, Jack mentioned, "Fine woman."

"Hmmm? Oh, yes. She is."

"Woman like that should make a man stay home at night."

Neil shot him a sour look. "Why do I feel a sermon coming on?"

"I don't mean to be prying into anything—"

"Then don't. It's none of your concern."

"Yes, it is." The words got out of him before he could grab onto them, and suddenly, Neil Marcus was giving him a long, hard look.

"How do you figure that?"

" 'Cause you're my friend and I owe Miz Marcus the leg I'm standing on, not to mention my very life. Guess that gives me a right to care about the two of you."

Neil gave a soft snort, then wrapped his arm about his sergeant's shoulders. He must have been drunker than he looked, because he was leaning heavily. "Yeah, you are a friend. A damned good one." He took a long pull at his flask and stared at his lovely wife. "She slept with them, Jack."

"What?"

"The Apache. Otherwise, she'd be dead."

"Neil, you can't hold that kinda thing against a woman trying to save her life and that of her child."

"I don't. Not really. But I can't look at her without thinking of it. I'd rather find out she'd whored with every man in camp than to picture her beneath some damned redskin. Apache cleaned out my whole family when I was just a kid. Didn't just kill 'em, they roasted them alive. A man can't just forget that kinda thing. When they took Emily and the baby from me, I just gave up caring about anyone else. All I want to do is see as many of those sons of bitches dead as possible. Would do 'em all with my bare hands if I could. Every last one of 'em."

And Jack went cold inside. How was a man supposed to get over that kind of hate? Quietly, he said, "But none of that's Miz Marcus's fault."

"No, suppose not." But he didn't look convinced of it. "Maybe when the girl comes home, things'll be different."

"My uncle will find her. Until then, you could try being nicer to your wife."

Neil downed the last of his whiskey and pushed away from his friend. "You be nice to her, Jack. You're more decent than I am. Damned near to being a saint. Bet such things wouldn't wear on you at all, would they?"

Jack didn't dare answer.

"Seems she's a bit more fond a you than me these days, anyway."

"Neil, I never—" he began in protest.

"No, Jack, you never. I know that." Neil put his hand on the younger man's shoulder and pressed fondly. "A man could trust you with his last dime."

But not with his wife.

Writhing under that truth, the ranger sergeant looked away.

"I'm going to get a refill. Sure you don't want to join me?"

Jack shook his head. He was looking for Emily and suddenly couldn't find her among the other couples moving about the dance floor.

"Neil—"

But his captain was gone, too.

Emily enjoyed the dance with Pete Meyers. He was funny and polite and seemed to have a great respect for Jack Bass. When their dance ended, another ranger was quick to step up for the pleasure of her hand. Before she could answer, the music started and she was carried off in a romping country reel. Breathless and having more fun than she'd believed possible, she had no time to decline when another man became her partner, this one a citizen of El Paso, a man she didn't know. His grip was tight and his steps were determined as he wheeled her about the room, away from the gathering of rangers and right out into the cooler night air.

"Was getting stuffy in there, don't you think?" he drawled with a sly grin.

"No, I don't. I'd like to go back inside." She started to pull away, but his hand closed about her wrist none too gently. She pulled harder, but he wouldn't give. He just kept smiling. A sudden panic spiked through her. "Let me go. My husband is waiting."

"Your husband don't care nothing about you. If he did, he wouldn't be a right regular visitor at Juana's place. Figure with him gone so much a the time, you must be real lonely for the touch of a man. Pretty thing like you must be used to getting it all the time, after being with them redskins."

A hard gleam came into his eyes, a nasty speculative stare that she was all too familiar with. With a harsh cry, she twisted free and lunged back wildly—bumping into another burly figure.

"Having some problems hanging onto her, Frank?" Big hands cuffed her upper arms. "She giving you trouble?"

"She'll come to 'preciate me once I give her what for."

"Gonna save some for me?"

"If there's anything left to be shared."

Emily lost control. With a raw cry, she flung herself about in the man's grip. Unable to pull loose, she kicked out at the other one, hearing his satisfying grunt of pain. Then he struck her, hard and flat-palmed across the face. Shock stopped her rebellion cold, shock and remembered terror. She went limp with a quiet whimper.

"There now. That's better," the man Frank chuckled. "Now let's take us a little walk."

"The only place you're going is to Hell in a hurry, unless you let her go right now."

The soft voice intruded, making both men freeze up in alarm. Jack Bass stepped out into the evening. When they saw he was alone and still empty of hand, Frank sneered, "This ain't your business."

"You're wrong there."

"Maybe you'd like to take it up."

In a tone even quieter, Jack said, "I done took it up already." He spared Emily a glance, noting the cruel mark on her cheek without a change in expression. "Now, gentlemen, I'm giving you one chance to let the lady go and make her an apology before I kill you."

"Right polite a you, mister."

"A man with manners is far more dangerous than a loudmouth bully when there's gunpowder to be burned. I asked you nice to comply with me."

The man holding Emily looked uneasy. "Frank, maybe we'd better—"

"There's only one a him. He can't be that fast."

Jack gave him a mild smile. "Only three things matter in a gunfight. The deliberation it takes to want a man killed, the accuracy to see it done, and the speed to finish the deed. Now, sir, I figure fast is the least of my worries, since I already want you dead in a big way and I can add an extra buttonhole to your vest with no trouble at all."

"The man's a ranger, Frank. I don't want to mess with no ranger. You tangle with one and then you gots all of 'em after you." He gave Emily a push. She crumpled into Jack's outstretched arms.

"Oh, Jack," she cried in a quavering voice. She was shaking all over, and the thought of any living being putting that much fear into the brave Mrs. Marcus was going to seal that man's fate with a 250-grain slug. Quick.

"Ma'am, you pull yourself together, now, 'cause I aim to bury these men without any further ado." He gave her a bracing hug, then set her aside, freeing up his gun hand. He kept his eyes on Frank. That's where he'd place his shot. He guessed the other would break and run for it when the going got rough. He hadn't stayed alive as long as he had by not being able to look a murderer in eye and divine his intentions. "Make your play and back it with lead."

"Keep 'em leathered, boys," came a firm command. Neil Marcus was quick to square up at Jack's elbow. "What's going on here?"

The nervous one paled when he recognized the ranger captain. "We was just funning with your missus, Cap'n. Didn't mean her no harm. Jus' wanted a couple of dances, is all."

"Liar," Jack seethed quietly. "Look at her face."

Neil didn't bother. His expression was hard and unreadable. When he didn't react, Jack shot him an impatient look.

"They made light of your wife's honor," he charged angrily.

"Honor?" Frank scoffed. "She's got no claim to honor. Not after she's been a whore for the 'Pache, and from what I hear, the Mexicans, too."

"Where'd you hear that?" Jack surged forward only to have his captain catch him up in a restraining hold.

"Back it down, Sergeant."

Jack went still with surprise. "What?"

"I said let it go. I won't lose a good man over another's right to speak the truth."

With a soft cry of shame, Emily Marcus fled into the darkness. When Jack would have followed, Neil kept his arms pinned.

"Now, there'll be no gunplay tonight. You hear me, Jack?" To the others, he said, "I suggest you fellas make tracks before I let him loose."

They didn't need another warning. They were gone.

"Jack, now you settle down, boy. You're not to go after them. You understand? That's an order."

Jack jerked free and turned to confront his commander. He was breathing hard, his expression stark with disillusionment. "I can't believe you'd do such a thing," he whispered in a tortured voice.

"C'mon inside with me, Jack. You look like you could use a drink."

Not even favoring him with a reply, Jack whirled away and stalked off in the opposite direction from the one the hardcases had taken. Neil gave a heavy sigh and went back into the glare of bright lights.

* * *

Emily dropped off the borrowed carriage at the livery. Her breath was coming in uneven gasps by the time she ran to her front door. The sobs strangled in her throat, caught up on the awful truth her husband had spoken. There was no more question of how he thought of her. He'd stripped his opinions bare and had as much as broadcast them with his failure to defend her. By letting her abusers go free, he'd said he thought she deserved what she'd gotten because of what had been done to her. And though it wasn't fair, she lacked the strength to fight against it anymore.

She collapsed against the door, overcome by exhaustion and despair. Just as she reached for the knob, hoping to lose herself inside the solitude of her unwelcoming home, a hand passed over hers and a quiet voice stayed her.

"Emily, he didn't mean it."

She sagged against the door, crying, laughing weakly. "Oh, Jack, don't defend him. Of course he meant it."

"No. He'd never have hurt you like that if he'd been sober." He reached out his other hand. He left it hovering above her shoulder, uncertain of what to do, of how to comfort her. "Please don't cry."

"He hurts me every time he looks at me because I know what he sees. And I can't blame him."

He took hold of her then and carefully turned her to face him. The sight of her tearstained and bruised face unstrung his emotions. "Emily, that's not true."

"It is," she argued with a weary resignation. "It's what Neil thinks. It's what those men thought. No white man will ever respect me, knowing what I've been through. And no man is ever going to want a woman like me."

"I do."

He said that quietly as his hands came up to frame her face. And even as she began to shake her head in denial, he leaned forward to prove it was true. His mouth touched to hers and pressed gently until the fit was perfect and complete. Then he angled his head slightly to cause an exquisite friction. Emily made a soft sound of wonder, and as he pulled back, she was gazing up at him with such longing, his will caved in around his heart. His fingertips caressed her damp cheeks tenderly.

"I know what it's like to be shut out by circumstance, Emily. I know how much it hurts when those you love don't love you back. But you can't give in. You can't give up. It'll get better. You have to give it time."

"I want to believe you, Jack," she said, in a fragile voice.

"You have to believe me, 'cause it's true."

"Then prove it to me again, Jack. Please make me a believer."

She reached up to lace her hands behind his head, drawing him down to where her lips waited, all damp and eager for the feel of his. Emily had never cared for kissing. With Neil, it was a hard, emotionless thing, and Apache adults didn't kiss one another. With Jack came her first real taste of passion, and she more than liked it. She loved it.

After a few soft, slanting exchanges, Emily wet the seal of his lips in a tentative inquiry. His parted obligingly and she slipped in to sample more untried delicacies. Then he did the same within the warm cavern of her mouth and the thrill of pleasure intensified to a frightening degree. Her fingers opened, meshing in his hair, plying the feel of it the way she'd appreciate sleek, mahogany-colored silk. As his kiss deepened until she felt surely he'd reached to her very soul, his rough palms roved over her upturned face, stroked down her taut throat, and skimmed her shoulders, pausing there. She wanted his touch to continue on as greedily as she craved the sweetness of his mouth and the sassy flirtations of his tongue. She would have given him anything he asked for as sensation pooled and thickened into a pulsing urgency. But the minute she moaned his name and readied to follow it with the words, "Make love to me," he moved away again, gently lowering her hands so he could step back even farther.

His pale blue eyes searched hers with a sudden yearning, and when she would have come to him again, he used their joined hands as a barrier between them.

"Emily, forgive him. I know he loves you. How could he help it?"

She didn't want to talk about Neil just then. She strained forward, trying so desperately to stretch up to him that he finally gave in and allowed her one more lingering kiss. He showed her more in that single moment of give and take than she'd ever dared dream possible.

"Jack," she whispered, against the luxurious feel of his mouth, "what about us?"

He snatched another quick taste, then stepped away, severing the temptation for more. His words were rough with tenderness. "It's wrong. But I'm not sorry. Goodnight, Emily."

She slumped back against the door and said, too softly for him to hear as he strode away, "I love you, Jack."

It took all of twenty paces for guilt to catch up to him. It was then reality dealt a crippling blow to his euphoria.

You are a friend, a damned good one. A man can trust you . . .

What kind of friend was he being a minute ago, taking advantage of a woman's weakness, shoving a man's trust back at him like a killing blade in the back?

What about us?

What was he doing, encouraging Emily to think of them in that fashion? There could be no "us." He had to start thinking with his head, instead with other parts of him that seemed to forget all about morality when she was near. He had to stay away from her. He wasn't doing her any favors by fueling her confusion. Or his own. He was just as vulnerable as she was, just as hungry for that taste of acceptance. Only they couldn't take it from one another. They just couldn't. He was fooling himself if he thought he could be a friend to Emily Marcus. He didn't want to be her friend. He wanted to be her comforter, her protector, her lover . . . her husband. But that spot was already filled. The best thing he could do for her was stay the hell away until this particular madness subsided. Then, she would turn to Neil; Neil would accept her back, and that would be that. The way it should be.

"Jack."

He jerked up short, startled by the sudden call of his name. Only one man he knew could come up out of the darkness like that, like a ghost.

"Uncle Harm."

Harmon Bass separated from the shadows. He was covered with trail dust and the weariness of a hard ride. But there was a questioning intensity to his gaze that made Jack squirm.

"How long you been here, Uncle Harmon?" How much had he seen?

"A while. Thought I'd wait until you were less occupied."

He said that blandly enough, but Jack cringed under the censure. He had no excuse, so he didn't try to make one. What excuse was there for kissing another man's wife?

"Got news for you."

Thoughts of shame and regret immediately fell away. "About the little girl? You find her?"

Harm nodded. "How do you want to play it, Jack?"

"Best be asking the girl's father. You want to take a minute to clean up and get a meal while I go get him?"

Harm shook his head. "I want to get this done and get home. I got a wife waiting." His voice lowered a notch. "And if I was to find another man had been sliding into my shoes while I was gone, I'd be cutting his throat and watching him bleed."

Jack paled. "Uncle Harmon, I—"

"Don't bother with me, son. It don't make any difference what I think. She's not my woman. You do what you want. Just wondering if she was worth dying for."

"Yes." That was said softly, soberly.

"Guess you don't need any advice from me, then. A man's honor is about all he has in this world. If yours don't mean nothing to you, then I won't waste my breath." And he started to turn away.

Jack hung back, head bowed, heart bruised beyond redemption, feeling all of fourteen again. His uncle's disappointment in him brought home a sense of shame that was crushing. He'd spent his whole life doing anything it took to gain the respect of those he loved. And it was gone in an instant—or so he thought.

Harm caught the back of his neck with his hand and gave him a gentle shake. But Jack couldn't look up at him.

"You'll do the right thing," Harm told him, with a quiet confidence.

"I don't know what that is, Uncle Harm," he admitted mournfully.

"Yes, you do."

"I'm in love with her."

"I know."

That brought his gaze up, all shiny and uncertain. "You know?"

Harm smiled thinly. "I'm the best there is at reading signs. And you're not very good at covering yours."

"What am I going to do?"

"Whatever you have to. You think of her, not yourself. You're going to do the right thing, but first, you're going to buy me a beer."

That won a faint smile. Then Jack grew sincere. "Having your respect means everything to me, Uncle Harmon. If I was to lose that—"

"You earned that a lot of years ago, Jack, and you haven't come close to changing my mind. Don't worry about keeping my respect. Keep your own. How 'bout that beer?"

Jack placed a hand on one dirty shoulder. "Where's your horse?"

Because the dance was still going full steam ahead, the barrooms were fairly empty, and they had no trouble securing a place at the brass rail in the first one they came to back in El Paso.

"Gimme a beer," Jack called, and when it was supplied, he carried it over to one of the tables with his uncle in tow. "Sit yourself down for a minute and cut the dust. I'll be right back with my captain."

When Harmon was situated comfortably, Jack strode out in search of Neil. His uncle's words pressed on him. The right thing. Finding Cathy Marcus was the right thing. Restoring her to her family was another. Stepping back and letting things heal naturally was a right thing, too. And that's what he would do. That decision cleared his mind of confusion and his soul of guilt.

Harm was just putting the finishing swallow to his beer when his nephew returned in the company of a tall, whiskered man. They stopped at the table, and Jack was quick with the introductions.

"Uncle Harm, this is my captain. Neil Marcus, Harmon Bass."

Harm stood and was already reaching for the outstretched hand when he looked up at Neil Marcus. He didn't give much away, just a short expulsion of breath as if someone had punched him in the gut, and the slight droop of his lids to shield the sudden, feverish glitter of his eyes. But inside him, everything came undone.

"Mr. Bass." Marcus took his hand in a firm clasp. Then his eyes narrowed, too. "Do I know you?"

Harm's drawl was soft and deceiving. "We've never been formally introduced."

But Harm knew him. He knew Neil Marcus well.

He'd been waiting twenty years to kill him.

Ten

"So, where is she?"

Neil posed that question as he took a seat at the table. Harm settled more slowly, and had Jack been paying more attention, he would have noticed the dangerous tension that settled with him.

"In the Bend."

"I knew that. Where exactly?"

"With a band of Mescalero. Nowhere you'd ever be able to find her."

"Tell me."

"I don't think so."

Jack followed the discussion, puzzled by the immediate antagonism. His uncle was not the most trusting of men, but he could see no reason for this sudden cool belligerence. Wasn't finding Cathy Marcus for her father and mother what he'd been sent to do?

"Uncle Harm, how can we get her back?"

Harm never looked at him. His gaze was fixed on Neil Marcus. "I don't know as that's my problem."

"Uncle Harmon, you said—"

"I said I would find her for you. I didn't say I would return her for him."

"I'm not asking you to," Neil rumbled. "All's I need to know is where, then my men and I—"

"Can what?" Harm put in, like the quiet shush of a drawing blade. "Kill them all and take her back? Or do you think you'll just ride in and they'll hand her over to you like civilized folk?"

"I'm talking about rescuing a white girl from savages, and all you're worried about is saving the skin of some of your relatives."

Then Jack understood. It wasn't who the two of them were, it was *what* they were—a ranger and an Apache. Aggravated and alarmed that such a serious situation could dissolve into a petty dispute, he spoke up reasonably.

"I thought the idea was reuniting a daughter with her mother. Gentlemen, we're losing the focus here. Uncle Harmon, would you go grab us up a round?"

Neil pushed a coin across the table. Harm gave it a long, narrow look, then chose to ignore it as he rose and went to the bar. Immediately, the ranger captain turned on Jack.

"He's an Apache."

"He's my uncle. And being part Apache is why he was able to find your daughter. Back down, Neil, or he's not going to help us."

"Don't need his kind of help. How do you know he's not going to lead us out there and get us all killed in some kind of trap?"

Jack gave an exasperated sigh. "Because I know. Harmon has a reputation with the rangers. Ask Will. Ask Cal Lowe. They know him."

"I don't know him."

"Well, he's not all that easy to get to know. I'm not asking that you trust him. I'm asking you to trust me."

Three mugs of beer smacked down on the tabletop. Harm resumed his seat, his mood no more malleable than it had been moments before. In fact, Jack had seen rattlers in the coil of a more friendly persuasion. It was something about Neil. Jack couldn't pin it down, but he knew his uncle well enough to know something wasn't right. Harm wasn't trusting, but he was usually fair about making judgments. He'd already made up his mind about Neil Marcus, and Jack wondered why.

"Uncle Harm, would you have any objection to taking me to where you found the girl?"

"Alone?" Neil interrupted. "No. That'd be suicide. I won't hear of it."

"Neil—"

"No. If you go, it's with a detachment of rangers, well armed and ready for anything."

It would seem to be a stalemate. Neil Marcus wasn't prepared to give, and Harmon had withdrawn behind an impassive face that even Jack couldn't read. There was one more thing he could try.

"Uncle Harmon, family should be together."

That pronouncement won a reaction. Harm's gaze flickered to him, softening slightly, but the wariness remained.

"I'll be in charge of the men," Jack continued. "They'll answer to me. It's just for the girl."

"I won't lead rangers against my mother's people."

"I'm not asking you to."

"Your word."

"You've got it."

Harm studied him, measuring the value of that word and the man who gave it. "All right."

"First thing in the morning, then. Have you got a place to bunk?"

"I'll be close by."

Just then, Juana Javier swayed into the bar. She had started to lean in close to one of the cowboys at the bar when she saw

Neil, then her purpose changed. Without pausing long
enough for a drink, she gave Neil a beckoning look. Then she
turned with a rattle of cheap jewelry, heading for the door.
Neil rose up at once. Jack ground his teeth down on his want
to comment. It wasn't his business. It wasn't.

"If you fellas would excuse me, I'm gonna turn in for
the night. Jack, see me before you ride out. Mr. Bass . . .
a pleasure."

"Yes," Harm replied with a small smile. And he continued to smile as he watched Neil Marcus make his way to
the bat-wing doors, his hot blue gaze detailing the other
man's back as if fitting him for a coffin. It wasn't a look
Jack could ignore easily.

"What's wrong?"

"What?"

"What's bothering you, Uncle Harmon?"

His gaze was still on the empty door frame. "Just thinking about the little girl. About bringing her home to him."
And that's all he would say.

Emily stood in the kitchen while her husband talked business with Jack and Harmon Bass. They were talking about
her child, her daughter.

With Cathy returned, perhaps there would be a chance.
She owed Neil that chance, even after he'd broken her heart
with his callous disregard. Maybe it was, as Jack had said,
because he was drunk. Maybe it was just the shock of her
return. Most men wouldn't have let her back into their house
at all. Neil, at least, was willing to provide her with shelter
and the illusion of a marriage. She hadn't been trying overly
hard to be a proper wife to him. She'd allowed the distance
between them to grow and knew it could not continue once

Cathy was home. Things would be hard enough for the child. She would need the strength of family in order to adjust to ways that would seem frightening to her. She would probably resist the change. But she was Neil's child. It wasn't right that the Apache should keep her.

Emily made coffee with trembling hands. It was good that Jack Bass was going. Now there would be less distraction as she turned her energies toward making her marriage work. If there couldn't be passion, at least there could be kindness and harmony. Neil was a good man, a strong man, a necessarily hard man. She owed him her loyalty. It wasn't his fault that he wasn't as gentle as Jack Bass, or as compassionate, or as giving. But he was her husband. And they shared a child. She would have to strive harder to make the past disappear from memory, both Neil's and her own. And she would have to forget the desire his ranger sergeant stirred inside her. Because above all, she was a survivor.

Jack Bass might have kissed her but he hadn't offered her anything else. He hadn't told her he loved her, even if that might be true. He hadn't suggested she leave her husband, or that he'd provide and care for her if she did. And she didn't believe he ever would. If he wanted her, it would be a hidden passion. If he loved her, it would be an unspoken longing. Because that was the kind of man he was. A man of honor, a man who lived by the code of loyalty to friend and family. He wouldn't break that for her. Not for the wife of his best friend and commander. And if he wouldn't, there was no point in thinking of him at all. She had to think of how she was going to live and provide for her daughter. It didn't matter if that required the loss of her pride or the denial of her heart. Rebecca Bass had put that plainly. She would do what she had to and make no apologies. The past was gone, and part of her heart had gone with it.

The men rose up when Emily entered the room carrying a coffee service. Purposefully, she didn't look at Jack as she poured, but when she leaned close to Harm to fill his cup, the tracker murmured quietly, "She is well."

Emily's gaze flashed up expectantly, thankfully. "You've seen her?"

Harm nodded. Then his voice lowered another notch and he shifted to the language of his mother's people. "And the other one, too."

Emily gasped. Coffee spilled out to swim in the saucer before Harm could tip up the pot's spout.

"How did you know?" she asked faintly in the same tongue.

"His mother's eyes."

"You haven't said anything?"

He shook his head slightly.

"Please . . ."

"What would you have me do?" was his quiet request.

"Please say nothing. He must stay with his father's family. He will be safe and loved, and I can't guarantee that here. Can you understand?"

Harm's hand eased over hers for a gentle press. "You are brave and wise."

"What are the two of you talking about?" Neil demanded, irritated by the grating sound of Athapascan syllables.

Harm slid him a cutting gaze, then looked at Emily Marcus for a long, somber moment. "You are his woman?"

Puzzled by his intensity, she said, "Yes."

Harm moved his hand and said very softly, "I am sorry." No other explanation. And Emily felt a shiver take her as she straightened and went to stand by her husband.

She was doing the right thing, the only thing she could

do. But she didn't feel brave or wise. She felt as if her mother's heart was breaking.

Because if Neil Marcus wouldn't accept the fact that she'd lived with the Apache, how would he deal with the knowledge that she'd borne a child with one?

Did any man have that kind of strength?

I do.

Her gaze was drawn to Jack Bass in a study of his tough features and the sensitive sweep of his mouth. No, she couldn't believe it, even of him. So she would say nothing and she would suffer the loss alone.

Jack had prepared for an awkwardness when confronting Emily Marcus in her husband's house. If there was any, it was all on his part, because Emily never so much as glanced at him. She hovered at Neil's side like a devoted wife, as if no one knew how his words had cut her to the soul. And while Jack was proud of her for the stand she was taking, he mourned the loss of her. She'd never seek out his kisses or his comfort again. When he brought home their daughter, the Marcuses would no longer be his concern.

How lonely that left him.

Only when the time came for them to rise up and go did Emily meet his eyes. Hers were wide and soft, as green as the prairie grasses, as strong as the mountain pines. He gave her a small, reassuring smile, murmuring, "We'll bring her back to you, ma'am."

"Thank you, Sergeant."

He fit his hat and started for the door, aware that once again she drew his uncle aside to speak to him softly in words only the two of them could understand. He didn't know what she said, but Harmon nodded and gave her one of the rare warm smiles he usually reserved for family.

"Please take care of Jack," she'd bidden him, and how could Harmon wish her any ill after hearing the tender concern in her voice?

Perhaps he wasn't Apache enough for what he had to do.

They traveled light and fast during the long daylight hours, sticking to the divides rather than the established routes, setting up their camps next to streams or watering holes after first crossing them. Horses were picketed on a stake rope as well as hobbled in the dangerous countryside and placed under cautious guard because a ranger afoot was no ranger and a man was only as good as his horse.

After the beans were parched and ground as needed and the coffee put on to brew, the rangers sat at ease around their fire in a comfortable camaraderie. While they were for the most part disinclined to talk of their own exploits, there wasn't a man among them not curious to learn a little something about Harmon Bass.

"Don't have much to say, does he?" Billy nodded toward the slight figure bedded down well off from the others, apparently asleep in his blankets.

"Harm don't go in for socializing," Jack explained.

"Shame," muttered one of the other men. "Shore would like to hear some of his story. If half of what I read was true, he's one helluva legend."

Jack chuckled. "If you're talking about that soft-bound trash fiction, that's just what it is. Fiction, pure and simple." When the men looked disappointed, he smiled and added, "The truth is better."

Their attention perked up, and to a man, they were eyeing

the wiry part-Apache tracker who was stretched out with his hat over his face.

"Pete said he rode with him once, years back. Was on the trail of some bushwhackers. Said he went afoot for two days to stay on the track, running it like a hound. Never once did stop for rest and took only water. Outran most of their horses. That true, you think?"

Jack just smiled blandly.

"Heard tell he took on ole Judge McAllister down Perdition way over some white woman. Kilt the sheriff down there in a knife fight. Cut him up so bad they're still looking for pieces of him. He do that, or that some fancy fiction, too?"

"That's true," Jack murmured. He knew. He'd been there for that one.

"What happened to the woman?"

"She was his wife, my Aunt Amanda."

"Rumored that he made a habit a tracking fellers down and butchering 'em up real messy-like without giving no reason. They say he don't need no fancy sidearm, not the way he handles a knife."

Jack slid a gaze to the speaker. "Clayton, for a fella with a half claim to a brain, you sure fall for every cock-and-bull story you hear."

There was a rumble of laughter, but Jack didn't share in it. Because he knew the rumors were true. His uncle had done things no white man could ever understand. No matter how much he loved his uncle, he never could.

Billy was studying the silhouetted figure with interest. He was young enough to be looser of tongue than most of the more experienced men and impressed enough to speak his questions plain. "Don't hear much a him anymore. Why's that? Man with his kinda reputation, seems a shame that he up and holed himself in away from the thick of it. He lose his nerve, or just his edge?"

"Why don't you wake him up and ask him?" Jack suggested.

"No, thanks. I seen that knife he carries. But answer me this, you being his family an' all. He still as good as they say?"

In answer, Jack picked up a small stick and gave it a toss so that it landed near Harm's feet. In the time it took for the dust to settle, his uncle had spun out from a full reclined ease into a low, taut-muscled crouch, his knife at the ready. The rangers blinked. Most of them hadn't seen him move.

"Yep," Jack concluded. "Uncle Harmon, you want some coffee? Seems you could use some. Were a might slow on the reflexes."

Harm relaxed his lethal pose and the rangers began to breathe easier.

"Son of a—"

"Dang!"

"Ain't never seen nobody human move like that."

The mutters quieted when Harm approached the fire.

"Might as well have a cup, seeing as how you fellers can't seem to hush long enough for a man to get his sleep."

Jack poured. "The boys were jus' wondering if you'd gotten slow and lazy in your old age."

"Were they?" Harm swept the group with a leisurely gaze and not a man among them appeared to have the slightest bit of curiosity left.

"Seems they all cut their teeth on dime stories about *the* Harmon Bass." Jack was grinning, enjoying his uncle's discomfort.

"You want an expert to talk on and on about *the* Harmon Bass, you should have asked your brother or your aunt to come along. They know things about me that I ain't even heard yet."

When he squatted down Indian fashion to accept the cup from his nephew, one of the men grew bolder.

"You really kill your first man when you was twelve?"

"Ten," Harm corrected softly, as he blew into the steam rising from his tin.

"How many men you reckon you killed since then?"

"None that didn't deserve it, and some jus' for asking nosy questions." He stood then, all the rangers rearing back slightly, the way they would if a rattler had risen up from its coil in their midst. But Harm paid them no attention as he took his cup and walked out of the circle of light until the surrounding shadows swallowed him whole.

Jack waited a moment, then followed. He found his uncle staring toward the mountains with a wistful look etched into the harsh angles of his face.

"Missing home?"

Harm laughed softly. "You'd think I'd appreciate the quiet." Then he sighed. It was a sad sound, like the mournful wail of the evening breeze. "Funny, how you just get used to having someone with you until they become like the air and the light and the sun. There's no living without them. Listen to me. Ammy calls it my romantic soul. I sound like a fool."

Jack slid his palm along his uncle's tense shoulders. "Sound like a man in love with the right woman."

"It don't get any better than what I got, that's for sure. An' I don't deserve a lick of it." His pensive look intensified. "If those men knew half the stuff I've done, they wouldn't be so amused. Before Amanda, I was in a world so dark and deep, I didn't know anything but killing. I was no hero. Nothing for them to admire, no dime novel legend. Your Aunt Amanda made me into a good man. She allowed me to bring three lives into this world to replace those I'd taken. I'd humble myself to no man, god or devil, but not a day goes by that I wouldn't go down on my knees for her."

Jack said nothing, moved by the strength of emotion in his uncle's words.

"I was taught it was bad manners to be too fond of a wife's company, that it showed a lack of discipline to desire her more than a couple of times a week, that it was unmanly to crave her comfort. I held my honor above my life until I met Amanda, and now it means nothing, where she's concerned. A man's will can't hold when a woman wants to have her way. I'da run like hell if someone had told me that when I was your age."

"I seem to recall you leading Amanda a pretty darned good chase."

"Yeah? The way I remember it, she had me snared and gutted out before I had the sense to get outta her way. A right dangerous and determined woman, your Aunt Amanda. She saw what she wanted and wouldn't let anything discourage her. Not even me."

"I envy you, Uncle Harm." That was said quietly, without spite or jealousy, and Harmon turned to let his knuckles rub under his nephew's jaw.

"Your time will come, Jack. When it does, you'll know."

Trouble was, he did know. And the time for him was already past. The woman for him was someone else's.

"It's good to be riding with you again," Harm said to distract him. "But your friends have no manners."

"Don't be too hard on 'em. They're good boys. Jus' awed to be in the presence of a legend. Not every day a man sits to a fire with *the* Harmon Bass."

"You might be taller than me, but that don't mean I can't smack you for giving me sass."

"Yessir, Uncle Harm." But he was smiling, not showing the least bit of worry.

Harm's mood altered subtly and it was as if a sudden cold front had settled in from the north.

"Tell me about your captain, Jack."

"What do you want to know?"

"Whatever there is."

"He's firm and fair. He's disciplined from being in the Army, yet there's not a man among us that he wouldn't invite to sit down beside him. I'd follow him into hell with a pail of water. I'm proud to think of him as my friend."

Harm took this in, his expression never changing.

"What is it? Do you know him from somewhere? I've never known you to take such a dislike to anyone."

Harm ignored the questions to continue with his own. "He's a lot older than his wife. I'd guess him to have a couple a years on your mama. What did he do before ranging?"

"I told you. He was in the Army during the war."

"Before that?" Harm's voice had quieted to a glassy calm, the kind that surfaced deep and dangerous waters.

"I don't know. What are you getting at, Harmon? There bad blood between the two of you or something?"

"Something," he admitted with a glacial brevity.

"What?"

"If something were to happen to him, would you take up with his woman?"

"Yes . . . no, I mean, why are you asking such a thing? Nothing's gonna happen to Neil."

Then Harmon gave him a look that set up cold and thick as ice in a January rain barrel. It froze along Jack's veins until the chill had him shaking. He grabbed onto his uncle's arm and squeezed tight for emphasis.

"If you're planning to make something happen, I won't

like it." His tone was low and full of threatening promise. Harm merely placed his hand over his nephew's.

"You are my sister's son and I love you as if you were my own." Then he moved from under Jack's grasp with a quick pull so he could turn and stride back toward camp.

Jack stared after him. "Uncle Harm? Harmon!" His breath came in soft, panicked chugs as the slight, deadly figure continued to walk away.

And as Jack stood alone in the darkness, one thought came, black and forbidden.

If Neil Marcus was dead, Emily could be his.

At the gateway to the Big Bend of Texas, there were three things: Will Bass's ranch, Harm's at Blue Creek, and the town of Perdition.

Though their conversations had been slightly strained since Harm's veiled comments concerning the length of his captain's future, the first thing Jack thought to ask was if his uncle wanted to swing by and check on his wife. Harm thanked him but declined, saying he'd rather finish with what he started. Besides, he said rather wryly, Amanda didn't cook up a meal a man would cross a desert for. Jack didn't press. He understood. It would be too hard for him to leave home once he'd gotten the taste of it again.

Then, when Jack declined the opportunity to visit his own family, Harm allowed him the same courtesy and kept out of it. But when Jack's sorrel pitched a shoe and he decided to make a quick detour into Perdition to get the animal reshod, Harm told Jack he could go without him. He had no desire to see the inside of that particular town again. He said he'd stick with the rangers and Jack could catch up as soon as he was able.

It wasn't much to look at, that was true. Jack had seen all kinds of dusty border towns, and this was as bad as it got. El Paso was no paradise of morality, but at least it had an energy of its own. Perdition had an attitude of cold disregard, a kind of bristling hostility that claimed, "Enter at your own risk, and leave if you're lucky!" And he was glad not to have to linger for long.

After dropping his sorrel off at the blacksmith's, he wandered into the first saloon to offer a meal and sampled a cold beer while devouring the salty fare. He kept his eyes to himself so as not to stir up any need for trouble. Still, it managed to find him.

"Heard tell a man sitting his horse like a ranger had rode in. That be you, mister?"

Jack glanced up, taking stock of a rail-thin man sporting a lush, drooping mustache and a sheriff's badge. "Yep. Do something for you, Sheriff?"

"Jus' wondering if I had cause for worry. You boys don't come in often, lessen it's in search of soon-to-be corpses."

"Just getting my horse tended. Nothing official."

The sheriff began to stare at him, studying his features with probing puzzlement. Then he blinked and took a step back. "What's your name, Ranger?"

"Jack Bass."

"Bass. As in Harm?"

"My uncle. You know him?"

The sheriff gave a wide grin and laughed loud. "I'll be damned. Name's Lon Pager, and I was a right good friend of your daddy's!"

Nothing could have caught his attention quicker. Jack sucked in a breath, then let it out slow and unsteady. "You know my father?"

"Sure. Used to be sheriff here. Hell, boy, you look just like him. Ain't nobody ever tole you that before?"

His uncle and mother had told him that many times, but never in so many words.

"When was the last time you saw him?" Jack's pulse was beating fast with nervousness as he awaited the reply. After all these years, all his wondering.

"The day I helped bury him six years ago. Or what was left of him."

He was dead. His father was dead. A sense of emptiness settled inside him, but also a strange, giddy relief. Now he'd never have to confront him. He'd never have to know. Except he did; he had to know.

"What was his name?"

"His name? You joshing me?"

"What was his name?" Jack repeated more forcefully, in no mood for games.

"Cates. Tyrell Cates."

What was so familiar about that name? Six years ago? What was he missing? He had the pieces, but they weren't fitting together in a recognizable picture.

"How did he die?"

Lon Pager hesitated. Then he began to look apprehensive. "Your uncle around here?"

"Not in town, but nearby. Why?"

"Then you ask him."

"I'm asking you."

Pager gave a low, rusty chuckle. "You want to know what killed your daddy? About thirty stab wounds. Hell, one or two would a done the trick, but after your uncle was done with him, they had to rinse him off the floor."

Jack collapsed back in his chair, his mind stunned by the

knowledge, the shock of it too great, too sudden to absorb all at once.

Pager smiled a slow, sneering smile. "When you see your uncle, tell the son of a bitch I said hello."

Eleven

It was nearly dark by the time Jack reached the rangers' campsite. Most of the ride he'd made in a state so numbed he couldn't recall holding a single thought. But once the thoughts started coming, there was no stopping them.

Tyrell Cates. He remembered now. He remembered the man's deceivingly easy smile, the chill of his laugh, the cold brilliance of his stare. Pale eyes, like his own. A wide smile, like his own. He recalled a time six years ago when Cates and his men had swarmed their ranch, had shot Will and held them hostage. Cates had worked for the powerful Judge McAllister, whose stolen jewelry had brought Amanda from New York in search of her brother, who'd disappeared while delivering it to West Texas. She'd hired Harm to find him. Too late. And Cates held his family as ransom for the jewels. Harm, Amanda, and Calvin Lowe had come to their rescue. It had happened so fast, the details had been lost to him. He'd been fourteen at the time. And he remembered dragging a badly wounded and bleeding Harmon Bass to his horse so he could ride after McAllister, who'd had the bad idea of taking Amanda to use as a shield in his attempted escape. Wounds Harm must have sustained in a fight to the death with Cates. His father.

Harmon must have known.

And his mother. His mother and Tyrell Cates, together at

least once some fourteen years before that meeting at Will's ranch. Had they been lovers? he wondered frantically. What? What had they been to one another? He had no idea. The subject had been forbidden, tied up tight behind Will's mumbling about bad blood.

His father had been a hired killer and his uncle had slain him.

"Hey, Jack, just in time for grub."

Clayton Wainright snagged his bridle. Jack couldn't remember pulling back on the reins. He rolled out of the saddle, oblivious to everything and everyone in camp until he caught his uncle's eye. Harm rose up from his bedroll and without a word began to walk off away from the others, knowing Jack would follow. Which he did as his comrades looked on in bemusement. When they were out of earshot, Harm came to a stop, but he didn't turn.

"Lon Pager sends his regards."

His uncle's slight build snapped taut. "That son of a bitch."

"Then the feeling's mutual." He stared at his uncle's back, chewing on so much anguish and upset he didn't know where to start or how to get over it. Finally, he asked hoarsely, "Why didn't you tell me?"

"Tell you what?"

"Tell me what?" He gripped Harm's shoulder and shoved him around to face him. "Why didn't you tell me you killed my father?"

"I killed your father," he said flatly. "He was a man who needed killing."

"And you didn't think I'd ever find out?"

"I love you, Jack." That was said in the same toneless voice.

"So you lied to me? You let me meet my father face to

face and didn't even tell me?" The grip he had on his emotions was coming undone. Wild, angry feelings were flying through his heart and head. And a helplessness so strong and frustrating that the need to strike out in response kept bunching tighter. "You killed him and you didn't even let me pay my last respects over him? Even if it was to spit on his grave? Why, Harmon? Why didn't you tell me?"

"You were better off not knowing."

"Says who?"

"Becky didn't want you to know, and I agreed with her."

Jack took a quick gulping breath, struggling with the hurt, feeling betrayed because they hadn't trusted him. "Why? It's not as if everyone didn't know Will wasn't my father. Did she think I'd rather go through life wondering if every man I met could have lain with her to beget me? Did she think I'd be ashamed of finding out she'd whored with a gunman out of wedlock?"

Harm's expression sharpened into a series of harsh angles. "Don't you talk about your mama that way."

"Why? Because it's true? Because she took a lover and bore a bastard son, and then couldn't stand the thought of one or the sight of the other? And then got to feeling so ashamed she let you cut him up and bury him deep before I was any the wiser? What were the two of you afraid I'd find out? That I'm just like him?"

"No!" Harm gripped the lapels of his coat, yanking him up for a fierce shake. "You're not!"

"How am I supposed to know that? Huh? How am I ever gonna know? Do I take your word for it? After you've lied to me for all these years? To protect me from what?" His palms smacked into Harm's chest, knocking him off balance, forcing him to release his jacket. "What, Harmon? What the Hell do you see when you look at me?"

"What do I see? You want to know what I see, Jack?"

"Yes! Tell me!"

"I see the face of the man who beat and raped your mother. I see the face of the man who killed my mama and tortured me, and threw me into a box on top of her after she was cold, and buried the both of us together. I see fourteen years of Hell, spending my every minute tracking down the ones responsible. But you know what? You know what, Jack? Your daddy died too quick. I couldn't make him live long enough to suffer half as much as I wanted him to. If I could bring him back, I would, just for the pleasure of sending him to Hell again. Now," he concluded savagely, "if that's all you wanted to know, I'm going to ride out and do some scouting up ahead."

It took long minutes after Harm's brisk footsteps receded for awareness to seep in.

A monster.

His father was a monster.

What did that make him?

Harm had already ridden out by the time he wandered back into camp. He was immediately beset by his men.

"Jack, there's a good chance we'll be squaring off with them Apache in the morning. What are we gonna do?"

"What?" Apache? He didn't understand. Shock was shaking up through him.

"Them Apache. They're the ones who did Foster. What're we gonna do about it?"

"About what?" he echoed in a daze.

"About the fact that they murdered a good friend. Jack, what's wrong with you?"

"The cap'n would want us to wipe 'em out to the last man."

"They kilt Foster. We jus' gonna let get 'em away with

that? What's the chance of us ever findin' 'em again? They know every danged cave and ditch and sand hole in these mountains. We'll never get this close again."

"Foster was your partner, Jack. You took two arrows and almost died."

Jack squeezed his eyes shut. His head was reeling with pain, with the sound of Foster's screams. The frustration rose up like a noxious bile, sour, bitter, needing to be expelled.

"Jack, we gonna ride on 'em or what?"

"In the morning. At dawn."

"All right."

"We're with you, Jack."

"For Foster."

He tried to sleep but couldn't. With every added minute of the long, tense night, his emotions notched that much tighter, preventing him from any degree of peace. He tried to hold to the only good thing he could think of, to the image of Emily Marcus, but it kept fading away beneath the ugliness of the rest.

He closed his eyes and he could see his mother's horror when looking upon him. He twisted within his blankets, picturing his uncle's slashing blade. He locked his arms over his head, praying frantically that the screams would stop echoing and reechoing through his mind; his mother's, his friend's. He couldn't tell the difference anymore. Finally, exhausted and drained to a fragile stretch of nerves, he dozed off, only to be awakened what could just have been a few minutes later.

"Jack?"

He opened bleary eyes. They felt gritty from lack of sleep

and the need for tears. He blinked to give them ease, then saw Harm crouched down beside his blanket roll. And he shrugged away from the hand his uncle pressed to his shoulder. He rubbed at his face and dragged himself upright.

"What time's it?" he mumbled.

"About five. You all right?"

His jaw set. "Fine. Did you find them?"

"They're camped in a small ravine by a waterhole. You can see it when you crest that next rise. There are about eighteen men, twice as many women, and some children, including the Marcus girl. My guess is there's a hunting party out, so if you want to go in, now's a good time. I can translate for—"

Jack stood, turning away, interrupting him with the brusque call of, "Get ready, boys."

Harm stood back and watched as the ranger unit prepared to mount up. There was a keen edge to them that made him wary. But he wasn't really concerned, because Jack wasn't concerned, and these were his men. Until he started watching Jack. He was stuffing rounds in his personal armaments, his features worn to the same ravaged symmetry as the surrounding buttes. Harm had never seen a look so hard shaping the familiar face as when his nephew brought a cartridge into play with the clank-clunk cycle of his Winchester's ejection-reload system.

"Jack?"

Still, Jack wouldn't look at him, and suddenly, he was very uneasy with it all. They had the deadly look of men fixing paint for war. But Jack had given his word, and that would mean—

"For Foster," Billy murmured somberly, rousing a chorus of agreement.

"For Foster," Jack affirmed.

Harm squared off in front of him. "You gave me your word."

Jack regarded him through eyes dulled by disillusionment. "I thought honor and retribution were things you understood, Harmon. You hid your lies behind them well enough."

Realization brought a stark fury to Harm's expression. A fury, and the terrible pain of recognizing treachery. Then both emotions were gone.

"I don't want to know you." He said that as if words alone could sever the tie of family. Then he struck Jack a staggering blow across the face with a snarl of, *"Tejanos sangrientos!"* and ran for the nearest horse.

"Don't let him give them warning!"

The cry went up and Jack swiped the blood from his mouth to yell, "Stop him, but don't kill him!"

Harm was snatched off the saddle, but he was scrambling for another the second he hit the ground.

"Cut him off!"

Circled by a body of rangers, Harm jerked his knife free, warning them back with deft feints and a hiss of *"Cabrones!"*

"Don't crowd him," Jack cautioned. "He'll gut you faster than you can blink."

"What're we gonna do with him, Sarge?"

Jack hadn't the slightest idea, but he knew what they had backed into a corner was the most dangerous thing any of them could imagine. "Harmon, give it up. We're not going to let you pass."

Harm spat on the ground. "An Apache does not surrender to his enemy. What a fool I was not to recognize mine."

"He's gonna kill somebody, Jack. We got no time for this now."

There was the sound of a revolver coming to full cock.

"No! Nobody shoots. Nobody gets hurt." Jack stepped into the circle, hands empty and spread at his sides.

"Jack! What're you doing?"

"He won't hurt me, will you, Uncle Harm?"

At that moment, he couldn't bet his life on it, though that was exactly what he was doing. He advanced slowly, steadily, making no quick moves. And Harm was posed in a crouch, as ready to spring as an unpredictable mountain cat.

"Uncle Harm, don't give them cause to shoot . . . please." Jack reached out for the hand that held the knife. He was close enough to be disemboweled, if that was Harm's desire, but the blade never moved. Jack's fingers closed gradually about his wrist. He could feel the thundering pulse beneath his grip, but he never looked away from his uncle's penetrating gaze. "Easy, now."

And abruptly, Clayton Wainright stepped up from behind to neatly smack the base of Harm's skull with his rifle butt. He went down soundlessly, Jack there to ease his fall.

"I'm sorry, I'm sorry."

"Sun's coming up, Jack. We're gonna lose the surprise."

"What're your orders, Sarge?"

Moving a gentle hand through the hair at the nape of his uncle's neck, feeling the awful swelling starting there, Jack replied, "Pick your targets carefully. There are women and children in that camp, and I don't want any of them injured. No one escapes. I want it done clean and fast, even though they didn't give the same courtesy to Foster. Wait on my signal and commence a crossfire. Watch out for the captain's little girl. If you're ready, let's go."

* * *

Mists lay heavy and low, cloaking the ground in elusive mystery as daybreak burned above them. Movement began as the Apache woke and started about their morning rituals.

From his concealment among the surrounding rocks, Jack studied the scene, growing more and more dismayed. The shrouding fog wasn't lifting fast enough. The figures moving through it were vague, indistinguishable shapes. As the time for action approached, a rational calm began to replace his fevered anticipation. And with that calm came the terrible insight that he was on the verge of making the biggest mistake of his entire life.

It was wrong, what they were doing. It was wrong what he'd done to his uncle. Why hadn't he been thinking clearly? The sounds of screaming and the agony of truth had veiled his mind just like the cold morning haze. Only he was waking from his now.

He had to stop it.

Quickly he scanned the ridge of rocks, wondering frantically how he was going to get word to his men. And then he caught the glint of early sunlight off someone's blued barrel. And so did one of the Apache below.

Once the first shot was fired, there was no stopping anything. The Mescalero men met them with a return fire, fighting fiercely, as men do when protecting their families. What followed was so fast and final, Jack had no time to do more than react as he'd been trained. Stay down, shoot low and to kill, and bring down as many horses as possible. It was a scene of confusion. All the Indians were running with blankets covering their heads. There was no way to tell threat from innocence as bullets flew, randomly seeking targets. Screaming; the bite of gunpowder; the scent of blood—that's what Jack would remember when it was done.

And blame, horrible gut-clenching blame, as he stood to survey the quiet scene of carnage.

"Some of 'em slipped through, Jack. You want us to go after them?"

To hunt them down like animals and kill them? He shook his head. "Let 'em go. We've done enough."

The cools mists had evaporated, exposing the campsite all too clearly. And as Jack moved between the still bodies, he felt the same roil of horror he'd experienced after ordering his first man hanged. Innocent blood, the first he'd spilled at his command. And he knew he'd never feel the same about himself or what he was doing.

He was his father's son, preying on the helpless.

The other rangers were going about their grim business, tearing off blankets that were now shrouds, to make sure the dead posed no threat. Several of the Indians had fallen into the water hole, discoloring it with the pinkish stain of death. They made coffee from that water, and Jack could swear he tasted blood in his cup, the way he'd tasted it when his Uncle Harmon had taken him on a hunt and had made him eat the raw heart from his first kill. To ensure success in future hunts, Harm had told him. And looking into his coffee, he had to wonder the same thing. *Tejanos sangrientos,* Harm had called them. The bloody Texans. Yes, they were. And he wanted no part of it.

Because when they returned to their camp, his uncle was gone. And because strapped over the back of his horse, bundled in his slicker, was the small body of Cathy Marcus, killed by a ranger bullet.

"Daddy! Daddy!"

The joyous cries brought Amanda out of the house at a

lumbering run, but her smile was quick to fade when she got her first glimpse of her husband. He was kneeling in the dusty yard, his arms filled with his two girls, eyes closed in a face etched with weariness and strain.

Something terrible had happened.

He looked up then and saw her standing on the porch. His expression gave nothing away, but she was too good at reading the other signs: the way he was hugging their children, the way he stared so long without speaking.

It was bad.

He got up slowly and approached the house, one of his girls hanging on either hand.

"Hey, Uncle Harm!"

Sarah raced up to circle his neck with an exuberant embrace and cover his face with kisses.

"Hey, *shijii,*" he murmured softly.

When she stood down, puzzled by his lack of animation, Harm bent down to address his daughters.

"Girls, you stay out here with your *sikis* Sarah for a minute. I need your mama."

Sarah was watching his face, beginning to frown, but she put an arm around either child and said gaily, "C'mon, girls, let's go down by the creek and see if we can spot some dinner."

Amanda waited until he'd come up onto the porch, then preceded him into the house, chattering aimlessly in her panic. "You look exhausted. Come in and I'll fix you up something to eat. Then I want you to wash up and get about three days' sleep before you—"

He caught her hand, halting her in the narrow hall with the sudden fierce clasp of his fingers. When she turned toward him in question, he angled his body to bump her back against the wall. His free hand tangled in her hair, anchoring her head as he kissed her with a hard urgency. He didn't say anything, and she didn't need to hear words as she led the way upstairs.

Harm took her down to the bed where the late afternoon sun pooled warm and golden across the coverlet, continuing the aggressive kisses, following them with rough, impatient caresses, until Amanda finally had to protest.

"Harmon, stop." She caught his hands, but he pursued her with the hungry pressure of his mouth: upon her face, over her breasts, until she had to grasp his head to pull him away. "Stop," she whispered. "You don't want to hurt the baby." When he began to lever away anxiously, she pushed him over onto his back with a husky, "Let me," and kissed him breathless beneath the attention of her sweet lips.

"I love you, Ammy," he panted against her mouth.

"Shhhh. I know."

Maneuvering aside the necessary clothing, she eased over him and worked out his tension with a slow, compelling rhythm. And afterward, he slept hard, without ever telling her anything.

Amanda made supper for herself and the three girls, but her thoughts were with the man sleeping in their shared bed. She tried hard not to betray her worry, but Sarah felt it, too. When the children were tucked in for the night and she finally slipped in next to her husband, he greeted her with a soft cry and a remembered nightmare.

"I can't breathe!"

"Harmon? It's all right."

He began to gasp noisily, as if suffocating in their darkened room. When she reached out to him, he jerked back with a raw, "No! Don't hurt me! Don't hurt my mama! Please . . ."

"Harmon—"

"No! I can't get out! I can't breathe!" He rolled from the bed, colliding with wall, pressing against it, palms flush to the wood, breath coming in hoarse moans of panic.

Amanda wasted no time. She headed first for the windows spanning the opposite wall. She'd had the house designed so they opened out to catch the inviting mountain breezes. Just in case. For the same reason she'd insisted upon the house's mammoth size and its spacious rooms—so Harm would never feel closed up when inside them. She flung open the casements, then went to her husband. When she touched his forearms, he gave a tortured cry and wrenched away.

"Don't! Don't shut me in here. I'll die in here!"

She gripped his wrists, pulling on them, dragging him. "Harmon, come with me. I'm going to let you out."

"Mama?"

"Come on. It's all right."

"Don't do this! Don't hurt me!"

He'd dug in, sliding down to the floor until he was sitting, scrabbling with his heels against the smooth planking as Amanda continued to tow him. Then he felt the air on his face and he was crawling fast, lunging forward, halfway out the second-story window before she could catch him. He hit the sill with his belly, Amanda pulling his hands up behind him, him wailing, "No! Don't!" before sliding to the floor on his knees and into Amanda's embrace.

"I won't let them hurt you."

"Make them stop hurting my mama!"

"I will."

"Becky—"

"Becky's fine. It's all right, Harmon."

"Ammy?" The fierce tremors were easing, the glaze dimming in his eyes, the horror beginning to recede.

"Yes."

"Don't leave me."

"I won't." She curled her arms around him, drawing him in close so that his head was resting on the curve of her abdomen. He moaned her name again and she answered with a soothing, "I'm here."

Then his tone altered, growling harsh and low. "They'll pay. I'll make them pay for what they did."

"It's all right, Harmon."

"When I find them, I'm going to kill them."

"Shhhh."

"Mama?" A small frightened voice sounded from the other side of the door. "Daddy?"

"It's all right, Leisha. Your daddy's fine. Go back to bed, honey."

"Amanda?" That was Sarah.

"Sarah, tuck her in, please. Everything's fine. Just a bad dream."

Only she knew it wasn't. As she stroked his damp hair, Harm quieted and finally slept. But Amanda knew she wouldn't, not until she knew what had returned this particular childhood terror to haunt her husband after a six-year absence.

⌣

She found out in the morning, as she was cleaning up the breakfast dishes. Amanda heard a horse in the yard, and with carbine in hand, went to see who'd come calling.

"Jack!"

He looked awful. He looked the way her husband had

when he'd ridden in, the day before. He dismounted and came toward her. His hat was tipped low, shading his face and his expression.

"Is Uncle Harmon here?"

"No. You missed him by about an hour. He took your sister home, and the girls went with him."

"Oh." He stopped, seemingly at a loss.

"Jack?"

"Could you tell him I'm—could you ask him to—just let him know I came by."

And he turned away, walking in a blind, almost staggering circle, until Amanda ran down to gently take his hand. His breathing was labored and broken by soft sounds of distress. He was as distraught as one of her children, and her heart instantly melted.

Then Amanda understood. Harmon had left because he knew Jack was coming and he'd taken the girls because he'd wanted her to talk to him about whatever had occurred.

"Come up to the house," she coaxed. "I was just about to pour some coffee." She tugged, and he followed with a numb obedience, dropping down on the porch swing when she said, "Sit." When she returned with the cups, he'd taken off his hat and was scrubbing his sleeve across his eyes. She could see his knees shaking.

Whatever it was, it was bad.

"Here. Careful, it's hot."

Jack took the cup, but he made no attempt to drink. He just stared into the dark liquid as if it contained something loathsome. "Did Uncle Harm tell you anything?"

"No. Will you?"

"You knew about my father."

"Oh, dear." She touched the back of his bowed head with a gentle caress. "Yes, I knew."

"Am I the only one who didn't?"

"Jack, none of us ever wanted to hurt you, least of all Harmon."

He didn't comment on that. Instead, he asked, "Would you tell me what you know?"

She did, speaking softly, sympathetically, as his head sank lower and lower into his hands.

"How could they stand to look at me?" he murmured, when she was done.

"They love you, Jack."

"I've tried so hard all my life to overcome something I didn't understand. I never knew why they were waiting for me to go wrong. Guess I do now."

"Jack, you're nothing like him."

"I killed Emily Marcus's little girl." The tortured confession made Amanda gasp in disbelief. Then, as he explained how things had gotten so out of control, she slipped her arms around his shoulders and hugged him.

"Harmon will forgive you. He knows good men can make mistakes."

"What about Emily? Will she? Would you, if it was Leisha?"

Amanda thought about that for a moment, thought hard, then said, "In time, I think I could. Because I know you, Jack. But I'd advise against telling her if she was holding onto anything sharp or primed."

He smiled grimly. "I gotta go. The boys are waiting."

She stood with him and embraced him over the tremendous swell of her belly. "Don't be so hard on yourself," she ordered. "You're a good man, Jack Bass, and your family loves you. Harmon will understand."

But she wasn't so sure when her husband returned later

that day with two sleepy little girls and an expression so somber, she wasn't certain of how to approach him.

She didn't have to. He came to her, wrapping her up in his arms and kissing her tenderly.

"Jack stopped by."

No reaction.

"At least now he knows everything."

"Not everything."

"What do you mean?"

"He doesn't know that his good friend, his captain, is one of the men I've been looking to kill for what he did to our family."

Twelve

She was brushing out her hair when she heard his voice at their front door. Forgetting her robe in her excitement, Emily rushed out to see her husband speaking quietly to his sergeant. Jack Bass was standing just inside the doorway, his hat in his hands. When he glanced up and she saw the sorrow swimming in his eyes, she knew. He didn't have to say a word.

Looking down at his crumpled hat brim, Jack muttered thickly, "Ma'am, I'm so sorry. This was the last kind of news I ever expected to be bringing you."

Emily came closer, drawn by a horrified need to know. "Where's my daughter?"

"Out front," he whispered.

She started to run toward the door and Neil caught her, stopping her cold with his stark words.

"Emily, she's dead."

She looked up at him, reading the truth in his somber dark eyes, refusing to recognize it. "Where's Cathy?" When neither of them answered, she began a soft, desperate panting. No, not her little girl. Not after all she'd done to keep her safe. Jack had promised. He'd promised.

"It's my fault, ma'am. My fault. She was caught up in a crossfire. She'd hidden herself under a blanket and—and no one could tell her from a hostile."

"Couldn't tell?" she challenged, in a taut little voice. "Couldn't tell a six-year-old child wasn't an Apache warrior? How close did you bother to look before you started shooting? There wasn't supposed to be any shooting." She stared at Jack, but he wouldn't lift his gaze. His hat kept turning, turning in his hands, hands that had been so gentle. "Your uncle promised there'd be no bloodshed."

"It wasn't up to him. I gave the order."

She slapped him.

"I'm sorry, ma'am."

She slapped him again and would have waded in with her fists if Neil hadn't grabbed onto her to pull her back. Jack hadn't moved to make the slightest attempt to protect himself from her anger. The side of his face was white, then a hot crimson.

"Emily, stop it," Neil ordered. "She's gone. This won't bring her back."

"He murdered our little girl, Neil!" She was gasping, nearing hysteria.

"It's not Jack's fault."

She went very still, scarcely breathing. "Not his fault? Not his fault that he gave an order to kill helpless women and children?"

Neil's answer was calm and cold. "Under the law of the Frontier Battalion, it isn't necessary to make the distinction. A hostile is a hostile."

Emily took a shuddering breath and with a soft cry, jerked free of him, running not to their bedroom, but from the house. Behind her, she could hear Neil speaking to his sergeant with a compassion he hadn't shown her.

"Put it behind you, Jack. You're not to blame."

Who does Neil blame? she wondered with a crazy grief as, she raced across the ranger courtyard. It wasn't his men.

It wasn't those responsible. He blamed her. As irrational and hurtful as it was, she knew it was true. Neil blamed her because she'd done what she'd had to so she and Cathy could survive among the Indians.

Her white nightgown fluttered up around her knees and her dark hair streamed loose. Anyone who'd touched a drop of liquor that night would have sworn he'd seen a ghost fleeing toward the stables. That's how she felt, like a disembodied spectre with no hold upon the real world. All distilled emotion; all detached pain. She grabbed up a saddle and slapped it down on the horse Will Bass had given for her use. At least the rangers couldn't track her down and hang her for horse stealing! She was halfway up when a strong arm cinched about her waist, pulling her down.

"No!"

"Emily, what are you doing?"

The sound of his soft-spoken words evoked a maternal rage. She twisted wildly in his grasp, slapping, striking, kicking, screaming at him.

"You *cabrone!* You coyote! You murderer! Let me go! Let me go!"

"Emily, stop."

She didn't want to listen to him. She didn't want to recognize the terrible anguish in his eyes. She wanted to hurt him because he'd taken something precious away from her.

"It *is* your fault! It's because of you! She'd be alive if I hadn't saved you. She'd be alive if I hadn't believed your promises, your lies! I wish I'd let them kill you. I wish I'd left you to their torture."

"So do I."

Then he spoke quietly, and she was stunned into silence by his words.

"They couldn't have put me through worse than this. At

least God would have had the mercy to let me die at their hands eventually, and it would have been with honor."

She gulped for air and choked on a sob. Then her arms were around his neck and she was swallowed up in his embrace. "Oh, Jack."

"I'm sorry. Emily, I'm so sorry."

He held her while she wept, so heartsick himself he could easily have joined her. But when her tears ebbed and she pulled away, he found himself confronted by a sober gaze and a startling request.

"Let me go, Jack."

"Go?" His arms tightened in protest. "Go where?"

"Back where I belong. Back with the Apache. I've nothing here to hold me. At least with them, I still have reason to go on." Then her voice broke off and she looked up at him with a renewed devastation. "Oh, dear God, I hope I do. Who else was killed?"

"What?"

"The others who were shot. Who were they?"

"Ten braves, four women, a boy . . . and your daughter."

She took a frantic breath. "The boy, how old was he?"

His answer was so faint, she could hardly distinguish the words. "About the age of my brother, Jeffery."

Twelve. His brother was twelve. That meant . . . her knees gave in relief, and it was the circle of Jack's arm that supported her. "The others got away? Safely?"

"Yes."

She leaned into him weakly, a soft spill of tears beginning again. "Then he's safe."

She felt his start of surprise and then heard his quiet question, asking that she confirm his understanding. "Your son?"

She nodded against his shoulder, afraid to look up, afraid

of what she'd see in his face as he put the pieces together and came up with a half-breed child.

"How old is he?"

"Four. His name is Kenitay."

"Who else knows of this?"

"Your uncle."

"Harmon? Neil doesn't?"

"No. What could I tell him? Do you think he'd be glad to learn that I'd borne an Apache child?"

"But he's your child, too, Emily. Why didn't you say something?"

She did look up then, bracing for signs of his contempt. "What difference would it have made? Things were bad enough already. And he's better off where he's loved."

A strange look came over Jack's face, and he asked, "You don't love him?" He was seeing his mother's expression as she stared at him and saw his father. He was feeling all the insecurities and isolation of a boy who had no true place in the world.

"Of course I love him! He's my son. Do you think it matters who fathered him, that I'd love him less because he's part Indian?"

He gave her a very small smile. "I was hoping you wouldn't." Then he leaned forward and kissed her, briefly, lightly, before pulling her in close again. "Don't go, Emily."

She let her arms go about him, let herself enjoy the feel of him, the warmth and strength of him. Her mouth was pulsing, her heart was hurrying. It didn't matter. To Jack Bass it didn't matter that she had a half-Apache son. Then his reasoning cut through her relief.

"You and Neil are going to need each other to get through this. You've lost a daughter. The grief can't help but bring you closer. In time, he'll be ready to learn of your son and he'll accept him."

"Oh, Jack, I don't think so."

"You've got to believe that, Emily. You've got to."

He sounded so earnest. Who was he trying to convince? Her? Or himself? She wondered if he was thinking of his own broken heritage and of the family who loved him. She wondered if he believed it because he didn't see things the way most men did, because he'd been raised with an open mind and an open heart, unaware of bigotry and blind hate. And she wondered if she should be the one to disillusion him.

Jack nuzzled his face against the soft tousle of her hair and his chest filled up with a mixture of mourning and tender elation. She felt so good, and he hurt so bad. But it wasn't his place to give her comfort.

"I'd better take you home."

Her reaction was immediate. Her arms squeezed tight about his middle. "Please, Jack, can't you hold me for just a little longer?"

What could he say? No?

He guided her over to a fresh mound of hay and tossed a blanket over it. Once she was seated, he unsaddled her horse and put the gray back in his stall. Then he sat beside her and slowly took her up to his chest, where she sighed sweetly and his conscience went straight to Hell.

As she lingered in his embrace, quietly weeping for her two children, one absent and one lost forever, they were unaware of a dark, spiteful stare.

Juana Javier had been strolling by the stable when she heard a familiar voice. Curious as to what kind of woman could stir the handsome sergeant's blood, she'd stepped closer and had nearly cried out in her surprise.

And as she watched the pretty ranger curl up with her lover's wife, a sly smile shaped her mouth as she thought of what to do with the information.

The house was dark and quiet when she returned. Neil had already gone to bed. She could see his long shape stretched out atop the covers. Soundlessly, she slipped in on the other side and lay there, so hollow inside that memories echoed back through the years.

She remembered the first time she'd seen Neil Marcus. He'd come riding into their yard wearing torn and dusty Confederate gray. That had been fifteen years ago, another lifetime. She'd been ten, and in her child's eyes, he was the most heroic figure she'd ever seen, performing the most sadly heroic deed she could imagine. He was returning her father's sword from the battlefield.

He'd served with her father and had only good things to say of the man whom he credited with turning his life from a wrong path onto a right one. He felt beholden to the slain man's family, and because times were so hard, Emily's mother had been grateful for his offer to stay on for a time. She was alone with six children to raise, her husband dead, her two oldest boys lost. Because he had nothing to go to, Neil just stayed on and on, working her family farm and watching her grow.

He wasn't much for words, so she never felt she knew him, but he was a strong man, and she liked the sense of security he provided. She was no stranger to hard work. With her mother still tending young ones, many of those duties fell upon her shoulders, but she never thought to complain. She accepted it as the way things were. There was no softness in her life, no joy, no affection. Getting by was just too darn hard to allow for those luxuries. And when she was almost fifteen, Neil Marcus asked her mother for her hand in marriage.

Emily smiled thinly into the darkness. She'd been so young. She'd known nothing about love or dreams. There was no reason for her to expect more from marriage than what he offered so straightforwardly in their kitchen. He wanted a woman to share the hardships of his day-to-day existence, the same way he'd buy a packhorse to carry an extra burden. Her mother was planning to remarry, and the family would be grateful for one less mouth to feed. It was only natural that Neil take his reward for work well done before moving on. So Emily went with him. Only now did she ponder over her lack of remorse at leaving her family. Perhaps because they'd never been much of a family, just a group of people struggling to survive as best they could.

Neil supplied no rescue, just more of the same she was used to; long, hard hours, without comfort or companionship. He provided for her and she made his life easier, a simple, practical relationship. She didn't complain because she hadn't known there was anything better. She'd been too young to appreciate the intimate aspect of their marriage; the first time had hurt and terrified her, and after that, she learned to endure his rough possession. It was the price of carrying his name. She didn't know anything about love until Cathy. Neil hadn't been pleased by the news. He'd been wanting to get out of Galveston. He hated farming. He wanted to move westward into the rough frontier of Texas, and now he'd have to wait until the baby was old enough to travel. Nor had he been pleased that their first-born was a girl. He'd never said as much, but his attitude betrayed it. He'd wanted someone to help him out but had had to settle for an extra hand in the kitchen.

While he waited impatiently to move west, Emily show-ered all her love upon her tiny child, but she'd never known what it felt like to have that feeling returned until Jack Bass. She couldn't remember Neil ever holding her tenderly. She couldn't recall him kissing her, unless it was a prelude to sating his needs. He'd never shown her one spontaneous act of affection and she'd never missed it because she hadn't known kindness existed. She hadn't known a man could want to give without receiving a quick and selfish reward. She'd never wondered if she should feel something during the act of mating because she assumed it was for her hus-band's relief and not for her pleasure. She'd learned no dif-ferent when she was with the Apache.

But she suspected it wouldn't be like that with Jack. Would he be a gentle lover? Would the sweet sensations he encouraged with his kisses continue to an even greater level of satisfaction? Yes, she decided, but she would never know for sure.

Restlessly, she shifted on her marital bed. The sense of sorrow returned so sharp and painful she felt the need to cry out loud. She ached for a compassionate word. She longed for a comforting touch. She wanted Jack.

Maybe Jack was right; maybe the shared grief would bring her and Neil together, if he mourned their daughter's loss. He would, wouldn't he? He must feel some of the same helpless longing. She tried to remember if she'd ever seen Neil express any fondness for their baby, and tears came to her eyes because she couldn't.

"Neil?"

He shifted, but didn't respond.

Slowly, determinedly, she edged up next to him. She touched his arm, then let hers encircle him as she burrowed against him. He was hard of body and warmblooded, and those things in themselves supplied a degree of comfort. He was her husband, and she had a right to seek it from him. She held to him, feeling his heart beating strong and steady beneath her palm, and she wondered if she should wake him and ask that he make love to her just for the physical closeness the act entailed. She'd never asked before and wasn't sure how to go about it.

"Neil?" Cautiously, she touched her lips to his flannel-covered shoulder.

Then, with a firm, dismissing move, he shoved her arm away and rolled onto his belly.

Emily lay back, swallowing down her want to weep, telling herself that he hadn't been awake, that he hadn't done it consciously.

And then she did what she always did. She reached deep inside herself, relying upon her own inner strength to get her through the long, lonely night.

Cathy Marcus was buried the following morning in a small churchyard outside Ysleta. Neil and Emily Marcus stood side by side, watching the small coffin descend into the grave. And from across that final resting place, where the rangers stood in ranks to offer their solemn respects, Jack watched the silent couple, wondering almost angrily why his captain didn't put his arm around the grieving mother of his child.

Emily stood straight and strong, though her features were wan with weariness and her eyes were swollen from privately shed tears. She didn't cry at the gravesite. She stood brave and so alone in her bereavement beside her stoic husband, flinching slightly as the first spade of earth showered down upon the smooth wood. Then she turned, along with

Neil, to accept the condolences of those who'd come. Not one of the rangers who passed in front of her to murmur expressions of sorrow would look up to meet her gaze. She showed no sign of resentment and was never less than gracious in hearing their sympathies spoken. If she hated them to a man for what they'd taken from her, she never let on. Nor did she betray how close she was to total collapse until she felt Jack's hand slide over hers for a gentle press.

She looked up at him through eyes lost and swamped with anguish. He fought against the need to pull her close, to crush her and cherish her, to kiss away the gathering brightness rimming her lashes, and to whisper words that might offer hope and consolation. But all he could say was, "I wish there was more I could do," in hopes that she would understand.

Her fingers laced through his, her hand shaking, her grasp tightening. She mouthed his name and leaned against him. For a terrible moment, he feared she was going to crumple, but she merely rested her forehead to his shirtfront in an instant of slacking strength, then stepped back to regard him with a glimmering gaze.

"Thank you, Sergeant. Thank you for coming." Then she looked to the next man and he was forced to walk on, away from her, without looking back.

The rooms of their house were hot and airless, as arid as Emily felt inside. On the table was a drooping bouquet Jack had delivered earlier, and in one of its chairs, her husband sat slumped over a glass of whiskey. He didn't look up when she came out of the bedroom, where she'd washed her face and unpinned her mourning veil. She paused to observe him deep in thought. Was he thinking of the child whose love was lost to them? Suddenly, her heart softened with the desire to provide him comfort.

Neil glanced up when she touched his shoulder. He didn't so much as blink as her palm charted the rugged angles of his face. Nor did he move when she sank down on her knees beside his chair to pillow her head upon his thigh. She remained in that submissive pose until she felt the light movement of his hand upon her hair, a gesture all too brief.

"I've got to go out for a while."

Emily looked up in dismay. "Now?"

"I've got work to do."

"But Neil, we've just buried our daughter." She hadn't expected him to be a fount of support, but she hadn't expected him to desert her.

"I can't bring her back, Emily, and maybe that's just as well. After five years, she'd have been more Indian than white, anyway."

Then he stood and she stayed crouched at his feet, looking up with such devastation it would have melted a heart of stone. But he reached for his hat and said, "I'll be back home later on."

After a while, she got up and moved about the house, absently tending the things that had to be done. She submerged the shock and the hurt to a depth where they could not trouble her. But repressing those emotions meant repressing all, so she was little more than an empty vessel as she prepared the evening meal for him.

She heard him come in. There was the rattle of a chair being bumped across the floor and a muffled curse. He was drunk. She supposed he'd taken his comfort from a bottle, and she tried not to feel resentful—until she stepped into the room and got a whiff of that woman's perfume. A dreadful coldness settled then, and it was all she could do to speak to him.

"Supper's ready."

"Put it on the table."

She served it up, strung so tight she would have snapped with the slightest extra strain. Here she'd felt guilty longing for Jack Bass's kind words, while her husband had found solace in the arms of a whore.

If he'd grieved at all.

She watched him eat his meal, the way he devoured it with a purposeful economy of movement. And she felt something new and powerful beginning to stir within her breast. It was hatred. She tried to excuse it. She was mourning. He'd hurt her with his callous rejection. That's all it was. Things would get better.

But then, things had never been better between them. Not even before the Apache had taken her.

She finished her meal in silence, then cleared the dishes away.

While she washed the pots and plates, Neil sat at the table, continuing his attention to the bottle. His stare burned with a sullen intensity as he watched her move about his kitchen. Because he was hearing malicious whispers and he was wondering if they were true.

Was his trusted sergeant, Jack Bass, riding between his wife's knees under the guise of their friendship?

"Set another place for supper."

Emily didn't question the order when it was given the following night. She gathered up the necessary utensils and laid them out, grateful that there would be a buffer to the silence settling between man and wife.

Until she saw whom he'd invited.

Jack Bass grabbed off his hat and offered a faint smile. "Hope I'm not putting you to any trouble, ma'am."

"I'm glad for the distraction, Sergeant. You're always welcome at our table."

"Sit down, Jack. We've got some talk to make if you're going to be ready to ride out in the morning."

Neil's words hit Emily hard, but she didn't falter as she served the men their meal. Jack was leaving. She tried to keep her eyes off him. She tried to hear what Neil was saying over the roar of panic in her ears. And she was too upset to notice how closely her husband was watching her.

"Bragg's gone down into Mexico. It's our feeling that he's holed up with Ramon Cota, down west of Ojinaga. They've partnered up before in carrying stolen beef across the border. I want him back to stand for his killings over in Van Horn. Now, I'll not order you to cross the Rio Grande, but if you were to take a man and slip across and have Bragg on the other side before I was the wiser, there wouldn't be much I could say about it, other than to publicly reprimand you."

"Yessir," Jack murmured. He had no problem with that. "This is mighty good gravy, Miz Marcus. Can I have my pick of the man who's to go with me?"

"Any one of them would ride anywhere in the world with you, Sergeant. Who would you like?"

"Billy Cooper."

"He's young, and still a little green. Are you sure you wouldn't rather have Wainright or Meyers?"

"No. He'll stick by me through the thick of it, I've no doubt. He knows the language some, and I have no worries that he'll do less than his best."

Neil nodded. "I don't think I need to advise you of the danger."

"No, sir."

"If you were to get yourself caught over there, we couldn't come and get you."

"We won't get caught. And I'll bring Bragg back to stand trial. Could I have some more of that, ma'am?"

"Yes, of course." Emily passed the platter, but her mind was feeding on the word "danger." He might not come back. She might not ever see him again, hear his soft voice, or feel the warmth of his gentle gaze. A terrible fright took hold of her. And she would never have the opportunity to tell him how much he'd come to mean to her.

All too soon the meal was over and Jack, with hat in hand, was heading for the door, thanking her for the meal. She followed him as far as the opening, trying not to tremble, trying not to reach out to him.

Her voice was low and full of untapped emotion when she told him, "Good luck to you, Sergeant. I wish you and Billy a safe return."

"Why, thank you, Miz Marcus. I'll do my best."

Because Neil was right behind her, Emily was able to look up into Jack's pale blue eyes, conveying all her concerns and fears with her taut expression. But Jack was helpless to do more than nod to reassure her. Then he fit his hat and looked to his captain.

"I'll see you in a few days, Cap'n."

"Goodbye, Jack."

Neil Marcus watched him go through heavily lidded eyes, waiting until the door had closed. Then he reached out to grab onto his wife's arm, pulling her around to face him. His words were like a gutting slice.

"Are you sleeping with him?"

Thirteen

"What?"

Emily was so stunned for a moment, all she could do was stare.

"I asked if you were lying with him."

Her fury blew up like a West Texas tornado.

"How dare you? You come home to me, stinking of your whore, and then you can stand there and ask something like that about a man like Jack Bass! He's your friend, and he knows the meaning of the word loyalty. He treats me like a lady, like your wife. You're the one who has trouble remembering that, not him. All he's done is be a friend to me, to be kind when I couldn't get a drop of kindness from my own husband. I hope by the time he comes back, you won't be foolish enough to confront him with this nonsense."

Neil gave her a long, chill look, and drawled, *"If* he comes back."

And then he stalked out of their house, leaving her shaking with shock and the awful thought that perhaps he'd knowingly sent Jack Bass to meet his death.

What could she do? Emily paced in restless terror. She could go to Jack and warn him—of what? That his captain was sending him to commit suicide upon his order? He already knew that. He knew the risk, and he was willing to take it. In his thinking, there was no matter too small to die for at Neil Marcus's command. So what could she say to him? "Please don't go, I love you and couldn't bear it if you were to die?" Would knowing that change his mind? She thought not.

And she writhed with guilt, because even though they were innocent, in fact, of what Neil had accused them, they were guilty in heart and mind. Jack had kissed her, and the only reason she hadn't made love to him was because he hadn't asked her to. Had the opportunity presented itself, she would have rolled with him in sinful abandon. And if anything happened to him down in Mexico, she would never be able to convince herself that it was not her fault.

How could she plead with her husband to change his order without making him believe her guilty of adultery? He would think she was trying to protect her lover. If only that were true! Part of her frustration was the fear that she'd lose Jack before ever knowing what it would be like to be loved by him. If she was going to be damned by thought, why not by deed? Except that Jack differentiated between the two. And she suspected he would rather take his chances in Mexico than risk his soul on the hope that they could hold onto their honor.

And maybe he was right.

Emily and Jack. Thinking of them together was making him crazy.

Neil bolted down his last drink and picked up the half-emptied bottle.

She said they hadn't done anything behind his back, but how was he supposed to believe that? His good friend Jack, with his tender heart and gentle manner. His sluttish wife, who'd allowed herself to be violated by heathens rather than accept a preferable death. He loved Jack Bass like a son and trusted him like a brother. There was nothing he wouldn't share with him—except his woman. Even though he couldn't forgive his wife, neither could he give her over to another.

Damn them both.

He reeled across the yard toward his adobe house, wondering what to do. If they hadn't betrayed him—yet—maybe he should just wander over and put a bullet in Jack's brain. That would spare them all the pain and disappointment. It would spare Jack his wife's seduction and the treacherous fall to come. Or he could strangle the bitch and be done with it. Except he knew Jack would never forgive him that.

And he owed Emily. He owed her father for pulling him out of hell and back onto the path of redemption. Through Emily, he'd tried to make up for the evils he'd done. He'd given her the best life he could, had been the best husband he could be. He'd let her come back to him when most men would have turned her out cold. And how did she repay him? By leading his best man astray.

There was something about Jack, always had been. When he'd come to join up with the rangers, little more than an eager boy, he'd touched a responsive chord. Maybe it was because Neil could feel the same inward struggle in the boy that he himself had gone through at that age; that want to do right against the lure to do wrong. Jack could have gone either way. If he'd fallen in with bad company, he could easily have been the one Neil was sending the rangers after. The balance was that delicate. But the desire for justice, for fairness, anchored Jack on the side of right, and Neil hated to think of him crossing that line in the other direction.

It was Emily. She was confusing the boy with her act of helplessness, with her beauty, with her dependency. Of course, he'd be sucked right in. He'd want to give her comfort and protection if he thought she was in need. That's the kind of man Jack was. It was his one big fault, that tender nature. What Emily needed wasn't Jack's big hearted devotion. She needed to be shown her place.

She was at the table, fussing with those damned flowers. She looked up at him through sullen eyes, accusing eyes, as if he had something to apologize for. Him! A deep, territorial anger started rumbling. His wife. His woman. She needed to be reminded of that.

Emily gasped as his hand flashed out, smacking into the pottery vase, sending it skidding across the tabletop to smash upon the floor. Bits and pieces of broken clay were scattered amid the strewn flowers.

"What—"

The sight of her confusion seemed to send him over the edge. It was time to reclaim what was his.

He grabbed her by the front of her dress. He could hear fabric tear, could hear her quick, startled breath. And he began towing her toward the bedroom. He knew the minute she knew what he was up to. She started fighting. That was something she'd never done before. If anything, she'd always been too agreeable to his lovemaking, never protesting, never participating, just letting him do whatever he wanted. Not this time.

She was at him like a wildcat, all claws and vicious snarls. He ignored her until she happened to land a surprisingly hard whollop. Then he was forced into a retaliation. He slapped her, and for a moment, it seemed that would be that. She sank down to her knees, sobbing while he continued to drag her down the hall. Then she came around, set her heels, and put up a renewed struggle.

"Neil, please! Don't do this!"

Her frantic cries left him unmoved. He jerked her to her feet and flung her bodily across the bed, where she rolled and quickly scrambled into a defensive crouch.

He was drunk, she thought wildly. Otherwise, he wouldn't do this. She tried to suppress the terror, the fear of what was to come. She was his wife!

"Neil—"

She wasn't prepared for his sudden violence. He hit her. The impact took her on the side of the face. Pain exploded. She tasted blood where the inside of her cheek cut on her teeth. She whimpered like a mad thing and tried to get away. His hand was on her ankle. His other one went up under her skirts. Her legs thrashed. She flung herself from side to side, trying to throw him off. He was too strong. She knew it. She wasn't going to be able to stop him. She was only going to make it worse for herself. Fighting him would only provoke a more painful retribution. Knowing that, she went still and lay panting beneath him.

"Neil, don't."

Her terror finally reached him. Or was it something else? He was looking at her as if he was seeing—she didn't know what. But he released her and backed off her. They regarded one another for a long, tense moment, then he growled, "Why is it you welcome any man but your own husband?"

"Neil, it wasn't my fault!"

He turned away from her angrily, but her plaintive cries continued.

"None of it was my fault. Please. Why can't you forgive me?"

He stalked out of the bedroom and she heard the front

door bang shut. It wasn't until she heard an unrecognizable sound issue from her own throat that awareness returned.

Jack.

Jack. Her thoughts fastened upon him in panic. She needed Jack. He'd hold her and make the horror go away. And then what? What would he do if she told him her husband had tried to rape her? That's what Neil had done. No different than the Mexicans, except the law told him such savagery was acceptable. She'd run to Jack and he would—what? What could he do? A man's wife was his property. No other could step in to challenge his right to do as he pleased. And if Jack chose to, he would be facing down his best friend, a man he admired. How could she do that to him? Involve him in something not of his making, where he had no right or reason to interfere?

He was leaving in the morning and she was staying behind, with Neil.

Determinedly, Emily pushed the tears from her face with the back of her hand, wincing at the tenderness beneath her left eye. Slowly, she crawled off the bed and washed before changing from the torn gown into her nightdress. Then she withdrew her pistol from its holster, checked the chambers calmly, and carried it back to the bedroom with her.

Neil wouldn't be coming back that night. She was almost positive. But the smooth, cold reckoning power of the revolver beneath pillow made her rest easier.

She heard them talking.

Leaning against the closed bedroom door, she could hear Neil, Jack Bass, and Billy Cooper. When Billy asked after her, Neil made some comment about her sleeping in late and no one questioned it. And when Jack asked him to

convey their regards, she almost wept in anguish. Because
she wanted so badly to see him. But she couldn't allow him
to see her.

Overnight, the swelling beneath her eye had turned a
vivid purple.

When she heard the two rangers leave, she rushed to the
bedroom window and cautiously parted the curtains. Her
gaze hungrily detailed the figure of Jack Bass as he limped
toward his sorrel.

Come back, Jack. You have to come back.

As he swung up into the saddle, he paused and stared
back toward the house. She started to duck behind the curtains but realized it was too late; he'd already seen her.
Keeping the left side of her face carefully shielded, she
smiled and raised her hand in a gesture of farewell, hoping
from this distance he couldn't see the dampness on her
cheeks. He reached up for the brim of his Stetson almost
as if he was adjusting it, tipping it in her direction. Then
he and Billy were gone.

Please come back!

After a time, she left the bedroom, warily skirting the
table where Neil was finishing up his coffee. He glanced
up at her and she noticed his slight recoil as he took in the
condition of her face as if surprised by the amount of dam-
age he'd caused. She met his look with a frosty challenge,
then continued on into the kitchen.

"I already made myself breakfast," he called in to her.
"There's coffee on the stove." His voice was surprisingly
subdued, probably due to a throbbing head.

She was pouring herself a cup when he came up behind
her. The feeling of threat was immediate. She turned toward
him, backing up against the stove, looking ready to climb
right over the top of it to escape him. When his hand lifted,

she cringed back and went rigid, as if waiting for the blow to fall. But all he did was touch her discolored cheek with unusually gentle fingertips.

"I'm sorry, Emily."

What was she supposed to say? "That's all right? I forgive you?"

"I got a little carried away last night. I didn't mean to hurt you or scare you. Too much whiskey."

She said nothing. Was he waiting for her to accept that excuse?

Finally, he let his hand drop away. "It won't happen again, Emily. I promise you."

His words sounded practiced, almost as if he'd said them many times before, and she wondered when and to whom. Up until last night, he'd never laid a harsh hand upon her. She wasn't reassured and her caution didn't ease. In her heart, it was hard for her to believe that it was an isolated incident.

He was studying the bruise. "Why don't you just rest today?" he suggested, then followed it with a meaningful, "and stay inside."

Where no one could see what he'd done to her.

But who was there who'd care? And what could they do about it if they did?

Wearily, she picked up her coffee cup. "I think I'll just do some mending. Some of the boys asked if I'd run a few seams for them."

"Sounds like a good idea." And he sounded relieved.

He hadn't asked her to leave his house, and she wondered why. If he really believed she was carrying on with Jack, wouldn't he have thrown her out? But he seemed content to let the matter go and let things return to their normal pattern. After all, Jack wasn't around to be a problem.

So she sat down to her mending, managing to numb her thoughts and fears with the rote busywork. Until she came upon a pair of Levis with an irregular hole sliced in the right thigh, the cut she'd made to remove two arrows. She stitched the gash together painstakingly, making the seam all but invisible. And then she sat for a long, long while with the denims draped over her knees, her eyes too blinded by tears to continue.

Time passed slowly, each second weighted with worry when they heard nothing from Jack and Billy. But no news was supposedly good news. If they'd been caught, not a man in West Texas would be unaware of it. And Emily had some small consolation. If the rangers wouldn't go in after him, she'd hire Harmon Bass to do it.

But she wasn't worried about Jack being captured. She was terrified that he'd been killed. Then there'd be nothing anyone could do to bring him back.

Neil was on hand for breakfast and supper, but she saw little of him between or after. He didn't come into their bedroom again, apparently finding it more pleasing with his harlot. Emily didn't care if the other woman had him. She had a roof over her head and a good name and a reason to wait for Jack Bass's return.

They'd just sat down to their evening meal when the disturbance reached them. Neil grabbed up his gun out of habit, but relaxed when the noise took on the definite sound of celebration. Emily went with him to the front door, having to grab onto the frame for support when her knees went to rubber beneath her.

Jack.

He and Billy rode in on spent horses, they themselves

showing wear in every dirt-caked crease and sweat-stained circle. And between them rode their prisoner, Neville Bragg, wanted on five counts of murder by the State of Texas. Over all the noise, Emily heard Jack's quiet command for Billy to incarcerate the prisoner while he filled in their captain. The younger ranger headed across the square, trailing half the men, while the rest lingered where Jack pulled up in front of the Marcuses' house.

He swung down off his sorrel, easing onto his bad leg as if not sure it would hold him. His comrades parted so he could come to the porch in his slow, bone-weary step.

"Cap'n, we brung in the fugitive."

"Where did you apprehend him, Sergeant?"

"Oh, down the river a piece."

"Exactly where?"

"A ways. Would you like to reprimand me now, or might I beg a cup of coffee first?"

Emily lost her sense of paralysis. He was back and he was safe. "Come in, Sergeant Bass. I'll put some coffee on."

"Thank you, ma'am."

As he walked between her and Neil, the temptation was so great to reach out and touch him that Emily had to bury her hands in her skirts and grip tight. Once he'd passed, she was able to relax. Then she started for the kitchen.

Jack drew up at the sight of their dressed table. "Oh, I'm sorry. I didn't mean to interrupt your dinner." He stood, hat in hand, staring at that service for two with the oddest expression.

No, he couldn't leave yet! Hurriedly, Emily offered, "There's plenty, Sergeant. If you're hungry, draw up a seat. If not, it'll keep."

"Jus' coffee'll be fine, Miz Marcus."

She put the water on to boil with shaking hands while rangers filled up her living quarters, eager to hear of the adventure firsthand. She listened to Jack's modest telling of the tale, wondering how much he glossed over in that casual narrative. He was underestimating the danger, of that she was sure. And when Billy Cooper arrived, more of the story evolved. Billy wasn't half so self-effacing and was proud of his part in the adventure. He loved to spin a yarn out in a colorful weave. And the more Emily heard, the tighter the anxiety bound up in her breast.

"They had Bragg living the high life down there. We spent a couple of days shading off among the border folk until Jack decided the time was right to strike. With me holding the horse for Bragg, he goes flat out right down into their stronghold, snatches the fella right off the lips of some sweet little Mexican gal, which of course riled him plenty, wheels around, and makes out of there before any of 'em can match two and two together. Old Bragg gets to wiggling like a tick on a hot plate while Jack's going full-out on that hard-jawed sorrel, him stretched out over the critter's haunches.

"Jack pulls up so we can get Bragg up on his own horse. When I commence to tying off his hands, the sumbitch knees me in the face and lights out with Jack hard after him. Not wanting to call any more attention to ourselves, Jack's forced to overhaul him without making a shot, and seeing this was so, Bragg turns his horse and comes at him in a charge.

"Now, the Sarge's sorrel is one bullheaded cuss, and with him a hauling hard on the reins, that animal causes him to go right out from under his hat while plowing into Bragg. The whole lot of 'em go down, and by then, we got a posse of men hot on us."

There was a chorus of concern and excitement from those gathered in a tight-packed circle, and Emily's heart was banging as hard and fast as anyone's. Particularly when she glanced up from the simmering pot of water into Jack Bass's pale blue-eyed gaze.

"How's the coffee coming, Miz Emily?"

"Just about ready. Shouldn't you be in there, reliving your moment of glory?"

He smiled and murmured, "Living it once was enough, and I don't recall it being as nailbiting a situation as Billy's painting it to be."

But she imagined it probably was, maybe even more so than the younger man depicted it.

For a moment, they stood in an awkward silence, close enough for the tension to flow like a river current between them, undercutting the best of their resistance. She'd never been so acutely aware of another person as she was of him in that instant; of the way the Texas dirt had embedded itself in the creases fanning from the corners of his eyes, of the way his breathing rocked in an enticing rhythm, of the way the hard hours of riding had molded his denims to the long line of his legs. He was dirty and potent, and about the most invigorating sight she'd ever seen. And if he'd been her man, she'd have been stripping off his strong-smelling clothes and taking him down to the kitchen floor for some desperate lovemaking.

But he wasn't.

"I'm glad to see you back safe," she said quietly. Just then, the coffeepot began to steam over. She reached for it at the same time he reached for it and the movement brought her in close under the bridge of his arm, beneath the angle of his chin. The unexpected contact froze both of them.

"Emily—" It was a hoarse sound, strangling up from his throat. Then he swallowed hard. "Here, let me help you with that."

"I've got it. Thanks. You go join the others and I'll bring it in."

But even as she spoke, her fingers were easing over the backs of his in an almost independent motion. His spread, allowing hers to lace between them, and they stood for a minute longer, hands entwined, as Billy Cooper finished up his vivid story.

"So here we are, running hard to the river, my horse failing bad under the weight of me and Bragg. So what does Jack do but circle that sorrel around, him yelling for me to make for the water, while he rides straight on them as they're coming up behind us. Well, now, those were some mighty surprised folks, let me tell you. Them being citizens, not soldiers, they scattered every which way, looking for cover. By that time, I was splashing up river bottom, hollering back at Jack to come on. He was across the river before any of them thought to fire off a round. When none of 'em pursued us, I waved my hat to 'em. We picked up another horse and rode on here."

"Not nailbiting?" Emily chided softly. She felt her pulse jerking like crazy, just envisioning how it must have been. Her fingers convulsed tightly about his. Jack shrugged and gave her his unassuming smile. Then he drew his hand away.

"I could sure use some coffee."

"Go, sit. I'll bring it out."

She waited a minute, then loaded up a serving tray. Rangers occupied every available surface. The ones at the table were finishing off the rest of her meal. She spoke each man's name as she prepared a cup to his liking, then paused when Billy Cooper smiled up at her. Touching her fingertips beneath his chin, she bent to place a light kiss on his brow.

"Good to have you back alive, Billy."

A hot blush flooded his youthful features, but he grinned and declared, "Well, shoot, ma'am. Getting that was worth the whole trip!" Then his gaze shifted to his partner with a sudden devilry. "How 'bout Jack? Don't he deserve some reward for his part in it?"

The boys snickered, anticipating their bashful sergeant's mortification. But he sat unprotesting as she touched her palm to one rough cheek and her lips to the other.

"Welcome back, Sergeant. Thank you for not bringing me anything to mend."

When she straightened and continued to serve up the coffee, talk continued and she was more or less forgotten. Except by two men; by her husband, who watched her with a subtle suspicion, and by Jack Bass, who watched her with a covetous desire.

Jack was tired, sore, and so filthy he could hardly stand himself, yet he lingered with the other rangers, listening to Billy tell and retell their adventure until he wondered if he'd been there at all, the facts had become so altered by exaggeration. But he didn't leave to seek out a well-deserved night's rest because the sight of Emily Marcus had him wide awake inside.

She was the first thing he looked for when they rode into Ysleta. Seeing her on the doorstep, her green eyes wide with relief and her lips shaped with a smile of welcome, he'd have given anything in the world if she'd been there waiting just for him. But the fact of that table set for two crushed that dream. He watched her silently and efficiently tend to the wants of the men crowding, rude, and dirty, into her home. She never complained that they'd been eating or that muddy boots were marking her furniture or that an occasional chaw of tobacco found the floorboards. She was a gracious hostess, and all the boys felt at ease around her. And he'd have been so damned proud if she was his wife.

But she wasn't.

He was ashamed of the growing envy he felt toward Neil Marcus. Neil was a good man, as fine a commander as a man could want. But to Jack's thinking, he left much to be desired as a husband. During the course of the evening, he never once glanced at his wife. He never once thought to tell the boys to mind their manners when their talk coarsened, the way men's tended to when they were together. He didn't offer to lift a hand when she sliced up freshly baked pies to pass around with more of her good strong coffee. Nor did he seem to notice how pale and weary she looked as the hour grew late and the talk showed no signs of abating. A man ought to notice those kinds of things, but Neil didn't. It was none of his business what went on beneath the Marcuses' roof or in any of its rooms. The bedroom was foremost on his mind as his thoughts evolved from the slow caress of his gaze as Emily bent and began to pick up the dirty dishes.

If Emily had been his, he'd have shooed the lot of them out and taken his woman to bed.

And that was another thing he begrudged Neil Marcus. What would it be like, having a woman like Emily waiting on his desires, keeping his house, filling up his heart with her small smiles, and shoring up his soul with her tremendous strength? How he wished for the chance to discover it for himself.

He was too worn down to protect himself against a mood

of melancholy. He wasn't doing himself any good, hanging out for another man's good fortune. He needed a good night's sleep and a new day's perspective. Dragging himself out of his chair, he collected up all the dirty plates within reach and carried them into the kitchen. He was separating china from silver when he heard her come up behind him.

"You don't have to do that."

"I don't mind. Habit. Too many boys in my family to get away with doing nothing. 'Sides, it was right nice of you to spoil us with a little home baking."

She smiled at that. "I don't mind. Habit. Too many kids in my family to have a minute to do nothing."

He lingered there at the sink, smiling faintly, having no reason to stay and no want to leave. And Emily wished she could offer him more than coffee and pie and a chaste kiss on the cheek.

"Well," he mumbled at last, "I'd best be going. Want me to clear out your living room for you? You and Neil probably want to get some sleep."

He couldn't miss the way her features stiffened, but her answer was generous. "They're fine, Sergeant. My father had a pack of hunting hounds once. Kind of makes me think of them. They were noisy and messy and sometimes smelly, but they were so affectionate and so hardworking, you couldn't help but . . . love them."

"Yes, ma'am," he murmured, dodging her stare and moving out of the kitchen.

Emily remained at the sink, rinsing dishes and holding onto her regrets as she heard Jack relay his goodnights to all. His parting seemed to break up the gathering, and within minutes, she had the cluttered house to herself. Even Neil had gone. Sighing, she picked up the discarded dishes, and when they were all scoured, she drank down the last cup of coffee and wondered how she was ever going to get to sleep.

She couldn't. Her nerves were wound too tight by the coffee and excited man-talk. A walk in the night air would do wonders for her wistful mood. So once she'd put the kitchen to rights and she'd strapped on her pistol, Emily took to the quiet back streets, walking aimlessly at first, then with a growing purpose.

The cemetery was still, its monuments moonwashed and almost glowing. There was a calming sense of peace at this late hour, and she let herself in the picket gate to move surely toward the spot where she'd buried a piece of her heart and history.

She hadn't gone far when she realized she wasn't alone in seeking comfort from the somber tombstones and gentle night breezes. A solitary figure stood at one of the newly spaded resting places, hat in hand, head bowed. Moonlight gleamed soft and burnished off the dark auburn hair. Emily drew up in surprise.

Jack Bass stood over her daughter's grave, his pose remorseful, his flowers laid gently upon the slight eternal mound.

Fourteen

He was so immersed in his own private thoughts, he didn't hear her until she was standing next to him.

"Jack?"

He gave a start of surprise, then angled his head away so he could dash his sleeve across his eyes before he turned to her. If Emily felt the slightest trace of lingering resentment for what he'd done, it was gone the instant she looked up into his face. His expression was stripped to a desolation so bare he couldn't attempt to hide it from her.

"I'm sorry," he mumbled thickly. "I probably shouldn't be here. I'll jus' be on my way. I'm sorry."

But to Emily, it seemed very right that he should be, so she caught his hand and held to it when he would move away. His fingers worked around hers in agitation until she tightened her grip, surrounding them, keeping them still.

"Thank you for bringing the flowers. Cathy liked flowers, and she'd be glad for the company. You would have liked her, Jack. She was such a bright little girl, always so curious and alive—"

She couldn't go on. Jack touched her shoulder and she instinctively moved into the circle of his arms. He'd cleaned up since leaving her house. His shirt was freshly laundered, and he smelled of shaving lather and sharp soap. And he felt wonderful.

"Oh, Jack, I miss her so much." Hers was a quiet summation, not a whimper, not a wail, and his embrace brought her in to fit snug and secure against him.

"I wish I could bring her back for you."

"I want to see my son, Jack." She hadn't known how much that was true until she spoke it out loud. Then the need was overwhelming. "I want to see that he's all right. I want to hold him in my arms, kiss him, and rock him to sleep. Just one more time."

"I'll bring him to you."

He had a way of stating the impossible as if it were within his immediate grasp. And a way of making her believe him. For a little while, anyway.

"Neil would never authorize it."

"Wasn't planning to ask him. I've got some free time coming—"

"You'd go alone?" She leaned away so she could look up into his handsome face and read the sincerity there. "You'd never get close enough."

"I could do my best. I owe you this, Emily."

"You don't owe me anything, Jack. Least of all the risk of your life."

"Yes, I do."

She wanted to argue with him, but in a corner of her heart beat the love of her child, and if he had the slightest chance to restore that love, to return that child . . .

"When would you go?"

"In the morning. As soon as I can arrange the time with Neil."

"You don't have to do this."

Yes, he did. Or everytime he looked at her, he'd see the little crumpled body on the ground. He'd taste the blood-laced coffee and hear his stepfather's prediction. *Just like your father.* No! He would break that cycle, no matter what it took. It was a terrible wrong that ached inside to be righted. And there was another wrong, a wrong he wasn't going to be able to keep from happening if he stayed in camp much longer. He'd wanted to kiss Emily in her husband's kitchen. He wanted to kiss her now. And one of these times, kissing just wasn't going to be enough for either of them. Better he put the length of West Texas between them.

"How are you going to find him?"

"Well, now," Jack said, drawing in a deep breath. "I aim to pay a visit to my uncle, and if he doesn't kill me right off, maybe he'll help me."

He could hear Harmon's voice: *You planning to just ride on in there, nice as you please, and ask if you can borrow one of their kids for a few days?* That was sort of exactly what he had in mind. And with Harmon's help, it would be a whole lot easier.

"Let me do this for you, Emily. Please."

What ever had possessed her to say yes?

What were the odds of Jack Bass surviving such an impossible quest?

Was that what he was counting upon?

Emily paced the night away, fretting over whether or not she'd done the right thing. The fear of not seeing Jack again warred with her desire for her child. Kenitay. She could smell the softness of his skin perfumed with yucca soap. She could hear his gurgles of delight and picture his haughty pouts of displeasure. And she thought of him growing up to live the hard Apache life. How long could he exist among a doomed people? Wouldn't he be safer living with her, even if that meant exile from her own people?

Neil would never accept the child into his home; she knew it without question. She wouldn't think of that yet. First, she had to see her son. Then would come the strength for such decisions.

She was scraping eggs from her skillet onto Neil's plate when the knock came on the door. Obeying Neil's command to enter, Jack slipped inside, apologizing for interrupting yet another meal. Neil shrugged it off and told Emily to bring in another plate for his sergeant. Emily complied without comment as Neil waved Jack into a chair.

"What's on your mind, Jack?"

"I need a favor, Neil. If the time's not good, jus' say so."

"Go on."

"I'd like about ten days off, if it can be arranged." He glanced up when Emily slid a plate in front of him and managed a polite smile and nod.

"Can I ask why?"

"Got some business I need to take care of with my family. Don't want to let it go too long."

Neil was studying him, noting his downcast gaze, his edginess, his obvious discomfort. "Things all right with you, Jack?"

The quiet concern in that question brought Jack's stare up. Inside he writhed around that half-lie. "Fine, Cap'n."

"Get it done and get back when you can."

"Thank you, Cap'n."

"When you leaving?"

"Now."

"Take what you need." He waved off the protest. "Take what you need."

"Thank you." He started to get up.

"Eat your breakfast."

"I'm not awful hungry. If you'll excuse me, ma'am." He

tipped his hat to Emily and strode to the door, anxious to leave their table and their house and to get to the business of fixing his mistakes.

He rode hard and he tried not to do much thinking. He had no particular plan in mind, just a lot of hopes hanging upon the word "loyalty."

What if Harmon wouldn't help? His uncle had no reason to trust him, no obligation at all. Amanda said Harm would forgive him. Well, maybe he would, maybe he wouldn't. Harmon was a hard one to figure, sometimes. Having bad feelings between them sat ill with Jack, like part of him had been cut adrift. Doing a wrong thing was hard enough. Doing it without having any hope of redemption was another thing altogether. It left an emptiness that was deep and scary to live with. It paved the way to more wrong things, and he didn't want to go that way. His family had taught him better, and he was clinging to their teachings. He wanted to go home in a bad way.

But how was he going to face his mother with what he knew was the truth?

Crossing through West Texas was lonely business, even with its cutting edge of danger. The spaces were wide, and everything was so far away. It was like being caught between yesterday and tomorrow, that sense of time suspended. It was like pursuing dreams, striving hard and never seeming to get closer. That was the problem with Texas. It was lousy with land; there it was too easy to just fall away from anything to do with civilization. With the shifting sunlight to set the faraway mountains in their sundry moods, it was enough to get a man thinking crazy things, things like stretching his arms open wide to embrace as much of

this desolate ground as possible. Cattlemen had a name for
it: they called it Big Bend fever. It was a homesickness for
a place that could never be a man's home, a longing to
possess something he knew he could never claim. It was
the way Jack felt about Emily Marcus.

It was a feeling that wasn't going to go away, so he would
have to.

He'd thought of little else while tracking down Bragg.
What he felt for Emily was a deep, undying love. Reason
had no hold over it. Neither did honor. It was the way his
uncle spoke about his wife. It was a terminal emotion. Jack
couldn't be near her without wanting her. Not just for a
physical satisfaction, but for his spiritual well-being. And
he couldn't feel that way about a man's wife without growing to resent the man who had her. It was hard to think
about Neil with any degree of his former fondness, and that
was tearing him up. It was pushing an unhealthy situation,
one that could be healed with a fatal dose of lead. He could
see that coming down the road. He was already lying to
the man; how long before he was doing worse? Like lying
with the man's wife? Not long, unless he separated himself
from the Marcuses right quick. He'd have to transfer out of
Neil's company or leave the rangers altogether. But first,
he would do this last thing for Emily, because he owed her
a child, because he wanted her to know how much he loved
her.

He rode until he was weaving in the saddle from exhaustion. Finally, his mount settled it for him. The horse drew
up short and dropped his nose into some bunchgrass as if
to say if his rider didn't have the sense to know when it
was time to quit, he did. Out of respect for his animal, Jack
dismounted and relieved the sorrel of his tack, then staked
him out. He was too tired to do more than build a small

fire and curl up in his blankets. The instant he closed his eyes, he was gone, sleeping hard and dreamlessly through the hours of the night, waking to the enticing scent of black coffee.

He came up out of his blankets as if someone had set them on fire . . . and found himself looking into Emily Marcus's calm gaze.

"Good morning. You're a heavy sleeper. Lucky for you I wasn't after your horse and your scalp."

He couldn't seem to prod his tongue into the necessary motions for speech. He just stared as Emily poured a tin and extended it to him.

"You look like you could use this."

He took the cup in hands so unsteady she had to take it back from him before he burned himself. Finally, he remembered the basics of language enough to gasp, "What are you doing here?"

"Making us breakfast. I'll just set this down so it can cool." She put his coffee on the ground, then went back to the cook fire as if it was the most natural thing in the world for her to be tending him.

"No."

She glanced up. "What?"

"No. Go back. You can't be here." Jack's breathing accelerated into a frantic panting. Emily Marcus, making him breakfast. An impossible madness seized him. It shook him right to the soul.

"I am here and these biscuits are just about ready. Are you awake yet, Sergeant? You look a bit strange."

Strange? He was so bewildered, he wasn't sure he was awake. And if he was dreaming, he didn't want it to end.

Emily smiled in the face of his confusion and explained,

"I did a lot of thinking after you left yesterday. I decided the best thing would be for me to ride along."

Best thing? For whom? Good Lord, he had to get her out of his camp, out of his reach, out of his heart! Had she any idea what she was doing? What she was doing to him?

"Emily—" he croaked.

"Drink your coffee, Jack."

"No. You've got to get out of here right now. Get on your horse and go back to Ysleta before Neil finds you gone."

"He must already know."

"Oh, God," Jack moaned.

"I left him a note saying I needed some time to think things out. I didn't say anything about you."

His laugh was almost hysterical. "You don't think he's gonna figure that one out? He's not stupid. He's gonna know you're with me."

"So what if he does?"

She said it so calmly, Jack was knocked for a hard loop. "But he's gonna think—"

"I don't care what he thinks."

"I care! He's gonna think I lied to him and ran off with his wife!"

"But you and I know that's not true. We just happen to be going to the same place for the same reason. I won't let him shoot you down, if that's all you're worried about."

That wasn't what he was worried about at all. He was worried that Neil would have reason to. "Emily, you can't be here with me like this. It's just the two of us."

She deliberately misunderstood. "I trust you to protect me, Jack."

But who was going to protect her from him?

"Anyway," she continued, in the same cool tone, "I want

to see my son. The Apache aren't going to let you take him, but they may let me in long enough to visit him there. It's the only thing that makes sense. You see that, don't you? And I have to return this horse to your father."

All he could see was Emily Marcus bending over his fire and the long days and nights ahead wrought with temptation.

When he didn't comment, she looked up at him through a somber stare. "If you don't want to go through with it, Jack, I'll understand. Tell me now if you want to go back."

"No."

"All right. Then eat your breakfast, I'll clean up, and we'll get going."

It was a miserable day. The sun was high and hot in the searingly blue sky. Jack was running with sweat, and nervous enough to start at the slightest sound. He tried to keep his attention focused ahead, but it was drawn back inevitably to the woman riding at his side.

She rode to the envy of any ranger, easy in the saddle, without complaint. She'd taken to wearing a split skirt, high boots, and a man's cotton shirt; Neil's, from the looks of it. Her dark hair was drawn back in a low knot, and her eyes were shaded by the tipped brim of an oversized Stetson. That was Neil's, too. The reminders made Jack uneasy. He was crazy to be doing this. He should have taken her back to Ysleta immediately, bound and gagged, if need be. But a part of him was thrilled with the idea of these days alone with her, with the illusion of them sharing a campsite and a trail and a common goal. If only he could remember the goal. It was the only time he was ever likely to have with the woman he loved, and selfishly, he refused to surrender it. If he couldn't have her for a lifetime, he'd settle for a week or two. If he couldn't enjoy her intimately, he'd make do with her company. The Apache couldn't have designed a more wicked torture.

What she said made too much sense. She did have a better chance than he did alone, especially where Harmon was concerned. She might be able to sway him much more easily from her mother's point of view. His uncle was terribly tenderhearted on the subject of family. As long as Jack kept focused on what was up ahead and didn't look back to what they were leaving, he was all right. But when thoughts of Neil Marcus crept in, his soul sank into despair. There was no going back for either him or Emily. Both knew it, though neither was willing to discuss it. So what did that mean? She was abandoning a husband and he a friend. He refused to think beyond that.

He pushed daylight to the limit until Emily called, "Jack, I can't see the end of my horse. Don't you think we ought to consider stopping?" He was considering running as far as his mount would carry him.

They made a quick camp and settled into a restless silence. He made the fire, she made the dinner. Then they stretched out on opposite sides of the fire and lay there as relaxed as desert mice in the talons of a hawk. That tense charade continued for an agonizing hour, then Emily cursed softly and snatched up her blankets. Jack stopped breathing as he heard her come around the fire. She flung her bedding down next to him.

"What are you doing?" he asked in a strained voice.

"We're going to make wretched time tomorrow if neither of us gets a second of sleep. With me over there thinking about you and you over here thinking about me, neither of us is going to get any rest." She dropped down on the blankets and almost angrily burrowed up against him. "There. That's better. Now go to sleep!"

He let out his breath in a shaky tumble. After a few tor-
turous minutes, he heard her chuckle.

"Jack, I won't try anything improper." Her palm eased
across his middle and up to rest over the rapid scurry of
his heart. Then she added, with a provoking devilry, "Unless
you want me to."

"Go to sleep," he growled. But he was smiling as he
nudged his arm beneath her head so she could have a comfortable pillow to rest upon.

He never would have believed it possible, but sleep he
did, deep and undisturbed, the minute he held her close, as
if all was right and he was relieved of worry. When he
woke, he was alone and she was already fixing him breakfast. Smiling with a lazy contentment, he thought what a
great companion she was to have on the trail. His relaxed
mood lasted all day. She was easy to ride with, and he liked
looking over at her. If she caught his glance, she'd smile,
sending him into a giddy fluster of emotion. He liked that,
too.

He'd just gotten comfortable with the whole idea when
he made the mistake of coming around to help her dismount
that evening. She stepped down with the support of his
hands upon her trim waist, and awareness of her seemed to
smack him right between the eyes. She didn't help the situation because she didn't move away. She stood, leaning back
against him, letting his hands rest on her, letting her head
fall back gradually until it was pillowed on his shoulder.
He shut his eyes and just breathed in the wonder of her:
the scent of her hair, the feel of her feminine form along
his harder contours. Then her hands covered the backs of
his, rubbing gently, taking them up in hers, shifting them
higher so his palms grazed her sleek torso and came up
beneath the underswell of her breasts. She made a low

moaning sound and he jumped away in a panic. What was she doing? He had a purely, paralyzing recall of his Aunt Amanda seducing Harmon with the same kind of subtle warfare. Women didn't fight fair. How was a man supposed to be ready with a good defense?

"I'll see to the horses," he mumbled fiercely. "You find some firewood."

Emily did so without comment, and by the time the flames were leaping nicely, so were Jack's passions.

He was angry with her for upsetting the delicate balance. Now he'd have to be on guard against her as well as his own traitorous desires. He'd just begun to feel in control when she'd driven all such notions from his head. His hands itched for the feel of her. His mouth hungered for the taste of her. And the rest of him was in restless misery. Why couldn't she have left it alone?

He was feeling surly as a snapping turtle by the time she brought him his dinner. He wouldn't even look up at her as she stood, plate in hand.

"I'm not hungry."

"Take it."

"I don't want it."

"Yes, you do."

"I don't."

"You need it."

"Don't tell me what I—"

As he lifted his head, his expression furious, she dropped down on his mouth with a truly startling end to their argument. He was hungry. He wanted it and he needed it. End of discussion. Their kiss was wild and wet and ravenous, full of desperate passion and frustrated longing. By the time she was finished with him, Jack was breathing hard and too dazed even to protest when she moved away and pressed his plate upon him.

"Eat. It's getting cold."

He ate.

He never tasted any of it.

He'd almost managed to calm himself down again when it came time for the spreading of their bedrolls. She put hers beside his and he was very aware that she made him no promises as she nestled in close.

He shut his eyes and tried to relax. Even his skin felt taut as a drying hide. Within the cage of his ribs, his heart was pounding madly. He didn't dare move for fear that he would act upon the pressures pulsing through him in hot, eager surges. He felt like an awkward adolescent with his first woman. But this wasn't his woman. Why couldn't he remember that? Why couldn't she?

She began cleverly enough with a soft sigh designed to penetrate his staunch reserve. Then she snuggled into him with an almost innocent contentment. Almost. Except she was touching him in a very knowing fashion. Her fingertips grazed his shirtfront, rising up to meet the warm curve of his throat. There, her touch feathered along his jaw, making light forays up and down his neck, making it impossible for him to swallow. When the soft pads of her fingers sketched over his parted lips, he kissed them restlessly, sucking them in for the wet lath of his tongue and nip of his teeth. Then, realizing what he was doing, he gave an objecting groan and rolled away from her, onto his side.

She gave no quarter. Her body melted against his, all liquid longing and rippling urgency. Her hand bunched in his shirt until it came free from his trousers. Then she was undoing his trousers and pushing them aside, her hand next to the warm furring of his belly . . .

"Emily—"

"Jack."

Her lips moved against the hair at the nape of his neck, nibbling there until a hard shudder wracked through him. Then she rose up slightly to taste his earlobe and the side of his neck.

"Emily, please, I can't—"

"I want you to."

What was the use pretending it wasn't everything *he* wanted, too?

He rolled toward her, surrendering to her kisses for a time, then taking control of their passions himself. He cradled her face between his hands and settled his mouth over hers, the movement slow, sure, a sensuous possession. When he let their kiss deepen, her arms went around him, her fingers spearing through his hair, holding hard so he couldn't pull away if he wanted to.

He didn't want to.

He broke off when neither of them could breathe. Even then, he continued to tease her with the gentle sweep of his mouth against her cheeks, against her brow, over her lips, again. Then he leaned up on his elbows so he could look down upon her. She was so beautiful, so vulnerable. He should have said he wanted her. That would have been enough to please her, but to him, it wouldn't begin to touch on what was stirring inside. So he spoke the truth.

"I love you."

And he watched her eyes dampen with emotion and darken with desire for him. And then she said something that purely amazed him.

"Jack, be good to me."

"I will be."

He put his whole heart into that promise and all his feel-

MORE PASSION AND ADVENTURE AWAIT... YOUR TRIP TO A BIG ADVENTUROUS WORLD BEGINS WHEN YOU ACCEPT YOUR FIRST 4 NOVELS ABSOLUTELY *FREE* (AN $18.00 VALUE)

Accept your Free gift and start to experience more of the passion and adventure you like in a historical romance novel. Each Zebra novel is filled with proud men, spirited women and tempestuous love that you'll remember long after you turn the last page.

Zebra Historical Romances are the finest novels of their kind. They are written by authors who really know how to weave tales of romance and adventure in the historical settings you love. You'll feel like you've actually gone back in time with the thrilling stories that each Zebra novel offers.

GET YOUR FREE GIFT WITH THE START OF YOUR HOME SUBSCRIPTION

Our readers tell us that these books sell out very fast in book stores and often they miss the newest titles. So Zebra has made arrangements for you to receive the four newest novels published each month.

You'll be guaranteed that you'll never miss a title, and home delivery is so convenient. And to show you just how easy it is to get Zebra Historical Romances, we'll send you your first 4 books absolutely FREE! Our gift to you just for trying our home subscription service.

BIG SAVINGS AND FREE HOME DELIVERY

Each month, you'll receive the four newest titles as soon as they are published. You'll probably receive them even before the bookstores do. What's more, you may preview these exciting novels free for 10 days. If you like them as much as we think you will, just pay the low preferred subscriber's price of just $3.75 each. *You'll save $3.00 each month off the publisher's price.* AND, your savings are even greater because there are never any shipping, handling or other hidden charges—FREE Home Delivery. Of course you can return any shipment within 10 days for full credit, no questions asked. There is no minimum number of books you must buy.

4 FREE BOOKS

TO GET YOUR 4 FREE BOOKS WORTH $18.00 —MAIL IN THE FREE BOOK CERTIFICATE T O D A Y

Fill in the Free Book Certificate below, and we'll send your FREE BOOKS to you as soon as we receive it.

If the certificate is missing below, write to: Zebra Home Subscription Service, Inc., P.O. Box 5214, 120 Brighton Road, Clifton, New Jersey 07015-5214.

FREE BOOK CERTIFICATE
4 FREE BOOKS

ZEBRA HOME SUBSCRIPTION SERVICE, INC.

YES! Please start my subscription to Zebra Historical Romances and send me my first 4 books absolutely FREE. I understand that each month I may preview four new Zebra Historical Romances free for 10 days. If I'm not satisfied with them, I may return the four books within 10 days and owe nothing. Otherwise, I will pay the low preferred subscriber's price of just $3.75 each; a total of $15.00, *a savings off the publisher's price of $3.00.* I may return any shipment and I may cancel this subscription at any time. There is no obligation to buy any shipment and there are no shipping, handling or other hidden charges. Regardless of what I decide, the four free books are mine to keep.

NAME

ADDRESS _____ APT _____

CITY _____ STATE _____ ZIP _____

TELEPHONE ( )

SIGNATURE _____
(if under 18, parent or guardian must sign)

Terms, offer and prices subject to change without notice. Subscription subject to acceptance by Zebra Books. Zebra Books reserves the right to reject any order or cancel any subscription.

ZB0894

GET
FOUR
FREE
BOOKS

(AN $18.00 VALUE)

ZEBRA HOME SUBSCRIPTION
SERVICE, INC.
120 BRIGHTON ROAD
P.O. Box 5214
CLIFTON, NEW JERSEY 07015-5214

ings into the kiss that followed. Even before he eased off, she was unbuttoning her shirt. He took over the task, then paused in some surprise. It was his shirt she was wearing, the one he'd given her that morning on the Rio Grande. The knowledge that she'd kept it, that she'd wear it, was an indescribable stimulant. She wore it next to her skin, his practical cotton over her satiny flesh, and his hand separated the two in a gradual unveiling.

She was even more exquisite than he remembered: full, firm, shaped just right for the cup of his palm.

"Nothing you haven't seen before," she said, sounding just a bit nervous with his scrutiny.

Jack smiled down at her. "I wasn't looking at you quite the same way then." He continued to caress her, but her agitation lingered. Then he considered that past situation and the harsh impression it had made upon her, and it caused him to add, "Emily, I would never hurt you."

That made her smile trustingly, and she relaxed. "I know that, Jack."

"Don't be afraid to tell me to stop, if I'm doing something you don't like."

Her smile grew small and tender. "I think I'm going to like everything you do."

"I hope so."

She liked the gentle kiss he gave her, and the deeper one that followed. And she liked the way his roughened fingers moved upon her skin, with an adoring brevity; learning her, not claiming her, which made her want to give to him all the more. And when his mouth moved down to sample from her bared breast, he created a sweet, tugging tension within her like none she'd ever experienced. She'd lain with two different men, had borne them two children. She wasn't unworldly, yet Jack made her feel that way, as if he was waking her to sensations, as if the restless yearning he was generating was a first-time emotion. In a way, it was. Neither of the men before him had bothered to encourage a response in her. It hadn't been important to their pleasure. Jack concentrated upon it, making her feel, making her succumb to wondrous delight with each provoking touch, with each pluck of his lips or slow drag of his tongue.

By the time he nudged his hand under her skirt, Emily was ready to beg for him to take her. She knew that was the inevitable end, but was totally ignorant of the journeys they could take to get there. She knew only the direct path and was eager to take it with him. But that wasn't what he had in mind.

What he'd planned was more sensory seduction, more nerve-shaking exploration, until she was writhing, thrashing with increasing anticipation. Her fingers clutched at his shoulders restlessly. Her breathing became an erratic panting.

"Jack . . ."

"Is this all right?" he whispered against her lips, as his fingers slipped inside her. Hot, moist flesh contracted about him.

"Oh, Jack, I don't know what it is you're doing to me, but please don't stop. Don't stop."

"I wasn't going to, not until—"

She gave a sudden cry as her body spasmed beneath him. It was a sound of surprise, of wonder, of discovery. A beautiful sound.

"Until that," he concluded.

Fifteen

Emily was so replete with satisfaction, she wasn't immediately aware that Jack had smoothed her skirt down over her knees or that he was just holding her, stroking her hair. When the languorous shivers ebbed, she looked to him in confusion.

"Jack?"

"Ummmm?" His knuckles rubbed along her cheek and jaw. His look was so tender, her soul dissolved beneath it.

"Aren't you going to—you know?"

Much to her surprise, he shook his head. "I wanted to give you something no one had given you before. Have I?" But he was smiling, already sure of the answer. And obviously pleased by it.

"Yes, but—"

"Shhhh! I love you, Emily."

Her brow puckered in bewilderment. "Jack, don't you want to make love to me?"

His laugh was soft and strained to the limit. "Oh, you've no idea how much I want that."

"Then why—"

He kissed her gently, but her question lingered when he lifted away. He was bringing the edges of her borrowed shirt together, buttoning them up with one hand. "Looking is one thing. Touching is another. Taking another man's wife . . . I can't, Emily."

"I don't love Neil."

He drew a short breath, but said, "That doesn't matter." It did, but then again, it didn't.

"Jack, Neil—Neil—" She wanted to say that Neil hurt her, that he scared her, that she slept with a gun under her pillow. Instead, she told him, "Neil doesn't love me, either."

"That doesn't change things, Em."

"He doesn't want me, Jack. Not really. Doesn't that matter? I haven't—we haven't—been together since my return. I don't want him to touch me. I'd rather he kept to his whore. Doesn't that matter, either?"

"No. I wish it did."

"Don't you want me, Jack?"

"It doesn't matter what I want! If I could have what I want, you'd be my wife, and I'd be filling you with my children, and I'd be so good to you, so good to you. But I can't, and you aren't. Neil is my best friend, Emily, but it wouldn't matter who it was. You're not mine. You're not mine."

"I want to be. Oh, Jack, I want to be." She pressed her face to the warm hollow of his throat and began a quiet weeping. He held her because he couldn't do or say anything else. Finally, she asked in a low, tragic voice, "What am I supposed to do?"

"I don't know."

"Am I supposed to go back to him? If he'd even take me now. Am I supposed to forget I have another child because the fact that he exists would displease my husband? Am I supposed to live out the rest of my life miserable, empty, and alone because I wed a man I didn't know when I was little more than a child myself? Is that what I'm supposed to do, Jack?"

He had no answer.

"I love you, Jack."

Somehow, that made it all the worse.

"What am I going to do?"

"What's right," he told her, but that sounded weak and unsatisfying, even to him.

It wasn't right that she should have to go back to a man she didn't love. It wasn't right that her daughter had died. It wasn't right that she couldn't be with her only surviving child. Or that they should have to deny something so special between them. He would never love another; Jack had no doubt of that. He would never want another woman in quite the same way: to the extremes of heart and soul and sanity. But doing what was right meant he could never, should never, have her. And that might have been right, but it was damned unfair.

"What are we going to do, Jack? Pretend we don't love one another? Ignore this chance—maybe our only one—to be together? Jack, I've never had anything nice before. I've never known anyone good before. I've never felt kindness or been in love . . ."

His hand forked beneath her chin, forcing it up. His mouth ravaged hers with a hard, hungry passion. She tasted of her tears, and no drink could be more bittersweet or act upon his sensibilities was such potent effect.

"I don't want to pretend anything," he told her at last. "Not now, not out here, where there's nothing but nothing for days around. Until we find your son, you're mine, Emily. We belong to each other. We can share each other's company. We can hold each other. We can go as far as conscience allows. Maybe that's all we'll ever have and maybe it won't ever be enough, but for a little while, I'll have almost everything in the world I ever wanted."

She looked at him through eyes wet as new grass after

a sudden rain, with a desperate hope. "And we won't talk about Neil or think about what's to come."

Foolish things to agree to, he knew, but he was nodding as if it were possible. As if they could really forget what awaited them. And as he kissed her gently, he wondered if they could just get lost out here in the West Texas scrub for the next forty years or so.

Except that Neil would find them. He would track them down and kill them both.

No use pretending that he wouldn't.

They slept entwined like lovers and woke to share a long kiss, then went efficiently about the business of breakfasting and breaking camp. The mood was easier because neither of them tried to hide his heart when looking at the other. Easier in some ways, harder than hell in others.

It was hard not to keep looking behind them.

They spent their fourth night out at the edge of a lazy stream. Jack hunted up their meal while Emily washed the grit of four days' riding off her skin and out of her clothes. She was bundled in Jack's Navajo blanket when he returned with a lean jackrabbit. His gaze restlessly detailed the fair skin peeping above the edge of colorful wool, then he declared he was going to wash up while dinner was cooking. The water wasn't cold enough.

When he returned to the fire, the rabbit was sizzling in its juices and Emily in hers. As he came down on his knees beside her, she opened the blanket with a slow, deliberate move, unveiling the perfection of her body. He feasted first on her succulent flesh and on the sounds of her completing pleasure, then upon the overcooked game he'd provided. It was the strangest meal he'd ever sat to: charred rabbit and naked woman. He had enough of the first, but couldn't get his fill of the second.

And when Emily lay back a second time and lifted her arms in invitation, he eased down into them, letting her absorb his weight in a torso-to-toe distribution. She was kissing him and he was moving above her, his hips rocking impatiently against the tantalizing spread of her womanhood. Her hands were at the seat of his jeans, encouraging the movement. It was too much for even a saintly man.

Breathing hard and half-mad with need, he rolled off her and onto his back, tense and trembling with self-denial. Had he thought it was going to be easy? That touching her was going to be enough? He figured as long as he kept his clothes on, there was no danger of them going too far. But Emily was of a different mind.

She curled against his side, one knee rubbing across his denim-clad thighs in a provocative rhythm. Her fingers played beneath his shirt, teasing through the mat of his chest hair, taunting his nipples into an arousal almost as fierce as the one that raged below. All the time she was doing these deliberately devilish things, she was speaking to him sweetly, kissing him softly.

"Oh, Jack, I never knew I was supposed to enjoy being with a man so much. I had no idea the things you make me feel even existed. I didn't know what I was missing. You're spoiling me shamelessly!"

"Someone ought to." He said that with a smile, then quickly clamped down on the image of Neil Marcus before it intruded into the moment. Too late. Neil should have. Why hadn't he? He'd given this woman a child but withheld the special joys of intimacy from her. Why?

"Jack?" Her finger stroked down his cheek to gain his attention. "Don't."

"What?"

"Don't think about it, all right?"

His smile was thin and unconvincing. Yeah, right. Don't think about it. Maybe if he was unconscious.

But Emily had another way of making him forget.

"Take your shirt off." When he recoiled from that suggestion, she began to nibble at his lower lip. "Please. I want to be next to you."

He stripped it off. The feel of her soft breasts flattening out upon his bare skin was an unimaginable delight. She eased down him, nuzzling, nipping, kissing him, all the way down to his belt buckle. He'd never had a woman do such things to him. When she tugged at that, his sensory shock ended.

"Em, don't."

She either didn't hear or didn't want to heed his hoarse command. She unfastened his belt and was trailing her fingertips over the mammoth jut of him packed safely away behind straining blue jean material. His breath altered, coming in short, savage snatches.

"Take these off, too." Her voice rippled along his overwrought nerve endings, eliciting a feverish shaking, but he continued to resist.

"Emily, don't. We can't do this."

"We're not going to do anything," she soothed, as her fingers deftly worked the straining fastenings. "Trust me, Jack."

He had little choice. His control was gone. He didn't want her to stop. That terrible feeling was back, that awareness of being right on the edge of a wrong thing. But she had a way of making it seem so good, so pure, so motivated by tender caring that he couldn't cling to the objection. Obligingly, he lifted his hips so she could peel down his Levis.

Her touch was like the whisper of cool raw silk over hot skin.

"You're beautiful, Jack."

Her husky murmur shot a shudder to his soul.

Jack closed his eyes, so far beyond coherent thought it took little more than her curious exploration and the sudden unexpected brush of her lips to wring an explosive response. Shattering sensations centered and shot through him, leaving him wonderfully dazed and dismayed. Then Emily was kissing his slack mouth, smiling in the face of his embarrassment.

"I wanted to give you something no one had given you before. Have I, Jack?"

He managed a nod, and with a gusty groan, gave himself over to an engulfing weakness of relief.

Her fingertips traced the soft swell of his lip. "Just imagine what the rest would be like."

She hadn't said it just to torture him, but it did. Yes, he could imagine. And even after such a splendid release, it made him crazy.

And long after she'd curled up to sleep in his embrace, Jack stared up at the stars, wondering frantically how he was ever going to let her go.

She didn't want it to end, but in spite of that fact, they made good time. Riding with Jack Bass, caring for him, cooking for him, loving him was like nothing Emily had ever experienced. There was a satisfaction in it that filled her heart to bursting, a pleasure in it that soothed all that troubled her soul. There was only one point of dissension: she wanted to make love to him. She wanted to have him in that most perfect and personal way. She'd never expected to hunger for a man the way she craved him. The more he gave, the more she wanted. She basked in his tenderness, she devoured his thoughtfulness, she fed upon his attentive touches until she was writhing for more—more everything. The warmth of his love lit her days and the heat of his passion scorched her nights. She was past considering what was right.

To someone who'd spent a lifetime in darkness, she was pulled helplessly toward his light. She was starved for what he so generously gave. And the thought of going without again stirred a panic in her that wouldn't go away. Even as he brought her to the pinnacle of pleasure with the devastation of his touch, she suffered for the nature of their relationship. It wasn't going to last. The shadow of that truth clouded everything, dimming the delight, depressing her joy, making their last day before reaching Blue Creek one of unbearable tension and testiness.

After feeling the snap of her temper over any little thing he said, Jack kept to himself. He was chafing from the frustration of restraint, but he didn't want to lose any of their time together separated by sharp words. He was at a loss with Emily. She was spoiling for a fight, and the more he tried to sidestep her ire, the more he felt the brunt of it. She criticized everything, from the quality of his coffee to the intensity of the blue sky. One second she'd be harping on the way he'd made the fire, and the next she was all over him with kisses. The minute he responded to them, she was shoving him away, stalking angrily to her horse. Edgy and upset by her inconsistencies, he followed. At a safe distance.

By mid-afternoon, the horizon was dark with storm clouds. Lightning flashed in dazzling strobes across the far mountains. Even miles away, they could feel the electricity in the air and scent the advent of rain, though it was unlikely that it would actually reach them out on the plain. The restless weather was a perfect companion to Emily's brooding silence, and Jack watched both with a respectful caution.

There was still plenty of daylight left when she decided to stop, complaining of weariness. Jack was reluctant to set up camp so early. They'd be at his uncle's the next day, and he was as anxious as he was apprehensive. His approaching confrontation with Harm had him less aware of Emily, and she was very aware of his distraction.

And she didn't like it. It made her wonder if he was looking forward to the end of their intimacy. It seemed the more she wanted lately, the quicker he pulled back. Had he tired of her demands and the impossibility of their situation? Hers were uncharitable thoughts and unworthy, from what she knew of Jack, but she couldn't help them. When he stepped off his horse with a preoccupied look toward the distance, she nuzzled in close, stroking his chest, kissing his throat. It took him a moment to respond to her, and that was a second too long. Her palms struck at him, knocking him back on his heels.

"Em?"

"I'm going to look for firewood."

"Emily—"

But she stalked off in a mood as violent as those approaching clouds. Sighing to himself, Jack set about securing the horses. He knew what it was. He'd seen the displays of alternate affection and annoyance before, between his uncle and his Aunt Amanda. And he knew what it would take to fix it. Something he couldn't give. She wanted him as her lover, and he couldn't commit to that final sin against his conscience. He'd told her that. He was telling it to himself in an angry, forceful undertone. He was almost glad tomorrow would bring them into the company of others. Then it would be easier to maintain a distance. Because all the small steps they'd taken—the words of love, the kisses, the touching, the spiraling pleasures—were nothing more than a prelude to that final plunge into the unforgivable. That which he desired more every time he held out against temptation. He wasn't going to last, and Emily wasn't helping matters. Yes, he'd be very glad to get to his uncle's house.

He was so deep in his own thoughts that it took him by surprise. The air had grown still, and a sultry odor like burning hay began to thicken without his being conscious of it. Then he glanced up by chance and was stricken with the sight. Low in the sky, a blue mist like smoke rolled in front of an inky blackness. The saddle he'd been holding fell forgotten.

"Emily!"

He ripped off a fearful oath and began to run in the direction she'd taken.

Only a fool would try to predict West Texas weather. It was as harsh and merciless as the environment, and just as deadly. One might joke about it, saying a norther could blow up fast enough to freeze a layer of ice on boiling coffee and so cold a man had to run backward to spit. They laughed because it purely terrified them, and a man always tried to make light of things that made him afraid. And Jack was full of that fear as he raced along the lip of a rutted ravine. He didn't know what nasty things those clouds intended, but he knew he wanted Emily close at hand.

She'd been picking up bits of wood in the bottom of the arroyo, chomping on her massing tension. In this desolate part of Texas, one had to dig for wood, as most of it was found in the deep and widespread root systems of the hearty desert plants. Down in the crevice, she found plenty exposed by eroding weather. She had an armload of it when she heard Jack calling to her. She was tempted to just keep walking. She wasn't ready to return to camp with him. To camp, where there would be more tantalizing kisses, more hurried breathing, more urgent coaxing of one another's passions. And then there would be that long interlude when Jack would hold her close and the wanting would be so tense and turbulent that she could feel it vibrating through him. Through her.

She never thought she'd want to make love to another man. Her past experience with it was far from encouraging: memories of pain and indifferent possession. But with Jack, it would be as wonderful as all that went before it; she just knew it. And he was holding back in the name of long-forgotten propriety. What did she know of propriety, she who had married for security to a stranger, then a savage? What kind of pride did she have left to claim? The only thing she could give that would be truly her own was her love, and she wanted to give it all to Jack Bass. But he wouldn't let her.

So she didn't respond to his first shouts. Then she heard how frantic he sounded. She stopped, puzzled.

"Jack?"

"Emily, where are you?"

"Down here. What's wrong? You sound—"

Then she heard something so terrifying she forgot the rest of her words.

It bore down on her like a freight train, sweeping around the bends and twists of the arroyo with a mad fervor, a sound like she'd never heard before. Like an approaching tornado. She let the wood drop and started scrambling up the crumbling bank, haste hurrying her actions and charging wildly through her heart.

She'd almost reached the top when she saw it: a wall of water, racing toward her like a tidal wave. It had started small somewhere up in the desert where the rains had fallen in a hard torrent, too fast for the hard-packed soil to absorb.

It began in a trickle and rose in volume and velocity to a frothing surge channeled by the walls of the ravine.

"Jack!"

"Emily, hang on!"

She actually felt his fingertips as they grazed the back of her hand. Then the water hit and she was jerked away from him. The current seized her, snatching her from the safety of his grasp, pulling her under and away within an angry riptide of debris.

"J-a-a-a-ack!"

Her scream was abruptly cut short as a swirling piece of wood struck her in the temple. Everything went black.

"Emily!"

Jack was left groping in mid-air. Before his wide, disbelieving eyes, she was sucked down into the seething flood. He saw her bob up some yards farther on, then watched helplessly as she was knocked unconscious. Without thinking, he jumped out into the raging waters. The pull was surprisingly fierce, but instead of fighting it, he worked with it, using the shove of the current to rush him toward where he'd last seen Emily's flailing hands. Panic as wild as the waters swamped him. He couldn't lose her now. Not like this!

He almost missed her. The water was murky with mud and clotted with all sorts of litter. He was almost swept by when he saw her limp form wedged in the crotch of an exposed root. He reached out desperately and snagged onto the back of her shirt. For one terrible moment, he felt fabric tear and give, then he had hold of the waistband of her skirt, and finally, his arms were around her. He tried to say her name, but it was drowned out by the rush and roar of water.

Struggling against the force, Jack angled himself around so his body provided a buffer. Then all he could do was hang onto her, hoping the root that anchored them wouldn't give way while he was battered by debris. He was assailed by the terrifying doubt that he hadn't come in time to save her.

She was so terribly limp.

Finally, after what seemed an eternity, he felt the fearsome current ebb. Within minutes, it slowed to an easy ripple; then, just like that, it began to recede into the accepting Texas soil. Jack lay back along the dirty bank, panting, eyes closed, Emily's slack form cradled to his chest. Her hair was plastered across his face in a wet tangle. As he brushed it away, he heard the most glorious sound.

She gasped.

That was immediately followed by a series of wracking coughs, and as he crushed her close, giving his thanks, she began to stir in his arms.

"Jack?" It was a weak cry, as weak as the curl of her embrace.

"I've got you, Em. It's all right."

"Oh, Jack."

And she burrowed into him, filling him with what had to be the most possessive tenderness he'd ever known. If he hadn't been able to save her . . .

Her shivering finally forced him to take action. They had to get back to their camp, in front of a fire. Jack managed to get Emily up the soggy bank; then, with the support of his arm about her, they started walking. The water had swept them practically a half-mile in seconds. By the time they found the horses, they were exhausted and cold. While Emily stripped out of her wet things and huddled in Jack's blanket, he gathered up enough wood to start a saving blaze. Emily was very quiet, watching him.

"You warm enough?"

"I need you under here."

He didn't argue. His damp clothes were quickly discarded

and spread to dry. Then he slipped beneath one side of the blanket and sighed as the sensation of warmth encountered his chilled skin. Then again as Emily filled his arms.

From where her face was pressed to his shoulder, she murmured, "I was so afraid."

"Oh, Em, you know I'd never, ever let anything happen to you."

She levered back slightly so she could look directly into his eyes. "I was afraid I would never see you again, that I wouldn't have the chance to apologize for the way I've acted today or to tell you—to tell you how much I love you." Her fingertips spread over the lean angles of his face, easing back until they meshed in the sleek dampness of his hair. Then she tugged him forward to meet her kiss. Her lips were soft and expressive, moving over his with a lingering wealth of emotion, slowing only long enough for her to claim again, "I love you, Jack."

He took the initiative then, building on her kisses with a tender intensity. She went down onto her back beneath his insistent pressure and there, welcomed within the spread of her thighs and the circle of her arms, he lavished her lips and the quivering tips of her breasts with his attentive mouth. The friction of skin on skin quickly warmed them and the feel of Jack swelling huge and hard against her had Emily forgetting all about the tribulations of moments ago.

Don't pull away now, Jack. Please don't pull away. I need you. I need you. These words pulsed from her heart as she strained to encompass him with all she had, with all she was. They'd come so close to losing each other; she couldn't let go now. It would be so unfair if this one chance for happiness was denied them after they'd struggled through so much to be together.

When she said his name in a breathy little voice, ready to

beg him if need be, his tongue speared deep to turn her words into a throaty moan around it. And at that moment, she felt the sudden surge of him pushing in and up inside her, filling her with an incredible flood of heat and strength, until every increment of emptiness was exquisitely conquered. All the fear, all the panic, all the loneliness was gone.

And when he began to move, she cried out in a thrill of awareness, clutching at him with trembling hands, encouraging him with the inviting lift of her hips. Each slow draw and hard drive of him honed that awareness to a sharper sensory degree until she was aggressively chasing the sensations, cupping his taut flanks, tugging to increase the fervor of their union. And just as unexpectedly, the sweet binding tension burst, releasing thousands of fragmented shivers through her system, culminating with the rewarding feel of Jack's hard shudders, above her, inside her, mingling with hers, and dwindling into a luxurious heaven of relief.

He remained unmoving for the longest time, stroking the side of her neck with his warm, uneven breaths. She didn't care if he ever moved. This was where she wanted him forever, surrounding her, completing her.

And she knew right then with a certainty that she would never, ever let Jack Bass go.

Sixteen

He was sorry.

Emily could feel it the moment Jack began to recover himself.

He didn't say anything. Maybe it was the silence. Emily didn't want silence; she wanted to laugh and cry and tell him honestly that what he'd just given her was the most fabulous experience of her life. Nothing even came close to that intensely personal sharing. But she was afraid to speak.

He withdrew both physically and emotionally, leaving her body even as she tried to hold to him. She said his name with something akin to reverence. He went still. She touched his averted face, cupping his chin, lifting his head so she could kiss him. He didn't try to hold back. His mouth moved with hers in a passionate complement. Then he whispered, "I love you, Emily," with such a sad tone of regret that she was nearly provoked to tears.

He shifted over onto his back, drawing her into the familiar hollow of his side and shoulder. He was caressing her hair and her arm with a gentleness that was her undoing. She couldn't stand the deepening melancholy of his mood.

"I'm sorry if I disappointed you."

Jack reacted with such a predictable urge to comfort her, Emily almost felt guilty in her ploy. Almost.

"Disappointed? How could you think that?"

She ducked her head and murmured, "I wish I knew how to please you better."

He expelled a sound, a sort of incredulous laugh. "Oh, God, Emily, you were—more than I ever dreamed. I've wanted you for so long, I've imagined what it would be like. But I never guessed that what we'd make between us would be magic."

Those were the words she wanted to hear, spoken with the love required to put her insecurities to rest. She cuddled up contentedly upon his shoulder, trusting him to keep her safe when she was at her most vulnerable. Knowing he wouldn't fail her, she was able to sleep.

But Jack couldn't rest. He felt a thousand times damned and disgraced, and so satisfied deep in his soul that it was a torment in itself. It shouldn't have felt so good to do something so bad. There should have been punishment, not this luxurious sense of reward. He should have felt worse than he did. But he felt like smiling.

And he felt like waking her up and making love to her all over again.

In the back of his troubled mind, a small spark ignited, fanning a terrible thought. Why didn't he feel more guilty about taking his friend's wife? A man of conscience would have. A man of decency could have stopped himself. He wasn't either of those things.

He was his father's son.

Jack was up and dressed before Emily even considered stirring. She thought about making coffee and starting breakfast, but before she could move upon the vague idea, Jack had done it. She felt unusually lazy, and so pleased with the world in general, she opened her eyes to greet the day with a smile . . . until she saw Jack.

" 'Morning," she called softly. He glanced at her furtively and murmured a like sentiment. He was quick to turn back to the tending of their animals. She sat up slowly, surprised by the many bodily aches and pains from the previous day's ordeal, and smugly satisfied by a more intimate chafing. With the blanket tented about her shoulders, she watched him, loving him so much it warmed her like the best fire. Like the red pepper he favored in his beans. And she could tell when he grew uncomfortable under her scrutiny.

"We'd better get a move on," he said to his saddle, securing the ties and their supplies. His movements were jerky and had his horse dancing.

"Jack?"

He paused, then slowly turned toward her. He looked almost fearful of what she would say.

"Thank you."

He stiffened. "For what?"

"You saved my life yesterday."

"Oh." Then he looked relieved. He shrugged. "Was I supposed to let you drown?"

"It might have been easier on you in the long run."

He looked dismayed by her words, but he didn't question her. He knew exactly what she was talking about. And he didn't argue. That's when her thoughts turned from romance to resignation. He wasn't about to come within ten feet of her this morning.

"Do I have time for a cup of coffee?"

"Sure. Help yourself." Oh, he was wary. She smiled wryly and reached for the pot. And couldn't keep herself from groaning as a sudden splitting ache shot through her temples. Jack was instantly on his knees beside her.

"Em? You all right?" He pushed her hand away and examined the swelling above her ear, frowning in concern. She leaned into his palm, finding his gentle touch a miraculous restorative.

"Just a little dizzy," she murmured. But she wondered if that was due more to him than to the split in her scalp. He eased her head down to his shoulder, his fingertips beginning a light massage of the sore area.

"That better?"

"Ummmmm." She closed her eyes and sighed.

"You want to just take some time and rest up this morning?" She could feel his lips moving against her hair.

"I'll be all right. In a minute."

The blanket had slipped lower, off the smooth skin of her shoulders, and it was there that his hand began to move in slow, easy circles. Then his mouth was brushing over that same soft slope. When she touched her hand to the back of his head, he seemed to remember himself, and he straightened.

"You'd better get dressed, Emily. We'll just take it real slow and cautious this morning."

She wasn't sure if he was talking about the riding or their relationship. Or both.

Amanda Bass was nothing like she expected.

When the very pregnant blond woman came flying into Jack's arms, Emily looked on in complete surprise. Why, Harmon's wife was hardly any older than Jack! She was a fragile-looking thing beyond the mammoth belly, all freckled skin and huge, dark eyes, with a crisped-toned northern voice that spoke of cultivation. What on earth was she doing with a tough Apache tracker like Harmon Bass?

Amanda Bass turned a generous smile upon her. "You must be Mrs. Marcus. Climb down and make yourself at home. We've got plenty of room. Harmon calls it our hotel." And when she said his name, her dark eyes glowed warmly and Emily knew without a doubt that this woman was madly in love with her renegade husband.

"Thank you, Mrs. Bass."

"It's Amanda. Come inside where it's cooler and I'll get you something to drink. The girls will be excited to have a guest and to finally meet their Cousin Jack, who has managed to make himself scarce since Leisha was an infant." She shot him a scolding glance and continued to rattle on. Emily found herself smiling. How did the stoic Harmon get a word in edgewise?

Two little girls came out of the house, one bounding and one toddling, both blond, like their mother, and with their father's swarthy coloring. Beautiful children. Emily's throat knotted up with unexpected emotion.

"Mrs. Marcus, these are my daughters, Leisha and Becca. Girls, this is your Cousin Jack's—friend, Mrs. Marcus. Why don't the three of us take her inside while Jack goes to find your daddy?"

Leisha, the older girl, gave Jack a long, quelling look that was so typical of Harmon. "He doesn't look like Sarah or Sidney or Jeffrey."

"He's their half-brother," Amanda explained patiently. "And you will like him very much, once you get to know him."

She pursed her lips in a doubting expression. "Is he the one Daddy calls a lying son of a bitch?"

"Leisha!" Amanda looked to Jack, her features stricken. Jack gave a small, thin smile.

"That's me."

Leisha studied him impassively. "Maybe he should go

away before Daddy gets back and gets unhappy all over again."

"That's not up to you, young lady," Amanda said sternly. "Jack, I'm—"

He waved off her apology. "It's all right, Amanda. Where's Harmon?"

"Out back with Sarah."

Out back could mean anywhere within a twenty-mile radius.

"Emily, you go on in with Amanda. Have her take a look at where you hit your head."

"Are you hurt, Mrs. Marcus? Oh goodness, and here I stand, yammering your ears off. I'll see to her, Jack. You go make up with Harmon. And if he's not of an open mind, tell him I'll discuss it with him later."

"Yes, ma'am."

"And Jack," she called as she put an arm about Emily's shoulders, "go easy. Remember that he loves you."

They were crouched down over some impressions in the dry Texas dust, Harmon looking so much more like Sarah's brother than he ever did. Jack smiled to himself. Sarah was finally getting her lesson. How well he could remember his uncle's patient instruction when they'd gone on their first few trails together. Of course, that was before he had become a lying son of a bitch and changed everything between them.

"Tell me what you see," Harmon said.

Sarah studied the track with a serious intensity. "Hummmmm. Small foot, shallow depth, walking there, running here. I see a thirty-year-old skinny Tex-Apache with blue eyes, about five foot seven, in boot heels, probably being chased by his hot-tempered wife, toting, from the look of the print, a scatter gun. Would be running faster if it was a Winchester pointing at his backside."

"Very amusing," Harmon drawled. His expression didn't soften, but his eyes crinkled at the corners. "How do you know it wasn't Amanda?"

"For one thing, she's not much for running these days and she has a few pounds on you, though please don't tell her I said that. She wears boots, and these are Mescalero moccasins, like those you've got on now."

"And?" he prompted.

She looked more closely. "And she walks heel first and you walk toe first. That was made by a cautious Indian, not a careless white woman."

"Good."

Sarah beamed up at him, then she looked over his shoulder and exclaimed in delight. "Hey, J—"

"You want to listen to me, or are you done learning?" Harm cut in brusquely. He never looked behind him. He'd been aware of Jack's presence for some minutes.

Sarah waved to her brother, then looked back at the ground. "What else do you want to know? What you had for supper, or what you were carrying in your pockets?"

He ignored her teasing with the infinite tolerance of a good teacher. "When were these made?"

"Oh, that's hard. Let me see." She drew her finger around the edge of the impression and tested the soil in the center. Her face was studious. "I'd say it was about five minutes after midnight."

Harm blinked in surprise. "How—?"

" 'Cause I followed you out here when you were making 'em. Hah! You never saw me. Some Apache you are." Her arms whipped around his neck and she planted a wet kiss on his cheek before jumping up and racing to her brother. Then she was wrapped around Jack in a tangle of long arms and legs. "How's my big, handsome ranger brother? You gonna be staying for a while? How's Mrs. Marcus?"

"She's with me, and I don't know for sure how long we'll be staying." His gaze was fixed over her shoulder on the slowly straightening figure of his uncle. "Why don't you run up to the house and say howdy to her? I need to talk to Uncle Harm for a minute."

"Okay. See you in a bit." And she ran, all lanky legs and coltish grace.

The two men regarded each other for a long, tense moment, then Harmon started for the house.

"Uncle Harm, I—"

Harm walked right by him without a glance. When Jack reached out to grab onto his arm, Harm jerked away with a fierce, "My heart does not recognize you. Go away from my family. You're not welcome here."

Jack stood up, stunned and as abruptly winded as if the breath had been struck from him. "Uncle Harmon . . ." His voice trailed off into despair.

The small figure paused, but only for a fraction of a second, then continued on to the house.

Amanda looked up at the sound of her husband's quick footsteps. "Harmon, we're in here. Come say hello to Mrs. Marcus."

He came into the front room and Amanda knew things had not gone well between him and Jack. There was a tension to him that defied any kind of reconciliation.

"Where's Jack?" Just in case, she glanced at the knife Harm carried. No sign that it had been used in the last few minutes.

Ignoring Amanda's question, Harm crossed to Emily

Marcus. He went down on one knee before her, took up one of her hands, and pressed it somberly over his heart. He spoke to her in the language of the Apache.

"My heart breaks for you. I didn't keep my word. I'll meet whatever payment you decide upon."

Emily's eyes filled up. She had no doubt that if she demanded his life, he'd give it up right there in front of his parlor sofa. But what good would that do? She answered quietly, in English.

"I don't want your sacrifice, Mr. Bass. I know you did your best and I'm grateful for it. I don't hold you responsible for Cathy." Then she glanced up to where Jack stood in the doorway, and the compassion in her eyes was plain to see. "It was a terrible thing, and more suffering won't bring back my daughter or ease her loss." She stretched out her hand, and Jack came reluctantly to take it. Her lips brushed over his knuckles in a forgiving gesture.

"It takes a big heart to accept another's failings, Mrs. Marcus." Amanda was looking at her husband as she said that. She saw his spine stiffen, and he rose up without acknowledging his nephew. "Forgiveness is the first step in healing."

He strode out of the room.

"Emily, we'd better go," Jack said softly.

"Sit down." The abrupt, authoritative crack of Amanda's voice startled them all. "Don't you move, Jack Bass." She dragged herself out of her chair in pursuit of her husband. "Harmon!"

He halted halfway out the front door, but stubbornly refused to turn.

"We have guests."

He responded to that soft command with the squaring of his shoulders and a gruff, "I am going."

"Harmon Bass, you leave this house and you'll find your belongings on the porch when you get back."

He looked at her then. "You don't mean that."

She looked serious enough to start his heart jerking.

"You walk out of here and I'll consider that you've chosen to walk away from me."

"Amanda, this is not funny."

"I am not laughing. I won't tolerate this."

"You would divorce me over it?" He was shaken, and his tone betrayed it. The thought of losing her, even if the threat was a bluff, purely terrified him. "Ammy, you wouldn't. You wouldn't put me out of my own house, away from my own family."

"Jack is family," she stated unyieldingly. "You will not hurt him like this in my house. That's not the kind of example I want set for my children."

"Ammy . . ."

"It's up to you, Harmon."

He stared at her, panic and uncertainty flickering through his gaze, then a cold pridefulness settled in. "I don't need a sharp-tongued woman telling me what to do. I'm better off walking away. I'm going." And he did, banging the door behind him.

Amanda stood in shock, pinching her lips together to hold back the frantic cry of his name. She let him go. Slowly, she returned to the parlor, where an agitated group awaited her.

"Amanda, are you all right?" Sarah cried out, dismayed by her sudden pallor.

"Oh, I'm fine, Sarah. I think I'll start dinner. You keep Jack and Emily company, if you would, please."

"Uncle Harm?" she began worriedly.

"He won't be joining us."

Amanda managed to get as far as the hallway, out of the sight of her company, before a soft sob of upset escaped her. Instantly, strong arms banded about her and a quiet, "Shhhh, *shijii*," whispered against her ear.

"Harmon." Her knees gave weakly as she grabbed for his hands. "I thought you'd gone."

"As far as the second step," he admitted with some chagrin. "I'm a fool. Don't you know that you could curse me and beat me with sticks and I would still come back to you?" Then he paused and said somberly, "You didn't come after me. I thought you would."

She bit back her reply. She'd wanted to.

He took an uneven breath. "I was scared."

She gave him a tremulous smile. "So was I."

"Ammy, don't ever say you wish me gone."

"I didn't."

"But you would have let me go."

She smiled with a bit more confidence. "I didn't think you'd get past the first step or I wouldn't have suggested it at all."

He smiled then, too. Just a little.

"I have dinner to make."

"I'll help."

His idea of helping was to stand so close, she bumped into him with every movement. Not that she minded. In fact, she finally gave up altogether, put her arms around his neck, and kissed him until he was content. But she was the one who came away breathless.

"Harmon Bass, I want to make love to you so bad."

He looked alarmed, "But we can't—"

"I know," she moaned in misery. "But as soon as I'm able, I'm going to take you at my convenience, whenever the mood hits me, oh, at least four or five times a day for a month or so." Her hands were rubbing over him restlessly. He caught them and squeezed them tight within his.

"And who will you get as a replacement when you've killed me after the first week?"

Her smile was completely wicked. "I haven't lived with an Apache for nothing. I can make you suffer a long, long time."

"Is it awfully hot in here, or is it me?"

"I think it's me. Get out of my kitchen, if you value your virtue."

"You stripped me of that a long time ago." He hopped up to sit on the edge of the table. "So, little girl, how do you plan to make me last for all these days and months?" he wanted to know.

And the dinner almost burned as she described some of the ways in detail.

Dinner was strained. Sarah returned home, and without her bubbly presence, silence settled in, thick and palpable. Harm and Jack never looked up from their plates, and Emily was looking at Amanda's daughters with a longing any mother would recognize. Amanda's heart broke for her. She was burning with curiosity over why her visitors had come; Jack was with another man's wife, and she was just as interested in the glances that passed between them. She recognized those looks, too. The same charged glances were still exchanged between her and her own husband, steeped in desire, longing, and mostly, love. She was trying to decide which of them to wrest the story from. Jack would probably perish of embarrassment, but she didn't know Emily that well. At least, not until she asked if the other woman would like to help her put the girls to bed.

Leaving their tense men at the table in hopes that they would find some way to break the silence between them, Emily followed the three blond Bass females upstairs. The children were giggly and less shy with her, and Emily found herself caught in a bittersweet joy. Leisha, at five, had all of Harm's arrogant posturing and his exquisite bone structure. She was going to be a dramatic beauty. Becca was more her mother's child, with huge, gentle dark eyes and hundreds of freckles. And her mother's gift of gab. She brought her hairbrush to Emily and climbed up on her knee, pointing out all the beautiful toys lining the shelves of the room she shared with her sister. Emily had never seen such lovely dolls and obviously expensive playthings.

"They're from New York," Amanda explained, as she wrestled her oldest girl into her nightdress. "From my relatives. Harmon does not approve." From her tone, neither did Amanda.

"I wasn't aware you had any other family."

"My family is here, Emily—may I call you Emily? Make no mistake about that. Harmon, his sister, Will, Jack, Sarah, the boys—they're all the family I need. Mine only take an interest because I'm rich and they don't want me to forget them." She started to braid her daughter's hair as her expression grew faraway. "Perhaps when this baby is old enough, I'll take the children to visit, just so they'll know another world exists out there. Then, maybe I won't. I'm not sure I could leave Harmon for that long."

"He seems pretty self-sufficient to me."

"Harmon? Oh, goodness, yes. He'd probably enjoy indulging in a little savagery while I was away. I'd return to find he'd strung up and roasted half the villains in West Texas in my absence." She smiled wryly, and Emily marveled at her. This was no shallow, silly woman.

"Take him with you."

"Harmon, in a city? That would be rather like dragging a wildcat out of the mountains, expecting it to purr in proper company. Harmon isn't quite—civilized enough. Besides, he'd be terrified. He'd face down a Comanche war party and a band of cutthroats with the bare blade of his knife rather than be forced to sit at a society table and pick the correct fork to use. I would never unman him with his own ignorance of such things. I find him man enough just the way he is."

Emily smiled wistfully. "You must love him very much."

"I chased him all across West Texas, and he can outrun most horses on foot. I have no intention of letting him get away from me now. Life is uncertain down here in the Bend. I want to take advantage of every second of it while I have him. Because once he's gone . . ." Her voice trailed off, and for a moment, Amanda Bass looked all too vulnerable. She took a cleansing breath. "Harmon and I protect each other. Ours is a spirit union. I like the sound of that. Harm says that's how the Apache believe, but then, you'd know that. He's a hard and dangerous man, and sometimes I think I must be crazy to stay with him. He may be wild, but he's like a wolf who mates once and for life. Jack's like that, too."

Amanda glanced up to catch Emily's expression, finding in it just what she expected.

"Is that the way things are between you and Jack?"

Her reply was very faint. "Yes."

"It broke his heart, that business with your little girl, you know."

"I know."

"He didn't think you could forgive him, but I told him you would. I told him Harmon would, too, but I'm not quite so sure as I was." And she wondered for just a moment if she should have left the two of them alone downstairs together. Then she got right to the point. "Why are you here, Emily?"

She was stroking Becca's pale hair with a trembling hand. "I have a son with the Apache."

"I know. Harmon told me."

"Jack thought your husband might help me get into their camp to see him."

"See him, or take him?"

"I don't know if I can see him without wanting him."

Amanda nodded. "And then will you be going back to your husband?"

Emily met her surprising shrewd stare. "No, I don't think I can go back. Especially not with Kenitay. My husband is—"

"I know what your husband is." She stood up abruptly, setting Leisha on her feet. "Come on, girls, time to go to bed. Go on down and give your father his kiss goodnight. And don't forget to tell him that you love him. He needs to hear that now."

When they scrambled off, Amanda confronted Emily Marcus. "Will you stay with Jack, then?"

"I don't know how that would be possible, Amanda. He's a ranger, and my husband is his captain."

Amanda shrugged as if there was no problem at all. "Then you and your child will stay here with us. We're all family, after all."

Emily stared at her. If only it could be that simple. "But Harmon—"

"Loves children, and we have plenty of room. And Jack could come see you whenever he likes."

"But I'm a married woman."

"You don't have to be." Amanda gave her another hard-eyed stare. "Divorce him."

And Emily began to wonder if maybe it could be just that simple.

"G'night, Daddy!"

The patter of bare feet and high-pitched girlish voices broke the uneasy silence between Jack and his uncle. They'd been sitting in a tense stalemate, Harm refusing to acknowledge Jack's poignant stare, Jack refusing to pretend the situation was acceptable. The arrival of his daughters brought an immediate thawing to Harm's manner. He bent and scooped both children up into his lap, hugging them tight, returning their kisses and their "I love you"s. He glanced over their golden heads at his dispirited nephew and spoke to the girls quietly in the Apache tongue before setting them down.

Becca came to Jack and reached up to him. Looking startled and heartbreakingly pleased, Jack leaned down to accept her soft kiss on his cheek. When he looked up, he was met with Leisha Bass's mulish frown and her glittery stare. When nudged by her father, she managed a stiff nod, then fled the room rather than display any further acts of civility.

Feeling like a son of a bitch, Jack stared down at his cup of cold coffee. He didn't look up when Harm rose. He didn't realize his uncle stood behind him for the longest moment with his hand outstretched, just inches shy of making contact with his shoulder, before pridefully withdrawing the gesture.

Silence settled in the house, and weary beyond words, Jack finally went upstairs to seek rest in the room Amanda had assigned him. He walked by one of the open doors, and glancing in, was arrested by the sight of Emily Marcus combing out her long, dark hair.

"Goodnight," he called in softly. She looked up and the longing pooled in her green eyes. He moved on quickly before he gave in and went to her. They were far beyond stopping at a chaste goodnight kiss. Better to leave it alone.

And alone was how he felt stretched out on the comfortable bed. His arms were so empty. He'd gotten used to a womanly shape filling them while he'd been on the trail. He forced his eyes to close and his body to relax. And he was just on the edge of sleep when a sudden, terrible cry had him grabbing for his gun.

Harmon!

He reacted instinctively to the threat of danger, racing to his aunt and uncle's room and flinging open the door, ready for anything.

Anything but the chill of madness in his uncle's eyes as Harm's knife blade slashed out for his throat.

Seventeen

"Harmon, no!"

Jack heard Amanda's frantic cry as he threw up his arm for protection. He felt Harm's blade slice through his palm instead of his jugular, and he was instantly grappling for his uncle's wrist.

Harm rode him down to the floor, snarling like a vicious wild thing, smashing the side of his head with an elbow, then stabbing with his knife again. Jack rolled frantically. The blade skittered across the wood floor.

"Don't hurt him!"

That was Amanda again, but Jack wasn't sure who she was trying to protect with her desperate plea. The last thing he wanted to do was hurt his uncle. But he wasn't about to let the man kill him!

Nor was Harm willing to settle for less than that. He'd seen the face of his nightmare. Hatred and horror blocked all else. He never felt Amanda tugging on his arm or heard her short cry as his hand flashed back, catching her across the face with enough force to send her sprawling. All he knew was his enemy. All he felt was the need for blood. And he went after it with a fierce determination.

Jack knew he was no match for Harmon Bass. The lust for killing had never been bred into him. Harm was smaller, lighter, quicker, and more deadly. It was like struggling with barbed wire. There was no escaping.

"Uncle Harm! It's Jack!"

His words had no effect. Harm slammed into him, knocking him back against the wall. His head hit with a sickening thud and everything swam behind a distortion of bright pin dots of light. Through that haze, he saw Harm's arm lift in a fatal arc. And Jack knew he was going to die for the sins of his father.

"No!"

Emily had only a second to react to the scene before her. She saw Jack sprawled back on the floor with Harm straddling him. She saw the wicked blade whisked up and saw it begin down in its killing stroke. Without thought, she grabbed Harm about the neck and yanked him back, off balance. He fell over and went into an immediate roll, coming up crouched on the balls of his feet, facing her with his knife at the ready.

"Harmon!"

He blinked, staring up at the dark-haired woman silhouetted in the dimness. "Becky?"

Emily was quick to take advantage of his confusion. "Yes, it's Becky," she soothed.

Harm sank to his knees, the blade falling from his hand, forgotten. "Oh, Becky . . . it was so real. He was so real. thought . . . I thought—" He looked up in a lost panic, reaching out with both hands. Emily knelt down, letting him draw her close into his desperate embrace. He was shaking, each labored breath sobbing from him. "I won't let them hurt you, Becky. I won't."

Emily held him easily, rubbing his tense shoulders until they sagged, rocking him gently, the way she would one of her children, until his head was heavy upon her shoulder.

She saw Amanda sit up to wipe the trickle of blood from the corner of her mouth. Her dark-eyed gaze was wide with concern.

"He's all right, Amanda. See to Jack."

Jack was leaning back against the wall, cradling his gashed hand, trying to overcome the whirling dizziness. Amanda took up his hand, stemming the flow of blood, and began to bind it with the flounce torn from the bottom of her nightdress, making quiet excuses as she did.

"Oh, Jack, Jack, I'm sorry. He didn't mean it. He didn't mean to hurt you. He didn't know who you were. He thought you were—"

"I know who he thought I was."

She touched his cheek gently, her dark eyes welling with despair. "I'm sorry."

"My God," murmured Emily with a quiet horror, still holding Harm's dark head against her shoulder. "Amanda, what did they do to him?"

"Terrible things." She remembered Rebecca's dire statement. *Unspeakable things.* "They beat him and tortured him, and I think they—did worse, but he never talks of it, and I don't think I really want to know. He was only ten years old. He used to have nightmares sometimes. He hasn't had them for a long time."

"It's my fault," Jack mumbled thickly. "It's my fault for coming here."

"It's not you, Jack," Amanda assured him. "Harmon loves you. It's—" She glanced at Emily uncomfortably and finished with a lame, "It's not you."

It was Neil Marcus.

But not knowing that, Jack didn't believe her.

Amanda went to her husband. "Harmon?"

"Ammy?" He looked up at her, dazed and disoriented. "I had an awful dream. Don't leave me."

"I won't." To Emily, she said, "I'll take him." But as she bent down awkwardly, Harm got a glimpse of Jack and started to panic all over again. His eyes got round and wild as he scuttled backward, dragging Emily with him.

"No. I won't let him hurt you, Becky. I won't."

Amanda eased between him and Emily. "Emily, take Jack out of here, please. Harmon." She put her hand to his rigid cheek, directing his face toward her. "Harmon, look at me. That's Jack."

"Jack?" No recognition.

"It's all right." She enfolded him gently in her arms. "I'll keep you safe."

"Don't leave me, Ammy."

Then Emily understood. They protected each other: Harm from the real threats, Amanda from the imagined ones. "Are you going to be all right?" she asked the other woman.

Amanda smiled. "We'll be fine. He's all right now. See to Jack."

Seeing to Jack proved another difficult problem.

He was numb.

Emily took him by his good hand and led him down the hall. Harm's frightened daughters peered out from behind their partially opened door. Emily smiled at them and said in a voice that was both gentle and authoritative, "Everything's fine, girls. Your daddy just woke up from a bad dream and your Cousin Jack had a little accident. Go back to bed now."

When their door closed, Emily continued to steer Jack to his room, where he stood at something of a loss, staring blankly at the crude wrapping on his hand.

"Does it hurt?"

"What? No."

But he was hurting clear through; Emily could see that. He had on a pair of long underwear liberally splashed with blood. Slowly she began to unbutton them. "Let's get you out of these. They're rather messy. Does your head hurt?"

"What? No, it's fine."

She began to wonder if that was true. He was acting very strange, almost in shock. He let her strip him down to the skin without the slightest blush, and that was not like Jack. He crawled under his covers without complaint, bundling up in them as if freezing on the balmy night.

"Stay with me," was all he said, and that was all it took for Emily to close the door and slide in beside him. Jack was shivering. She put her arms around him and held him tight until the tremors stilled. Then, very quietly, he said, "I love you, Emily."

Before she could respond in kind, he was kissing her, deeply, almost desperately. She encouraged him with the parting of her lips and the answering dance of her tongue over and around his. She felt the push of him through the thin barrier of her night clothes and knew a moment of urgent excitement. She whispered his name and his hands slid up, bunching her nightgown to her waist. Then he sank himself deep, gasping softly at the tight fit of her, at the fiery embrace of her around him. He began to move, plunging into her mouth in tandem, reaching as far as he could, as if searching out her very soul. She gave it up gladly, first with quick little pants of his name, then with low, full-bodied moans of anticipation, and finally, with the clutching spasms of her body.

"Let me give back the life I took from you."

She heard him say that as he drove hard and spent deep. And she wondered on a dazed periphery if he was referring to the child she had or one he would seed as he emptied life within her. Or both. She would have taken either or all.

"I love you, Jack," she claimed in quiet amazement, as he withdrew and continued to hold her tight. Then, just as she was relaxing into sleep, he woke her with renewed caresses and the sudden rough thrust of him. He loved her hard and fast until he was smothering her cries beneath his hungry kisses, wringing their passions to an explosive end. And sometime later, closer to morning, he was so slow and sultry sweet with his loving, she was weeping with pleasure before he was through.

And Jack was weeping with a silent sorrow as she drifted to sleep because he knew he was never going to see her again.

Amanda woke to a flood of brightness through the windows blocked by a still figure. Harm stood staring up into the hills, his arms wrapped tight about himself. She was familiar with the stance.

"Whose blood is on the floor?"

Amanda wiped the sleep from her eyes and struggled to sit up. She felt like an Overland stagecoach.

"Whose?" he repeated with a deceiving quiet.

"You were having a bad dream. Seeing Jack startled you."

"How badly did I hurt him?"

"He cut his hand."

"On what?"

"Your blade."

She watched his shoulders rise and fall and his posture tense. "And your face?"

"An accident."

Her evasion was his answer.

"I hit you?" His voice was soft with the horror of it. "I hurt you?"

"It was just an accident, Harmon. I know you'd never hurt me."

He leaned his cheek against the glass, his eyes closing. "Oh, God. I can't go through this again, Ammy. I thought it was all done with. But I should have known it wasn't. Not as long as any of them are living."

"Harmon, you promised me." Amanda clutched at the sheets, going cold as death inside.

"I made another promise, too."

"But no one wants to hold you to it."

"I made it on my mother's grave." Then he smiled horribly. "Or should I say, in my mother's grave."

"Harmon, let it go."

"I thought I could. I did, for six long years. I made everything here my life. And now this ugliness, this horror, is back, taking control of my life. Ammy, what am I going to do? Nothing?"

"Killing Marcus will solve it?"

"I don't know. I can't think of anything else. I see his face, I hear his voice, I see him on top of Becky." His eyes squeezed tighter and his features twisted. "And yet he lives unpunished."

"He lost his child. He's losing his wife. Isn't that enough?"

She knew before he answered. His eyes opened, glittering like cold steel.

"No."

"What are you going to do about Jack?"

"Jack?" He looked puzzled.

"What's he going to think when he hears you've gutted

out and fried his friend and captain? Chances are, he'll be one of those who come after you. Do you want him there when the rangers catch and kill you?" Her words snagged up on that last fateful phrase.

"I'll tell him the truth."

"Isn't he hurting enough already? What good is it going to do? Marcus is a ranger now, a man sworn to uphold the law. A law Jack's sworn to follow."

"A law he didn't mind breaking when he was torturing and killing us!"

"Harmon, please. What about Emily?"

"I'm thinking I could settle quite a few things with the simple pull of a knife blade." How cold and cruel he sounded, like an Apache walking the trail of vengeance, a path she'd gotten him to step from six years ago. And would again, if she could.

"What about me?"

He looked at her with his heart breaking in his eyes. "I love you."

"How am I supposed to hold to that for comfort when you're dead? They'll kill you, Harmon. They'll hunt you down and they'll kill you. These aren't the old days, when a man could get by doing whatever he pleased. You murder a ranger captain and they're not going to let it go. What am I supposed to tell your children when we put you in the ground? That their daddy thought more of his revenge than his family? That the hero in those books really was a lie?"

He looked away, not saying anything.

"They need you, Harmon." And more softly, "I need you, Harmon. Please."

He sighed heavily, broken by her eloquent argument. "What do you want of me, Amanda?"

"Don't act on it, Harmon. At least, not now. The baby's

due next month, and I'll curse you till the end of time if you die before you see it."

"Things'll only get worse if I do nothing," he warned soberly.

"I can take care of you."

"What if I hit you harder? What if I knock you down? What if—"

"Harmon, I'm not afraid to be alone with you. I never have been."

"Maybe you should be."

"Why would I suddenly develop common sense after all these years? Harmon, come here to me." She put out her arms. He did so and let her hold him, but he was far from compliant in fact or form.

"It's more than the dreams, Ammy. It's everything that I am. A man is nothing if he doesn't take care of his business and his family. A man is obliged to avenge the death of a loved one. It's the way of my mother's people. It's my way. Killing calls for retaliation. If a man takes a life, he is killed, or someone in his family is killed in his place. If a man rapes and murders your woman, you rape and murder his wife or mother or sister or daughter. If he kills your son, you torture and kill his. It's an eye for an eye, and the Apache aren't the only ones who practice it, so don't label us as savages. I can't rest because my mother's spirit can't rest until I do what I must do. Ammy, you knew what I was when you married me. You've seen what I do and you chose to stay with me."

Amanda leaned away from him, stroking his lean face between her palms. "Harmon, if it would cleanse your soul, I would have you bring the man here to our home and I would *gladly* spend a day or two filleting him over a fire in the way of a good Apache wife for what he did to you and your family. He deserves every cruel punishment you can imagine. If it would erase those memories, if it would bring back your mother, if it would take away Rebecca's pain, I would say, go find him, go kill him, with my blessing. But Harmon, it won't. It won't. I love you. I will not lose you. I would live with you as a madman before I would choose to live alone. Please let it go. If you love me and your children, let it go."

He looked at her long and intensely, then told her, "I'll let it go."

But when he got up off the bed, she grabbed his hand. "Harmon, you're lying to me."

"An Apache doesn't lie."

"Yes, but what part of you was just speaking?"

"If I go out and kill him, would you refuse to let me come home?"

She had him there, and she knew it. All she had to do was say yes. But Amanda couldn't lie to him. She couldn't withhold the comforts, the security he depended upon. And she couldn't give him up. "No, Harmon . . . I can't imagine you doing anything so terrible that I would not welcome you back into my arms."

He took her chin in the vee of his hand and bent to kiss her expressively. "You are a good wife to me, Amanda. I give you my word that for Jack's sake, I will not act against the man he calls his friend. Does that satisfy you?"

"*You* satisfy me." And her hand cupped behind his dark head, pulling him down for another kiss.

Emily and Jack came downstairs together to find Harm and Amanda sitting on the front steps, watching their daughters race about the yard. Harm spoke to them without turning.

"Who is the father of your Apache child?"

Emily drew up in surprise, then she clutched at Jack's sound hand, squeezing it tight. "His name is Kodene. Do you know him?"

"I know of him. He's a man of consequence among the Mescalero, a force in leading them from the reservation to follow Victorio's path."

Jack knew the name, too. He was one of the renegades responsible for most of the raiding throughout the Bend area—and for many of the deaths. Emily's husband. A man who had lain with her to beget a child. He tried not to think of it. He tried not to think of anything beyond his objective.

Harm continued. "This child—?"

"Kenitay."

"Kenitay. A good name. You want him returned to you?"

Emily trembled with anticipation, her eyes on the two children playing in the yard. "Yes."

"They have let you take one child from them already. Why would they give you another, one of their blood?"

"He is my son."

"A boy belongs with his father, his uncles, his grandfather."

"He belongs to me. Are you saying you won't help me get him back?"

"I'm saying it won't be easy. We have no army of brave fools to rush in and tear him from their arms this time."

Jack winced at that, but he spoke up with a firm conviction. "We don't need an army. I want to talk to Kodene."

Harm did turn then, and he stared at his nephew through fiercely narrowed eyes. "Why would he listen to anything you say?" His glare said, *Why should I?*

"Because you're going to ask him to. I'll go alone and unarmed."

Emily grabbed onto his arm and looked up into his set face. "Jack—"

"It's all right, Emily. I know what I'm doing." He was going to right a wrong. His gaze never left his uncle's. "Uncle Harm, will you take me to him? Just for a talk?"

Harm stood. He glanced down at the wrapping around Jack's hand, but the hardness of his features didn't alter. "For talk. And if I find you are hiding behind me for some kind of treachery, I will cut your heart out myself and save them the trouble."

"Fair enough."

"Let's go."

He started for the barn, his daughters halting their play to run gleeful circles around him until he scooped up one in either arm and carried them along with him.

Jack started after him, but he found Emily in his path, her expression all caution and concern. He didn't want to linger. It was a time of action, not regret.

"Jack, what will you say to him?"

"Don't worry, Em. You'll have your son back; I promise. I owe you."

He wasn't answering, and Emily was uneasy with his evasion. "Jack—"

"Emily, things will work out. You stay here with Amanda, and if all goes right, that little boy will be in your arms by nightfall."

"And you?"

"I love you."

He saw more questions gathering, so he circumvented them by cupping her face in his palm, by kissing her with all the considerable passion in his heart. She made a soft sound and put her arms around him, hugging to him hard, burrowing against him, and refusing to let him go until

Harm walked back up to the porch leading two horses. He regarded the embracing couple with an impassive face.

"Let's go."

Emily moved from the cove of Jack's shoulder, kissing his neck, his jaw, his mouth, whispering, "I love you, Jack. When you get back, we have much to talk about."

He stared down into her eyes for a long moment and Emily wished she could read what went on behind the intense play of emotions there in his gaze. He gave her one last quick kiss and pulled away. Then he went to kneel beside his aunt, leaning in to hug her close.

"Take care of her, Amanda. I love her." Then he straightened and went to mount up. Leisha Bass was sitting in his saddle. She regarded him through wary eyes, then reached down to him. He lifted her down, touched to the soul when her arms stayed about his neck for a brief hug. He swung up onto his sorrel.

Harm nodded to Emily, then exchanged a speaking glance with his wife.

"Harmon, be careful."

A smile quirked his lips. "I'm always careful. And I will always come back to you." He leaned down to touch his lips very gently to the slight discoloration at the corner of her mouth. Her head turned to capture his kiss fully, drawing it out into an expression of unequaled devotion. Then he went to lift Becca down from his horse, challenging sternly, "You girls see to your mama for me," earning a chorus of, "Yes, Daddy."

He swung up and jerked the reins to one side, and he and Jack were gone.

* * *

They'd ridden clear of the house and lands when Jack said to his silent companion, "I want to swing by Will's to see my mama."

Harm muttered, "Fine by me," but he began to study his nephew with an uncomfortable suspicion.

The cry went up the minute they rode into the yard.

"Mama! Jack and Uncle Harm are here!"

Rebecca Bass came out onto the porch, smiling in welcome. "This is a surprise. Where are you two boys off to? Got time for some breakfast?"

"Not just now, Mama. Got some business to tend. Just wanted to stop in and say—and say howdy."

Rebecca came up between the two horses, clasping her brother's knee with one hand and her son's hand with the other. "Just put some coffee on. Sure you don't have a minute?" She looked up at Harm hopefully, but he was studying Jack. So she turned to him, too. "Jack?"

He slid out of the saddle and into her arms, hugging to her frantically, his face buried against her shoulder.

"Jack?" She touched his hair, frowning as she felt the hitch of his breathing.

"I love you, Mama. I'm—I'm so sorry."

"Sorry? About what? Jack—"

But he wrenched out of her embrace and was back on his horse before she could stop him, wheeling the animal away, kicking it into a canter. She looked to her brother in alarm.

"Harmon, what's wrong?"

"He knows about Cates."

"Oh, God. Harmon, you tell him I love him. You make sure he knows that."

"I will."

"Tell him—tell him I'm not sorry."

Harm nodded and went after him.

When Harm finally caught up to him, he found Jack leaning low over his sorrel's neck. Hearing his uncle's approach, he straightened, dragging his sleeve across his face. Harm fell in beside him, not speaking for a long while, snatching covert glances at the unyielding set of his nephew's face. Finally, he couldn't keep quiet any longer.

"What are you up to, Jack?"

Jack drew a deep breath and kept his eyes straight ahead. "Righting some wrongs, Uncle Harm, as best as I know how."

Eighteen

The Mescalero band was camped deep in the Chisos. Harm led the way through a snaking canyon, lifting his hand at intervals to signal guards Jack never saw. Had he come alone, he would have been a dead man within twenty yards. He felt the hair bristle at the nape of his neck, that feeling of being watched crawling all over him. He didn't look around him, knowing he'd see nothing if the Apache didn't want to be seen. Instead, he focused on his uncle's straight back and he tried not to think about the steady run of sweat beneath his collar.

The Apache were on them before Jack had a chance to react. They swarmed down from the rocks, out of hidden crevices, and up from unseen gullies. He'd been expecting it, but still it made him think of that time, riding with Foster Richards. He couldn't help the way his hand twitched toward his empty hip or the way every sinew in his body tensed as the Indians converged upon their horses. Some were afoot, some on horseback, all were well armed, but none made a threatening move against the two riders. He felt like a calf taking a stroll with hungry wolves. Several of the braves must have known Harm, because they engaged him in an easy conversation. His uncle sat relaxed in his saddle and Jack tried to do the same, but these were not his people, and only a fool would not be afraid in the same situation.

Harm nudged his horse forward and Jack followed, the Indians flanking them on either side. Then, suddenly, the canyon opened wide and a camp of about twenty extended families spread out before them.

Calmly, without looking around, Harm called back to him, "Take that ranger star off your coat, 'less you want 'em using it for target practice."

Moving carefully, Jack unpinned his badge and pocketed it. He felt naked without his sidearm and hoped Harm's reputation was enough to hold his enemies at bay until he'd accomplished what he'd come for. And soon, he would know if his plan was possible, for the entire Mescalero camp turned out to eye their visitors. There were mostly women and children, and they looked lean and hungry, and far from friendly. He could hear Foster Richards's screams echoing through his memory.

"Get down and come with me."

Jack dismounted and fell in slightly behind Harm. His uncle addressed several members of the tribe in an amiable manner, then came to a stop before a tall Apache warrior. He was bigger than Harm, toughly muscled, and wearing a traditional buckskin shirt, loincloth, and high moccasins, with his bag of magical powders about his neck and dangling earrings. He was striking, but not handsome, with a shock of black hair left hanging loose about broad, round, and rather flat features. He regarded Jack through carefully hooded eyes.

"This is Kodene," Harm told him. "Talk to me, look at him. I'll relay your words."

This was the man who'd given Emily a son. Jack felt a territorial tension rise within him and saw no reason to make small talk. "Tell him I've come for Kenitay, to take the boy to his mother."

Harm translated and listened to the casual reply. "He wants to know why Emily didn't come herself."

"Tell him she is safe with my family and I am acting for her."

That had little effect on the stoic Kodene.

"He says he doesn't know you and would not entrust you with his son. He says if Emily wants the boy, she can come live with him here."

"Tell him that she lives with me. Tell him I am her man now."

Harm glanced at him, then relayed the words. Kodene's black eyes swept over the young ranger with a slow deliberation. He muttered something to Harm and gave a soft snort.

"Never mind," Harm told him, when Jack gave him an impatient look. "Loses something in translation. He questions that you're fit for the job."

"Say it's enough that she's with me and not with him. Tell him I want to see the boy."

"Kodene says no."

"Ask him what he wants for the boy."

"He says his son is not a slave that can be bought or sold. Jack, he's not giving him up. If you've got some other idea, you'd best be getting to it."

"Tell him I am the man responsible for the ranger's raid on his camp."

"Jack—"

"Tell him."

The words brought an instant stiffening to all who heard. And the mood was suddenly very ugly.

"Tell him down in Mexico I am worth fifteen hundred dollars alive, five hundred dead."

"Jack—"

"Tell him."

A rumble of interest went up through the gathering and a hard glint of speculation gleamed in their dark stares. Kodene waved down the talk and prompted Jack to go on with the lift of his head.

"Ask him if he will take a ranger in trade for the child. I'll give myself over to them if they let you ride out with the boy."

Harm didn't look at him. "No."

"Uncle Harm—"

"They'll kill you or turn you over to the Mexicans to be hanged."

"I know. Tell him what I said."

Harm spoke the words with obvious reluctance, then said, "Kodene asks why they should not just take you, now that they have you."

"Because they respect you, and I am of your blood, and to do so would dishonor you."

"Nice bit of Apache logic," Harm mumbled; he repeated the sentiment to earn some grumbling, but no one made a move on Jack.

"Tell Kodene I can see that his people go hungry. With the money I'll bring in Mexico, they can feed themselves— Uncle Harmon?"

Harm had turned away, breaking off communication. Kodene was frowning in puzzlement.

"Uncle Harm?"

"I won't let you do this." His voice was soft and thick.

"But—"

"I won't speak the words that will get you killed." He

looked up then and his gaze was steeped with emotion. "I won't lose you, Jack."

"Speak the words. I have to do this."

"Why?"

"To right a wrong."

"What wrong? Your father's?" He sounded angry then, and the Apache shifted in uncertainty. He seized Jack's arm, fingers indenting flesh and muscle. "I atoned for him."

"Tell that to my mother when she looks through me and sees him."

Harm hesitated, hearing the truth in that, feeling the pain. "Jack, Becky loves you."

"I know."

"Then don't make me have to tell her that I let them kill you."

"It's more than just that."

"Then let's talk. This isn't the place. We have hurts to heal between us. Things that have gone unsaid for too long already. We—"

The pressure of his hand was intense, and Jack slipped his over it as he interrupted firmly. "I love you, Uncle Harmon. You have always been there for me. Do this for me now. Please. Speak the words. Let me follow the path I've chosen."

Harm cursed quietly and bowed his head. After a moment, he began to relate Jack's offer in low syllables, his grip never lessening on his nephew's arm.

"Tell Kodene he can use the bounty to buy weapons, to fight their enemies, but he and I both know the time of the Apache is almost gone." That won a lot of agitated murmurs, but Jack continued. "His son will be safe with his mother and his line and his pride will continue. If the boy stays, he will suffer as his people suffer and no one will live to carry tales of their honor. This way, he will live to fight another day." That was one important lesson he'd learned from his uncle. But it no longer applied to him. This was the only way he could fight against the wrongs he'd committed.

"Kodene wants to know why you would exchange yourself for a half-Apache child." Harm met his gaze. He wanted to know that answer, too.

"Tell him I owe Emily a life and a child."

Very quietly, Harm related, "He asks if you have any idea of what they will do to you before they take you below the border to trade."

Jack gave a dry laugh. "I'm trying real hard not to think about it, but tell him yes. And tell him I have your blood, the blood of his people, so they needn't worry that I won't supply them with plenty of pleasure and power."

Harm repeated the words, his voice growing gruff and guttural. "He says you are a brave fool."

Jack looked the Apache in the eye and smiled thinly. "Tell him thank you."

Kodene turned away from them to bark out a command, and soon an elderly woman brought forward a small child. Jack smiled in spite of his dire situation. Kenitay was a sturdy boy with Apache features and green eyes that regarded the goings on with curiosity rather than alarm. Jack reached out his hands and the woman reluctantly gave him the child.

Jack took a moment to hold the boy close, despite the way the child began to wiggle in protest. This was Emily's son, a child they might have raised together had circumstances been different. A swell of tenderness rose up inside him as he breathed in the fresh scent of yucca and young skin.

"Take care of your mama for me," he whispered into the black hair, knowing the boy didn't understand him. Then he handed the child to Harm. He repeated the words to his uncle, "Take care of Emily for me."

Harm accepted the boy with the ease of a man who was a father, but his eyes were on his nephew. "I will." Then he spoke to the child in a calming voice, telling him in his own language that he was taking him to his mother. Kenitay looked up at Harm trustingly and put his small arms about his neck, apparently satisfied with the explanation of why his father allowed him to be given over to strangers.

Jack looked at the two of them for an emotion-crowded moment, then added, "And I release you from your vow of vengeance against these people for whatever they might do to me."

Harm took a quick breath and murmured, *sotto voce,* "I will not let you linger long."

Jack was hearing Foster's screams, and he swallowed hard. "I'd be obliged to you for that." It was then he realized that Harm would soon be gone and he would be alone to face the horrible fate he'd prescribed for himself. He struggled to shore up his courage. He refused to appear afraid, but he told Harm with a meaningful intensity, "I hope to God that you're a good shot."

"Trust me. I won't let you suffer." He put his hand to the back of Jack's head and pulled him tight against his free shoulder, hugging hard, clutching tight, then letting go. "I am proud of you."

Jack supplied a faint smile, then drew his ranger star from his pocket, pressing it into Harm's hand. "Give this to Will. Tell him I tried to wear it as well as he did."

Harm nodded, his fingers clutching the badge until the edges of it drew blood.

"And tell Neil that I never meant for things to happen the way they did, and that—"

A sudden loud cry interrupted the rest of that as an Apache brave swooped down upon them on horseback. Caught by surprise, they had no time to react. The arc of the brave's war club caught Jack above the right eye, nearly smashing his skull. Harm grabbed him up as he staggered back, reeling, bleeding fiercely from the split in his brow. Kodene leapt forward to snag the warrior's bridle, shouting at the man in unrestrained fury as Jack went down to his knees, sagging in his uncle's embrace. He was barely conscious when Kodene approached them, all stiff apology. Harm relayed the words as he worriedly examined the wound. It was a nasty one.

"He says he is shamed by Ahkochne's actions, but that the man lost his wife and son to your rangers."

Jack nodded, the ache in his head growing tremendous from the move. He hung on to Harm, struggling to keep his senses clear. "I understand." His voice was a ragged whisper.

Harm looked up and met the seething warrior's glare. He pointed his little finger at Ahkochne and his thumb to himself, then made a slashing motion across his throat. The brave tossed his head in contempt.

Knowing his strength was failing fast, Jack gave a feeble push away from Harm and the boy. "Go now."

"Jack—"

"Harmon, go now. Please."

Harm's hand fit to Jack's cheek, staining red with his blood as his palm moved in a gentle caress. Then his uncle rose up and strode for the horses, not looking back. Jack watched him go, smiling slightly, grateful for the daze of pain that took the edge off his fear. He floundered for a moment and managed to get his feet under him, standing with a wobbly dignity.

Harm mounted, holding Emily's son, Kenitay, in front of him. His heart was so heavy, it hurt to breathe. He wondered how he was going to ride away. He wondered how he would pull the trigger to mercifully end his nephew's life. But he knew he would do both things. He gathered up the reins and jerked them hard to one side, holding the leads to Jack's sorrel in the other hand. And as he started away, down that long, winding canyon, he heard a savage cry rise up behind him, a cry of retribution. Twisting rapidly in his saddle, he was in time to see Ahkochne's war lance driven into Jack's body with such force that its tip tore through the back of his jacket.

Emily spent the day trying to think of nothing beyond the reunion with her son. She looked past the worry, over the fear, to the joy of holding her child again. Amanda stayed close, chattering ceaselessly as a sign of her own anxiousness. She, too, was watching the yard, but if Emily caught her at it, Amanda would pat her arm and say confidently, "Harmon will bring them back."

Then her smile would fade and she'd go back to watching the yard.

Emily forced her mind to think about the future. When Jack came back with Kenitay, then the three of them could have a life together. If a man could be accepting of another's son, Jack was that man. He had the goodness of heart and generosity of soul to embrace her half-breed child. And he would have an understanding of what the boy would go through because of his own uncle, because of his own past. She wouldn't go back to Neil. She would see about getting a divorce. She and Kenitay would have Jack Bass. And he would be good to them.

She was washing the supper dishes when Leisha's cry rang out.

"Mama, Daddy's back."

Emily let the plate fall carelessly into the soapy water and ran for the front door, drying her sudsy hands on her skirt. As she pushed out onto the porch, Amanda grabbed her by the arm, jerking her to a halt.

"Emily, wait."

But Emily had no patience with the flat caution in Amanda's voice. She saw no farther than the child perched upon Harm's saddle and she raced out, sobbing joyously. Her son! She lifted eager arms, and Harmon settled the boy into them. Only after she'd hugged and thoroughly kissed the child in maternal abandon did she think to glance around, then up at Harm in confusion. A confusion that turned to the beginnings of a horrible understanding.

"Where's Jack?"

Again, her gaze flew frantically about, but Harm was alone. Then she looked up at him, really seeing him. His features were expressionless. His black hair had been chopped off by his own blade until short and unevenly ragged, and he smelled of sage smoke—signs of Apache mourning that Emily refused to recognize. And even when Harm said it, she didn't want to believe.

"He is gone."

"Gone," she repeated blankly. She drew a quick, spasming breath. "Where's Jack?"

But Harm nudged his horse ahead, leaving her standing out in the yard alone, her child clutched to her breast, her wild gaze searching the trail he'd traveled. With a terrible cry, she sank to her knees.

Amanda caught the reins to Harm's horse. Her anguished eyes were on her husband's face, trying desperately and to no avail to see beyond the tight Apache facade.

"Harmon? What happened?"

"The one who was called Jack is gone."

He was dead. That was as close as Harm could come to saying it.

Amanda watched him swing down off his horse. She touched his arm, but he didn't respond. Without looking at her, he started toward the creek. She stood in a quandary, looking between her husband and Emily, torn between the want to help them both deal with their pain and her own great sense of loss and disbelief. She let Harm go for the moment. He seemed to be coping, considering. But Emily was huddled over her son, shaking with shock.

"Leisha, Emily's son's name is Kenitay. He's about the same age as you are. Could you take him inside and fix him something to eat and drink?"

"Sure, Mama." The girl's solemn gaze was on her father, but she did as she was told, coming to take the little boy by the hand. Emily hung onto him for a moment until Amanda knelt down beside her, touching her shoulders.

"He'll be all right, Emily. Leisha will see to him."

So Emily's hands dropped away and she watched Amanda's daughter lead her precious son to the house, speaking to him in familiar Apache gutturals. Then everything came apart inside her.

"Jack," she moaned. "Oh, God, he can't be dead. He can't be dead." Her eyes lifted to Amanda's sympathetic gaze, begging her with that teary look to tell her there had been some mistake. "He loves me, Amanda. He wants to marry me. He's going to be good to me and Kenitay. Oh, Jack! Oh, God, what am I going to do?"

Amanda held her, crying her own silent tears because she'd loved Jack, too. Because she was thinking how it would feel if it had been Harmon who hadn't returned to her. But Harm was safe.

And Jack was not coming back.

Harmon finally came in when it grew dark. Emily was sitting in the parlor rocker with Kenitay asleep on her shoulder. She didn't glance up when Amanda rose from the nearby sofa to see to her husband. Wordlessly, Harm let her lead him to the kitchen, where she washed Jack's dried blood off his hands and tried cautiously to pry the truth from him. It wasn't easy.

"Did he suffer?"

"No. It was quick."

"Was it Emily's husband?"

"One of his band. I will settle with him."

"Did you bury him?"

"Just the horse. Burned everything else. He won't be poor on the other side."

Knowing her husband's inbred fear of the dead, she asked gently, "You couldn't bring him home?"

He closed his eyes momentarily, summoning the will to overcome his distress. "They're taking him to Mexico for bounty."

"Oh, Harmon." She leaned into his shoulder, but he didn't embrace her or offer comfort. He wasn't able to. "Please don't tell Emily that."

A small hand fit into Harm's and he glanced down dully at Leisha.

"Why didn't Cousin Jack come with you?"

He bent down so their eyes were on the same level and

told her gravely, "You must not speak his name again. He is gone, and it would be bad to invite his ghost to return with the call of it."

"Then why are you crying? I didn't think you liked him very much."

Harm drew a soft breath and placed his hand over his heart. "I loved him. I will always hold his name in here. You should do the same."

"Leisha, it's time for bed," Amanda instructed quietly.

The girl's arms went around Harm's neck for a tight hug, her childish voice quivering with upset. "Don't cry, Daddy. You still have all of us to love."

"And I do, *shijii,* but a woman wails and a man cries at such a time. There is no shame in it. It is to honor those who are lost and to free those who remain."

He let Amanda lead his daughter away, unable to move for long minutes as trails of dampness streaked his face.

Emily tried to sleep, but there was no comfort in the small presence beside her. A four-year-old boy was not the ranger sergeant whom she loved. Her heart and mind still couldn't absorb the enormity of his loss. After being isolated within herself for so long, she couldn't imagine not knowing the gentleness of his smile or the searing sweetness of his touch. Or the bright promise of a future with him in it. Without him, there was nothing. Nothing but Kenitay. If it hadn't been for her child, she would have ended her life upon hearing the news. Part of her died with Jack. But now she was denied even that bittersweet sacrifice.

Her soul was a well gone dry. And when she heard a similar echo of despair on the warm spring breeze, she responded with a shared spirit of misery. Leaving Kenitay sleeping soundly, she went downstairs and out onto the porch, where she found Amanda wrapped in a bed quilt, sitting on the steps. The pregnant woman's shimmering stare was held by the figure kneeling in the yard. It was Harmon singing Jack's death song; half-wail, half-exultation, moaning with grief and howling for revenge. It was only in times of crisis and loss that an Apache expressed full emotions, and Harm's were raw and aching for relief.

Without a word, Emily touched a hand to Amanda's shoulder, then she went out across the yard to where Harm rocked in the throes of his bereavement. She knelt down beside him, letting the sense of sorrow swell. Harm didn't object to her intrusion. His hand went out, his fingers curling about hers in a crushing grip, joining their spirits, though he didn't look at her. And she began to mourn for Jack, her desolate weeping playing harmony with his low, undulating wail, until they were leaning against one another in search of solace. And there they stayed until morning.

Amanda made them coffee when the sun came up. There was little else she could do except tend the children and suffer for their pain. Finally, she lumbered out to where they sat. Harm looked up at her through eyes dry and red. Emily was asleep against his shoulder, clearly exhausted. Amanda eased down on the other side of him and he took her up in the curl of his free arm, ready to accept her tender compassion, now that the wracking ritual of grief was done. He returned her gentle kiss and held her close, rubbing his cheek against her soft golden hair. She spoke to him quietly.

"Rebecca is supposed to stop by today. I'll tell her if you like."

He nodded.

Just then, an unfamiliar little voice broke through the silence, a child's voice calling in Apache for his mother.

Emily jerked into wakefulness and stumbled up, heading for the house. Amanda watched her go, her tender heart twisting.

"Oh, Harmon, what are we going to do about Emily?"

"I told J—I promised to care for her."

"She could be carrying his child."

That casual statement brought Harm rearing back in surprise. Amanda smiled at him sadly.

"Oh, Harmon, don't be so naive. They were in love with each other."

"But she—"

"Is a woman. How long would you have stood off the temptation?"

"Forever."

Amanda rubbed his narrowed lips with her thumb. "I don't recall that being the case. Leisha was a very quick nine months."

"That was different. I—"

"What?" She waited patiently, but he could come up with no answer to that argument other than the truth.

"I was too in love with you to care about honor or anything else."

She kissed him. "Come in for some breakfast and we'll talk to her."

But Emily had her own ideas.

"I need to go back to Neil."

"What?" Amanda choked out the word. "Oh, Emily, you can't."

"To tell him about Jack. I owe him that much, at least. Jack was his friend. He's still my husband. Perhaps he'll be more forgiving—"

Perhaps not, Amanda concluded to herself. In the last six years, she'd come to know the men of Texas and their rigid moralities. No Texan, no ranger, was going to welcome a half-breed child. Jack was the exception. She was about to point out the obvious when Harm spoke up.

"I'll take you to him."

And Amanda was immediately suspicious of her husband's toneless offer.

"I have a message for him," Harm continued. "You can ride along."

Amanda looked between the two of them, not liking the idea of either of them making the journey. "At least, leave Kenitay here. It's a long trip for a little boy, especially when the outcome is uncertain. You'll make better time, and you'll want to speak to your husband alone. We'll see he's well cared for, Emily."

Emily hesitated. She saw through all the varying shades of Amanda's offer. Her chances with Neil would be better without the evidence of her liaison with an Indian. If Neil would not accept the boy and she decided to stay with him, the Basses would keep Kenitay for her. And it would be a good home, perhaps better than any she could provide him. But having just been reunited with him, she was reluctant to be separated from the only thing in the world she loved. Until Amanda said gently, "We'll care for him as if he were our own."

Then Emily nodded. She looked to Harmon. "When will we leave?"

"How soon can you be ready?"

"I'm ready now."

He gave her a long look. She was ragged and weary, about as torn up as he felt inside, but he understood her need for haste, the need to get it all behind her. And he admired her for it. "Finish up and we'll go."

And as she readied for the ride, Amanda confronted her husband.

"Harmon, why are you going to see Neil Marcus?"

"I told you, I have a message for him."

She regarded him narrowly. "How do you plan to deliver it? On the point of your knife? Did you think by having Emily along that I wouldn't guess what you were planning?"

Well, he'd hoped so. But it would seem his wife knew him too well.

When he wouldn't look at her or argue that, she grew afraid. Fear stripped away the need for pretty words. She put it plain. "Harmon, are you going there to kill him?"

"I gave you my word."

Yes, he had. For Jack's sake. And now Jack was dead. She wasn't sure what to make of his word now. But she did recognize the savage tension within him, the darkness of mood, the fierceness of purpose. He was going hunting. What more could she say? She started to gather up the breakfast dishes and he grew quiet watching her. Until he saw the dampness pooling in her eyes.

"Ammy—" He took her arm and she tried to pull away. Very gently, he drew her up against him. "I love you. You are my life. But you know who and what I am, just as I know what I must do, even if my heart is here. It's my soul I must satisfy. Can you live with the things it calls me to do? Tell me again that I can come home to you."

She leaned back to look up at him, her face tearstained, her expression hard as West Texas. "Do what you have to do. Do it quick and clever so no one can trace you. And come home to me."

Nineteen

Rebecca Bass stood on her brother's front porch, her son's ranger star clutched in her hand. All evidence of her weeping had been wiped away, but sorrow etched deep into the lines of her face.

"He was saying goodbye to me. I didn't know, Amanda. If I'd known, maybe I could have stopped him. There must have been something I could do. Something I hadn't done. Something he needed from me."

Amanda stepped up behind her, rubbing her hands over her sister-in-law's tense shoulders. "You can't blame yourself, Rebecca. Jack and Harmon, they carry their wounds buried deep. Men like that need something we can't give them. They need something they find on their own, a sense of personal honor, a sense of rightness with their soul. I don't know—something. All we can do is wait and hope and love them."

"But you changed Harmon."

Amanda laughed softly. "I didn't change Harmon. I gave him a place to belong, a place to come home to, but nothing's different. I've been able to keep him safe here with me only because he had no temptations. But once something starts eating away at men like him and Jack, they can try to push it away, to pretend it doesn't exist, but sooner or later, they have to act on it. They can't stand the confusion.

They need things clear cut, and that's why Jack did what he did. He couldn't face what had been done to you and Harmon, and he couldn't live with what he wanted from Emily. He couldn't find a solution for either of those things, so he took care of them the only way he could—with self-sacrifice and violence. The same way Harmon does, and Will, and all those other stubborn West Texas fools."

"But what you did for Harmon—"

"I did nothing for Harmon except make him feel better about who he is. He still carries around all his old demons. And they flare up the second he's put back in the same situations."

Rebecca caught the edge in her voice and glanced sharply at her sister-in-law. "Amanda, what's happened?"

"Harmon's found another of those men." She saw Rebecca pale and continued unhappily. "All his nightmares are back, and his fear of the dark and of being indoors. He hasn't slept through the night for months now. The children are upset, I'm upset, and he's half crazy. I couldn't help him, Rebecca, and now he's gone to help himself to Neil Marcus."

"Emily's husband?"

"Harmon's going to kill him."

"Does Emily know?"

Amanda shook her head. "She's with him."

"With who?"

"Harmon."

Rebecca grasped her arm with a sudden intensity. "Are you saying that Neil Marcus's wife is out there in the desert, alone with Harmon? Oh, my God."

"Why? What's wrong?"

"What's wrong? Harmon is Apache. He thinks like them,

he reacts like them. The Apache code of retribution has been ingrained in him since he was a baby."

"I know, but—"

"Neil Marcus raped me and my mother, tortured us, then killed her. To avenge the women in his family, an Apache man would strike at the women in the other man's family first, to do to them what was done to his."

Amanda remembered Harm telling her that, but she didn't understand—

"Amanda, Harmon is somewhere out there alone with Neil Marcus's wife."

"No." Amanda shook her head to deny the suggestion. "Harmon wouldn't."

But she'd seen—she'd *seen* the terrible things he was capable of in the name of revenge. Against men. Not helpless women. But Jack's death had shaken him, pushing him even further into the precarious despair he'd been walking with. He'd been too long without sleep, too long without everything that kept him on an even keel. Ordinarily, she'd swear he'd never hurt a woman. He was a man with children— daughters. And he was so gentle with her. But if anyone were to touch her or one of the girls . . .

"Oh, Rebecca, he couldn't." Then her gaze lifted in a panic. "Could he?"

Rebecca was looking out over the harsh land, her features carved into the same unyielding lines. "An Apache would. Without thought. Without remorse. I wish I could say I didn't think my brother could do that. I wish I could, but I can't. I know he *could*. I just don't know if he *will*."

Amanda stood helpless. If she hadn't been so far gone with child, she would have mounted up and ridden out after him, to save him from that strain of viciousness he'd inherited. But she couldn't; she could only stand and pray that he was too civilized for such ruthlessness, that he wouldn't risk what he had with her. But she'd promised—hadn't she?—that she would accept him back no matter what he did. Rape and murder of a woman had never occurred to her when she made him that vow. He wouldn't be motivated by lust or the need for violence, but by a simple fact of duty.

And Harmon Bass was an honorable man.

Amanda wondered with a dreadful anxiety if she could let her husband come back to her if he took his revenge through Emily Marcus.

"Where are we going? This isn't the way to Ysleta."

Emily had been studying the landscape for some time and she was certain they were heading farther into the Bend, south instead of west.

"I have a stop to make first. It won't be a long delay. Just a debt to settle."

"With whom?"

"With a man who stole something very precious from me."

They were heading toward the Mexican border.

"Are you after the one who killed Jack?"

"He acted without honor, so I am freed from my vow."

She had no problem with him seeking retaliation. She had no desire to see the man who'd taken Jack from them go unpunished. So she rode on with Harmon Bass, as somber at heart as he was as he began to track the Apache southward.

They camped near the river in some of the most explosively beautiful country Emily had ever seen. At another time, under other circumstances, she might have appreciated it. But she was numb to her surroundings as she made a fire and cooked up what Harm provided. Then she sat in a morose silence with the one man who probably had loved Jack as much as she did.

She watched him. He seemed well recovered from his grief. Or at least, he'd hidden it deep. He stared into the fire with an intensity as hot as the flames. And she knew she should pity the man who'd slain Jack Bass, because Harm was going to kill him ugly. But she didn't feel sorry. All she felt was frustration and undirected anger. Mostly, she was angry with Jack. How could he have risked himself so foolishly? If only she'd known what he'd intended. She would never have allowed the sacrifice. Not for anyone, not even her son. She'd have longed for her child, but she'd have known he still lived. Now, she could only mourn for Jack. And it was so unfair. How could Harm have allowed it, loving him as he did?

"Why didn't you save him?"

Harm glanced up. The firelight reflected in his eyes, giving them an unnatural brilliance. "He didn't want to be saved."

"What are you saying? That he went to the Apache knowing he would be killed?"

"Yes."

That stunned her and made her all the angrier. "Why? Why would he do such a thing?"

"Because of who he was. And who you were."

"You're saying this is my fault?"

"No. Not yours or his. I know whose fault it is, and I'll settle with him soon." And his eyes glittered, one minute hot steel, the next cold metal. He stared at her until she felt uncomfortable. There was something very big behind what he wasn't saying.

"I don't understand."

"Twenty years ago, a group of men invaded my family's ranch, killing my mother, raping my sister, leaving me for dead. Jack was fathered by one of those men. And you are married to another."

Emily stared at him, for a moment at a loss for words or even argument. Then, she gasped, "What? Neil? I don't believe you. You're mistaken."

Harm's smile was slow and sinister. "Oh, no. I'm not mistaken. You don't forget a man who does those kinds of things to your family." And his gaze flared hot as he sat, remembering. His features were all harsh angle and shadow when he looked toward her. Again, his intensity gave her a shiver. And his next quietly spoken words gave her reason for a deeper dismay.

"It's good Jack died before finding out what kind of a man his friend was. I don't think he could have forgiven me for what I must do. I'm not even sure Amanda will." Then his expression went rigid. "But he's got to pay, and it's my right and my duty to see that he does."

Harm surged to his feet so suddenly that Emily shrank back in alarm. He stalked away from the fire, into shadows as dark as those within his soul. Emily stared after him, confused and shocked. Neil . . . she didn't want to believe it, but it made too much sense. It would explain too much of what she knew of him. And it surprised her that she wouldn't feel denial more vehemently. Except deep down inside, she knew Neil was capable of what Harm suggested. What she didn't understand was why Harmon would take her along when he was planning to kill her husband.

Unless that wasn't all he was planning.

She hadn't lived with the Apache for five years without learning their ways. She never accepted them, but she knew them. And revenge was what they knew best. She was no stranger to their methods of getting it. Unlike the Mexicans, the Apache didn't rape their female captives. They felt it improper to sexually mistreat women. Unless it was to avenge a wrong, and then they were unbelievably cruel.

Harmon Bass was going to kill her. Eventually.

She sat paralyzed for a long moment. Her gaze scanned the darkness nervously. No sign of Harm. They were miles and miles from anything, from anybody. From any help. And she was at the mercy of a man half-crazed by his thirst for vengeance.

There wasn't a lot of time for reasoning or rationalization. She could either wait to find out exactly what he had in mind, or run far and fast while she had the chance. She had a son waiting for her, a future watching him grow into a man. Emily wasn't about to lose that. She wasn't ready to die out here in the desert without seeing her child again. She had no intention of suffering for Neil Marcus's sins.

Quickly, silently, she slipped away from the fire and dashed for the horses. She wouldn't bother with a saddle. Jerking the tether loose, she went up on the gray's back and from out of the darkness came a quiet, "What are you doing?"

Emily lashed back with her heels, startling both Harm and her horse into jumping. Harm snatched up the animal's lead, commanding it to stand. With a desperate cry, Emily leapt off the other side of the gray and ran straight out into the night. It was a frantic flight. She knew she couldn't outrun him, just as she knew she wasn't strong enough to fight him or well armed enough to kill him. But she had to try.

She had gone fifty yards when Harm grabbed the back of her waistband. She screamed and stumbled, taking them both down hard to the ground. She tasted dirt and felt his weight stretched out over her, pinning her. She knew what would come next. Too stunned and scared to do more than sob for breath, she let him roll her onto her back, her wrists imprisoned by the cuff of his fingers, her hips straddled by legs like tensile steel.

"What the hell's gotten into you?" he was shouting, breathing as hard as she was.

"Please don't do this. You can't do this." Terror and a terrible anticipation reduced her words to a panicked quivering.

"Do what?"

"Don't rape me. Don't hurt me."

Harm went slack with surprise; then she could see the flash of his wry smile. "Ma'am, my wife would frown on me running around doing those sorts of things, and I try very hard not to rile her unnecessarily these days. She's a mighty tolerant woman. She'd put up with a lot of things, but that's not one of them."

Emily took a hitching breath and ventured, "You're not going to kill me?"

"Hadn't planned to. Might choke you, if you don't tell me what the Sam Hill set you off running like a jackrabbit with such nonsense in your head."

"You said you wanted revenge on Neil."

"Oh, yes, ma'am and I—I see. And you thought—oh."

He relaxed his grip on her just a little. When he spoke, his words were steeped in sincerity.

"Emily, you listen to me. I might fillet a man and stake his raw flesh out over an anthill, but I would never, ever hurt a woman. I could never do that, Apache justice or not. I couldn't. So you just take it easy and I'll let you up. I give you my word, I won't hurt you. In my heart, you are like family. You were loved by one I loved, and I promised to keep you safe. That vow is sacred to me. All right?"

Emily nodded weakly. Harm eased back and she sat up, shivering nervelessly. "But you're going to kill Neil."

"After I settle with Ahkochne."

"Then what happens to me?"

"I'll take you home with me." He looked very uncomfortable for a moment, then asked her, "Could you be carrying Jack's child?"

"Yes." She refused to act ashamed. Then she realized he was more upset about the subject than the circumstance.

"If that's so, and I hope it is, you will be of our family. If not, you may stay as long as you like. You and Kenitay will be welcome. It would have been his wish. Now, come back to the fire. I won't do anything improper."

Those words tore through her in a way his big blade couldn't. She made a soft sound of pain and she found herself clinging within the embrace he offered. She hadn't believed she had any tears left, but there was a sudden flood that had to be cried out.

And Harm held her, not saying anything. Because he understood pain and mourning better than he understood anything else.

Finally, Emily found the strength to wipe her eyes and lean away. And she asked what was puzzling her. "Why did you let me come with you? Aren't you afraid I'll give Neil warning?"

Harm smiled thinly. It was a frightening gesture. "I would just as soon he know I'm coming."

Despite all that preyed upon her heart and mind, Emily slept deep and wonderfully well, waking to a cool, misty morning and an odd inner calm. The ache of missing Jack wasn't gone, but it was absorbed throughout her, making the pain easier to manage than when it was concentrated with such a wrenching ferocity within her heart. She knew it was a pain she would never lose, just like the loving was something that would never fade, but she would adapt, and she would go on because she had a child to think of. Perhaps two. Jack's child . . . the idea pleased her tremendously. She would pray that it was true. That would make her future so much easier; a reminder of the man she loved, the Bass family to belong to.

Harm was already up seeing to the horses.

"Good morning."

"Coffee's hot. Help yourself, then let's get moving."

She poured and watched Harm's quick, efficient movements. "Will we catch up to them today?"

"Yes. Then I'll find someplace safe for you, while I do what I must." He wasn't going to offer a ringside seat to the killing. That was all right with Emily.

She hadn't decided how she felt about Harm killing Neil. She knew she should feel something, but the emotions were clouded and not easy to ascertain. She didn't love him, had never loved him, but she owed him a certain loyalty. He was her husband, but that didn't necessarily make him a good man. She remembered too clearly the weight of his hand and the flame of his temper. And she wondered if she would ever be safe if Harmon didn't take his revenge. She and Jack had undercut his pride, and a man like Neil didn't let that go. Jack was beyond his retribution, but she feared her husband would exact that payment upon her. Out of principle, not from any feeling. He would make life with him living Hell.

And wasn't Hell what he'd put the Bass family through?

"You drinking that coffee, or telling fortunes in the grounds?" Harm wanted to know.

What she wouldn't give to know her future. "I'm ready." She dashed the rest of the cold coffee onto the fire.

They came upon the Apache band around noon. It was a broiling day, and a dust cloud followed the southward movement of horses and travois. It made them easy to track. Harm allowed Emily to stay with him as he worked along the perimeter of the procession, seeking its weakest spot and the warrior Ahkochne. Finally, he nestled down along a ridge, stretched out on his belly like a sunning snake to watch and wait. Emily lay beside him, trying not to look upon the people passing below as family she'd lived with for five years. It was hard when she knew most of them by name. And she knew Ahkochne, the brave that Harm meant to kill, as an arrogant man, but a strong and clever warrior. She hoped Harm would choose to pick him off with his carbine rather than challenge him hand to hand. Harm was wiry and tough, but Ahkochne was brutal.

Suddenly Harm came up on his elbows as if he didn't care if he was in full view of those below, had they chanced to look up. He was staring, his breath gusting from him noisily.

"Harmon?"

He didn't respond. He seemed frozen.

Emily grabbed at his shirt sleeve, jerking him down. He dropped flat, burying his face in his hands. Worried, she touched his shoulder. He was shaking. A low, strange sound was muffled within the cup of his palms. It sounded like— like wild laughter. Emily withdrew a bit, wondering anxiously if he'd lost his mind. His bizarre behavior and the tears she could see wetting his face when he finally lifted up had her truly alarmed. He answered her perplexed gaze with a wobbly smile and pointed toward the Apache caravan. She followed his direction, not understanding, looking along the string of warriors until her puzzled stare touched upon a slumped figure lashed atop a scruffy pony. Then her breath pulled in sharply. Harm's hand sealed in her cry of disbelief before he dragged her up to his chest for a rough embrace.

It couldn't be . . .

Then she was hugging Harmon about the neck, sharing his tears and his silent joy, because somehow, miraculously, Jack Bass was still alive.

It wasn't the pain that tormented him; he'd grown numb to that. It was the thirst. The awful dryness and ache swelled up in his throat and made even breathing a chore. He was so hot. Sun baked him on the outside, fever from the inside. He felt like a brittle bit of jerky.

He couldn't believe they'd let him live. Mature men were always killed when captured. Perhaps they figured he posed no danger. Or perhaps they were so hungry, they needed the extra thousand dollars his breathing would bring.

He wasn't sure how long it had taken him to come around that first time. Harm was gone. It was dark, and he hurt bad. His head felt like a blacksmith's anvil, ringing from impact. He couldn't see out of his right eye and wasn't sure if he'd been blinded, or if swelling had sealed the eye shut. Ahkochne's lance had gone clear through his shoulder, and as long as he didn't move, it caused him surprisingly little discomfort. But it was hard not to move. He was on his knees, his hands lashed behind him, a thong about his neck tethered to them so that if he bent forward, the rawhide choked him. It was not like he was going anywhere, anyway.

He had to lift his head to look around, and that wrought a price that was dear to pay. He was on the outskirts of the camp, for the most part ignored, except for the single guard assigned to him. He could see their fire burning brightly and wondered why he wasn't hanging over it. He knew they could keep him alive for a long time without coming close to killing him. Maybe they were afraid he was already too far gone and didn't want to risk the loss of bounty. Fine by him. At least the Mexicans would hang him quick and be done with it. Or maybe they'd try to ransom him for Bragg's release. Then Neil could kill him for running off with his wife. There was a thought, and it kept him busy while misery ravaged him. So many pleasant options.

He wondered if Emily was even now holding her little boy. That made him smile to himself, and it was worth the pain the tug of facial muscles caused him. He had damn little to be grateful for at the moment. Was Harm out there somewhere, waiting for the opportunity to kill him? It didn't much matter if it was here in the Apache camp, or at the end of a Mexican's rope. Soon would be nice. Soon, Harmon.

A figure approached, and he saw it was a woman. Alarm prodded through him, but he was too weak to act upon it. He'd heard Apache women were more bloodthirsty than their men and that captives were often turned over to their fiendish care. He'd heard of men being chased through camp with their hands tied behind them while the women ran after them with axes and knives and finally rode them down on horseback, impaling them on their spears. That gave him something else to think about as the woman came to kneel before him. Had she lost a loved one to the rangers, too? He felt too bad to be more than just mildly curious. He wasn't afraid.

But the feel of cool water against his face was a surprise. She was very gentle, and he was confused by her kindness.

Sometime later, another woman came. This one tended his shoulder wound, washing it, smearing it with a cooling salve, and packing it tight. When he managed a hoarse, "Thank you," she merely nodded and hurried away. His guard made no attempt to halt their attentions. One brought him water to drink, one fed him from her fingers. Another carefully bathed his face. He couldn't figure it out.

"You are spoiled, for a prisoner."

Jack slit a glance up at Kodene. "You speak English." It was a raspy accusation.

"Some. I was taught by reservation missionaries."

"Why are they doing this?"

"You do not recognize them?"

"No."

"They know you. They say you are the ranger who freed them from the Mexicans and took my woman even after those pigs had her."

"Oh." And now they were returning the good deed. That made sense.

Kodene squatted down so they were eye to eye. Jack was at a disadvantage there. He could hardly see at all. The Indian seemed puzzled. "You are not like most rangers. They say to us, 'Go or be exterminated,' yet you saved our women."

"My uncle taught me respect for your people."

"Ahhh. Bass. He walks well with us."

"He'll see to your woman and son."

Kodene nodded, satisfied by that arrangement. "And when the People grow strong again, I can always go steal them back from him."

Jack gave him a faint smile. "Thought you learned your lesson with my aunt's horses."

Kodene laughed and straightened. "A shame to have to let you die, Ranger."

A shame it may have been, but not so great that it halted their exodus to Mexico. The camp packed up early and began to move. He was loaded onto a pony and tied there to keep him from falling—ridiculous to think it was to keep him from escaping. Time was reduced to the bob of his body in rhythm with his horse's stride. He was beyond thought, beyond care, beyond pain. And when they stopped for the night, he stayed where he fell, unable to eat or swallow the water he was given. He was going to save the Mexicans the trouble of hanging him. He was dying by gradual degrees.

It was a dream; he was sure of it. He opened his eyes to the sight of Apache moccasins and heard a soft voice saying his name.

It sounded like Harm.

A broad palm fit to his face and a sturdy shoulder nudged under him for support. Jack leaned loosely.

"Uncle Harmon?"

"Shhhh."

A tremendous relief flowed through Jack. The comfort he drew from his uncle's presence was indescribable. Harm had come to see to his word. Just in time. Jack viewed the gleam of his big knife blade as his salvation.

"I'm hurting in a real bad way, Uncle Harm. Make it easy for me." And he rolled his head back along his uncle's shoulder, exposing his throat to simplify the task.

Harm gave a quick pull of his blade, separating the strands of Jack's bonds.

"Nothing's easy, Jack. I've come to take you home."

Twenty

It was taking forever.

Emily stood with the horses, her anxious gaze scanning the field of darkness for any sign of movement. Her heart was beating in frantic anticipation.

Even watching as carefully as she was, Harm's sudden appearance near her elbow startled her as he moved in from the night like a ghost. Then Emily gave a quiet cry.

"Jack! Oh, Jack!"

Her arms flew about his neck and she was kissing him desperately, over and over, as he sagged within the circle of Harm's support. It didn't matter to her that he was too weak to respond. What mattered was the warm feel of his breath, the taste of his dry lips, the heat of his fevered skin. He was alive.

Harm grabbed her shirt collar and hauled her off.

"Later."

Emily stood back, panting and trembling. Then she gained control of herself and gave her love an appraising study. One side of his face and the area around that eye were grotesquely distorted. His shirt was drenched with dried gore. He looked like Hell. He looked wonderful. He looked as if he had no idea of what was going on.

"Can he ride?" Emily asked dubiously.

"He's gonna have to."

"Put him up with me, then. I won't let him fall."

"C'mon, Jack. Up you go."

Jack lifted his foot obligingly. It wobbled about in mid-air for a moment, aiming at nothing. Harm gripped him by the trouser band and heaved him up onto Emily's gray, holding him in place. She scrambled up behind him, winding her arms about his slumped figure, grabbing up the reins and kicking back her heels without waiting for Harm's instruction. She didn't need it. They were running for their lives.

They pushed the horses and themselves, riding hard through the night, pausing at dawn to let the animals blow. Harm prowled the perimeter of rocks restlessly, watching behind them. He'd slipped into and out of the Apache camp with Jack without calling attention to himself. He'd left the guard bound and gagged in the shadows. There was no telling how long he'd go undiscovered. And when they found Jack gone, they'd be in pursuit. The only question was whether or not they could be outrun. There'd be no hope in fighting them off. Harm wasn't one to consider odds, but in this instant, if he had, he wouldn't give them a spit-in-the-wind's chance of making it without being forced to make a stand. And if caught out in the open, all three of them would die. Because he wasn't about to surrender Jack up to them. And he didn't think Emily would, either. As much as he hated to bring trouble to his family's door, he could see no other way around it.

Below him, Emily sat crosslegged on the hard ground, cradling Jack's head and shoulders in her lap. She was stroking his face, speaking to him softly. She didn't know whether or not he heard her. He was slipping in and out of a fragile consciousness.

"Don't you dare die, Jack—not after all this. I love you.

We're going to be together. We are. And we'll be so good to each other."

"Emily."

She looked up through a glaze of tears to see Harm's silhouette framed against the rising sun.

"They're coming."

Her fingers clutched reflexively in Jack's shirt. "I need a gun."

"You need to get mounted up and as far from here as you can. I'll hold 'em."

"Harmon—"

"I don't want to lose him, either. Just do what I tell you." Emily nodded.

"C'mon. Help me get him up on my horse. You'll make better time if you're not doubling."

"What about you?" She was levering beneath Jack's slack weight, pushing while Harm lifted.

"I got two good feet. Take him to my place and tell Amanda I'm on my way. Tell her to batten down tight." He shoved Jack up into his saddle and began to lash him down like a sack of goods. Then he paused, his hand resting atop Jack's head. "Tell her I love her."

"You tell her when you get there," Emily challenged, as she swung aboard her mount.

Harm smiled up at her and nodded. "Get going. Don't stop for anything." He slapped his palm down on the rump of her horse, and by the time she glanced back, he'd already disappeared.

And about fifteen minutes later, she heard the first sound of gunshots.

* * *

"Amanda, two riders coming in. Hard and fast."

"Who is it, Sarah?" Amanda reached down for the Winchester she kept propped next to her broom in the kitchen. She started for the front of the house at a graceless waddle, one hand pressed to the small of her back.

"Looks to be Emily and Uncle Harm."

Emily and Harmon. Amanda gave a gust of relief, all her overwrought worries of the past few days expelled in an instant. He hadn't. . . . She should have known. She should have trusted in the man she'd married. But why were they back so soon? They couldn't have gotten very far. Then Sarah shouted the answer, and it purely terrified her.

"Amanda, he's hurt."

She broke into an ungainly run, panic tightening about her already constricted lungs. By the time she reached the porch, she was wheezing. Sarah was racing out to meet the two riders, hurrying around the horse Emily led by the reins. Then there was a moment of tense silence and the girl's shrill cry of, "Jack!"

Amanda grabbed onto one of the support posts, weaving dizzily. Not Harmon. It wasn't Harmon; it was Jack.

Jack?

Emily slipped out of the saddle and rushed to where Sarah was already loosening Jack's bonds. Jack's sister was sobbing freely, touching him, kissing him, as if unable to convince herself that he was real and here. Between the two of them, they managed to ease him down from the saddle and drag him up to the porch.

"Oh, my goodness!" Amanda gasped. "It is Jack! Get him out of the sun. There, on the swing. I hope you're going to explain all this to me, Emily. How bad is he? Sarah, quick, get some water."

Emily sank down to her knees beside Jack's still figure,

unwilling to leave him even for a minute, and briefly described how they'd found and freed him while Amanda opened his bloodied shirt to check his wound. It was oozing, but not badly. The shock of travel had probably put him into worse danger. That and the fever. With rest and care, if they could get the fever down, if there was no infection . . .

"And Harmon?"

Emily was tormented by the memory of gunfire as she looked up at the pregnant woman. She made her answer vague, lessening the magnitude of Harm's act. "He stayed back. He said for you to burrow in and wait for him."

"We've never had trouble with the Mescalero before." But Amanda was practical. She was mentally inventorying all the firearms they had on hand. Two women, a girl, three children, and a half-dead ranger. Some defense. But then, when Harmon got back, the odds would even out. Harm Bass was better than any ten armed men.

Suddenly, a cry went up from Sarah, and the women on the porch jerked around to see her cut off between the house and the windmill by several mounted Mescalero braves.

"Sarah, don't move!" Amanda yelled to her.

As silent as spirits, two dozen more riders drifted into the yard, ringing the house with a bristle of rifles and lances. Amanda went to the edge of the steps, hissing to Emily, "Keep the children in the house until I find out what they want."

Just then, one of the warriors cantered through the circle, riding right up to the porch. Over his pommel, Amanda could see the drape of denim-clad legs and moccasined feet. Her world started to whirl even as the brave reached across to grip a handful of raggedly cut black hair, lifting and carelessly slinging the body of her husband to the dirt at her feet before he rode back to line up with the others.

Amanda's legs went out from under her. She felt the hard bump of the top step beneath her and the jar of impact knocked his name from her lips.

"Harmon."

"Daddy!"

Emily grabbed up Leisha Bass as the child shot out of the house.

"Hold her, Emily," Amanda said vaguely. "I don't want her to see."

She didn't want to see, either, but she had to know. Amanda edged down the steps, breath jerking from her. The threat of the Indians was completely forgotten. Six years . . . was that all she was to have? Just six years with him? She could see blood on his shirt. Oh, God. On her knees, she moved up beside him, touching him with shaking hands.

"Harmon."

She reached for his averted face, turning it toward her, swallowing down her sob of horror as she saw more blood, a river of it, streaming from where a jagged furrow creased him just above the ear. A gash, not a hole. It took a long moment for her to comprehend what the difference was. Until Harm groaned softly and began to stir. Then she lay her head upon his slow-moving chest and shuddered with a desperate gratitude, looking up only when another horseman approached them.

"I am Kodene. Your man, Bass, he is too good a fighter. We could not afford to lose any more horses to him or to wait until he started aiming for our men. He is a hard man to put down, but it was not our wish to see him dead. I would have you know this."

As hard as it was to be charitable with her husband bleeding on the ground, Amanda managed a stiff, "Thank you for bringing him home to me. Sarah, I need that water."

"Get outta my way," the girl growled fearlessly at the Apache blocking her path. She smacked her palm into his horse's shoulder and the animal shied violently, nearly upsetting its rider. She took advantage of the distraction to hurry across the yard.

The first touch of cold water shocked Harm into wakefulness. He blinked slowly, focusing in on Amanda's smile, responding faintly with one of his own as awareness gathered. Then his blue eyes snapped wide open. He twisted and rolled onto hands and knees with the suppleness of a cat, then moaned mightily, clutching at the side of his head, swaying into the quick support of Amanda's arms.

"Easy. Easy, Harmon. Take it slow."

"Jack?"

"He's all right. He's up on the porch. I was just getting ready to talk with our guests."

He lifted his gaze with obvious difficulty to assess their situation. He remembered picking his shots from behind an outcropping of rock, bringing down the horses of their pursuers. Had they been a passel of white soldiers or Mexicans, he could have stood them off for hours. But the Apache were a wily foe, well matched for his skill. They scattered, becoming vague and brief targets to draw him out so they could fix on his position. That was all right. It gave Emily and Jack time to get to safety. He heard just a shuffle of sound, looked up, and felt as if half his head had been blown away. Apparently, that had not been the case.

They'd shown him an unusual mercy by bringing him to Amanda alive, but they were far from out of danger. They might have let him live, but that didn't mean they were willing to let him get away with what he'd done. He'd snuck in beneath their defenses, then shamed them by stealing a captive out from under their noses. They wouldn't take that kind of thing lightly without dealing out some sort of lesson. And Apache lessons were harsh, oftentimes fatal.

"What do you want?" he demanded of Kodene, showing no fear even as he huddled at the man's feet, injured, unarmed, and defeated. At least for the moment.

"The ranger. He is ours."

"No. No more. That coyote there has broken the vow of faith." The warrior Ahkochne stiffened at the insurmountable insult as Harm glared at him, then continued. "We will not give him up to you."

"Who will stop us from taking him?"

"I will."

"I will."

Emily's voice came as a strong second. Kodene looked to her narrowly, frowning at the sight of her hovering over the motionless ranger. Then he turned back to Harm.

"It is a matter of debt. You understand these things, so why do you argue against them?"

"I see no debt." In a low aside, he asked, "Help me up, Ammy." Once on his feet, he faced the warriors squarely. "You have killed one ranger and wounded this one."

"He led an attack upon women and children."

"And warriors. It was a fair exchange."

"He took my woman."

"She walked away from you. You have no claim here."

Kodene glared up at Emily and at the small boy now huddled into her skirts. He could feel the anger of his people demanding that he take action. As did his pride. "There are those who say I do. Give me the ranger and we will ride out. Try to hide him behind your woman's skirts and

I will have your whole family slain right before you. This you know we will do. Is that what you want?"

"No!"

That wobbly cry came from Jack. He spilled off the swing onto hands and knees, then pushed away Emily's hands to drag himself upright. "Don't hurt them. I'll go with you."

"No, Jack." Emily clutched at him frantically. "No, I won't let you. I'd rather die here than lose you again."

He tried to struggle free but was far too weak. Emily restrained him, pulling him back, where he collapsed upon the swing, panting shallowly for breath while she positioned herself in front of him, ready to fight the Apache, to keep him safe.

"You took the boy. It is our right to take him," Kodene restated firmly. "Are your words untrue, Bass? Have you been white too long to remember how to keep vows once spoken with honor?"

"No," Harm argued. "My word is always good. I've forgotten nothing. It is your right to demand satisfaction for your losses. But not with his life. And not with my family's blood. I'll make that payment to any who feel they have been wronged."

He felt Amanda's hands bite fiercely into his arms, but she didn't speak. Gently, he set her aside and began to strip off his shirt, using it to swipe the blood from the side of his face. Then he cast it away and drew his big blade. He pointed the tip to Ahkochne. "I'll start with you, Son of Many. Get down and face me like a man, if you are one."

His slur was met with a roar of fury and the brave leapt from his horse's back, stripping down to his loincloth for battle.

"Go inside, Amanda."

"No," she argued. "I won't leave you." And Leisha came

to tuck in beside her, looking up at her father with the same stubborn expression. What was a man to do with such willful women?

He bent down to kiss his oldest daughter, smiled at Becca, who clutched at Emily on the porch, and then embraced his wife. Amanda clung to the hard contours of him, stroking his bared skin, her facade brave, her eyes wide with fear.

"I love you, Harmon."

It was then that Ahkochne decided to strike.

Catching the movement from the corner of his eye, Harm quickly angled his body to protect his wife and child. The warrior's blade scissored across his ribs, opening a thin line of red. Harm countered with a vicious backhanded blow to the other man's face. Ahkochne's nose smashed flat from the impact and he stumbled back.

Pushing Leisha and Amanda to a safe distance, Harm turned to address his foe with a seething fury. How dare the man attack with his family so close at hand, placing them in danger? He glided easily out into the yard, where he'd have greater room to maneuver. He made slow figure eights in front of him with his blade, beckoning to Ahkochne with his other hand.

"You have my attention now. C'mon, you *cabrone*. I'm ready."

But Harm's words were stronger than his ability to back them. Weakened by loss of blood and still dazed by the head wound, he wasn't as fast as he should have been. He managed to keep away from the flashing knife, but the Apache landed several massive blows to the head and body until Harm was plainly staggering, shaking his head from side to side as if to clear it. His timing was poor, his power ebbing. And at the threshold of their home, his wife stood watching, impassive as any Apache after purposefully turning their daughter's face away. Her lips moved faintly in what might have been a prayer, but Harm knew what she was whispering.

Harmon, be careful.

And so he was, crouching low to be a more difficult target, jabbing out fiercely with tightly controlled arcs of his blade, circling with the bigger, fitter Ahkochne, planning his moves and retreats with a deadly precision. Even so, he was drawn off by a feinted swing and was driven to his knees by the force of the Apache's fist against his temple. Ahkochne had an instant lock on him, one arm crooked about his neck from behind while his other brought his knife into play.

Harm lashed back with his head, smacking his enemy full in the face, but it wasn't enough. He dropped and rolled, yanking the other off balance, escaping the choke hold but leaving himself splayed out on his back and vulnerable. Ahkochne dived in with a victorious war cry, lunging upon the downed man with the plunge of his knife. It was a cry cut short as he found himself impaled upon Harm's blade.

Harm heaved the dead man off him and swayed up to his feet. His breath was chugging with exhaustion, his eyes blinking to clear the sweat and fog of faintness.

"Who else?" he cried out, staggering as he surveyed the silent horsemen. "Who else would have a claim upon my family?" Weak as he was, there was no mistaking the fact that he was still a dangerous man. His grip on the dripping blade was strong, and the fire in his stare hadn't dimmed. And the Apache were impressed. What an honor, to be allowed to kill such a man in battle. "No one? No one among you?"

Then, slowly, Kodene came down from his saddle.

"No," Emily called out. "No. I'll go with you." Purposefully, she didn't look behind her, where Jack was sprawled out on the swing, unaware of all that was happening because of him. "Kenitay and I will go back with you if you'll ride out and leave these people alone. He can't fight you. He has nothing left to give."

"I have plenty," Harm drawled out, assuming an aggressive stance. "I'll give you a good fight."

"But you will not win," Kodene stated with grim conviction.

"We'll see."

Harm started to shift to one side, and to his horror, his legs wouldn't support the move. His knees buckled and he was forced to shuffle quickly to catch himself. But the weakness just kept swelling, ignoring force of mind or dire circumstance. He had nothing left to give but heart, and Kodene was about to carve that out of him. He wobbled and went down on one knee, bracing his forearm atop it as he gulped for air. Kodene drew his blade and began to advance upon him in quick, fatal strides. It was then that Amanda decided she'd seen enough.

"No more!"

She flung herself between them, her arms going about her husband so that her body was a shield. Harm tried to pry her away, but even that was too great an effort.

"Amanda, no. Get away. Please. Ammy—"

She wrenched the knife from his slack hand and turned awkwardly to confront the big Apache. It should have been an amusing sight, a woman huge with child brandishing a blade as if she could actually defend her man against such a superior force. But the blaze in her eyes said she would do her best until her last breath.

"Enough," she declared, holding Harm behind her. "How

will your honor be served if you kill him? Will it change anything? Will it bring back any of those who've died? No. It won't. It'll mean more killing. Jack will come after you, and after him, his brothers and the other rangers, and they will kill you or you will kill them. Then who will feed your families? Who will give your wives children when you are all dead?"

She paused, panting furiously. The Indians held back, not sure what to make of her tirade. The ones who knew English muttered soft translations to the others. Then all were silent. Kodene had halted his advance. He had no desire to slay a breeding woman any more than he wanted to murder the noble Harmon Bass. But honor was at stake and atonement had to be made. Then Amanda continued.

"You say we've wronged you. I say if we have, we are sorry. We have been friends to the Mescalero for years. Harmon's blood mingled with yours long before you sought it with your knife. He is of your family. No justice is being done here. What are you fighting for? To get back a woman who doesn't want you? What man wants to keep a woman who prefers another? You speak of the women and children the rangers killed in an accidental crossfire. I say Jack gave you back the women of your band when the Mexicans took them. If payment has to be made, it won't be in blood. Too much of that has been shed already. This ground is red with it. The mountains run with it. If you want payment, take something that gives life."

Harm was leaned against her back, his head heavy on her shoulder. She took his hand and brought it around to press the palm down over her belly.

Not unmoved by the sight, Kodene murmured, "What would you give?"

"I have one hundred and twenty-eight head of fine

horses, enough to carry your people and feed them through the summer. Take them and go in peace as our neighbors. Let our dead find rest."

Kodene thought a moment, then he glanced back to see how the rest of his followers received that offer. They looked inclined to accept. It was a good deal, offering the survival of many—the small, the old, the weak, who had no other to provide for them.

And his pride could not stand keeping a woman who didn't want him.

"The payment is fair. We will take one hundred horses."

Amanda let Harm's knife fall from her hand and she turned to hug him tight.

"Ammy, the horses—"

"Are just horses, not pets or family. You told me that once. I can get more horses; I can't replace you."

She took his face in her hands and kissed him hard, breaking off halfway through it to pant heavily. Her fingers were clutching his.

"Ammy, what's wrong?"

"Well, Harmon, if all the talking is done, I think I'd better go inside and have this baby."

Twenty-one

Randall Bass entered the world to a strange audience. His mother barely had time to lie back on her bed before he made his appearance. He was delivered by a runaway wife while her lover lay unconscious on the porch below, while his father kept silent company in the front yard with two dozen Apache that minutes before had been ready to kill him. When the baby gave his first lusty yell, the cry was answered by those in wait, and moments later he was carried by his beaming cousin to be placed in his father's arms.

"A son," Sarah claimed.

And Harm lifted the child high to proclaim it proudly. Shouts of congratulations greeted the news then his guests filed away, taking with them one hundred horses and a vow of friendship.

Because he didn't trust his strength, Harm gave the boy back into Sarah's safekeeping so he could go up to his wife. Amanda greeted him with a smile and the stretch of open arms, and he sank into them, into her kiss, murmuring, "Ammy, *shijii,* I am so proud of you today, my warrior wife."

She smiled, but her concern was for him. She touched his temple with gentle fingertips. "Are you all right, Harmon? That looks so sore. Let me get up to tend your cuts."

"No, Ammy, I'm fine. You rest."

"Harmon—"

He compromised. "I'll rest with you. You've given me a beautiful son."

"He looks just like his father." She edged over and coaxed him down beside her, urging him to curl up close. When his dark head pillowed on her shoulder, Harm gave an expressive sigh, and by the time it was fully expelled, he'd surrendered up his awareness of all. And with her husband within the circle of one arm and her new child in the curve of the other, all was well in Amanda Bass's world.

Watching them, Emily was tormented by a bittersweet longing. Twice she'd borne children, but neither time to such a gladsome circumstance, into such a surrounding of family love. How different would it be if she was to bear a child with Jack Bass?

She walked out onto the porch. Her son was standing at the edge of the steps, looking out uncertainly in the direction his father's people had taken. When he looked up at her through great green eyes, she gave him a reassuring smile, wishing she felt as easily comforted as her small, trusting child.

She went to sit beside Jack. He was her future, and it was far from secure. How was she supposed to feel safe with a man so torn by guilt that he would surrender himself up to a horrible death to ease the pain of conscience? How could she become such a burden to the man she loved?

It was cool.

That comfort was the first thing Jack noticed: the absence of heat from inside and out. When he opened his eyes, the fact that he could see out of both of them was the second thing. His confusion over where he was and how he'd come to be there was overshadowed by the sight of Emily Marcus at his bedside. She was curled up in a chair, her head tipped at an awkward angle as she slept. Nothing else mattered for a long while, except that he was alive and she was with him. He edged his hand out from under the sheet that covered him until his fingers brushed over Emily's where they rested slackly upon her thigh. His curled hers within them. And he enjoyed the feel of her waking beneath his touch, of her hand turning, tightening about his before she was even aware of it.

"Jack."

He tried a smile. It didn't hurt too badly. " 'Morning." His voice was hoarse and faint. "Or is it evening?"

She looked about, not sure herself. "It's morning." Then she leaned forward to stroke her fingertips along his stubbly cheek. It was the most wonderful sensation. "How are you feeling?"

"Surprised to be breathing."

Emily withdrew. It was a slight thing. Her hand pulled away. She sat back in her chair, and a remote look settled in place of other emotions. "I'm sure you are. You did your best to see it otherwise."

He wasn't certain how to answer that, so he glanced about and murmured, "Where am I?"

"Your aunt and uncle's. We brought you here. Don't you remember?"

"Not much." He closed his eyes and tried to bring the memory back. He remembered Harm with Kenitay, and then the sudden impact of Ahkochne's spear. He remembered the pain and thirst. The sound of Harm's voice: *I've come to take you home.* Emily's kisses. Apache in Harm's front yard.

He gave a slight gasp, his gaze flying open. "Is everyone all right?"

"Enjuh. All is well."

Emily stood and moved aside as Harm came to touch the back of his hand to Jack's forehead, cheek, and neck.

"Your brain fever is gone. Good."

Emily slipped from the room before Jack could protest, so he settled for his uncle's company. He gave Harm a curious look. "That's an awful haircut."

Harm put a hand self-consciously to his close-shorn locks and smiled wryly. "I'll be happy to let it grow."

"How long have I been here?"

"My son is a week old today."

"Son?"

"Randall. For Amanda's brother." He looked uneasy, not comfortable with using the name of the dead, but it had been so important to Amanda. And he couldn't deny her anything. To appease him, she'd altered it from Randolph to Randall, and he was getting used to it.

"What else have I missed?" Something big. He could tell by Emily's cool mood. "Kenitay?"

"Is here. A fine boy."

"And the Mescalero?"

"They're satisfied." He didn't mention the horses. In his mind, it was a good trade. No sense disturbing Jack over it. "The one who acted dishonorably toward you, I've slain," he concluded matter-of-factly.

Jack stared at him. He knew incredible understatement when he heard it. He could see how gingerly his uncle moved and the remnants of a healing wound at his temple, and wondered what the fight had cost him. It was hard to believe the same man who'd claimed not to want to know him less than two weeks ago had come close to giving up his life to save him. And that reminded him of other un-finished business.

"Uncle Harm, I made a big mistake, breaking my word to you."

Harm halted the rest of his apology by pressing his thumb to Jack's mouth. "You were wrong and I was wrong. I'm at peace with it now. Say no more. You rest and I'll do the same while the baby's sleeping." He smiled thinly, but with an obvious fondness. "The boy talks as much as his mother."

"Harmon?"

"What?"

"Thank you." Great sentiments, expressed with powerful brevity and answered in the same fashion.

"You're family."

Family. Jack absorbed the strength of that notion and con-centrated on his recovery. It took him time to work through all that had happened, piecing together action with conse-quence until he could reorder it into something he could live with. His falling out with Harm, the killing of Cathy Marcus, the days with the Mescalero—he managed to put them aside as painful events. And as he came to terms with each thing, the focus of his thoughts narrowed and chan-neled into one specific area: Emily and Neil.

What was he going to do about Emily?

He loved her. He'd made love to her. And yet he was no closer to possessing her. The longer things hung unsettled and unsaid between them, the more the tension mounted. There wasn't a time when he awoke that she wasn't with him, sitting in that chair beside his bed. He didn't know when or where she slept. However, the minute he tried to draw her into conversation, she found some excuse to leave. And he chafed in her absence. He didn't know what was wrong. He didn't know how to fix it. He lacked the strength to grab onto her and demand she give him some answers. Perhaps she didn't owe him any. Perhaps her self-imposed distance was an answer in itself.

Now that her son was with her, had she no more room in her heart for him?

He liked the boy. Kenitay was inquisitive and feared nothing. He'd come up and perch upon the edge of the bed to regard Jack through lively green eyes as if to ask where he fit into his mother's life. Jack wished he had an answer. He was growing less sure by the day. He started to teach the boy English, and once the lessons began, he was popping up every few minutes to ask the name of the thing that brought up water from the ground, of how to describe the color of the sky and clouds, of how to interpret Becca's shy words of friendship and Leisha's curt orders. He was plainly awed by Harmon, but it was Jack he felt close to and comfortable with, and he spent hours each day stretched out across the foot of his bed, demanding words for everything in sight.

There was where Emily invariably found him, with one or both of them asleep, and it seemed to trouble her no little bit.

What was he going to do about it?

He was healing fast. Each day his strength was flowing back, taxed only by a visit from his family. His mother's tears were like torture to bear. She tried to talk him into returning with them, but he insisted that he was still too weak to travel. That wasn't true. He didn't want to leave the safety of his uncle's house. It had become a buffer to returning to the rest of his life, where nothing was certain. As long as he lingered abed, there was no pressure for him to make the decisions preying upon his mind. And if his body was rapidly mending, not so the confusions of his heart. His mother gave him back his ranger star, reminding him that he was betraying his friend and captain by keeping his wife from returning to him, and Jack was tormented because he didn't want to do anything to remedy it. He couldn't let her go and he couldn't deny his own conscience by keeping her.

"So, how long are you going to lie about my house?" Harm's blunt question forced Jack to consider that which he'd been trying to ignore.

"Have I overstayed my welcome?"

Harm smiled. "I could never have enough family under my roof. That's probably why I agreed to this mansion, so I'd have a place to put 'em. A man is nothing if he's alone."

Jack ruminated on that for a moment, his features reflecting his melancholy until Harm couldn't stand it.

"None a my business, but I seem to remember some big talk about Emily being your woman. When you gonna do something about that?"

"She's got two husbands ahead of me, Uncle Harm. Hard for a man to hold out any hope when he's that far back in line."

"Only if he's content to wait there."

Jack sat up against the headboard and began working his arm at the elbow. The pull against torn muscle still pained him, but he could tolerate it. What he couldn't stand was the pull upon his heart. "What do you suggest I do, Harmon? Blast my way through the other two?"

"Kodene is no problem. Emily has walked away from him. They're no longer married."

"Oh." He thought about that for a moment. One step closer, but still a million miles away. "She's still married to Neil. Walking away isn't gonna change that, and I'm not

the kind of man who can just forget that the woman I'm
with belongs to someone else."

"I'll take care of Marcus for you."

Harm said it so calmly, Jack thought at first that he'd
misunderstood. Then Harm glanced in his direction with a
slow cant of his eyes. The blue of them glittered with lethal
intent. What in God's name had happened between Neil and
his uncle to earn that degree of animosity?

"I thought we'd already discussed that."

"He'd be dead now if I'd gone to Ysleta first. But then
you'd have been dead, too, so I guess I'm glad I waited.
It's just a matter of time, Jack. Just a matter of time."

"Damn it, Harmon! You let me take care of it!"

But Harm only smiled. "He owes me, Jack. It's not something you could handle for me."

"I don't want to step over his dead body on my way to
Emily!"

Harm shrugged. "My way is easier. Cleaner. Final."

"What did he do to you?"

Harm ignored the question. "You talk to Emily. Find out
what's in her heart."

"Kinda hard to do, with everyone coming and going."

"I think I'll pack up my family and head over to Terlingua. Be gone for a couple of days. Baby's old enough to
travel, and I want to show him off to the Lowes. 'Sides,
Ammy's about to drive me crazy with her—" He broke off,
and Jack could swear he was blushing. "Anyway, if you're
smart, you'll make use of the time."

"Harmon?"

"Ummmm?"

"Don't make any sidetrips to Ysleta."

Harm bared his teeth in what might have been a smile

but didn't have the feel of one. "I don't take my kids on hunting trips. Rest easy, Jack."

Rest easy. Harm was out for his best friend's hair and he was stealing the man's wife away. Of the two, Harm's was probably the more honorable intention.

True to his word, Harm had Amanda and the children packed up to go by mid-afternoon. They stopped in his room to say their goodbyes. Becca kissed him shyly, Leisha begrudgingly, and Amanda with a gentle affection.

"You take care, Jack," she fussed, leaning down to touch her lips to the colorful split at his brow.

He grinned at her and glanced toward Harm. "You two behave."

Amanda supplied a smile so wicked, he knew his uncle's plan was useless. She was going hunting, and the nights were long out on the Texas plain. When she walked by her husband, her fingertips grazed down the length of his arm, and Harm was quick to catch at her hand, allowing himself to be pulled along behind her. Jack smiled to himself. She wasn't going to have to work very hard to snare the elusive Harmon Bass.

And as he heard them drive away, he began giving serious thought to going hunting himself.

The house was very quiet. With Kenitay down for a nap, Emily prowled its rooms restlessly. Without the Basses, all distraction was gone. There was her, and there was Jack. And she was nervously aware of it.

She'd have to see him eventually. He'd want his dinner, and it would be unkind of her not to supply it. But how was she supposed to serve up his food when she was so hungry for a different kind of feast? She couldn't look at him without wanting him. She couldn't see him stretched out on that bed without wanting to be in it with him. And as she went toward the kitchen, she came face to face with that desire.

He looked so good for a moment she couldn't tear her gaze away. It was easier to dismiss the potent attraction when he was abed and healing. But standing at the foot of the steps, all mended and wonderfully virile in snug jeans and clean cotton shirt, he was enough to weaken her knees. She didn't want to feel helpless around him—at least, not now. Now was a time to stand by her convictions.

"Should you be up?"

"Should have been up and around a while back. Kinda nice being spoiled, though. Thought I'd come down for supper. Didn't want you to go to any trouble."

Then they stood staring at each other, just dying for the taste and feel of one another, though neither was willing to make the first move toward it.

"I was just going to start dinner."

"Oh. Don't let me get in your way."

But as she started past him, somehow they both got re-routed into each other's arms.

Emily welcomed the heat of Jack's kiss. It was as if he breathed life back into her and seeded it with passion the instant his tongue plunged deep. She moved against him in a way that could leave no doubt. And his response was just as hard to miss. Her hands rubbed over him restlessly, assessing each swell and plain and ridge with greedy appreciation. It was as if she hadn't touched him during these last long weeks. But those had been gestures of care and cherishing compassion. These were fueled by longing and ripe with anticipation, just as she was.

Jack broke from their kiss, breathing hard into his desire,

the taste of it sweet upon his mouth, the need for it beating hard within his chest and pooling with a collective urgency beneath the provocative stroke of her palm. But it was more, so much more, and it always had been.

"I love you, Emily."

She went suddenly still.

Jack nuzzled his face into the spill of her dark hair, fighting down the panic that he was losing her. He didn't know why, but he could feel it, feel her pulling away even as she remained in his arms. His embrace tightened as if to prevent it, and he said again, with a touch more desperation, "I love you, Em."

"You love me."

There was something very wrong with the mocking way she said that, and Jack began to tense all over.

Emily jerked away and glared up at him, her green eyes flashing. "You love me. And I suppose that's the reason you couldn't wait to go get yourself killed."

He looked so blank, she lost all patience with him. All the horror, all the pain and frustration she'd suppressed as he was close to dying in her arms, surged up with a vengeance, demanding to be addressed. And she wasn't about to spare him.

"If you loved me, you wouldn't have done such a cowardly thing."

She turned and stalked away. He heard the front door bang shut behind her.

Cowardly? That's how she saw his sacrifice?

He stood for a moment, panting in confusion, wild with upset. How could she think such a thing? He'd gone to face his fate without a whimper! How could she accuse him of being less than brave? Her words pierced his pride, her actions put a powerful panic in his soul. He couldn't dismiss them lightly, so he went after her to demand an explanation.

Emily was standing out on the porch, her back to him, her posture all starchy and inapproachable. But approach he did. He came up behind her, hurting for the way he could see the tension increase within her stance. He didn't touch her.

"Em, I did what I thought was right."

"Right for whom, Jack?"

"For all of us."

"Really? Oh, yes, I can see how you throwing your life away would solve everything—for you. But what about me? What about me, Jack?"

"I asked Harmon to take care of you." He was insulted to think she would believe he hadn't considered her welfare. But her welfare wasn't what had her so furious.

"Harmon. And was Harmon supposed to lie with me at night and hold me in his arms and make love to me so I wouldn't feel so horribly alone? Somehow, I don't think that's what he had in mind when he agreed to take me in."

"Emily—"

"Did you think that all I'd need was a roof over my head and food on the table? Oh, living here would have been the perfect solution. Your aunt and uncle would have made it a wonderful home for Kenitay. He could have grown up happy while I grew old mourning you."

"Em—"

"Or did you think I'd go back to Neil if you were gone? That he'd let me move right back in, knowing I'd run off after you? That he'd say, 'Oh, sure, bring your half-breed son, and I'll raise him like my own and I'll treat you so good.' Is that what you thought, Jack? Well, you thought wrong.

"I don't want security, Jack. I want to be loved. How much satisfaction did you think I'd find in your grand gesture? Would it keep me warm at night? Would it give me children? Is it something I could grow old with? It almost killed me, thinking you were dead. When Harmon came back without you. . . . How much courage did it take to leave me with nothing but emptiness? How was I supposed to feel, knowing you'd rather die than take responsibility for me and my child, that your pride was more important than our happiness?"

"That's not true."

"Isn't it? Then why were you so willing to give our care over to someone else? If the thought of loving me is such a strain upon your conscience, why don't you just go over there and jump down that well?"

Jack's hands settled lightly upon her shoulders, tightening when he felt the tremors running beneath them. He stepped in closer so she could feel the warmth and strength of him. He could hear her tears in the jerky way she was breathing.

"Emily, I love you so much. I never wanted to hurt you. I didn't know what else to do. I wanted to make things right for everyone, and there just didn't seem to be a way to do it."

"I know you did, Jack." She placed her hands over his. It wasn't a passionate touch. "You're a boy who wants to play at being a hero. You want to fill your stepfather's expectations and live up to Harmon's legend. You're living to please everyone else, and as long as you are, you'll never know what it's like to walk in your own shoes. You've already jumped down that well, Jack. You just haven't hit bottom yet."

And she pushed his hands off her, moving around him without ever meeting his anxious eyes to disappear into the house.

* * *

Dinner was a strained affair. Emily served and Jack ate without ever lifting his eyes from his plate. And Kenitay looked between them in confusion. He liked the soft-spoken ranger. It had taken him awhile to get over his fear of the word "ranger," but the gentleness of the man had finally conquered it. He liked the warmth of his smile, the patience of his instruction, the playfulness of his mood, and the way his pale eyes followed his mother. He'd been afraid when his father and everyone he knew left him behind in this strange house of walls, but he was gradually forgetting all that came before in his excitement of what was coming up ahead. As he looked between his mother and the ranger over that silent supper, the fear was back and he held to his tears as he'd been taught. But he couldn't hold in his worries when he and his mother were alone later that night.

"What's wrong, Kenitay?" Emily asked, as she tucked him in bed.

"Are you mad at Ranger Jack?"

"No." But her eyes shifted downward, and he knew it was not true. Why would his mother lie to him?

"Are we going away? Back to my father?"

"Would you like that?" The caution in her voice alerted him and he was more afraid than ever.

"I like it here."

"It's not our home."

"He who is called Bass said we could stay. I want to. They are nice to me here. The food is good. She with yellow hair smiles and talks much. I like Ranger Jack. He teaches me English. Leisha is wise and Becca is my friend. Can we not stay?"

"No. I don't think so."

"Where will we live? In Ranger Jack's camp?"

"No."

Dampness began to collect in his big green eyes. "We will have no home? No family? Ranger Jack doesn't want us?"

She stroked his hair and smiled gently, sadly. She had no answer for that. Did Jack want them? Yes. Would he make the move to keep them? She didn't know. "He hasn't asked us to stay."

Kenitay glanced down, but not before she saw the first glimmering tear line his cheek. "Is it because I am of the People and he is White Eyes? I have heard they hate us. Does he want me to go away?"

"No. No, of course not. Ranger Jack is not like most white men. Harmon Bass is of the People, and Jack is his family. He doesn't see you as Indian. He sees you as Kenitay."

"I would like to stay with him." He lifted his head, his expression one of somber sincerity. It broke Emily's heart because that's what she wanted, too.

"You go to sleep. I'll talk to Ranger Jack."

"He likes you," Kenitay confided, as he snuggled under his covers.

"I know he does."

"And you?"

"I like him. Now, sleep."

"Ask him if we can stay."

How simple it all was from a child's point of view; how complex from her own. But yes, it was time to talk to Ranger Jack. She and Kenitay could rely no longer upon the Basses' charity. She wanted her own home, her own man.

And she wanted that man to be Jack Bass.

Twenty-two

Jack was standing in the moonlight, looking down into the shadows of the well.

The loneliness of his stance gave Emily pause, but she couldn't afford to soften to it. There'd be a lot worse misery to come if they didn't settle things. She couldn't afford the luxury of time. Jack was a thinking man, one who weighed and studied and pondered, but now was the time to take action. He said he loved her. She had to know how much.

"Not going to jump, are you?"

He gave a quiet chuckle. "Not after all the trouble Harm and I went through to sink it. He'd never forgive me if I was to contaminate his water supply."

"How's the arm?"

"Fine."

He wouldn't look at her. Emily could see the tension working along his jaw and the sudden acceleration of his breathing as his distress multiplied. Knowing she was the cause of it wounded worse than anything she could think of. She had him poised on the edge of a figurative well, and she was going to ask him to jump: either across, to continue his life the way he'd planned it before being stopped by those Apache arrows, or into it with her, where the fall was long, uncertain, and possibly fatal. Part of her needed to push, to know which way he would go, the other to hang on tight to the sureness of what they had, tentative as it was.

She wanted to do the right thing. She was a married woman who'd lost one child to tragedy and had borne another of an Apache. She'd toiled all her life and was scarred by its necessary cruelty. She'd lived among the Indians, had been violated by the Mexicans, had run away from her husband to commit infidelity with his best friend. Jack was a twenty-year-old Texas Ranger, old in the ways of the world, yet so painfully young in matters of the heart. He was struggling with a sense of honor so strong it forced him almost to make an unforgivable sacrifice. She was tearing his world apart, and she had to give him a chance to right it. It had to be his choice. He was so young, with so much ahead of him. If he took in a wayward wife and half-breed child, nothing would ever be the same for him again. Her biggest fear was that he would regret it. And she couldn't live with the idea of his remorse. She'd rather live without him.

"Jack, I'm taking Kenitay to Ysleta."

He jerked as if she'd plunged Harm's big blade into him. After a moment, he asked, "When?"

"Tomorrow. Before Harmon gets back."

"Oh."

She waited, her breath suspended, her hopes teetering on what he would say next, but he said nothing. She couldn't blame him. It was an opportunity for him to back away with dignity. It was a long fall for a man his age. She'd been asking him to give up everything. It was too much. She understood, and she would let him go. Because she loved him too much to insist he make a mistake that would ruin his reputation and his self-respect. Those things were important to a man wearing a ranger badge. Hadn't she learned that from Neil?

"Thank Harmon and Amanda for me. They've been very gracious with their home and in all they've done for me. I'll tell Neil you were sidelined by an Apache lance but that you'll be back with the company as soon as you can make the ride. He should accept that without too much question because he'll want to. Well, I guess I'll go turn in. It's going to be a long day tomorrow."

Jack stood there listening to her words, words that absolved him, that would allow him to return to his ranger life without stain, words that severed all obligation. He heard them and felt a whisper of relief as he let her walk away. Now he could go back to ranging, to being Neil's trusted friend, to being a good man, to . . . nothing.

What was wrong with him? What was he thinking?

"No."

He grabbed Emily by the arm and yanked her around. She looked startled and so beautiful with her eyes sparkling like green bottle glass.

"You're not going anywhere without me. You're mine, Emily—you and that little boy in there. I fought for you, I almost died for you, and I'm not giving you up to anyone!"

She surrendered with what sounded like a sigh to his savage kiss and encouraged a dozen more with unashamed eagerness. Then her hands were tugging his shirt tails free, pulling up the fabric so she could push her palms in next to the crisp mat covering his belly. His right hand was meshed in her hair, twisting to take up the slack so he could angle her head with the slightest movement to meet the downward slant of his as they continued to kiss wildly out in the Basses' front yard.

"Oh, Jack, I love you so much. I want you so."

Her breathless words inflamed him but when he tried to

gather her up more completely, the shock of pain in his shoulder made him wince.

"Jack?"

"I'm fine."

She was mouthing hot kisses along his throat, and his pulse rate was going like crazy.

"Jack?"

"Ummmmm?"

"Are you strong enough for this?"

His hand spread wide to cup her bottom, dragging her up against him and rubbing hard with a lusty impatience. "I'm not strong enough to resist it."

"Then don't." Her hands dropped to his belt.

"Em—Emily, don't you think we ought to move this inside?"

Her fingers were spearing inside, next to the heat of his body. He groaned. "Who's going to see?" she challenged huskily. "The moon, the stars, a coyote or two?"

"Your son, if he looks out the window."

"Oh." She withdrew her tormenting hands and let them run restlessly up and down his chest, as teasing as her next words. "Kenitay says you like me."

"I do like you."

"I told him I like you, too."

"Show me how much."

She grabbed him by the belt and started hauling him toward the house. He didn't balk at being led. They made it as far as the porch steps. As she stood a step above him, Jack turned her to face him and the hungry kissing started up again.

"Here's fine," he growled with a low urgency.

Jack pressed her back into one of the support posts and began hiking up her skirt and petticoat. It was an awkward business with one hand, but he didn't let it handicap him. When he had them waist high and she felt his palm caressing her, Emily went practically mad with need. Stretching her arms overhead so she could grab onto the post for balance, she hooked one leg over Jack's hip and around his waist, tugging him in tight against her ready heat. He needed little encouragement to fumble briefly with his Levis. Then he was thrusting up hard, devouring her gasp of welcome with an open-mouthed kiss.

Theirs was a short, rough ride, full of precarious pleasure to a stunning destination. Their hoarse mating cries eased to soft sighs of shared wonder, and for a long moment they stood, hearts and souls joined. Jack was leaning full length against her, the pinch of his fingers around her bared thigh slowly relaxing until she could lower her leg in a long caress down his. Then she just held him, enjoying the rhythm of his laboring chest and the weight of his head atop her shoulder. She kissed his auburn hair gently and murmured, "You'd better sit down before you fall down."

He nodded in agreement and let her tug him over to the swing. She settled first, then coaxed him to stretch out over the top of her so he was cradled within the spraddle of her legs, with his head upon her breast in a comfortable huddle. He was relaxed to the point of bonelessness. She adored the angles of his face with the ridge of her knuckles.

"Jack?"

"Ummmm?" He didn't open his eyes.

"I'm going to divorce Neil."

There was a short pause, then his quiet, "All right."

"I have plenty of grounds. The whole camp knows he's practically living with that woman. We haven't been—intimate since my return. And then there's physical and mental cruelty."

Jack gave a start of surprise and twisted to look up at her. His features were drawn into a frown. "You didn't tell me that he hurt you." It was almost an accusation.

"It doesn't matter now."

"He'll never have the chance to do it again. You file. I'll stand by you."

"Jack," she cautioned gently, "it could get very ugly. He could countersue, charging abandonment and adultery."

She felt him tense up at that, then he said, "Let him say and do whatever he wants. He had his chance to be a good husband to you. Now it's my turn."

Emily drew a quick breath. "Jack—"

"I want you to marry me, Em. I want to be your husband and a father to your little boy. I want us to be a family. All I've wanted my whole life was to belong somewhere. I want to belong to you."

"Jack—"

"I love you, Emily. Please say you'll have me as soon as things are final with Neil."

It was hard to be practical when her heart was beating wildly with joy. "Jack, it could take a while. As much as a year."

"I don't care. I'll wait. As long as I've got you to look forward to, it'll be worth it. Marry me. They say the third time's the charm."

And it was just as hard to be optimistic. "What if Neil makes trouble?" she asked anxiously.

"I'll convince him not to." That was said with gritty promise.

Then Emily's resistance gave way with a sigh. "I love you, Jack. I want to spend forever with you."

"Then be my wife."

"I will."

Ignoring the quicksilver agony it sent coursing through his shoulder, Jack drew her into his embrace, kissing her long and thoroughly, with a boyish exhilaration that had her smiling against his moist lips.

"Oh, Em, I'll make you a good husband. I will. I haven't had any experience in it, so you'll have to tell me what's expected."

"I've been married twice and I never knew anything about love until you. We'll learn as we go along."

"Sounds good to me."

And as they lay curled together skin to skin up in Jack's bed, he kissed her again and murmured, "If you can wait until Harmon gets back, I'll take you to Ysleta."

Emily frowned slightly. "I don't know, Jack. You being there might just cause more trouble."

"If there's trouble, I aim to be there for you. I'll be resigning from the rangers."

"Oh, Jack—"

"It's all right, Em. Cal Lowe offered me a deputy spot if ever I should want one. Might just take him up on it. It's not like I'll have a problem finding work after running as a ranger for four years."

He said that modestly, but she knew it was true. She kissed the bare flesh of his shoulder and started to believe things could work out.

"And while we're waiting for things to end with Neil, I think it's better we not live together."

"What?" Emily came up on her elbows to glower at him. "What do you mean?"

"I mean I want us to go about this as honorably as possible. I don't want anyone to have a bad thing to say about you. And . . . and I want you to have some time to yourself to make sure that . . . that you want me."

"Oh, Jack, I'm sure now." Then her eyes narrowed. "Aren't you?"

He chuckled softly. "Em, I was sure the minute you climbed up on that Apache pony behind me after cutting those arrows outta my leg. I'd have gone through Hell for you from that second on."

She stroked his beloved face gently. "And you have, haven't you?"

"I want you and Kenitay to stay here with Uncle Harm and Amanda. That way, I'll know you're in good hands and I won't have to worry about you. They won't mind it. They won't be needing this room for at least another nine months. And it'll give me reason to visit home more often."

"I'll miss you, Jack, every second we're apart."

"Good."

"Jack?"

"Ummmm?"

"Do we have to start being respectable now?" She eased her knee across his thighs and followed until she was astride him. Her breasts grazed the furring on his chest. Her lips nibbled along his jaw.

"We can start in the morning, if you'd rather."

"I would."

And she settled up and over him, riding slowly, steadily toward mutual ecstasy.

Jack woke gradually, soaking up the feel of Emily in the curve of his elbow, of her softness half draped over his chest. She was a warm, lush armful, and something other than lethargy began an immediate stirring—until he opened his eyes to the curious stare of her son.

Kenitay was sitting cross-legged on the foot of the bed,

observing them with an all-too-knowing smile. Jack adjusted the covers a notch higher, feeling his color rise apace.

"G'morning."

Kenitay nodded his dark head.

"Up kinda early, aren't you?"

"You and my mother are friends again?"

"Yes, we are. Hope that's agreeable to you?"

Kenitay smiled and nodded with more enthusiasm.

Just then, Emily gave a luxurious stretch and Jack tightened all over in a misery of restraint.

"Ummmm, Jack—"

"Look who's here, Em."

She blinked and glanced in the direction he nodded, giving a gasp. "Young man, what are you doing in here?"

"I came to say hello to Ranger Jack, and I thought I'd wait and say hello to you, too." He looked between them and she could see the beginning of confusion, as if she and Jack together excluded him. Emily smiled to reassure him and spoke to him in the tongue of his people.

"Kenitay, what would you say to having Ranger Jack for your father?"

The boy regarded Jack candidly. "I like him. Would I have to give up my own father?"

"What did he ask?" Jack prompted. When Emily told him, he met the child's worried stare and answered in a slow English. "No, you would not. You will always be your father's son. But you would be my son, too."

"And my mother?" he asked, haltingly.

"Would be with us as my wife." When Kenitay looked perplexed, he simplified it. "She would be my woman."

"Ah." He nodded and smiled wide. "I would like that, Ranger Jack."

"Good. And it's Jack. Just Jack." He beckoned with his

hand and the boy scrambled up between the two of them, nestling into a hollow between their bodies. And Jack had never felt such satisfaction as within those cozy covers with the two he'd grown to love more than his life.

They spent the next two days as if the three of them were family. Jack was strong enough to see to light chores around the ranch, and Kenitay was his self-appointed shadow. When he wondered where all the horses had gone, Kenitay explained they were now belly timber for his father's camp. As they sat to Emily's meal, she explained what had happened and eased away the furrows of concern on Jack's brow with a gentle kiss and a vow that everyone considered it a good trade. And she further convinced him of it when they lay in bed that night by loving him lavishly until he was lost to all but pleasure. When they were through, they dressed and Emily opened the door so Kenitay would feel free to come in. The boy had no difficulty accepting them together. In his eyes, they were already wed. A tremendous price of horses had been paid for his mother, and he was very proud. To him, the moment Jack invited them under his protection, all was binding. Of course, he knew nothing about Neil. That he never would have understood.

But Harm did. He understood everything as he paused outside Jack's open bedroom door, seeing his nephew tucked in nose to nose with the lovely Mrs. Marcus, both of the them blissfully asleep.

"Guess he took my advice," he whispered over the bowed heads of his daughters.

"Good advice," Amanda murmured back, her eyes taking on a lambent glow as she nudged up against her husband's lean flank. "Put those children down and come to bed, Harmon. I want to know exactly what you told him. In detail."

"Yes, ma'am."

* * *

It was the enticing scent of coffee that woke them.
Coffee?

Jack and Emily exchanged bewildered looks, and they
were quick about dressing and getting downstairs. They
turned into the kitchen to the sight of Harmon with his
back to them. He was standing up close to the table, and
all they could see of Amanda was the knot of her bare
ankles at his belt line and the twist of her fingers in his
short black hair. They must have been involved in some
pretty intense communication, because even Harm's sharp
Apache hearing failed to pick up the intrusion until Jack
cleared his throat diplomatically. Harm jumped back but
Amanda refused to release him, hanging about his neck and
peering over his shoulder with a sultry smile.

"Good morning. Didn't know you were awake."

"Obviously," Jack mumbled.

"Ammy, get down," Harm muttered fiercely, and she finally allowed him to pull her away. By then he was blushing
and bulging like a newlywed. "You got no manners, little
girl. We have company."

"I'm sure I didn't embarrass *them,*" she chided naughtily,
as she rubbed the dampness of her kisses off his narrowed
mouth. He was scowling, but his arm remained curled pos-
sessively about her waist.

"Well," Harm drawled out, as he eyed their two guests.
"You two sure made yourselves at home while we were
gone."

That did embarrass Jack, but his fingers laced through
Emily's and he proclaimed, "Emily and I are getting married . . . as soon as she gets a divorce."

"Oh, Jack! That's wonderful news!" Amanda hugged him tight and supplied a warm kiss.

Harm wasn't quite as boisterous, but he was no less pleased. He nodded to them both. "You'll be good for each other. It's a fine match. Welcome to our family, Emily." He embraced her in somber Apache fashion, then Jack.

"Well, now, if you'll all get out of my kitchen, I can bring out some breakfast and you can tell us everything." But when the three of them started out at her order, Amanda snagged the back of Harm's jeans. "Not you. I could use some help, Harmon." And her bare foot was rubbing over the top of his.

Looking amazingly stoic in the face of such tantalizing seduction, Harm mumbled, "You two make yourselves—"

"At home," Jack finished for him. He grinned. "Take your time and give Amanda all the help she needs."

"Sassy kid," they heard Harm grumble, as they went into the dining room.

As they were finishing up Amanda's overcooked breakfast, there came a ruckus from upstairs as the children discovered each other, then a loud squall from Randall Bass as his rest was disturbed. Amanda went up to him, chasing the older batch down. Kenitay came right to Jack, climbing up on his lap to bestow an affectionate hug. When Emily gathered up dishes and took them to the kitchen, Harm followed her in.

"He'll be good with the boy."

Emily glanced at the part-Apache tracker. "Yes, he will be."

"Not many men would be accepting under any circumstance. Jack has a very good heart. You won't break it, will you?"

She smiled. "Your sister said the very same thing to me.

Harmon, I love Jack. I know he's a good man, and I know how lucky I am to have him. I've given him every opportunity in the world to walk away from me if he had the slightest doubt. I've told him it isn't going to be an easy life. He won't budge."

"He's not afraid of what's to come."

Emily nodded. She began cleaning off the dishes and Harm remained, lingering at her elbow until she looked to him in question. "Something else on your mind, Harmon?" She was warned by the sudden narrowing of his bright blue eyes.

"What have you told him about your husband?"

Emily tensed, then went back to scraping plates. "Nothing."

"Why?"

"Why? Like I said, I love Jack. How can you ask such a question? Look what this obsession has done to you. How can you think it would be good or right for him to know? What purpose would it serve? Jack's almost buckling under the guilt of his past as it is. What do you think it would do to him if he found out his best friend had a part in the nightmare you and his mother went through? It would kill him, Harmon. It would tear him apart. If you love him as you say you do, you won't hurt him with a truth he doesn't need to know."

"What's going on?" Amanda came up behind them. She could feel the rigid tension in her husband's form as she rubbed her palms along his arms. "Harmon?"

"Where's Jack?"

"He's outside with the children. What are you talking about?"

"Marcus." He spat the name.

"Oh." And her arms went quickly and tightly about his taut middle.

"You know?" Emily asked.

Amanda nodded, hugging Harm close, all sweet, strong support. But her opinion was firm. "Don't tell Jack. Emily's right—it can only hurt him."

"He's man enough to handle it. It's his right to know."

"Oh, Harmon, please. Of course he is, but why should he have to? There are things I gladly would have kept from you if I could have."

"Like what?" he growled suspiciously.

She rubbed her brow along the hard ridge of his cheek and kissed his jaw. "Like the truth about McAllister. I would have spared you that. If I'd found out about Neil Marcus first, I would have done everything I could have to keep it from you."

"Why?"

"Why hadn't you told Rebecca?"

He scowled and said gruffly, "She's gone through enough pain."

"Exactly. So have you. So has Jack. Harmon, please don't force him to act on this. He will if you tell him. Think of your sleepless nights. Do you want that for Jack?"

"No."

"Then say nothing."

Harm looked between the two willful women. In his head he wanted justice, and he wanted Jack to share in it. In his heart he knew they were right. And his love for Jack proved stronger than his code of duty. He nodded.

"One more thing," Emily began, and Harm knew he wasn't going to like it.

"What?"

"I know you have just cause for wanting to kill Neil;

I'm not arguing that. Just please wait until after Jack and I settle with him. I don't want my life with Jack beginning in the pool of my husband's blood. Jack would never be able to separate the two things."

"All right," Harm agreed.

Emily gave a tremendous sigh of relief. "Thank you, Harmon. Well, I'd better get the rest of those dishes."

Alone in the kitchen with his wife, Harmon hugged her close and kissed her hair.

"It's the right thing to do, Harmon."

"I know."

"I'll help you get through it."

"I know."

"Harmon?"

"What?" Her hesitation prompted his soft, "What is it, *shijii?*"

"When you were taking Emily to Ysleta—"

"Yes?"

She tucked her head against his shoulder, hating the lingering curiosity, her need to know. "Harmon, knowing that Emily was Neil Marcus's wife, were you ever tempted to—to—"

He tipped up her chin with his forefinger, forcing her to meet his wide blue gaze. "To what? To toss her down and take her like a savage while my wife waited, full of my child? To torture and murder her, knowing Jack cherished her?"

"Oh, Harm, I'm sorry I—"

"Yes. Yes, I was tempted."

Amanda went very still, caught in the intensity of his stare. "But you didn't."

"No. Ammy, everything I was raised to be told me to do it, that it was my right, my duty. I was angry enough, my blood was hot enough with the judgment of my people. But everything that you've made me would not allow it. I'm not such a fool as to think you'd ever let me come back to you after doing something like that. You might love me, but you wouldn't understand that it wasn't sex or anything like it. You aren't Apache. I could never hurt you like that. Never. You are the only woman for me, Amanda. All that I am is yours, and I would not betray that trust."

Her eyes were shiny with emotion, her voice small and tight with it. "I love you, Harmon. I would have understood."

He smiled faintly. "No, you wouldn't. You would never have let me touch you again. That's too great a sacrifice to make for the sake of honor." He kissed her gently and held her close. She rode out his massive sigh. "Ammy, I've seen terrible things. I've watched those I love suffer—"

"Harmon, don't."

"It's all right. I just want you to know. I could never do those things. I am not like them. I'm not Cates or Marcus. I couldn't live with such horror on my conscience. It's not right that the innocent should suffer men like that."

"I love you."

"You are my life, Amanda, you and my family. Without you, there's only darkness. I won't be lost in it again."

He heard Emily return to the kitchen and stepped back from his wife. He stroked the wetness from her cheeks and kissed each one tenderly. Then he strode from the room, all filled up inside with the look of love radiating in her dark eyes.

And he decided right then.

Neil Marcus was a dead man.

Someday soon he would find the excuse to slip over to Ysleta. It wouldn't be a satisfying vengeance, but it would have to suffice. A quick pull of his blade; nothing grand or messy, nothing that would bring suspicions home to his family. Amanda would know, but she would understand. Maybe Emily, too. But Jack and his sister would be protected.

And he could sleep nights.

Jack watched the three children race around the yard. It was like looking back into his own past, at his own half-brothers and sister. The blissful existence of a child. How he envied them that. How he hoped it could be preserved a while longer. No one should have to grow up as fast as he did, as Harm had. It wouldn't be easy, protecting a child like Kenitay from the harshness of a white man's West Texas, but he would. He swore it as he watched the boy racing on strong little legs after his uncle's lively girls. He wasn't naive enough to think he could shield the boy from prejudice, but he could gift him with a strong foundation of love and the power to rise above such petty ugliness. Harm had. His mother had. And his soon-to-be-son would, too.

He was musing over these things as he sat on the porch rail with his back to the side yard in the warm morning sun. His mind was easy. His heart was calm. He was at peace with his surroundings until a sudden and very distinctive hard circle pressed meaningfully against his spleen. He knew the feel of a carbine when it was prodding his vitals.

"Howdy, Jack. Don't go making any moves, now. I'd hate like Hell to put a bullet in you."

Twenty-three

Jack took the advice. He didn't move. He kept his hands still and his posture relaxed. It wasn't easy.

"Hey, Billy. What's going on?"

"Should be asking you that, Jack. You're the last one I'da ever suspected of desertion."

"Desertion?"

"You was due back in camp three weeks ago, Sarge. Ain't heard a word from you. Cap'n tole me while I was out scouting ahead that I should swing on by and see what you was up to. And that I was to bring you back, in shackles, if need be."

"I don't think that'll be necessary," came a low drawl from behind them. Billy Cooper froze solid as a blade lined up under his Adam's apple. It wasn't the knife that unnerved him, it was the man.

"H-howdy, there, Mr. Bass."

"Mind redirecting your piece? Jack, take it from him. I know you, don't I?"

"William T. Cooper, sir. I'm a friend of Jack's. We range together."

"You come up behind all your friends like this? A wonder you're still breathing."

"I could breathe a might better without that thing at my throat."

"Jack?"

"Let him go, Uncle Harm. It's all right—just a misunderstanding."

"Those kinds of misunderstandings get folks dead in a hurry." But Harm backed down, lowering his knife, and Billy Cooper gave a gusty sigh of thanksgiving. "What are you doing here, boy, coming onto my land looking to ventilate my nephew?"

"Well, hell, Mr. Bass, I wouldn'ta shot Jack, him being my pard and all. Well, I wouldn'ta wanted it to go down like that 'less he forced my hand."

"You're a true prince among men, Mr. Cooper."

"Uncle Harm," Jack cautioned. Then to Billy, he said, "Neil sent you after me?"

"In a roundabout sorta way. Bragg slipped his jailors and is heading for the border. We're riding to overhaul him and were in the neighborhood. Cap'n's been right surly about you not showing up for duty without giving reason."

"Being next to dead a good enough reason for you ranger boys?"

"Uncle Harm!"

"What?" Billy's gaze sized up his comrade. "Jack, you all right?"

Harm reached up for Jack's shirt collar, tugging it aside to expose evidence of the near fatal wound. "Good enough, or do you want to check the matching one in back?"

"Dang, Jack! It's a wonder you ain't toes-up somewheres! Bullet?"

"Apache lance," Harm supplied.

"Son of a bitch! You shoulda said something."

Harm went all flinty eyed. "A muzzle in the kidney tends to inhibit conversation some."

"If you two are finished." Jack scowled between them. "So who you riding with, Billy?"

"Better part of the company under the cap'n's command. We was sure hoping you'd be the one leading, seeing as how you know the way and you know Bragg. Glad to know you ain't quit us, and if you're up to it—"

Just then he broke off and his eyes went round as silver eagles. Jack glanced around.

"Hello, Billy."

"Ma'am." He tipped his hat to Emily Marcus and muttered, "Son of a bitch," under his breath.

Emily hesitated, looking to Jack for direction. It was a pivotal moment, and he didn't let her down. He extended his hand, and she was quick in joining him at the rail to press her own within it.

"Neil's on his way," he told her.

"Good," was all she'd say. "Billy, would you like a drink of something cold?"

"No, thank you, Mrs.—ma'am. I'd best be getting back to camp."

Harm smiled thinly. "Tell your captain he and the boys are expected for supper. I'll do some quick butchering and make it a proper welcome."

"Why that'd be right nice, Mr. Bass. The boys would enjoy a break from trail rations."

"The pleasure's mine, Private."

"Well." Billy affixed his hat and stole another pie-eyed glance at Jack Bass and Emily Marcus joined at the fingertips, bold as can be. "I'll be going."

"Billy?"

"Yeah, Jack?"

"I'd be obliged if you'd keep Mrs. Marcus's being here to yourself."

"Why, sure—"

"I want to be the one who talks to Neil about it."

"Fine by me. See you for supper."

There was a long silence after the ranger rode out.

"Guess I'll go carve up a couple of cows."

"Harmon?"

Harm looked back at his nephew, brows lifted in question.

"Make sure that's all you carve up tonight."

He gave Jack his bland could-mean-anything smile and continued to walk away, leaving Jack feeling far from secure. But then, his uncle wouldn't enact any kind of violence in front of his whole family . . . would he?

"Jack? What are you going to say to Neil?"

He thought a minute and while he did, he eased his arm in an intimate bridge along Emily's shoulders to draw her up tight against his side.

"I don't know, Em. The truth."

She burrowed in close to the beat of his heart. "He's not going to like it."

"But he's gonna have to live with it. We been friends for a long time. Maybe it won't be so bad." He was being optimistic. If anything, that would make it worse. "At least now it'll save us the trip back and everything will be out in the open. I want to move ahead on this. I'm tired of sidestepping."

"Jack, are you sure?"

The tentative quality of her voice melted him down inside like honey in a comb. "I've never been more sure of anything in my life. Em, what are you gonna tell Kenitay? About Neil, I mean?"

"The truth. As much of it as he can understand." She waited, wondering how to phrase it, then just said it plain. "Jack, I don't want to be alone with Neil." She was thinking about the truth no one had told him: that Neil Marcus had a ruthless past and a streak of viciousness he knew nothing about.

"You stick to me like a saddle burr, then. Or with Harmon. You're safe here, Em. You're with family."

She squeezed her eyes shut, hoping that was true.

Succulent scents rose from Harm's cook pits. All day, Amanda had been making veiled comments about her husband's skill when it came to slow roasting, until he grew plainly annoyed with her and threatened to give her a few turns over the fire if she didn't turn her tongue to something else. Then Sarah showed up in mid-afternoon, thrilled to learn they were to have a party and promising to help if she could stay at least until close to dark. Jack could swear he saw his thirteen-year-old sister's eyes sparkling when she heard there'd be rangers in attendance. Surely she was too young to be thinking of men in such a fashion. Then he began to give her a long, hard scrutiny. Emily caught him scowling darkly.

"What's wrong?"

"My sister. She's growing up. Kinda snuck up on me."

"She's very pretty. You'd better remind your friends that she's just a baby."

"Some baby. She's got—she's developed—she's pretty darn shapely for a baby!"

Emily laughed at him and squeezed his arm. "Let her have fun, Jack. You're young for such a short time. None of the boys will hurt her."

Jack grumbled. "You wouldn't be so easy if she were your daughter." He saw Emily take a step back in surprise, then he realized what he'd said and would have given his right arm to take back the words. "Em, I'm sorry."

She put an unsteady hand to her neck as if to force a swallow down. She touched the other to his shirt front, stroking gently. "It's all right, Jack." Then she took a deep breath and managed to smile. "Leisha reminds me of her. I can watch her and almost see Cathy. It makes her feel closer." Then the play of her fingertips grew more intimate. "Jack, I want you to give me lots of children."

He smiled, pushing down the thickness that had risen in his throat. "You mean I have to build you a hotel?"

"Just a couple of rooms for now. We can always add on." She stepped up close and rested her head upon his sound shoulder. He smelled good, of clean shirt and shaving soap and warm skin. He felt good, all starchy cotton, muscle, and man. Desire rose up so swift and strong, it undercut every other emotion. She lifted her head and guided his face toward her. His inquiring look altered the second he saw the damp part of her lips. He sank down upon them without delay, basting them with the wet drag of his tongue, seasoning them with sharp little nips of his teeth, teasing, tasting, and finally feasting with a ravenous pleasure until they heard a soft gasp. He turned guiltily to face his sister.

"Jack! What are you and Mrs. Marcus doing?" Her features were pale with shock.

"Sarah, Emily and I are going to be getting married as soon as she's free to have me."

"Well! Nobody told me!" Then her arms were around him and around Emily, hugging them both impartially. "Oh, this is wonderful! Can I tell Mama?"

"We were going to ride on over and—" He caught Emily's nod. "Oh, all right."

She squealed in girlish delight and set to hugging and kissing him until he was squirming and wincing.

"Back down, girl. And don't you let me catch you behaving like this with any of those ranger boys, or I'll have your—Sarah, what's that you're wearing?"

She stepped back and pirouetted proudly. "Amanda let me borrow it. Isn't it beautiful?"

"You're not wearing that! It's too—too adult for you."

"I am too wearing it, Jack Bass, and you can't make me take it off. Amanda said I looked like a proper young lady."

She did. She looked lovely in the strawberry-colored gown, with her black hair swept back from her tanned face and all too much of her browned torso showing. When the tired, homesick rangers got a look at her, they'd think they were seeing an oasis out in the West Texas desert. And he wasn't about to have any of them tempted to plunge right in.

"You go right back upstairs and tell your aunt that I said—"

"Tell Amanda what?"

"Oh, Uncle Harmon! Jack's being so mean! Don't you think I look pretty?" She turned her big, dark eyes on him and he melted down to mush.

"Why, *shijii*, you look pretty as a sunset. Your brother needs to have his eyes checked. That bump on the head musta knocked something loose."

She was grinning at him, reaching down off the top step to put her arms around him, when he happened to glance down to where her gown gaped away and he went dead still. He blinked, then roared, "Amanda Bass, you get this girl a coat!"

"Oh, you boys are just as contrary as ole mules," Sarah cried out angrily, but her eyes were filling up with adolescent misery. Emily came up to put her arm around her, frowning severely at both men.

"Come on, Sarah. We'll run a quick tuck in that neckline and it'll be fine. Your uncle and brother are just afraid they're going to have to spend the whole night shooing the boys away from you."

"Really?" She beamed up through the collected tears. "You think so?"

"I know so." She shot the baffled men another withering look and shepherded the girl inside.

"What did I do?" Harm wanted to know.

"Haven't a clue," Jack conceded.

And if they were perplexed by Sarah, they were poleaxed when the women finally appeared together.

Amanda had been into her trunk of eastern clothes. Her gown was of ivory silk, detailed with ruched lavender ribbon. Its neckline was cut low and square and filled over capacity with her ripe, nursing mother breasts. Suspended on a velvet cord was her brother's gold watch fob, just enough to keep her Apache husband off balance between uneasiness and unbridled lusting.

Emily was her vivid complement in deep wine-colored moiré, its modest collar offset by a snug-fitting bodice and the tiniest waist imaginable . . . something a man just longed to fit his hands to. Jack's were sweating.

Amanda breezed past her husband, tantalizing him with the scent of her perfume and the quick cant of her look-but-don't-touch gaze. Emily followed, walking by Jack as if he didn't exist. Harmon groaned.

"Oh, Jack, we're being punished for everything we've ever done or thought of doing."

Jack was too busy trying to pry his tongue off the roof of his mouth to think of a response. Emily slid him a look that sucked the air from his lungs. Harm laughed at his stricken expression and gave him a shove toward the barn.

"C'mon. Pretend we're not just dying to throw them down on the closest stretch of ground. No one can torture like a woman. Think I might have a cure for what ails us."

Jack followed him, then watched him tap into a barrel. He took the cup curiously.

"Drink up."

He drank and drank some more. "What is this?"

"Tiswin. Apache beer. Showed up on my doorstep a few nights back. Forgot to mention it to Amanda. Have another. It'll make the evening pass easier."

They drank in a companionable silence until Sarah came down to find them. She seemed to have forgiven them completely in her anticipation. She sidled in beside Jack, hugging him impulsively.

"What are the two of you doing out here? We have guests coming. Uncle Harm, our dinner is burning."

"I was just getting something to baste it in." He slid Jack a wink and carried his pitcher of *tiswin* up to the house, where Amanda was waiting impatiently. Her freckled nose crinkled up.

"Harm, have you been drinking?"

"Drinking in all that I see." And he let his gaze rove over his wife's splendid bosom. "A married woman with three kids and a jealous husband oughtn't to look that good."

"I won't tell the jealous husband if you won't."

"Well, from what I hear, he's a right nasty customer. *The* Harmon Bass, you know. Wouldn't want to mess with the likes of him."

Amanda hooked her forefinger between his shirt buttons to draw him closer. "How about messing with me?"

"Little girl, I'd say you were the more dangerous of the two. That's a right deadly dress you're wearing."

She smiled. "How long do you think it'll take you to get it off me?"

"Oh, not long, once I put my mind to it."

"Well, you be thinking on it, Harmon."

His fingertip rode slowly over heavenly hill and valley while his blue eyes simmered. "I will be."

"Good." And there was a wealth of meaning behind that

word as she watched him walk away. Harm would need all
the distraction she could offer, if they were to get through
this night unscathed. Because the devil was coming to their
front door, and she had to protect her own.

The rangers arrived just as the sun was nudging down.
The Basses stood tensely at the front steps, watching them
ride in: Sarah with anticipation; Jack, Harm, and Amanda
with trepidation. Eighteen dusty riders filed into the yard,
led by Neil Marcus. Amanda's hand became an anchor at
Harm's elbow as the man swept off his hat to them.

"Ma'am, Mr. Bass, we appreciate the invite. You boys get
on down and behave yourselves. Jack, I need to talk to you."

Short and to the point.

"C'mon inside, Neil. Howdy, boys. This here's my Uncle
Harmon, for those who haven't met him, his wife, Amanda,
and my sister, Sarah. She's thirteen, and I'll not like it if
you go to forgetting that fact."

Sarah shot him a killing glance, then aimed a sweet smile
that struck Billy Cooper right between the eyes. The boy
blinked and almost forgot how to get down off his horse.

Neil swung down and thumped the grime from his traveling clothes. When he came up to the house, he was very
aware of Harm's hard scrutiny. But the Apache tracker
smiled a bland greeting and stepped aside to let his enemy
pass, the breath hissing from him as Neil walked by within
striking range.

Jack led the way into the front parlor.

"Hear you're after Bragg. That ole boy's more trouble
than he's worth."

"You and Billy shoulda strung him up on the trail. Would
have saved us a lot of wear on saddle leather."

The easy talk ebbed and the two men regarded one another for a long, complex moment. Friendship and respect stretched thin beneath the pull of suspicion and regret.

"Billy tells me you took one through the shoulder. Have a bad time of it, did you?"

Jack wanted to squirm under the sincerity of his concern. "Not too bad. It's fine now. Just took some time to mend, is all."

"Well, good to see you fit and ready to ride. I need you to head up this outfit. You're my best man, Jack, and I'd feel a lot better going into this situation with a man I can trust at my side."

"Neil—"

"Hello, Neil."

There was an instant of total silence as Neil made the connecting glance between Jack Bass and his absent wife. Then he drawled a soft, "Well, well. Can't say I'm all that surprised."

"Neil, let me explain—"

"Shut up, Jack," he snapped dangerously. "How much explanation do you think I need? Funny thing, here for these last few weeks, I didn't know whether to worry over you being dead or to hope that you were. Good thing my wife just happened along to help with your healing."

Emily stood her own ground, making no move to take refuge at Jack's side. "Neil, I asked Jack to get his uncle's help in finding my son. I didn't think you'd allow it."

"Son?" Neil looked confused, then a curious expectation lightened his taut expression. "You didn't tell me we had a son."

"He's not your son, Neil," Emily explained gently. "His name is Kenitay."

That made everything crystal clear. Neil gave a soft

laugh. "Boy, the two a you are just full of surprises. What next? You gonna be breeding his bastard, too?"

"I hope to," Emily told him. "Only it's going to be a legitimate child."

Neil absorbed that with eyes narrowed. "Really? You want to spell that out for me? Jack?"

"Emily's fixing to divorce you so the two of us can marry."

Neil stared at him, and when Jack didn't drop his gaze, he gave another low chuckle. "Well, ain't this something? My good friend Jack and my sweet wife. Well, congratulations to both of you. When did you decide all this, when she was living under my roof and you were a guest at my table?"

"Neil—"

"Shut up! You son of a bitch." That moaned from him with incredible pain.

"Neil, I—"

"I trusted you."

"Neil—"

"I trusted you with my men, with my friendship, with my life! And this is how you repay me. I took you in when you were nothing but a green, scared kid and made you into the finest ranger I've ever known. I let you share my fire, my blankets, my rations, my experience, and this is the thanks I get. You were the one man I never, ever doubted. How could you do this to me? For her?"

"I'm sorry—"

"Sorry? What the Hell have *you* got to be sorry about? Look what you're getting." He gestured to a very pale Emily and sneered, "You're getting yourself a pretty little thing that will lie down for any man who'll provide for her. I'm the one who's sorry. I'm sorry for you, you stupid, stupid kid. You're throwing away everything I gave you. For what?"

Jack's features firmed. "Neil, don't—"

"Don't. Maybe you should have said that to yourself. *Don't. Don't look. Don't touch. Don't take.* But you didn't, did you, Jack? You just helped yourself. After I would have given you anything! Damn you, Jack! Damn you to hell!"

The silence was so loud, it hurt. Emily stood apart, weeping to herself for all the pain she'd caused. Neil was wild with rage and upset; Jack was drowning in sorrow. He flinched when Neil's hand settled on his shoulder and couldn't for the life of him look up to meet his gaze.

"Jack, you're the closest friend I've ever had, the best man I've ever shared a trail with. She's got you all confused. Open your eyes, boy. Think about what you're tossing away. A career, a good life. For what? Let's just drop this. You go on out with the other boys, I'll give my wife a talking to, and we'll forget any of this happened."

Emily stiffened. She could see what Neil was trying to do and she was scared, so scared that Jack would fall right in with it out of loyalty and guilt. She could see the remorse tearing through Jack Bass, but to her relief, he shook his head.

"Jack, you don't want to do this. Not over a woman."

Jack drew a deep, unsteady breath. "I'm sorry, Neil. I love her. I didn't want to. I never meant to let anything happen; it just did. And I'm sorry that it had to hurt you."

"Hurt me?" He moved his hand, spearing his fingers up into the hair at the back of Jack's head and clenching into a tight fist, yanking back so their stares were even. "Hurt me? You didn't hurt me, Jack. You destroyed me. You think I care about losing her? I wouldn't have come after her. I would have let her go without a second of regret. But she had to run off with you." His hand twisted cruelly, but Jack didn't wince. He didn't even feel the pain. "I kept waiting, hoping that you'd come back, that I was wrong. I kept praying I wasn't gonna have to chase you both down to kill you. Why couldn't it have been anyone else, Jack? Why did it have to be you? It wouldn't have been so bad if it had been anyone but you."

"I'm sorry, Neil," was all Jack could say, through everything choking up inside him.

"Sorry," Neil snarled, shoving him away. "You are a sorry bastard. To hell with you both!"

And he stalked out, past a pale, teary-eyed Emily, who took a quick step back when his glare cut through her. The door slammed out front and another silence settled.

Emily waited, uncertain of what to do. Jack stood all alone in the center of the room, his eyes shut, his expression screwed up tighter than the broken watch Amanda wore. She wanted to go to him but wasn't sure if he wanted her to. After all, she was the cause of his wretchedness. She had no right to offer sympathy . . . until he held out his hand to her. Then she came quickly into his arms and held to him with a fierce possessiveness, riding out the hitch of his breathing and the hard tremors of remorse.

"Jack?" She was fighting back tears.

"Shhh, Em. Don't say anything. Just let it go. Okay?"

She nodded. What could she say? That she was sorry? She wasn't. She wanted Jack, and now she had him. But she regretted the unavoidable pain it brought, both to him and to Neil. Because Neil had cared for Jack, even if he hadn't cared for her. And she knew how hard it had to be for Jack to tear away from years of loyalty and service. But he had. For her. And she would see he never, ever regretted it as much as he did in this emotional moment.

Finally, he drew a calming breath and she felt his lips move gently against her brow.

"I love you, Emily."

Oh, how she needed to hear that just then! And she believed him, but still she wanted to protect him. "We don't have to go out with the others."

He stood back from her and lifted her chin in his palm. "Those are my friends, and you're going to be my wife. I'm not hiding in this house. I've been hiding for far too long. Step on out with me. Let's get some dinner."

There was no way to verbally express how proud of him she felt, so she stretched up to kiss his mouth softly and then took his arm. And together they went out to where the other rangers were making short work of Harm and Amanda's meal.

There wasn't a man among them who didn't know their sergeant had been keeping house with Neil Marcus's wife. The minute Neil and Jack went inside to have words, Billy figured his vow of silence to be at an end. So when Neil stormed out of the house, no one confronted him with so much as a look. He stalked away from the gathering, presumably to return to their camp at the creek. Then, when Jack and Emily emerged together, suspicions were confirmed. But not a one of them knew how to react to it. Had it been any man other than Jack Bass, they would have cursed him for a no-good womanizer and homewrecker. But they knew Gentleman Jack and knew him to be one rung below sainthood when it came to holding to decency. They could have blamed Emily Marcus for being loose and immoral, but they'd all come to respect her for her cool bravery and gritty gentility. That left Neil, and while they all knew he could be hard, he was a man and therefore could do pretty much what he liked with his woman without repercussions. So that left no true villain in the curious triangle of friend, wife, and lover.

On the porch, Emily hung back. "Oh, Jack, they're all looking. Everyone knows."

"So?" he challenged gently. "You look 'em right in the eye and smile big. You've been through worse than this."

She smiled and said through gritted teeth, "I don't remember when."

"Hey, Jack!" Billy stood and waved him over where a dozen of the men had gathered. "C'mere."

He crossed the yard, guiding Emily with a firm hand on her elbow. The rangers all jumped up and doffed hats with murmurs of "Ma'am." And they were wishing to a man that they could pry the truth of the situation from their close-lipped sergeant.

"Hey, boys. How's the food?"

A chorus of affirming contentment.

"Jack, I was telling the fellers what happened, how you took an Apache lance and are here to tell about it. So tell about it."

"Not much to tell," he mumbled, looking uncomfortable with the attention.

"Not much? Well, hell, boys, take a gander at this." And before Jack could protest, Billy grabbed onto his shirt and wrestled it right over his head. "Look at that. Front and back."

A chorus of mighty impressed murmurs.

"Gimme my shirt, Billy. This ain't no sideshow." He struggled to put it back on, and no one missed the way Emily Marcus stepped in, familiar as you please, to help ease it up his injured arm. Not a one of them would have minded being the one she smiled up at . . . if it hadn't been for stepping on Neil's toes.

"So," Clayton Wainright demanded, "how'd you come by that souvenir?"

"Just got careless about where I was standing."

That was met with grumbles and moans of, "Oh, c'mon,

Jack." It was then that Emily spoke up. If he didn't mean to boast, she meant to brag for him.

"He got it standing up to Kodene and his warriors. He went to them to trade himself for my son and was ambushed by a brave who'd lost his wife and child to you rangers. They were going to trade him to the Mexicans for the bounty when Harmon stole into their camp and snatched him right out from under their noses."

It was the kind of story frontier men thrived on, all danger and derring-do, and they were bombarding Jack with questions when Kenitay nudged up beside him to get a closer look at the rangers. Jack didn't notice him at first until one of the men muttered, "Who does the 'Pache brat belong to?"

Kenitay might not have understood all the words, but he understood the meaning well enough. He shrank back against Jack, trying to hide from the narrowed speculative gazes. Seeing the boy's fright and confusion, Jack bent to take him up in his good arm. He smiled reassuringly at the child, then gave his companions a look that cracked hard enough to shatter stone.

"He belongs to Emily, and soon enough, to me. Any of you boys got a problem with that?"

Kenitay's little fists were balled up in Jack's shirt front. He was afraid to be the focus of attention, but he felt secure enough in Ranger Jack's arms to return the curious looks with a somber intensity. Billy grinned at him.

"I gots me a nephew 'bout that age. Pesty little cuss. Into everything. Tore into my rations last time I was home and had chewed up enough green coffee beans to be belly-aching for a week." He put out his hands and Kenitay burrowed tighter into Jack. "What's his name?"

"Kenitay." He smiled gently at the alarmed child.

"C'mere, Kenny. Cute kid."

Kenitay allowed Jack to pass him over and Billy dandled him fondly. "Let me borrow him for a second. Ladies got a soft spot for fellers who like kids. How old did you say your sister was, Jack?"

"Old enough not to trust you."

"Let's take a walk, Kenny. You can introduce me to your soon-to-be Aunt Sarah."

And Billy strolled off, relieving all the tension in the group. Emily touched Jack's shoulder.

"I'm going to give Amanda a hand in the house."

Just then Harm brought out the barrel of *tiswin* and all the rangers got to praising him for being a marvelous host. He smiled at them narrowly and went back to turning his spit.

"Hey, Jack," Clayton whispered. "You think he'd come on over and join us for a drink? The bunch of us, we're feeling mighty bad about the last time—you know."

He did know. And he was a little surprised Harm would allow any of the rangers to set foot on his property, let alone invite them for a feast.

"Ask him, Jack," another man urged.

"You ask him."

"Hell, no. What if he's still holding a grudge?"

Jack smiled. "If he was still holding a grudge, he'd be turning one of you over that fire. Hey, Harmon, c'mon over."

Harm approached them with an impassive face, looking first to Jack for explanation, then to each man in turn to observe their varying degrees of discomfort. Clayton finally cleared his throat.

"We was hoping you'd tip one with us, Mr. Bass. We're all mighty sorry about what happened before and would like it if you was to hold no hard feelings."

Jack pressed a mug of beer upon him and waited hopefully. Harm supplied a small smile that they took as a sign of for-

giveness and he drained the cup. The mood instantly lightened. Harm sat down at Jack's side and allowed his nephew's
comrades to pry his part in Jack's rescue from him. On occasion, he could be a pretty good storyteller, too.

From the porch, Emily watched them. She gave a bittersweet sigh. These were Jack's friends—the men he'd ridden
with, was comfortable with, had relied upon in times of
trouble, and joked with in moments of ease. And he was
giving them up for her. She wished it didn't have to be that
way. She liked the rangers. They were generally boot-sole
tough and somewhat ill mannered, but most were shy
around her and truly gentle. She wouldn't have minded living among them, doing their mending, patching their bullet
wounds, cooking an occasional dinner, or conceding to a
high-spirited dance. But that was impossible now. And she
wondered how much Jack was going to mourn the loss of
the camaraderie she could see between them.

She went inside, unable to watch any longer without indulging in melancholy, and as she walked down the hall
toward the kitchen, her arm was gripped in a sudden painful
clench.

"Just who I was looking to find." Neil Marcus gave her
a feral smile. "We got some talking to do."

Twenty-four

Terror leaped in an instant, for she was seeing not only her enraged husband, but the man who had tortured Harm and Rebecca Bass and had helped kill their mother. Emily cast a desperate glance toward the front door.

"Don't even think of yelling for him. This don't concern Jack. It's a private matter, between a man and his wife. Step on in here, wife. I'd like a word with you."

He gave her arm a cruel yank, jerking her into the shadowed dining room. He swung her about so she bumped painfully into the edge of the table and was trapped there by his crowding superior size.

"Pretty proud of yourself, aren't you?"

"What do you mean?" She could smell the liquor on his breath, and even though she didn't back down, she was afraid.

"Finding yourself a man like Jack, someone who'd overlook all the things you been and done. Even a bastard Injun baby. If you were looking for a kind-hearted, soft-headed fool, you found one. How'd you do it, Emily? What did it take to make a man like Jack shred his decency and reputation for a used-up slut like you?"

Fear gave before fury. "I don't have to—"

He pushed her back against the table, almost sprawling her back upon its polished surface. "Yes, you do. You will listen. What's the matter? You jealous of Juana? That it? You thinking to get back at me through Jack? You think by acting the whore, I'd be more inclined to stay in your bed? I could kill you right here and no jury in the state of Texas would convict me of any wrongdoing. You think I'm just gonna let you humiliate me? You think I'll let one of my men steal you away from me? Think again! It'll never happen. Never!"

She tried to convey a calm she didn't feel, tilting up her chin and saying, "It already has, Neil."

His hands slammed down on the tabletop on either side of her, and she jumped in nervous alarm. Violence seethed through him, each savage pull of his breath drawing him closer to a loss of control. "No, Emily. You are mine. You belong to me. I earned you out on a battlefield, fighting beside your father. I earned you grubbing on a dirty little piece of land for your mother. You were my reward." He gave a harsh laugh. "Kinda ironic, when you think on it. I mean, after all I tried to put behind me, look what I get in return. My sweet little wife, betraying me to the Apache, betraying me with my own men. Guess I deserve it, but that don't make me any more inclined to let you go."

"I won't go back with you."

"Yes, you will. And it may take some time, but you're gonna settle into your lot. You shamed me in front of my men. You made Jack out to be the better man. I can't have that. I can't have my men laughing at me behind my back, and if I was to let you run off with him and do nothing about it, they would. How can I command their respect if my own wife and my sergeant show me none at all? Huh? Answer me that. You forced me to it, Emily. If you'da just run, I'da said good riddance. But you had to grab onto Jack, you had to push the fact of the two of you together into my face. Now I'm gonna have to do something about it."

And now, suddenly, Emily was no longer afraid just for herself. "What are you going to do?"

"I'm gonna teach you a real hard lesson to forget. I'm giving you a chance right now to save yourself a lot of misery by just coming with me quietly. Make me do it the hard way and you'll regret it. Push me too far and I'll take you down across the border and sell you to someplace so dark and ugly you'll wish I'da killed you."

"You can't—"

"Yes, I can. You're my property. Who's going to stop me?"

"Jack—"

Neil smiled and the cold confidence of that gesture froze her solid inside. "Jack's not going to be a problem. You won't be seeing him again after tomorrow."

"Emily?" Amanda's voice sounded from behind them. "Is everything all right here?"

Neil backed away, never taking his fierce stare from his wife's fear-glazed features. "Everything's jus' fine, Mrs. Bass. My wife and I were jus' having a little talk."

"You'd better go out and rejoin your men, Captain Marcus. I don't want you in here under my husband's roof."

Neil turned his attention to Amanda Bass and was momentarily stunned by the chill fury she focused on him. "I beg your pardon, Mrs. Bass. I didn't mean to intrude."

"Don't beg to me, Mr. Marcus. You'll find I have very little sympathy for you. Please go. Or do I have to call my husband?"

"Ma'am." He tipped his hat to her, then pinned Emily with his meaningful glare. "Remember what we were talking about, Emily."

As if she could forget.

When he'd gone, Amanda's hostility melted into concern. "Are you all right, Emily? Do you want me to get Jack?"

"No. No, it's all right. He was just making some threats, trying to bully me into coming back to him."

"I can't abide a bully." She came to slip her arm about Emily's shoulders. "C'mon. Help me take some coffee out to the boys. The last thing I want is a bunch of drunken rangers rolling around my front yard. And I've got to chase Sarah home before it gets too dark. You just stay close to me. I've handled tougher than Neil Marcus. He doesn't scare me." She was thinking of Tyrell Cates. After him, even Lucifer himself was a distant second.

Emily wished she could say the same. But Neil did scare her; he wasn't issuing idle threats. And when she looked down into the yard, to where the rangers had grouped around the fire, she had reason for a deeper terror. Because Neil was addressing them as a unit. And Jack was listening.

"Howdy, boys. You all enjoying yourselves?"

The men looked up at their captain, murmuring affirmatives.

"I got a few things to say, then I want you to thank Mr. Bass for his hospitality so you can turn in. We got a long day tomorrow."

As they started devouring and swallowing whatever they could finish, Neil circled around the fire and came down on his haunches directly across from Jack. He regarded his sergeant impassively, not unaware of Harmon Bass's glittering glare from where he crouched at his nephew's side. Jack soon grew uncomfortable under the unblinking scrutiny and rose up, planning to quit the fire and the rangers at that moment.

"Sit down, Jack."

He regarded his captain somberly. "I'd best be heading out. You got business to attend and it's not mine anymore."

A quiet tension took hold of the men as they feared their captain and sergeant were about to come to words. But Marcus turned his hand palm up, gesturing to the ground. "Sit," he instructed softly. "It's ranger business, and as you're still wearing your star, you're obliged to listen."

"Cap'n . . ." There was resignation all over that deep-breathed beginning, and Neil wasn't about to hear any more of it.

"Jack, sit yourself down. You're the best man I have, and I'm not about to let you back out unless you don't think you're fit enough for the task. We're heading down into Mexico after Bragg. You're the man who knows the territory. We'd like you in on this, if you're up to it."

Jack hesitated, feeling the expectant gazes of the men he'd ranged with for four years and the man he'd served under with unswerving allegiance. And he sat.

"Mexico! Jack, you can't go to Mexico!"

"Em—"

"No!" She pushed away his hands as he reached to comfort her and scooted back toward the center of the bed they'd been sharing. They were nowhere near to sharing it now as tensions flared and emotions stretched taut. There was no way to overlook the fact that Neil Marcus was camped at the edge of Blue Creek with the rest of Jack's company. He might as well have been in the room with them.

Jack spread his hands wide and paced to the window. He

could see the fires from the ranger camp and he felt a stirring restlessness. He didn't want to, but he did. Emily wasn't making it any easier. "If you'd just listen—"

"I listened. I heard you tell me that you were done with the rangers. I heard you say we'd get a fresh start, the two of us. That's not what I'm hearing you say now. I don't like it, Jack."

"Em, it's just this one last time. They need me."

"I need you!"

He sighed, trying to explain in a way that she could understand. How did a man explain a sense of driving loyalty, the camaraderie that formed when you shared meals and saddlesores and minute-to-minute danger with men you were proud to call your friends? How could he explain the way they all counted on one another when the going was tough? And it didn't get much tougher than what they were going up against tomorrow.

"I have to do this, Emily."

"No, you don't."

"Em, I'm the only one who can take them where they need to go to find Bragg. I know the countryside. I know the man. Billy doesn't have the experience to lead them. It's got to be me. Can't you see that? I owe them. They're my friends. If they go without me, a lot of them might not be coming back."

"And what about you? Have you forgotten the price on your head?"

"I haven't forgotten anything."

"Except your promises to Kenitay and me."

"That's not fair, and it's not true. As soon as this is done—"

But she turned away, denying him with the stiff set of her back and shoulders.

Jack sighed again. Obviously, reason wasn't going to work, but there were other means of persuasion. He walked over to the bed and sat on its edge. She went immediately tense with wariness. He could feel her rigidity when he placed his hands upon her shoulders and began a slow, kneading massage.

"Emily, I love you and Kenitay. You're going to be my family, my future. Nothing is more important than the two of you."

"Then don't go, Jack." She said that as a flat-out ultimatum.

"I have to go. But when I get back—"

"You're not going to be coming back."

"Of course, I am." He began to caress her arms in warm, easy strokes. She kept to her resistance.

"Neil isn't planning to let you come back to me."

He gave a soft, disbelieving laugh. "Em, you make it sound like he's planning to kill me."

"He is."

"That's ridiculous. If he'd wanted to do that, he'd have called me out this evening. He's a ranger, Emily. We've got a job to do, and even though I don't like what he's done to you, he's still the best commander a man could ask for. He's not going to let what's personal get in the way of what's professional. He's not a killer."

She revolved up onto her knees to confront him then. Her expression was stark and serious. "Jack, you have no idea what he is."

"I know he's losing you and I'm getting you and I owe the man this much. I can't just turn my back when he's asked me for my help. We've been friends for years. I respect the things he stands for. I respect the man he's made me into. I feel damned bad about taking his wife. Let me do this much to even things out." He took his ranger star and pressed it into her palm. "That's yours. I'll go as a guide, not as part of the unit, and I'll be back as soon as I can."

She didn't say anything at all. When it became obvious that she wasn't going to, he leaned forward to kiss her. She turned her face slightly so that his lips touched her on the cheek. Then he took her in his arms. She didn't try to pull away, nor did she respond. There were no tears, and that's what disturbed him most. She leaned into him, trembling fitfully, as if already resigned to mourning him. He felt awful, yet what was he supposed to do? Let men who trusted him die because of her unreasonable fears? He'd make it up to her. He swore it to himself as he kissed her brow and gradually lowered them both to the mattress. He lay there with her shivering and withdrawn within his embrace, feeling desperate and alone, wanting to comfort her, needing comforting himself, but there seemed no way to bridge the sudden distance that Neil Marcus's request had put between them.

"I love you, Emily. Please believe that."

She did. She believed him. That wasn't the problem. He also believed Neil was an honorable man. Jack was going to Mexico and he wasn't coming back to her. How could she stand to grieve for him all over again?

And with Jack dead, where did that leave her?

At Neil Marcus's mercy.

Jack finally slept, deep and hard. Emily remained quietly within the slack circle of his arm just watching him for some time. Such a nice face, a strong, handsome face, yet with hints of a trusting innocence that was going to get him killed. Then it got too hard to do nothing but worry, so she slipped out of bed and went downstairs, out into the silence on the porch. She leaned against the rail, wondering if she could find the courage to go down into the ranger camp and shoot Neil before he had the chance to murder Jack.

"Solve anything with all your yelling?"

She glanced around at Harm and gave him a bittersweet smile. "Do you Basses ever listen to anyone?"

"Only when they're fighting in the next room loud enough to keep a man from getting a decent night's rest."

"I'm sorry if we—"

He smiled then to show he wasn't annoyed, but his gaze was intent and concerned, seeing much more than she'd planned to say. "What's wrong?"

"Neil's taking Jack down into Mexico to kill him."

Harm never for a second doubted it. "How?"

"I don't know. Maybe in some accidental crossfire. Maybe he'll just accidentally fall into Mexican hands. I don't know. Jack won't listen to me. He's insisting upon going. He's not going to come back, Harmon. Neil told me I'd never see him again." Her voice caught and the tears she'd refused to shed upstairs now rimmed her lower lashes.

"Well, then, we'll just have to do something about it, won't we?"

"How can I protect him if he doesn't believe he's in any danger?"

Harm rubbed his knuckles along her cheek, catching the advance of moisture. "I believe you. I guess I'll just go along to see that he makes it back all right."

Emily took a hopeful breath. "Would you?"

"I'm not about to give up any more of my family to the likes of Marcus. If someone's not coming back, it's not going to be Jack."

"Oh, thank you, Harmon." She put her arms around him and impulsively kissed his lean face, and he squirmed away, blushing every bit as boyishly as his nephew. Then he smiled at her with a new and surprisingly deep fondness.

"You're family, now, too, and my responsibility. I'll bring him home to you."

She believed him, and a great weight of anguish dropped from around her heart.

"Now, go up to Jack and spend this time with him. A man needs to know his woman is there to support him, even if she doesn't like it."

Jack sighed contentedly and murmured as he roused from sleep. Wondering what had awakened him, he blinked his eyes open and found himself staring up at Emily. Her face was only inches away, and again he felt the sweet brush of her mouth over his. That was what had caused the delicious disturbance of his rest. He didn't mind it at all.

"Did I wake you?" she whispered in feathery kisses.

"I think you meant to."

"Ummmm. Could be I did."

"Why? Not for more arguing, I hope." His hands came up to cup the curve of her ribcage. His palms slid on soft, bare skin. She wasn't wearing anything. All that stood between them were his clothes and their earlier words.

"No. No more arguing." She was balanced on elbows and toes, and the way she was moving along him was wildly arousing. Obviously, she intended it to be.

"Good, because I hated to think that I'd have to ride out remembering an unhappy parting."

"Shhhh." She sucked lightly on his lips. "Don't talk

about leaving. Don't talk at all. Can I take this off you?" She plucked at his shirt.

"Please do. Take all of it off, if you like."

She did. While he lay back with his eyes half-closed and his breathing shallow, she undressed him, taking an inordinate amount of time to kiss and caress each area she uncovered. Jack Bass excited her like nothing else could. She loved the taste of him, the texture of him, the tone and tensile strength of him. She could have spent a lifetime adoring each treasured inch, but she only had until dawn to absorb as much as she could and to share as much as she was able.

"Come back to me, Jack," she murmured against the flat, furred plain of his belly.

"I will."

And then he moaned softly as her attention shifted lower. Then he was shifting, restlessly, helplessly, his hands twining in her loose, dark hair. She lifted up when the pleasure grew almost more than he could stand so she could enjoy seeing him all glassy-eyed and frenzy-flushed.

"Jack?"

"What?" he panted.

"I love you."

And she settled down upon his mouth, kissing him deeply, settled atop him, drawing him in deeper still. Moving slowly. Rocking gently. Loving as completely as a woman could love a man. And still it didn't seem enough to give him. Until he rolled up over her to control the rhythm of their union, of their breathing, of her heartbeat. She gave herself up to him, content to hold to him, to let him stoke their passions high. He kissed her again and again, each time deeper and harder. He slid into her again and again, each time deeper and harder. And as she cried out his name, she couldn't have cared less if she was keeping Harmon Bass awake next door.

It had been his idea, after all.

And a good one.

Harm was awake.

Amanda watched him from the bedcovers, appreciating the way moonlight gleamed along the hard lines of his compact build. He was naked, and she liked looking at him. She'd never lost her fascination for the tough little Texas half-breed whose legend was bigger than life and surpassed only by the truth. He'd given her three children and was probably working on number four, had shared her table and her bed for six years, had smiled blandly in the face of all her chatter, had provided for and protected her and loved her to the limit of emotion, but he'd never ceased to be that wildly dangerous and totally unpredictable man she'd fallen in love with. And she didn't want to change that. What she wanted was to give him ease.

To the casual eye, he'd appear relaxed, the way he was leaning against the window's edge, seemingly looking out at nothing, but Amanda knew him intimately and well. She noticed the plays of tension along his bronze scarred back, the way his hands clenched and unclenched in a restless pattern at his sides. He was anxious to be elsewhere.

He gave a slight start when she slipped up behind him to pepper his shoulder with spicy kisses. Then he did relax as her palms soothed over his sleek middle.

"Harmon, where are you going?"

"To Mexico."

There was a pause, then she asked, "For how long?"

"I don't know. Not long."

"Harmon?"

"What?"

"Keep both of you safe."

"I will."

"Good."

No argument, no questions, no whining, just flat-out acceptance. God, he loved that about her. She knew him and she trusted him enough to let him go, and because of it, he could never stray.

"I'll leave you with everything you need, plenty of food and firewood."

She stroked him. "When you come back, then I'll have everything I need. Until then, I'll make do."

"You're a helluva woman, Amanda."

"You keep me on my toes, Mr. Bass."

She was silent for a time and that wasn't like her. Her cheek was rubbing along his shoulder and she was still caressing him, but those were absent gestures. Her mind was on something else. That wasn't like Amanda, either.

"What is it, Ammy?"

"I wanted to ask you—"

"What?"

"I don't know how to say it." She hesitated, kissing his shoulder, his throat, his ear, his jaw; they were possessive rather than passionate kisses. And she said softly, "I don't know if I should."

Now he was curious. Harm turned within the circle of her arms to question her with the lift of his brows.

"Harmon, I know what I've said before and I meant it, I really did, but I think—I think I was wrong. Harm, I love you. I want you here with me always. I want us to live together, happy, with no taint of the past. I hate this. I've always hated this, but I can't ignore it. Something has to be done and you're the only one who can do something about it."

"About what, *shijii?*"

"Kill him, Harmon."

"Who? Marcus?" Of course, Marcus. Harm's blood thickened just thinking about him. And now Amanda was opening the door to his cage of civilized restriction, turning him loose to be what he'd always been inside.

"He's dangerous. He's going to hurt Emily and Jack, I know it. I can feel it. You've got to put a stop to him before he kills one of them." Her vehemence surprised him. What a savage thing his dear little eastern wife had become. But not without good reason.

"I won't let him, Ammy."

"Good. God forgive me, but I'll be glad when it's done." She touched his face, molding her palms to the rugged contours. "You're a good man, Harmon Bass, but sometimes good men have to do bad things."

"I won't mind doing this one."

"You look out for Jack and you watch your own back. Don't take your eyes off that man."

"Ammy, just because a big snake's been sleeping under your porch for years and hasn't bitten you doesn't mean it's lost any of its poison. I'll be careful and I'll stay out of striking range."

"Do you want me to come with you?"

She said that so sincerely, he was twisted up by tenderness. "You stay here and protect what's ours. That way, I can go do what I have to do."

"Harmon, don't let him hurt you."

"He couldn't do any more to me than he's already done." He smiled then, a savage baring of his teeth. "I'm not ten years old anymore, Ammy. He's going to beg me to let him die."

She pulled him to her and kissed him hard, exulting in his urgency as he carried her back to bed. He was rough and ruthless in his lovemaking, but Amanda understood it. It was his war dance as he readied himself on the eve of battle, all fierceness and drama and highly focused energy. She encouraged him with her kisses and soft cries, and when he was through, he was once again all gentle passion. And the second time, she enjoyed it every bit as much as he did.

"Good morning."

Emily looked up from her fourth cup of coffee to see Rebecca Bass coming up onto the front porch. She was already so wound up with nerves, it was an effort for her to sit still. Rebecca was a welcome distraction as she waited to see Jack off.

"Sarah came home with some surprising news last night. I thought I should stop over and see if she was exaggerating. But I can see she's not."

Emily took a deep, composing breath. Family was everything to Jack, and if she was to be accepted in his, she was going to have to win Rebecca over. The only way she could think to do it was with complete honesty. She wanted to fit into the Bass family in the worst way, but she couldn't force that fit, and she knew it. They'd have to give her a place. She had one here with Harm and Amanda, but she needed a welcome at one other very important door. And here was where she had to start.

"I know I'm not what you had in mind for Jack. I can't imagine any mother being overjoyed to learn their son is wedding a woman not yet divorced with a half-Indian child, a woman who is older and a lot more worn than he is. I know he's young and sweet and it would be easy for a woman in my position to take advantage of that. But that's not what I'm doing. I plan to work hard to make Jack a very good wife."

"Are you in love with him?"

"I was in love with him the first time we had this conversation."

Rebecca thought about that and considered her for a long moment. She was a tough woman, used to protecting her own from all sorts of dangers. Emily didn't want to be classed as a danger, but that was Rebecca's decision. Then Jack's mother smiled at her.

"Well, you're wrong, Emily. I happen to think you're just what Jack needs. You can take care of each other, and that's important. And you love each other; that's vital. As far as your son goes, I'm the very last one to hold a bad opinion there. Jack will be a good father to him. You won't have to worry about that."

"I know. That's one of the reasons I just couldn't let him go. He means the world to me, Rebecca, and I want to be his wife. With your blessing."

"You don't need my blessing, but you have it." And she reached over to embrace Emily. "Just love him, Emily. Love him and support him and be there when he needs you."

"I will."

Then Rebecca stepped back, wiping away the moisture from the corners of her eyes. "Where is he this morning? Sarah said something rather breathlessly about a bunch of rangers passing through."

"Jack's riding out with them as soon as they assemble. Harmon, too."

Emily's mood clued her and she felt a shared anxiety. They were her son and brother, after all. "Riding into something bad?"

"Aren't they always?"

Rebecca nodded. "A word of advice about being married to a ranger. Let him do his work by day, don't ask too many questions, and keep him home and happy at night. You'll get used to him being gone, and when he's home, he'll make you forget you had any complaints." At least, that was how she was remembering it, if her small smile was any indication.

Emily saw no need to tell her that Jack was leaving the rangers. There'd be plenty of time for making those decisions when he got back.

"Where's Amanda?"

"She and Harmon are inside, saying their goodbyes. Again. The children are all still in bed, and I think they wanted a little time alone."

"Well, I won't interrupt them. I really came over to see you. After the boys leave, stop on out and see us, get to know Will and Jack's brothers better. I'm sure you know Sarah well enough already."

"I'd like that. Thank you." And the sense of finally belonging swelled up sweet and tight around her. It was a wonderful feeling and yet another reason for her to love Jack Bass.

"Tell Harmon to take care of Jack for me."

"I already have. He will."

"Good. Then I won't worry." But of course she would. She was a mother.

Then Rebecca turned away and came nose to nose with Neil Marcus as he started up the steps.

Twenty-five

Rebecca made a raw sound in the back of her throat and stumbled from the shock of horror. Neil froze where he was and stared with recognition but not recall. And Emily, realizing the awful potential of the moment, grabbed onto Rebecca's arms. It was like gripping the porch post. Every fiber of Rebecca Bass was petrified. Then a low, moaning cry escaped her, escalating into a wavering wail.

"Harmon!"

"Becky?"

Harm exploded from the house and Rebecca flew into his arms, clutching at the protection he offered and weeping frantically into his shirt front. He held her tight, demanding, "Becky, *silah,* what is it? What's wrong?"

Then he saw Neil.

And one look into Harm's killing blue eyes as they lifted from the black-haired woman in his embrace connected everything.

"Oh, my God." His mind numbed, Neil retreated from the steps, sure he was seeing a ghost.

"Oh, Harmon, Harmon. Why didn't someone tell me he was here?"

"Shhhh, Becky. Shhhh, *silah,* don't cry. Don't be afraid. I won't let him hurt you. Not this time. I can stop him this time." And he kissed her hair and brow with infinite gentleness as darkness rose inside. Rage bubbling up like hot rock from a yawning cavern that had torn through his soul, scalding his senses, burning through his veins, searing with the power of hate, the pressure of fear, and the need for revenge from where it had been simmering and steaming for twenty years.

"I thought you were dead," was all Neil Marcus could think to say.

When Rebecca quieted in his arms, Harm eased back and handed her over into Emily's care so he could face his enemy. "You thought wrong. Just like the seven before you thought wrong. Before I killed them."

"Hey, what's going on?"

Jack approached a scene so charged that the tension crackled like heat lightning. Neil and Harm were squared off and Emily and his mother were on the sidelines, hugging to each other. He couldn't tell who was comforting whom. They both looked upset, and he wanted to know why.

"Uncle Harmon?"

The lethal mood defused in an instant. Harm looked to him with a thin smile. "Jack. Your captain and I were just discussing how we both thought it'd be a good idea if I rode along on this trip."

Jack bounced an uncertain glance between them, feeling the undercurrent that lingered like an emotional residue. "Why, you know I'm always happy to ride with you Uncle Harm, but—"

"Good. It's settled. I'll get my things. This way, Captain Marcus and I will have plenty of time to rehash the old days." And he smiled wide, showing white teeth the way a wolf would with the curling back of his upper lip. It wasn't a friendly gesture.

"We're riding out, Jack. You coming?" Neil began to back

away from the Basses' front porch, his eyes never leaving the trio gathered there.

"Be down in a minute. I want to say goodbye to my mama."

And as Jack walked up to the house, Neil stared at him, seeing him for the first time through opened eyes before practically staggering back to the ranger camp beneath Harm Bass's deadly glare.

"Mama?"

Rebecca swept him up in a needy embrace. Feeling her despair and the tremors rippling through her, Jack hung on tight, confused and alarmed.

"Mama?"

He felt her gather control, and slowly, her grip relaxed. She continued to hug him close, her head pillowed on his shoulder. "I'm all right, Jack. Just being silly. Your uncle's taking care of it for me."

He was far from relieved to hear that. More secrets. What were they all keeping from him? Then he looked to Emily and saw the poignant tenderness in her gaze. She knew. And she was keeping it from him, too. But before he could push for any answers, his mother straightened and kissed his cheek with a whisper of, "I love you, Jack. I have always loved you."

The words struck him like a punch. He murmured back, hoarsely, "I know you have, Mama."

She looked up into his face and all she was seeing was the goodness of the man he'd become as she stroked his cheek. "You were the one bright thing that came from a very dark time, and you'll never know what a comfort you were to me. I am so proud of you—both Will and I are. We'll see to Emily while you're gone, and when you get back, you make time to visit."

"Yes, ma'am." He closed his eyes as she kissed his face.

"Now, you do as your Uncle Harmon tells you."

He smiled at that and chastened, "Mama, I'm not fourteen anymore."

But she didn't smile back. "Listen to your uncle."

"I will, Mama."

Then she gave him one long last look before embracing first Emily with all the fondness she'd give a daughter, then her brother.

"Take care of him, Harmon," she pleaded softly within their embrace.

"I'll take care of both of them," Harm promised meaningfully.

Then the porch was crowded with family as Amanda came out, leading the parade of children. She'd missed the excitement while getting them dressed upstairs, but she felt it immediately through her husband. There was no time to ask as Harmon scooped up his girls and Kenitay reached for Jack and all of them were trying hard not to act on any of the emotions edging up beneath the surface.

After kissing his daughters fondly, Harm set them down and bent over his sleeping son. He nuzzled the soft black hair, then lifted his blue gaze to Amanda.

"Harmon—"

"I will." And he kissed her brow quickly. "I'll saddle up the horses."

"I'll go with you," his wife volunteered. She wanted to know what had put more smoke into the morning air than an Apache roasting. And she wanted just a little more time with her husband.

But Harm laughed. "You stay put. We want to leave sometime this morning."

She made a face and pretended to pout just until his back

was turned, then her gaze followed him hungrily all the way to the barn.

Jack curled his arm behind Emily's neck, drawing her up beneath his chin. "Will you chase me that shamelessly after we've been married for six years?"

"For sixty years," she promised, kissing his throat, his jaw, and finally his mouth, until Kenitay started squirming and she had to step back so Jack could put him down. Then she nestled in close again, realizing that this would always be the most difficult—not the packing of his things, not watching him ride away, but the actual, physical act of letting go. She didn't want to. She didn't want to separate herself from him even for a minute. Her palms pushed under his short roundabout jacket, next to warmed cotton, and she tried not to cling or cry. Then Harm rode up to the porch leading a second horse and he levered away.

"I gotta go."

"Wait. Here."

Jack looked puzzled as she affixed his ranger star to the front of his jacket.

"Wear this."

He smiled wryly. She'd pinned it over his heart. "As what? A bull's-eye?"

"Body armor," was her elusive reply. It was the only protection she could give him. Behind a ranger badge he'd be safer from his captain's vengeance.

"Let's go, Jack."

The ranger company was approaching the house at a casual lope with Neil in the lead. With no more time left them, Emily grabbed Jack's face between her palms and kissed him hard enough to make her passion felt all the way down to his boot heels. Then she stepped back, giving him a firm push.

"Go."

He hesitated.

"I love you, Jack."

Then he was able to move, supplying quick hugs for his mother, Amanda, and the children before he stepped up to the horse. He studied the unfamiliar animal and borrowed tack, then glanced up at Harm.

"Where's my sorrel?"

"Be glad you're not on him," was all Harm would say. "Consider these a replacement."

It was one of Amanda's fine quarter horses, so he had no complaint, just a lot of questions. But it was going to be a long trail. He climbed aboard as the first of the ranger ranks moved up alongside them. Neil passed him without a glance. His dark gaze was fastened upon his estranged wife for a meaningful moment as he inclined his head for a stiff nod. The rest of the Basses he ignored altogether, though he was well aware of their reaction to him.

"Fall in, Jack," was his brusque command.

"We'll be back soon," Harm assured his anxious family, then he readied to ride.

"Harmon!"

Harm circled his mount around as Amanda passed their son to Rebecca so she could go down to him. She slapped at his foot and he moved it out of the stirrup. She slipped hers in and swung up and over the pommel so that they were face to face and her leg was riding over his. By the time the rest of the rangers converged around them, she still had him locked in a sizzling kiss.

"Hey, Bass, I'd stay home if I was you!"

"Yeah, you can always catch up in an hour or so!"

Trying to control his horse with his knees and his wife

with his hands, Harm muttered, "Ammy, you're embarrassing me."

She looked him deep in the eyes. "Do you want me to stop?"

"No."

And she kissed him again, slowly, searingly. When she released him, there was a collective gasp for air. The onlookers had been holding their breath.

"Put me down, Harmon. I won't humiliate you any further."

He was smiling. "I should thank you for adding fuel to my legend. Now these boys'll be believing everything they read."

Amanda wiggled naughtily. "And the best parts aren't even in the books. I could tell them things they'd really envy."

"They'd never believe a man could survive what you put me through, little girl."

"But then, they don't know *the* Harmon Bass as intimately as I do." She gave his lips another quick kiss and slid off his lap, holding onto his hand so he could ease her to the bottom porch step, not letting go.

And watching them, Emily wished mightily that she was at liberty to share the same demonstrative send-off with Jack. But she couldn't, not until she had her release freeing her from Neil.

Soon. Soon she would be free.

The rangers began to file out, tipping their hats to the ladies on the porch and smirking at the hard-as-nails Harmon Bass, who couldn't seem to wrest himself free from his pretty little wife. Finally, Amanda pressed his knuckles to her cheek then released him.

"Take care of my family," he told her.

"Take care of yours," she challenged in return.

Then he kicked back his heels and galloped in pursuit of the other riders. That left Jack.

"Come back," Emily called to him from where she stood with her arms hugged about herself.

"I will," he promised. He started to rein away when she cried out his name in a frantic voice. As he looked back, she jumped from the porch and ran out to him. He bent so her arms could encircle his neck as they shared a slanting of lips and hurried tangle of tongues.

"Come back to me, Jack. Please."

"I will."

"Don't bring me back anything I have to stitch up."

"I won't."

"I love you."

"I know."

Then she pushed away and ran back for the house so he wouldn't see that she was weeping. And she didn't stop crying until long after he'd gone.

"Keep him safe, Harmon. Keep him safe."

They put in a long first day's ride, but none of the men seemed to mind it. They were in unusually animated spirits: well fed, well watered on Harm's beer, well rested, and well stoked by curiosity. Subtle bets began exchanging hands on how long it would take for the simmering tension between the two men in charge to ignite into fists or gunplay. A second pool was going on who'd be left standing and on whether or not Harm Bass would stay clear of it. All were aware that the hard-eyed tracker held back purposefully in ranks, not flanking his nephew, but skimming the loosely formed group slightly to the rear of Neil Marcus. And all, especially their captain, were aware that his narrowed gaze seldom shifted from between the man's shoulder blades. The men were unanimously glad they weren't sitting in Marcus's saddle. They knew and had seen enough of Harmon Bass not to want to be on the business end of his blade.

Of all of them, Jack was the only one paying any attention to the purpose of the trip. He was half listening to Billy go on about his sister's virtues until the boy's typical exaggeration made him begin to wonder if Billy wasn't talking about someone he'd never met.

"So what do you think, Jack? Would she?"

"What?" He glanced at the eager youngster. He hadn't heard the question.

"Do you think your sister would be of a mind to take interest in someone like me?"

Jack grinned. "My sister would rather be a ranger than marry one."

Billy looked as if he'd swallowed his saddle, horse and all. "Marry! Hell, I ain't said nothing about marrying. Ain't even thought in that direction."

Jack's pale eyes affixed him unswervingly. "If you're thinking about my sister, you'd better be prepared to."

Billy snorted and shook off the notion. "She's only a kid. I got no use for somebody's kid sister." Especially when that somebody could shoot as accurately as Jack Bass and had absolutely no sense of humor when it came to dallying lightly with the ladies. " 'Sides, I can wait until she puts some meat on her bones."

"That better be all you're thinking of putting on her bones," Jack mumbled, with enough menace for Billy to turn his talk to something else. But he kept daydreaming of fiery little Sarah Bass, and it kept him smiling for the better part of the afternoon. He enjoyed ignoring Jack's pointed stares. It wasn't like his sergeant could shoot him for thinking.

Could he?

They camped at the Rio Grande on the United States side, dining well on what they'd carried away from the feast at the Basses', but the mood of sitting on a sack of dynamite lingered as sergeant and captain set up perimeters on opposite sides of the camp. When Harm squatted down beside him to offer a cup of coffee, Jack couldn't keep his questions to himself.

"Why are you here, Uncle Harm?"

Harm considered spinning some yarn, but he knew the boy wouldn't go for it. So he did what he preferred to do and told the truth. "To take care of you."

"Harmon, I'm not a kid. I can take care of myself."

"Not when you don't recognize your enemy."

Jack frowned. He glanced across the fire and Harm followed his gaze with one of malice. "Emily been talking to you?"

"She didn't have to."

"And you're thinking along the same lines? That Neil's brought me down here to kill me?"

Harm didn't answer. His impassive regard said it plain: *You bet.*

"I stole the man's wife." Jack lowered his voice when it drew curious glances. "If he'd wanted to kill me, he could have done it on the spot. I wouldn't have blamed him. He'd have had every right to. Why would he drag me all the way to Mexico? Why go to the trouble? You think he's gonna gun me down in a camp full of rangers?" Then he fingered the star Emily had pinned on his coat, beginning to understand her insistence that he wear it.

"He's too clever for that. He's the kind of man who

watches for a glimpse of your back. That's why I plan to keep it covered."

"You're wasting your time, Harmon."

"It's my time."

"Wouldn't you rather spend it doing—other things?"

He grinned blandly. "I needed a rest from those other things. Are you asking me to leave?" Oh, he'd leave if Jack asked, and he'd trail them out of sight. Marcus was in his coil, ready to strike, and Harm meant to be there to knock off his head before he sank anything deadly into Jack.

"Stay or leave, it's your choice, Uncle Harmon. Might as well get some sleep."

"You sleep. I'll sleep when I get home."

Jack chuckled. "I doubt that. G'night, Harm."

Harm got comfortable with his coffee cup in one hand, his carbine resting in his lap. But his eyes never lost their alertness. Especially when all who were supposed to be sleeping were sleeping and Neil Marcus got up and came around the fire. Harm watched him come, the ease never leaving his posture, but the sinews tightened along his limbs.

Neil came to hunker down near Harm, but not too close. He nodded to where Jack was slumbering. "He's Cates's boy, isn't he? Damn, I should have seen it. I always thought he had a familiar look about him." He mused for a moment and Harm watched him, saying nothing. "Does he know?"

"About what? That his father was a rapist and murderer? Yes. That his best friend is, too? No."

"Why didn't you tell him?"

"It's not something a man enjoys telling another. There didn't seem to be a reason for it."

"But you recognized me right off, didn't you?"

Harm smiled. "Oh, yes."

"So long ago."

"Had you forgotten the details? Or would you like me to remind you of them?"

"I remember. They aren't pleasant memories."

"I'm sure yours are better than mine."

Neil stared at the other man, trying to read beyond his impassive gaze. Such a deceiving front: mild expression, small build, no sidearm. Not like any assassin he'd known. And he'd known plenty. He was curious. "So, you killed them all."

"The first two right after they rode off with my sister, the rest over the years, until just you and one other are living."

"Who else? Cates?"

"No." And Harm smiled grimly. Then his eyes chilled. "I don't know his name. It wasn't exactly a tea party where everyone got introduced. But maybe you know it."

"Why would I tell you? So you can track him down and cut him to pieces?"

"I could make you tell me. I'd enjoy that."

Neil smiled thinly. "I bet you would."

"Tall man, black hair, dark eyes, full beard, accent not like Texas."

"Westfall."

Harm repeated the name, storing it away where he kept all the other dark things inside him.

Neil had had enough dancing around it. He put it plain, needing to know. Already suspecting. "So, why are you here, Bass?"

"To see that you don't kill Jack." Then he looked directly into Neil Marcus's soul. "And to kill you."

The ranger captain tensed at that clear-cut narrative, but he wasn't afraid. Not of one man, in his own camp. "Pretty damn bold of you to say so. What's to stop me from putting a bullet in you right now?"

"Me."

Marcus laughed. "Right in the middle of all my men? You think pretty highly of yourself, don't you?"

"I'm not stupid and I'm not careless. And you'll never know when it's coming."

"Want to tell me what I have to look forward, too? Or is it a secret?"

Harm could see the man didn't believe he was a serious threat. That made him a fool. Or maybe he did believe it. That made him a brave fool. Death wasn't something to be mocked—especially not one's own.

"Oh, I don't mind telling you. I haven't really decided. I could skin you and stake you over an anthill. I could burn you alive. I could bind you to a big cactus with green rawhide until it dried, impaling you on the spines. I could just get bored and cut your throat. Or I could do all the things that were done to me."

"Do it now."

Harm shook his head. "Part of the torture is the waiting. I want you to think about it, Marcus. I want you to know it's coming, but not when."

Marcus rose up, laughing softly. But for all his casual dismissal, Harm noticed he lay in his blankets with his pistol cocked. And he never closed his eyes.

It was a grueling day, hot and airless, as they rode over some hard, inhospitable countryside. The men grew tired and snappish, especially Neil, who seemed to have something contrary to say about every decision or suggestion his sergeant made. The powder keg was sizzling, and that made for nervous trailmates. And Harm Bass flitted along the edge of their group like a silent shadow.

Late afternoon, they overhauled a furtive Mexican. Jack recognized him as one of Ramon Cota's men. When asked about Bragg, the man had nothing to say beyond colorful expletives, calling the rangers *los Diablos Tejanas*—the Devil Texans.

Neil glanced at Harm, who was lounging easy in his saddle. "Would you like to convince him to talk? Hear you're pretty good at persuasion of that nature."

"Just along for the company," Harm drawled. "You'll have to do your own torturing. Hear you're pretty good at it, too." And above his mild smile, blue eyes gleamed like bared steel.

Marcus lost patience about then and told the boys to find a suitable tree. With the prisoner's hands bound behind his back and one end of a rope around his neck, the other over a tree branch, the Mexican was pulled up off his toes until he was an interesting shade of blue and asked calmly if he'd reconsider talking about Bragg. About the third time his neck was stretched to the point where his eyes bulged, he was only too eager to choke out the information. Bragg was holed up in Cota's stronghold, and without further ado, the man gave them all the specifics.

"Well, boys, guess we'll be planning a visit tomorrow." Neil looked at the wheezing bandit dispassionately and called, "Make that rope fast and put him on a horse. We can't have him spreading the alarm."

It was quickly done, and just before the horse was swatted out from under him, the Mexican shouted, *"Tejanos sangrientos!"* Then came the slap and gallop and the slow creak of hemp. Jack turned away from the necessary savagery and when he was offered a cup of coffee, he couldn't take it. He was afraid of how it would taste to him. The Bloody Texans. Was he the only one bothered by that truth?

His shoulder ached clear through to the bone, his conscience to the soul. His mood was low and he was missing Emily and her little green-eyed boy. He could never ride under Neil's command again. There was too much friction, just as Emily had predicted. That saddened him, because these men were the best kind of friends to him. The weight of his Texas star was heavy over his heart as the Mexican was dropped into a shallow grave and they readied to break their temporary camp.

Harm was sitting his horse like a rocking chair, eating canned peaches off the point of his knife. His presence chafed Neil Marcus into a raw disposition. He was ever aware of the man's speculative stare and of the taunting nature of the dangerous game they were playing. There wasn't much Neil could do about Jack Bass. Even if his uncle wasn't watchdogging him, Jack was operating behind the ranger badge that aligned the men behind him. Personal animosity had no place in their camp, yet theirs was ripe with it. Every order Jack gave felt like a jab at his authority. Every breath he took became an insult. The man had betrayed him with his own wife and yet was accepted within the fold of their ranger family as if he'd committed no wrong. And that wore on Neil. Jack—the man he thought of like a brother, like a son. The boy he'd spent so much time with so he wouldn't be led astray, the way he'd been when he was young. He'd worked so hard to make Jack into the kind of man he'd wanted to be. The symbol of everything he was trying to atone for had become a sobering reminder.

Jack Bass was Tyrell Cates's son. The irony was inescapable. The more he tried to bury the past, the more it rose like a restless soul to haunt him. Harm Bass was a vengeful spirit from that past, and now Jack was the living proof of it. All the good things he'd tried to do with his life were nothing as long as the two of them were there to stain his pure motives with his sins of long ago. He had to plant the memories deep if he was to go on, and if that meant planting Jack and Harmon Bass alongside them, so be it.

He had to think, and he couldn't with Harm's glare seeking out his vitals. The man made the hair on the back of his neck quiver and sweat run. Neil didn't like waiting. He didn't like not knowing. He was a man of action and quick decision, and Bass's cat-and-mouse game was making him crazy. If the man wanted to kill him, why didn't he just make his move? Why the provoking suspense? Torture, he'd said. Yes, it was. And Neil was tired of it.

"Bass, make yourself useful and go scouting up ahead."

Harm skewered a piece of fruit with a fierce jab of his knife and sucked it off the tip indolently. "I don't recall signing up under your command, Marcus, and I'm very disinclined to following your orders."

Neil stepped up close and put his hand on Harm's knee in what would look like a gesture of camaraderie to those who were too far away to hear their discussion. His voice was low and his words were goading. "It wasn't always that way, was it, Bass?"

Harm went very still, his eyes squinting into thin slits.

"I seem to remember when you'd do anything you were told. I seem to recall a runty little half-breed boy begging for the chance just to go on living, crawling like a sniveling coward. How does a man live with that? 'Course, you being Injun, that explains it. Whimpering cowards, all of you. Can't fight man to man, have to hide behind rocks and run away."

Harm gave him a slow smile. "I'm not a fool, Marcus. I jump on you and those rangers'd have me full of holes. You're not pushing me into anything until I'm ready."

"Come on, Bass. Let's settle this now. I'm sick of waiting. Man to man."

"I'm eating right now. I've waited twenty years for you. I plan to kill you at my convenience."

"You son of a bitch. Get down."

"No."

"Coward. Gutless Apache coward. Got no pride, do you? If you did, you'd have let us kill you quick." He glared up into the impassive face, as impressed now as he had been then by the man's tremendous tolerance and control. Coward? Not hardly. Even when he was outnumbered and facing a terrible death, none of them had ever seen fear in his eyes. He'd put nine grown men to shame, and that's why they'd done some of the things they'd done. They hadn't been able to break him then, and he had one last chance to do it now. Angry and afraid his nerve would fail if he had to wait for Bass to make his move, Neil prodded the stoic tracker to make him strike.

"Funny how ole Jack would pick a woman jus' like his mama. I liked your sister, Bass. A lot of spirit, even after all the boys were through with her." He paused, waiting for a reaction, but Harm gave him none, just the same flinty stare. So he took it one step farther, easing in close, pitching his voice low and sneeringly intimate.

" 'Course, a couple of the boys said they liked you better."

Then Neil Marcus got more reaction than he'd planned on.

Twenty-six

Jack was caring for his borrowed horse, watching the interplay between his uncle and his captain with a wary eye. It all looked to be civil enough. They were talking easily. Harm was eating peaches. Then everything went to hell so fast, Jack hardly had time to grasp it.

Harm let the can drop. His other hand blurred with lethal movement, switching his knife from a casual eating tool to aggressive attack weapon with one quick flip. And he was off his saddle and on top of Neil Marcus before the other man had time to draw a breath.

They fell together, Neil managing to twist around so Harm landed on his back, winding him just long enough for Neil to knock the knife from his hand. But Harm made no attempt to recover it. He went after the ranger with his bare hands, swinging fiercely, landing enough hard blows to topple Marcus. Harm was instantly astride him, pounding relentlessly, wielding his fists with a driving purpose, not to punish but to kill.

The other rangers were as stunned by the sudden violence as Jack was, but when they responded, it was to grab for their guns.

"No!"

Jack shoved his horse aside and ran toward the grappling pair.

"Put 'em down! Put 'em down! I'll take care of it. It's not your fight. You boys back down!"

Not pausing to see if they were obeying, Jack waded right into the middle of the savage brawl. Neil was obviously getting the worst of it. His face was bloodied past recognition, and Harm showed no sign of letting up. Jack gripped him by the arms and was tossed off as if he was a bothersome insect. By then, Harm had Neil docile and was groping for his knife with deadly intention. Reacting from instinct rather than intelligence, Jack flung himself between his captain and the descending blade.

"Harmon!"

And the tip jerked to a stop a half inch above Jack's heaving shirt front. With a growl of, "Get outta the way, Jack," Harm shoved him aside, meaning to complete his butchery. So Jack hit him hard. Hard as he could. Hard enough to stun him and set him back on his heels. Then Jack dived at him while he was off balance, wrestling the knife away, hanging onto him so the well-armed rangers wouldn't see him as a threat. It was like hugging a mountain lion. Harm was howling with rage, twisting, writhing furiously in his attempt to escape Jack's hold. Finally, Jack got a headlock on him, wedging his uncle's windpipe into the crook of his elbow and wrenching one arm halfway up his back.

"Stop it! Harmon, stop it!" But still he struggled. Jack realized then that short of knocking him unconscious, the only thing that was going to quiet him was getting Neil out of his sight.

Bulldogging his uncle, Jack nodded to the battered form of Neil Marcus. "You boys get him on a horse and head on outta here. Go on! Billy, you take charge. Run on up ahead a couple miles and plant down for the night. I'll catch up. Now!"

Used to taking their sergeant's orders, the men hurriedly did as they were told. All except Billy, who was regarding Harm somewhat uneasily.

"You gonna be all right with him?"

"Fine. Go on."

"What if the captain wants to come back after him when he wakes up?"

"Discourage him," Jack instructed grimly.

"All right, Jack. You be careful now."

With Neil slung loosely over his saddle, the men departed, and only then did Jack even think of trying to reason with his uncle.

"Harmon? Uncle Harm? Settle down, now. They're gone. He's gone. Easy, now. I don't want to hurt you." But the second Jack relaxed his hold, Harm was lunging toward his horse, forcing Jack to restrain him all over again. "Harmon, stop it! I'm almost breaking your arm! Now quit! Quit."

And finally he did, sagging in Jack's grip, panting hard with labored gasps, shaking fiercely from the strain of tension. After a minute or two, Jack took him by the shoulders and levered him away.

"All right, you tell me and you tell me now, what's between you and Neil? Harmon, you answer me!"

But he wouldn't, and when Jack shook him, he wobbled and went down on his knees, head bent as he gulped noisily for air.

"Uncle Harm, talk to me. You tell me, or you get the hell outta here. You go home. I got enough on my mind without worrying about some crazy debt—"

"There were too many of them."

"What?" Harm had moaned the words so low and faint, Jack wasn't sure he'd heard him right.

"I was one and they were nine. Twice my age. Three times my size. I—I couldn't stop them. I tried. I did. They—hurt us, Jack, your mama and me. They hurt us so bad."

"Who did?"

Harm caught Jack's forearms and clutched at them as he rocked back and forth with the hard push of his breathing. His gaze was fixed on the ground, his thoughts twenty years in the past. He started to shake his head, but Jack insisted.

"Who, Harmon? Who hurt you? My father?"

"Cates. And Franks." That name meant nothing to Jack. "Six others."

"You said there were nine."

"And Marcus."

"No." Jack said it without thinking, giving his head a denying shake as he did.

Harm looked up at him through eyes dazed and dulled by a terrible anguish. "And Neil Marcus."

"Oh, God." Then they were hanging onto each other; Harm crippled by despair, Jack weakened by shock.

"Jack, they—"

"I don't want to know! Damn it, Harmon, I don't want to know!" He shoved away and staggered to his feet, walking in aimlessly agitated circles. Neil . . . it was too much. He couldn't take it in. First the news about his father and the fact that Harm had killed him. Now this. He wanted to curl up someplace to protect himself from further hurt, from thought. But his mind was already spinning ahead in dizzying loops. "And Mama—she recognized him the other morning."

"Yes."

"And Emily knows?"

"Yes. I couldn't let her go back to him after we thought you were—gone."

"And Neil? He knows who you are? Who I am?"

"Not until he saw Becky." Harm wiped at his eyes. He was watching Jack, all sympathy and sorrow now. The anger was gone, but not the grief. "So . . . now you understand."

"I don't understand anything, Uncle Harm."

"I'm sorry."

Some of the wildness of confusion left him then and he gave his uncle a long look. Harm was on his knees and more vulnerable than Jack had ever seen him. His uplifted gaze was fragile with expectant self-blame. And Jack thought suddenly of Emily and her mournful confessions of unjustified guilt: *I tried to fight, but they were stronger.* Then he grew angry at those who would victimize these two that he loved. "Why are you sorry? It's not your fault."

"I just always felt that it was."

And Jack saw for the first time what a terrible burden his uncle had carried for such a very long time. And the burden of his own, as well. "It wasn't your fault and it wasn't mine or my mother's. We weren't given much choice, were we?"

Harm blinked, taking in Jack's quietly forceful words. And he answered from a tortured soul that desperately sought absolution. He sounded almost surprised by his own conclusion.

"No."

"Oh, Harm, you were right when you said nothing was easy."

"So, what now?"

Jack sighed and tried to think. He was churning inside, but a deeper calm was beginning to prevail. "We catch up to the others. I have a job to do, and you need to get us both home alive."

Harm nodded. "And Marcus?"

"I don't know yet." He took off his hat and ran distracted fingers through his hair. His hand was shaking. "I don't know what to think."

"Give it time."

"Do I have it? Harm—"

"I'll wait. I won't act until we talk again."

"Are you all right? I hit you pretty hard."

"Amanda's hit me harder than that." But he worked his jaw gingerly and rubbed at the start of a tender swelling. "Are you all right?"

"No. But I'm glad you're here. He really is going to try to kill me, isn't he?"

"Yes."

"Well, I don't plan to let him."

"Neither do I."

It was dark by the time they approached the ranger fire. They drew up at the perimeter and Jack called in to alert the guard.

"Hello in camp."

"That you, Jack?"

"Sandy."

"You got your uncle with you?" He sounded uneasy, and Jack couldn't blame him.

"He's with me, and everything's all straightened out. No trouble. Can we come in?"

"Sure, ride on ahead."

They intruded upon a cautious group gathered by the fire. Jack had no idea how difficult it was going to be until he saw Neil Marcus sitting on the other side, his face lumpy with contusions. When the man stood, Jack was assailed by emotions too big to identify. This was the man who'd befriended him and taught him discipline and pride. The man he'd sworn by the State of Texas to follow right up to death's door. The man who'd abused the Bass family and the woman he meant to marry. It was hard to know what to think or feel. He wished for numbness, instead of this engulfing tide of turmoil. Then he felt the pressure of Harm's hand upon his shoulder and his world steadied. Whatever confusions he was feeling now, how much worse they must be for his uncle. If Harm could hold them in, so could he until the time came to act upon them.

" 'Evening, boys. Still got some coffee?"

"Sure, Jack." Clayton began to pour. "He want some, too?" He glanced nervously at Harm.

"Ask him."

"Coffee, Mr. Bass?"

"No." Then softer, "Thank you."

From across the camp came a brusque, "Jack, we need to talk. Bring your cup."

Jack looked at his captain and said, "Yes, we do."

And as he started around the fire with Harm on his heels, Neil ordered curtly, "Just you. This don't concern him."

"Yes, it does," Harm argued quietly, but Jack waved him off.

"It's all right, Uncle Harm. Get some coffee and some grub. This'll only take a minute."

But Harm had no intention of taking his eyes off them as they walked to the edge of the firelight. He went to get himself coffee, not noticing how the rangers scooted over to give him plenty of space.

"Jack, it's about your uncle."

"What about him?" Jack drawled softly.

"The man tried to kill me."

"Why would you be surprised about that? Considering. I just might beat him to it." Then, as Neil turned toward him, Jack's voice lowered into a low, lethal rumble, "You bastard. How dare you talk to me about what's decent after what you did to my family?"

"So, he told you."

"Yes, he told me."

"What are you going to do about it?" He challenged the younger man with a narrowed gaze.

"Damn it, Neil, I don't know. I didn't want to be a part in any of this. It would have been a helluva lot easier on everybody if Emily had just let those Apache skin me. Then your daughter would still be alive, and those other women and children; Harm wouldn't be after your hair; and I'da died still thinking you were somebody I could respect."

Neil's hostility ebbed in the face of Jack's pained frustration. They'd been close, and that was a hard thing just to put aside. He found himself wanting to console Jack in his distress, to explain away the unforgivable. To earn back just a grain of that respect that had meant so much to him.

"It's hard to accept the fact that folks aren't perfect, that they make mistakes—bad ones, that they don't live up to what you think they should be. I was sixteen years old, Jack. My family had been wiped out by Apache. The only thing I lived for was evens. I got a job from a man named McAllister, range work mostly, but his headman, Cates, your daddy, came to me and asked if I had the stuff it took to ride on a little ranch and get rid of a breed family that was squatting on water right-of-way. I was up for it. Just a woman and a girl, dark as any Apache. I kept seeing what those savages had done to my folks and I never saw 'em as anything else. I wanted to make someone pay for what had happened, and there they were."

Sort of like Harm's Apache code of retribution, Jack realized with a chill.

"Then the boy came outta nowhere, cut your daddy, and would have taken us all on." Neil gave a soft, almost admiring laugh. "Hell, he was a wild one, a little kid fierce as any full-grown Indian. We were all drunk by then and in no kind a mood to take nothing off some breed kid. I was passed out through most of it, but I remember seeing plenty, doing plenty. When I came around after we'd burned the place and buried the boy and his mama, I can remember feeling a sickness so deep I didn't think I'd ever get over it. I couldn't believe I could have done any of those things— not ever."

Part of Jack was making excuses for the man; he'd been young, crazy drunk, wild with grief and hate. Part of him would take no excuse, remembering the terror in his mother's eyes, the panic of his uncle's nightmares. Emily's fear of him. He kept waiting for that blind surge of fury to rise inside him that would feed him with the same lust for killing that blanked Harm to all else. He shouldn't have felt hesitation. He shouldn't have felt sympathy for the boy this man had been or sorrow for the circumstances. What was wrong with him?

Neil continued, not looking at Jack, but off into the darkness, back into his troubled life. "The war came along and I joined up. Found myself serving under Emily's father. He was the first honorable man I'd ever known, the first to take an interest in me. I learned things from him that turned my thinking all around. And I got to hoping that maybe I could do something with my life, something that would right wrongs. And when that good man went down in battle and I carried his sword home to his family, I saw a way to start over." Then his tone grew savage. "You took that away from me, Jack. You took my chance to make up for my wrongs."

But Jack wasn't having any of it. "No, Neil, you gave that chance away yourself."

Neil spun to confront the younger man, his expression fierce, his glare hot. "And I suppose you're gonna tell me I just gave my wife to you."

"Yes. In a way, you did. She tried to come back to you, but you just couldn't let go of the hate. You held her accountable for the things that'd been done to her, things she couldn't have prevented any more than my mama could have. You pushed her away with that hate when she needed you. She wanted to do the right thing, we both did, but you just wouldn't let it happen."

"So it's my fault. My fault?"

"I was wrong to fall in love with your wife, Neil." He said that quietly, with a deep-felt sincerity, then he followed it with an even stronger sentiment. "But I'm not sorry."

Jack staggered from the suddenness of the blow Neil sent crashing against his jaw. And at the ranger fire, those who'd been covertly watching the confrontation escalate readied to move to pull the men they respected apart, if the need arose. And Harm's hand rested on his knife hilt. But the violence of the scene dissipated.

"You will be sorry," Neil spat at his young sergeant. "I'll make sure you're sorry."

Jack let him walk away, back to the ranger fire, where he was left alone by the uncertain group gathered there. Jack stood in the darkness, feeling dark and lost inside. Then, after a while, Harm came to spread their bedrolls out next to where he was standing. Without comment, Harm took to his, lying back with apparent weariness, leaving his nephew to his thoughts. Jack figured he'd fallen asleep until the sound of an approaching footfall had him snatching for his carbine.

"Rest easy, Mr. Bass. It's just me, Billy Cooper."

Harm's fingers relaxed.

"Jack, I come to let you know about tomorrow. We'll be taking Cota's place at dawn." He pressed a strip of white shirt material upon him. "Tie this off around your arm so you won't be mistaken in the dark. You riding in with us, Mr. Bass?"

"No. It's not my business."

"Well, I'll feel better knowing you're out there, anyway." He gave his sergeant a long look. Damn, he'd hate to lose Jack Bass to the Mexicans. Or to Neil Marcus. He hesitated, torn between his dutiful loyalty to his leader and his friendship with this man who'd given him a chance to rise in the ranks of distinction at his side. Jack was more than a friend; he was the man Billy aspired to be, and this pull between him and the captain was a difficult moral dilemma. Then Billy recalled clear as day Jack Bass turning his horse toward those Mexicans, riding down on them at the risk of his own life so he could get their prisoner to safety. And suddenly, the decision wasn't so difficult anymore. "If you need me, Jack, for anything, I'm with you."

Jack seemed all choked up for a moment, then he murmured, "I appreciate knowing that."

"See you before sunup."

"Billy?"

"Ummm?"

"My sister'd make a lousy wife. Can't cook a lick."

The boy grinned wide. "That's all right. I can. 'Sides, there's more to life than a good meal. 'Night."

From his blankets, Harm gave an agreeing chuckle, wishing for a little of that 'more' right about now. His wife made a most pleasant trail companion, despite her inability to cook meat evenly over his fire. Billy Cooper and Sarah Bass: a pair of hellions. Interesting thought.

"Sit down, Jack. Rest what you can."

After a restless second, Jack settled down on his back, rubbing the ache in his shoulder. The struggle with Harm woke it to all kinds of misery.

"What's on your mind?" Harm asked. "After six years with Amanda, I'm a helluva good listener."

Jack smiled faintly, then gave a heavy sigh. "I hate him for what he did to us, to Emily, but I can't hate him enough to wish him dead."

"And that bothers you?"

"Shouldn't it? I mean, with you, it's so clear cut. Me, I'm still going in circles."

"Good."

"Good? Why's that good?"

"Because it tells me you were listening to what I taught you. Jack, your mama and I saw the worst mankind had to offer, and we swore not to let you know that world. Apache kids grow up thinking there's no other way to die except through violence. It's a hard way to live, believing that. I go to bed every night expecting to die the next day. I wanted you to be stronger than that. I wanted you to look past tomorrow in a way I never could. I'm a weak man, Jack."

"You? No—"

"I am. My strength is in Amanda, and I know it. She makes me believe there'll be a tomorrow. You, you're strong. You don't need anyone to tell you that. You look ahead and see things you want, things to work for, good things, powerful things. I try, but there are demons that won't let go of me."

"Things like Neil."

Harm nodded. "I don't have the strength to forgive or forget. I can't let go even if I know it will kill me. Marcus knew that. He could recognize that weakness in me because it's in him, too. But you, Jack, you're better than we are because you look with open eyes and see with a big heart and clear mind. You see a circle, I see a wall. You can go around, I have to go through."

"You're going to kill him, aren't you?"

"I have to, Jack, before he does you and me. Because for Marcus and me, we can't go around. We have to end it. And I am very glad you don't feel the same way. I am proud of the man you are. I would raise my son to walk in the same steps and hope you will raise yours the same way. There's no hope in me or in my people, and that's why we can't survive."

"Uncle Harm, you—"

"Oh, don't worry. Ammy has every intention of dragging me into the next century with her. She'd never let my spirit rest if I were to leave her. She'd make my eternity hell, so I might as well enjoy the here-and-now."

"She's a good woman."

"She's my woman. And when this is done, you'll know exactly what I mean. When you ride in and yours is there for you, you'll see tomorrow in her eyes."

Jack thought about it, and he smiled. "I like that."

"It's my romantic soul," Harm drawled, then he gave a soft snort and closed his eyes.

"You're a good man, Uncle Harmon."

"Only because those around me force me to be. You, you're a good man because it's the way you are inside. Go to sleep. We have business to finish tomorrow so we can go home. I'm looking forward to my own bed and a wife who won't let me get enough sleep in it."

And Jack lay back, closing his eyes, imagining Emily waiting for him with tomorrow in her eyes.

The hours before morning were dark, still, and cold, with just a sliver of moon to stir the shadows. Jack awoke, not really surprised to find Harm gone. He'd be nearby, watching, and unseen protection was the best kind.

The rangers broke camp quickly, without coffee, without talk. They moved across the mile that separated them from their target with a swift efficiency, a job to do. While blackness still crouched alongside them, they ringed the hacienda where Neville Bragg sought refuge. And in those few stark minutes, Jack knew a true trickling of fear; not from what lay ahead, but from what could be lurking at his back. He felt alone and exposed in those predawn shadows, and he knew why Harm had said he had to end it. Jack couldn't imagine going through the years with that feeling of vulnerability crawling up and down his back. He and Emily would never be safe as long as Neil was out there with a grudge and a gun. And while Jack knew he couldn't force a showdown with his former friend, he was also glad Harm wasn't of the same conviction. Neil stood between him and his tomorrows, and if Harm didn't do something about it, he'd have to. He wanted those tomorrows with Emily. And if he'd learned something else from his uncle, it was that a man did what he had to to protect his family.

Dawn seeped over them gray and clear, and with it came Neil's firm command.

"You in the house, we've got you surrounded. We're

Texas Rangers come for Neville Bragg. Turn him over to us and there'll be no trouble."

He was answered by gunfire.

It was a waiting game. The rangers were protected by cover and able to move around. The Mexicans, on the other hand, were trapped in the adobe house with water a yard and a world away. Occasionally, there'd be bursts of fire from the stronghold, and once in a while a brave soul would make a dash toward that well, but he wouldn't get far. The sun rose high and hot, and the Mexicans began to bake beneath their tiled roof.

"Jack."

He lifted up to see Clayton Wainright, who was holed up behind a neighboring outcropping.

"Cap'n wants us to rush in on his command."

"What? Across all that open ground? We got nothing to lose but time if we stay put."

Clayton shrugged. He wasn't a man much inclined toward thinking for himself, and one order was pretty much as sound as the next to him, but Jack thought it suicidal and said so. But he would obey it.

About then Neil rose up with a shout of, "C'mon, boys. Follow me." A quick scramble of men brought a welcoming wave of bullets, but miraculously, no one was hit in that mad dash across to the outer walls. The Mexicans must have been too stunned by the audacity of the attack to shoot straight, Jack decided, as he hunched down behind the high surround. He took a deep breath and went up and over the wall, dropping down on the other side with his pistol at the ready. He'd gone some ten feet, running in a low crouch. He was safely out of sight from the gunmen in the house and was set on his approach when his attention was caught by a ranger rifleman jumping up onto the far wall.

The man was Neil Marcus and the rifle was pointed right at him.

The children saw it first: dust rising up from the approach of horsemen. Their excited cries alerted Emily, who'd been shaking a rug over the far porch rail.

"Amanda!" She shouted over her shoulder as she ran to the edge of the steps, straining to see the nature and number of the riders. They rode in a cluster, so she knew it wasn't Indians. The Apache always rode single file to confuse an enemy as to their true size. "They're back!"

A single rider separated from the rest, cantering up to the house, and from behind her, Emily heard a joyous cry. "Harmon!"

Amanda flew off the front steps and was wrapped around him before he reached the ground. For a long moment, they just clung together, neither moving. Then Harm said something to his wife and she stepped away, letting him come up to the porch alone. Emily waited, trying frantically to read something in his expression so she'd know whether to feel happy relief or crushing sorrow. But she couldn't tell what was behind the impassive set of his bronzed features.

"Harmon?"

He reached out his hand and hers went to meet it. She didn't need to look down to know what he pressed into her palm. It was a ranger star.

And she heard him say from what seemed like years away, "He died well."

Twenty-seven

From his carefully chosen position, Harm had a perfect view of Neil Marcus. Harm was a patient man. He'd sit back and wait for an opportunity. Sometime during the next few minutes of confusion, Marcus was going to become a ranger casualty on the end of his knife. He spent a moment paring the calluses off his palm to test the sharpness of the blade. Satisfied, he wiped it clean against the denim of his jeans and held it at the ready.

When Marcus yelled for his men to move in, Harm moved forward in unseen tandem. Marcus rode down across the stretch of ground, Harm covered the distance afoot. The ranger angled his horse up to the wall, swinging from the saddle to the top with his Winchester in hand. The second his leather was empty, Harm was up and over, right behind him.

From where he paused, moccasined feet poised confidently upon the saddle skirt, Harm caught a look across the yard, spotting Jack at the same time Neil did from up above him. He saw the Winchester swing into play, and just as he was about to drive in with his blade, he also saw a Mexican flanking Jack with pistol drawn, undetected by the young ranger. In that second, Harm knew a terrible helplessness, he himself armed only with a knife, and the distance impossible. If he took the time to kill Marcus and take his gun, Jack would be dead. All Neil had to do was nothing.

But suddenly Neil Marcus shouldered his weapon with a purposeful intent, squeezing off a shot. The man behind Jack was knocked out from under his hat, dead as he hit the ground. Before Jack could acknowledge the fact that his captain had saved his life instead of taking it himself, a shotgun blast from the house took Neil in the chest, toppling him backward, into Harm, and they both went down to the ground behind the wall.

For the next minutes, Harm sat with his enemy in his arms, watching the man breathe his last. Marcus's eyes were open, fixing on his in a recognition of his own death.

"Sorry to deprive you of the pleasure, Bass." He tried to smile, but it turned into a grimace.

"Dead is dead. I'll be satisfied."

Marcus's hands gripped his forearms, pinching tight as a cough rattled up through his shot-riddled chest. Harm allowed it. His spirit was calm now, and he felt no anger toward this man who had been his nephew's friend.

"Would you have killed him?"

Marcus took a gurgling breath and laughed. "Funny, I was ready to shoot him down until I saw that other feller fixing to do it. Just couldn't let it happen that way. We rangers protect our own. Crazy, huh?"

Harm nodded. About as crazy as him hearing his mortal foe's last confessions.

"Would you—would you tell Emily something for me?"

"I will."

"Tell her—tell her I died like a ranger."

"I will."

"And tell Jack I was—was proud to ride with him."

But Neil Marcus never heard Harm's last soft-spoken, "I will."

Through the roaring in her head, Emily heard Amanda cry, "Harmon, catch her. She's going to faint."

Strong hands caught her at the waist, but there seemed no way to stop the spiral down into darkness and despair. She was vaguely aware of the firmness of the porch steps beneath her and of curling into Harm, hiding from the truth by pressing her face up against the warm pulse of his throat, clinging to him in a daze of disbelief. But she didn't cry; the grief went too deep for tears. Her life was over. All she could do was moan his name.

"Oh, Jack."

"Emily."

She lifted up her head in answer to Harm's compelling command. He was smiling faintly and she grew confused.

"Emily, Jack's all right."

"W-what?"

She stared up at him, unsure of what to believe until he nodded his head toward the approaching rangers. She turned slowly, almost fearfully, to follow his gaze. Then the support of his arms cinched up tight again as she sagged with relief.

"Jack."

He was at the head of the ranger column, dirty, weary, but no worse for wear. And behind him, on the horse he led, was a blanketed shape. Then she understood: Neil was dead. It was *his* badge Harm had given her, and from what the other rangers observed, she'd collapsed from the news of her husband's death. To a one, they swept off their hats to pay their respects to their captain's widow, but Emily was only faintly aware of it. Neil was dead. She felt no stir of emotions at that knowledge, not when heart and soul were absorbing the sight of Jack Bass as he swung down and, hat in hand, approached. His expression was somber, his step slowed by remorse.

With a soft cry, Emily started to rise up to run to him, but Harm's grip suddenly intensified, holding her in place.

"No," he warned quietly. "Let him come to you. It will look better."

She was almost too numb to make sense of that, but she'd grown used to listening to Harm Bass's wisdom. So she stayed where she was and let Jack come to them. She was shivering from the effort of restraint by the time he halted. But when he looked up at her and she saw the terrible sorrow in his eyes, she was glad she'd heeded Harm's suggestion. If it had been any man other than Jack Bass coming to tell his lover of the death of the man who stood between them, no one would have believed him sincere in his distress. But no one doubted that the dampness on Jack's face was genuine or that his mourning was real.

"I'm sorry, Emily," he said in a grief-thickened voice. "He died saving my life."

With Harm anchoring her to the porch step, she could do no more than respond with tears of her own—not for Neil Marcus, but for Jack Bass, who'd lost a man he'd once admired and considered a friend.

Amanda came up to put an arm around Jack, supplying a gentle squeeze. To the rangers, she called, "Why don't you boys set up camp down by the creek, clean up, and rest. I'll see about fixing some supper."

There was a murmur of collective thanks and the quiet group filed by, taking their fallen leader and Jack's horse.

"Come inside, Jack," Amanda coaxed, and he moved beside her without a fuss. Then Harm released Emily and she was up racing after him, Neil's star cutting into her palm as she unconsciously clutched at it.

In the cool quiet of the parlor, Amanda let Jack go, rubbing his back comfortingly before shooing the curious children out and allowing Emily in.

"You kids go dig some potatoes," Amanda ordered. "We've got a lot of hungry men to feed." Then, as Emily led Jack over to the sofa, where they sat side by side so he could tell all that had happened, Amanda reached out for Harm's hand to tug him upstairs. She was met with no resistance.

Once in their room, Harm turned into her arms, holding tight, simply breathing in her soul-saving sweetness.

"It's good to be home."

And she kissed his dusty hair, his brow, his cheek, and finally his mouth, glad to have him.

"You didn't kill him?"

Harm shook his head. "The bastard ended up saving Jack to earn himself a way outta hell."

"Are you all right with that?"

He nodded. "He's gone, and I don't want to talk about him anymore." His hands were moving over Amanda, and she sighed at his touch. She started with his shirt buttons, moving rapidly downward, but her gaze never left his. When everything coated with trail dust lay at his feet, she tugged him toward the bed.

"I'm all dirty."

"I don't care where you've been, just that you're here." And she swayed against him to prove it with her eager kisses and urgent caresses. "Oh, Harmon." Then she gave him a push away. "Stretch out, get comfortable. I'll be right there."

She heard the creak of their bed frame and his luxurious

groan of contentment as she went to latch their door. She started back toward the bed, unfastening the small buttons that held the front of her gown together. Then she paused.

"Harmon?"

He didn't move.

"Harm?"

She came up to peer over his shoulder, looking upon the relaxed contours of his face. He was sound asleep. Fighting the want to moan in frustration, Amanda smiled instead. She drew a light sheet over him and bent to place a kiss on his warm shoulder.

"Sleep well, *shijii.*" Then she touched his short black hair and strong jaw, concluding, "It may be the last I let you have for nights to come." She kissed his brow. "I love you, Harmon."

Then, rebuttoning her bodice, she went to tend to her dozen-plus guests.

Emily sat listening to Jack tell of Neil's death and their subsequent success in storming the Cota stronghold. Bragg had been killed in the effort, and Jack remarked somewhat wryly that many would see it as a case of *ley de fuga,* saying the rangers deliberately killed the prisoner as he was "escaping" with immunity from their home state so he couldn't evade justice again. What Jack didn't tell her was whether or not that was true.

Emily watched his face and tried to decipher his odd hesitation. He was remote, not looking at her, making absolutely no attempt to touch her. It was Neil. He was sitting between them, and knowing that, she didn't push across that barrier. Jack needed time to heal the rawness of loss and to discard his guilt. How much time, she didn't know, and though the sense of separation scared her, she would endure it for his sake. And she could only hope that in his grief, he would attach no insurmountable blame to her.

"Jack, why don't you go see to your men while I help Amanda with supper? We can talk more later. All right?"

He nodded wearily but still didn't look at her. She found she couldn't be quite so noble. Her palm cupped under his rough chin, angling his head around so she could kiss his mouth softly with a brief tenderness. Then she left him quickly, while his eyes were still closed, before she was tempted beyond what was wise.

It was a much more subdued group gathered in the Basses' front yard than that of a few days ago. They fed on a savory chicken stew and drank down the last of Harm's Apache beer, not caring that it was warm or that it had gone flat. When every crumb that could be considered food was gone, they went back down to their camp after mumbling thanks and extending regrets to Emily Marcus. They seemed relieved in their acceptance of her, as if by dying with honor, Neil absolved them from having to make a choice between their respected captain and their popular sergeant. With his death, the tension was forgotten. All of them left in silence, even Jack.

Back inside, Emily started to scrape plates when Amanda shooed her out.

"Go tuck the children in. Let me do this. I need to keep busy. Harmon's sleeping, and he's safer if I stay down here."

Emily smiled wistfully, her yearning for Jack so severe it was like heartbreak. She gathered the clan of youngsters and herded them up and through their washing and prayers, but the Bass girls wouldn't go down until they'd seen their father. They slipped in quietly and up to where Harm was slumbering, the covers rising and falling gently over his chest. But the second the girls leaned down to hug him, his arm came up to circle his daughters, pulling them in close so he could kiss both blond heads.

"Where's your mama?" he murmured sleepily.

"Downstairs," Leisha volunteered. "Want me to go get her?"

Harm smiled and let his eyes close. "She knows where to find me."

"G'night, Daddy," the girls called in unison.

Harm was already back to sleep, secure enough in his world to let it move on around him.

"Where's Ranger Jack?" Kenitay asked, as Emily finally drew up his covers.

"He's with his men."

"Will he leave with them in the morning?" A sudden anxiousness came into his eyes and Emily recognized it, feeling the stir of it herself.

"I don't know. We'll have to see."

"Is he still going to be my second father?"

"We'll have to see," she repeated, sounding much more confident than she felt. "Go to sleep now."

She turned down the light, kissing his brow before crossing the hall. As she reached in to close the door, she gave a slight gasp as arms encircled her from behind, drawing her up close to a familiar form.

"Goodnight, Ranger Jack." The boy sounded very pleased.

"G'night, Kenitay." And he pulled the door shut, turning Emily as he did and greeting her with a long, thorough kiss. Then he just held her and they absorbed the feel of one another. Emily nestled close, sighing his name. He'd washed up and changed clothes. He smelled as good and fresh as the Texas Bend after a rain shower.

"Jack . . ."

"I love you, Emily." And he kissed her again, this time with considerable passion and enough fancy tongue tangling to have her pulling him toward their room. He was half undressed before he got the door closed behind them.

"I just put these on."

"You can get back into them. Later."

Her mouth was hot and eager as it moved from throat to chest to flat belly as she skinned off his jeans, then back up again to reacquaint itself with the sensuous shape of his lips. Treating her to the same tantalizing play, Jack disrobed her and went down with her upon the bed.

"Marry me," he whispered into her starving kisses. The past was gone and she was his future.

"When?" She was shifting beneath him, her hands impatient, her body arching, opening.

"Come back to Ysleta with me, you and Kenitay. I don't want to be without you." His mouth trailed down to one aching peak. Emily cried out softly from all his exquisite attention. Her hands twined restlessly through thick auburn hair. She couldn't answer until he lifted back up expectantly. She smiled, panting hard.

"It's a long trip in separate blankets."

He smiled back. "Then we'll have to get it all out of our systems tonight, won't we?" His palms caressed her, filling up with her softness. The soles of her feet stroked up and down his legs encouragingly. He nudged closer to what they both were craving. "Emily?"

"What?"

"Do you know what I see when I look at you?"

She touched his face, rubbing her fingertips across the spread of his cheekbones, her thumbs brushing over his mouth. "What do you see, Jack?"

"I see tomorrow and a whole lot of other tomorrows."

Her gaze simmered and shimmered damply. "That's lovely. But could you tend to tonight first?"

And then she gasped into his claiming kiss as he plunged deep to fill her body and soul with everything she could wish for.

A smiling Amanda and a spent yet smug Harmon Bass saw them off in the morning, but it was Leisha who surprised Jack with a quick embrace and warm kiss.

"Goodbye, Cousin Jack. I decided to like you after all."

Amanda was all teary kisses and Harm supplied rib-creaking Apache hugs. Emily squeezed him back, whispering, "Thank you, Harmon," to which he replied, "be good to one another, *silah.*"

He and Jack exchanged a hard embrace, then Jack told his uncle's wife, "You take care of him."

Amanda smiled confidently and cuddled up against her husband. "Oh, you can count on it. We'll see you soon. We have horses to buy."

Harm rolled his eyes heavenward, but his arm never slackened its hold upon the impetuous woman at his side as they stood watching the rangers ride away.

"They'll be fine," Amanda concluded.

Harm's forefinger stroked down her damp cheek, bringing her gaze up to his. "So will we, *shijii.*" And he kissed her convincingly.

"Ummmm, Harmon . . ."

"More horses." He snorted. "Are you sure?"

Her fingers were doing enticing things with his shirt collar. "Yes. You never know when they might be needed to buy more of your relatives out of trouble."

"You're trouble, little girl."

"And you're mine, Harmon Bass." After a lengthy discussion without words, she panted, "Let's go inside. We have two more rooms to fill."

Neil Marcus was buried with ranger honors in Ysleta. His body was carried in a black hearse by two fine black horses to a final resting place next to his daughter. His company of rangers marched behind on foot, along with a compliment of U.S. soldiers who fired farewell shots over the grave as Juana Javier threw herself prostrate on the fresh earth with a heartrending wail.

As soon as Emily Marcus changed from her black gown, she became Mrs. Jack Bass in a small solemn ceremony witnessed by Billy Cooper and a puzzled Kenitay. He didn't understand the words or the meaning. To him, Jack already belonged to his mother. What he did understand was the special nature of the newlyweds' first night together. It was spent in a hotel room in El Paso, the three of them curled up as family, with nothing but affectionate words and gentle kisses exchanged between man and wife and a very happy boy excluded from none of it.

The adjutant general himself had come from Austin to be present at the burial of his noted captain. The next day, he sent for Jack, and while a very nervous ranger sergeant went to stand before him, Emily and Kenitay went to the adobe home she'd shared with Neil to remove his belongings before a new commander was appointed.

Kenitay amused himself with a stray dog that followed him inside while Emily was faced with the task of folding away Neil's clothes. She felt a strange detachment from the duty, almost as if she was picking up after someone she didn't know. In a way, that was true. She had never really known the man Neil Marcus had been, and she wasn't sure how to feel, now that he was gone.

Then she heard her son cry her name and turned to come face to face with a dramatically black-garbed Juana.

"He loved me," she claimed harshly, as her black eyes glared resentfully at Emily's hands upon his coat.

Emily was in no mood to argue with the distraught woman. "Perhaps he did. If there is something of his you would like, you can have it."

"I want all that was his. I should have it all."

Emily dropped the jacket upon the bed. "Fine. Take it." She edged past the vengeful figure into the main room, where Kenitay waited anxiously. "There's nothing for us here," she told him quietly. She took his hand and had started for the door when Juana put herself in the way, fuming darkly.

"I want his guns. Where are they? And his star."

Emily stared at her blankly.

"Give them to me!" Her hand flashed back, readying a slap. And was caught firmly about the wrist.

"No."

Juana spun to glare at Jack. "I want them!"

"No. Have anything else you want. Pick the bones clean as soon as we're out of here. But you're not going to sell a ranger's guns, and his star is mine."

The Mexican harlot fumed, but she wasn't fool enough to think any amount of verbal or physical display would change his mind. So she planted her feet and snarled, "Get out. Get out of his house, you and your whore."

Jack put out his hand to Emily, drawing her safely past the seething woman who spat at their heels.

"Cabrone. Puta!"

They walked for a ways, the three of them, with hands linked. Emily was trying hard not to cry, but she was so disheartened. Jack was clearly angry, and Kenitay, confused. Not a wonderful way to start family life.

"I hope you got everything you wanted from back there, 'cause there's no way I'm ever letting you return."

"I did."

Hearing the desolate quality in her voice, Jack said nothing more. He led them down the row of ranger barracks to the one he'd shared with his friends. It was empty and his things were stacked in an orderly fashion on his bunk, topped by Neil's armaments. Kenitay observed the surroundings with rounded eyes. Emily did so glumly, knowing she was taking Jack from a life he loved.

"What did the general want?" she asked at last.

"Apparently, Neil had sent him a letter recommending me for promotion." He looked away from her empathic gaze. "They want to commission me to first lieutenant in command of my own company down in the Bend area. I'm authorized to pick whichever men I want with me and to select from any other applicants until the positions are filled. I have ten days to assemble the men and move out."

"So you told him yes." Her tone was carefully neutral until he looked over at her.

"I told him I would discuss it with my wife."

"What do the men think?" She didn't know if there would be any hard feelings following Jack after Neil.

"They've all said they'd follow me wherever I wanted to go." But his eyes were on her, asking what she thought.

Emily stepped in close, her hands gliding up his chest, tracing over the star he wore. "Well, Ranger Jack, I think you should get a corporal commission for Billy Cooper. You'll need a good right hand down in the Bend. And it'll probably help to have a wife who speaks Apache and relatives practically on the doorstep, especially ones who have reputations like Harmon's."

He studied her face, looking deep into her eyes, seeing the love there, the trust, the encouragement. "You're saying yes, I should take it?"

"Do you want to?"

"More than almost anything."

"Then I'm saying the State of Texas needs a man like you almost as much as I do, and this one time, I'm inclined to be generous—under one condition."

Jack was smiling. "What's that?"

"Texas can have you by day, but I get you by night."

He started bending down for her lips. "I can live with that." He kissed her, then lifted up to adore her with his gaze. "For today and all my tomorrows."

And her arms went around him tight, sealing that promise in with her kiss.

Please turn the page for an exciting sneak preview of Dana Ransom's next Zebra historical romance, Wild Texas Bride, *to be published in February, 1995.*

One

"Don't nobody move! This is a robbery!"

Those rough words woke Sarah Bass from her indifferent dozing. Disbelief was shaken from her when the train gave a hard lurch and shuddered to a stop on the tracks. Immediately a wail of panic arose from some of the passengers, who were sure they were about to die at the hands of desperadoes, a din taken up by the large Mexican woman seated opposite as she clutched her son and called upon the saints for mercy in shrill Spanish. The young man beside Sarah had gone rigid with shock. Beneath his derby hat, his face was as white as the scarce clouds in the West Texas sky above. He clutched his new travel case in his lap with hands that trembled. Sarah also gripped her bag, comforted by the hard contour of the revolver she carried in it. She wasn't frightened. She was mad as hell. She wanted to get home in the worst way and had no patience with the interruption.

"Elevate your hands so's we can be about our business," came the easy voice from the back of the car. "Present your valuables when asked and nobody'll get hurt."

Sarah felt a sudden prickle of recognition. That voice—she knew it! Straightening in her seat, she craned her neck, trying to see back to where the train robber stood. She'd started to rise up when the man across the aisle, who'd previously been sleeping under the tilt of his Stetson, rolled out of his place and clapped a hand upon her shoulder. In his other hand, he held a Colt Peacemaker.

"Nothing to see, ma'am. Plant your bustle and keep yer eyes front."

He forcefully shoved her back into her seat, driving an indignant "Oof!" from her as she gave a hard bounce. He paid her no mind as he drew his neckerchief up over his nose and joined the looters.

"Cabron," she growled, and instantly regretted it when he stopped and gave her a reassessing glance.

"Now, that may be true, ma'am, but it don't sound nice coming outta a lady's mouth."

Chastised but no less furious, Sarah settled on the bench seat and stared sullenly ahead, her chin taking an independent tip that made the outlaw chuckle as he moved on.

"Miss Bass," the young Easterner beside her whispered. "You shouldn't anger men such as these." He touched her arm with a soft, unblemished hand, and his passivity rankled her sorely.

"What do you know of men such as these, Mr. Blankenship? I highly doubt that you've come into the acquaintance of any while selling your snake oil in the city."

Herbert Blankenship blushed and drew back his gesture as the deceivingly fragile Sarah continued her soft tirade.

"These men are cowards who hide behind masks and steal other folks' hard-earned dollars. My brother will hunt them down and grind them beneath his boot heel."

The smooth-faced salesman looked heartened. "Is your brother a sheriff, Miss Bass?"

"My brother's a Texas Ranger."

Sarah had the satisfaction of seeing the young man's eyes go round with awe. And she would have the further satisfaction of seeing these lawbreakers brought to justice. But first she would have to endure the humiliation of being robbed, and that sat ill with her. She clutched her bag. There were only two of them. A couple of well-placed shots . . .

Just then, there was a groan as the front door of the coach was thrown open and two more bandits entered. So much for heroics, she thought grudgingly. She was impulsive, yes, but hardly suicidal. She wasn't carrying anything of worth, other than trinkets and gifts for her family. If they'd wanted money, they should have robbed her on her way to Austin, not as she came home from there. None but a fool brought a fortune into the Bend of Texas.

The woman across from her was crying again, her sobbing prayers upsetting the child held to her breast. Sarah leaned forward to pat the mother's heaving shoulder, murmuring comforting words in Spanish. As she did so, one of the bandits strode by her toward the others at the front of the car. His long canvas duster was tucked behind an impressive brace of pistols. He was a tall man with a swaggering walk, a familiar walk. But she wasn't sure until he turned slightly and the coat swung away from long, long legs. She didn't have to see his face. Sarah would never as long as she lived forget that expansive stretch of denim-hugged limb.

What in heaven's name was Billy Cooper doing robbing a train?

Surprise subdued her more efficiently than any threat. Collapsing back against the seat, Sarah watched him as he spoke to the others. He, too, was masked behind a triangular bandana fold and wore his hat pulled low atop a head of unruly shoulder-length blond hair. But no amount of disguise could fool her. How could she mistake the man who'd given her the spectacular taste of her first kiss? How could she not know the young ranger who'd captured a thirteen-year-old's heart? She remembered every detail of that first meeting in her uncle's front yard. Seeing Billy Cooper seated on his horse in the company of his fellow Texas Rangers had started her pulse racing with an unknown excitement and she'd savored that sudden breathlessness. He'd been little more than a green kid then, a couple of years younger than her brother, Jack, who'd been a lean, hard twenty. She'd known the minute she looked up into those dark, daring eyes that this was the man she wanted to teach her all about kissing. At thirteen, she'd been dying to know what it was like. At seventeen, she was no less eager to learn other things. And she'd never given up hope that Billy Cooper would teach her all of it.

But that was before he'd gone from being her brother's trusted second-in-command to a lowly train robber.

What would turn a man from an honorable life's mission to passing a hat to relieve folks of their valuables? Sarah wondered and frowned as Billy moved from seat to seat, coaxing her fellow passengers to dig deep with the same charismatic cheerfulness as a tent evangelist. How could she have been so wrong about him? By the time he reached her seat, she was seething with a confused outrage. His dark eyes touched upon hers and she held her breath, waiting for a shock of recognition. Then he looked away without pause.

He didn't remember her!

"Your contributions, if you please," he drawled amiably. He gave his hat a shake, rattling the coins and jewelry he'd already collected.

"And if we don't please?"

As Sarah spoke up boldly, the young man beside her pinched her so hard she almost yelped.

The dark eyes gazing down at her crinkled up at the corners and she could see the creases of his devilish dimples over the edge of the bandana. "Why, I'm sure a little lady as pretty as you would want to be obliging."

"Not when it comes to sniveling, underhanded, sneak thieves like you, sir."

Herbert Blankenship gasped and appeared close to swooning, but the bandit's good humor never faltered.

"I'm right sorry you feel that way, missy. Could it be you prefer I was to search your delightful person myself?"

An unexpected tremor shook through her. Sarah refused to recognize it as anticipation. She'd liked his handling well enough at one time, but those were different circumstances. He hadn't been thinking of stealing anything but a kiss from her then. Her reply was tart. "That won't be necessary." And she dug into her handbag to withdraw what few dollars she had left. Instead of putting them into the proffered hat, she dropped them to the aisle runner.

There was a low chuckle from behind Billy.

"That sweet thing giving you trouble, kid?"

Billy looked back at the man who'd spent most of the trip snoring across the aisle from Sarah. "Naw. I think she's flirting with me." He bent and scooped up the bills, never taking his eyes off Sarah's defiant features.

"Whatcha got in that there case, slick?" the second robber wanted to know. Herbert automatically hugged it to his chest.

"Just samples, sir. I'm a traveling medicine salesman," he stammered out in a thin voice.

"Then maybe you got the cure for what ails me."

"He doesn't have anything you want," Sarah spoke up tersely in defense of her pallid companion. He didn't look pleased with her protectiveness. He was expecting to be shot at any minute and was eager to appear very cooperative, lest he rile the men.

"You two traveling together?" Billy drawled out softly, with just enough implied menace to have Herbert quaking.

"Yes," Sarah snapped, wanting him to believe that.

"No!" Herbert yelped, praying he wouldn't be associated with the young woman's boldness.

Dark eyes went back and forth between the unlikely couple as if trying to understand the connection, of why a tough Texas beauty would link up with a simpering salesman. The other bandit had no such curiosity.

"Empty yer pockets. Now!"

And with the six-shooter shoved under his nose, the young passenger fumbled to do as he was told, coming up with a shiny gold watch and a sterling money clip thick with folded greenbacks.

"I'm feeling better already," the robber confided. He relieved the man of his goods, then deliberately knocked the sample case to the floor. There was the unmistakable sound of shattering glass and various colors of fluid seeped out onto the floor between the salesman's patent leathers.

"That was hardly necessary," Sarah said. She hated bullying almost as much as she hated lawlessness. A pair of chill blue eyes cut over to her. The man was no longer affable, and she swallowed quickly. She recognized danger when she saw it, and this man was a rattler in the coil.

"A regular razorback, ain't you, miss? You think he'd be as quick to come to your rescue? I think not. You forgetting something?"

When a gloved hand reached for the locket she wore around her neck, Sarah covered it with her hand.

"It's not worth anything," she protested. "At least, not to anybody but me."

Still, he caught her hand, compressing it until she gasped in pain and let go. With his other hand, he snatched up the pendant and broke the slender chain with a jerk. Sarah sat back, panting in fierce frustration.

"Lemme see that." Billy took it from his criminal associate. He flipped the catch with his thumbnail to open the triple hinges and regarded the small portraits held inside. A man and woman, the woman an older image of the one before him. A pale-eyed handsome man. Two boys, both dark and similar. Another couple, the woman blonde and delicate, the man swarthy, with light eyes. She held a baby in her arms. He looked uncomfortable. And there was no way Billy Cooper couldn't have recognized her family.

Yet he closed the locket and let it drop indifferently onto her knees. "Junk," he proclaimed callously, then, to the other man, said, "Let's get a move on."

Sarah scooped up the treasured locket. Junk? How dared he spit on her cherished memories! Or had he just saved them for her? She clutched the heirloom, wondering if she should be furious or grateful. Surely Texas etiquette didn't require thanking one's robber. She stared up into the unblinking dark eyes, trying to force some sort of reaction from him. He betrayed none. Then, with an impersonal nod, he readied to walk away.

The bully angled by to take up the collection, but before Billy could continue after him, Sarah decided she couldn't stand it any longer. She grabbed the sleeve of his coat. When he glanced down at her, she hissed, "Why are you doing this?"

"Man's gotta eat, ma'am."

"That's not what I meant and you know it."

"I'm afraid I know nothing of a kind, ma'am. You must be mistaken—"

"I'm not!"

Then his fingertips touched to her mouth, effectively stilling any further argument she thought to give. His fingers were rough and warm, the gesture gentle as they moved along the line of her lips as if to seal them shut. His dark eyes delved straight to her soul.

"You don't know anything," he corrected quietly. And before she could think of a retort, he was moving down the row of seats with his hat full of stolen treasures.

"Billy!" she called after him in an intense whisper. He paused for just an instant, then strode on without looking back, following his fellow outlaws out the rear door of the coach.

Within minutes, the train was wheezing and gathering steam again, the straining chugs evening out into the strong rhythm of the rails. The passengers began to chatter with a nervous exhilaration, grateful to be alive and grumbling about their losses and the boldness of the desperadoes. Sarah sat silent, fingering her locket.

He'd known who she was. Was he just too embarrassed to admit it? Too shamed that she'd caught him at his nefarious work? Or had he truly forgotten a starry-eyed youngster who'd teased him for his kiss four years ago, having to be reminded of her by the picture she carried of her brother, the best friend he was betraying by opposing the laws of Texas?

Beside her, young Blankenship was moaning over his case of ruined goods. Nearly all his sample bottles had been broken, yet he had a frail smile for her when he saw her notice.

"You were very brave, Miss Bass. That villain was right in what he said. I'd have never had the nerve to stand up to him the way you did." He didn't say he thought what she did was sensible, only that it impressed him. His eyes were warm pools of admiration. "You must have learned courage from having a brother in the Texas Rangers."

Sarah smiled. That was part of it, part of a long Texas tradition of heroes. But she didn't speak of it to Herbert Blankenship. Her father, Will Bass, had been a legendary ranger until he'd been crippled by a bushwhacker's bullet just before the Texas Frontier Battalion had disbanded at the end of the War Between the States. Her uncle, Harmon, was equally well known as a part-Apache tracker who'd gained fame in a series of dime novel exploitations. Jack, her half-brother, had followed his stepfather's path in the rangers, joining up at sixteen when they were reformed and earning a lieutenancy in the Big Bend of Texas by the time he turned twenty. She'd grown up surrounded by examples of bravery. Even her mother and the two women who'd married into the Bass family were grit to the backbone. Sitting through a train robbery was next to nothing compared to the stories told around their kitchen table, tales of when the Texas frontier was truly wild and dangerous, like the men who tamed it. Those were the feats she'd cut her teeth upon in her younger years and why she was more annoyed than terrified by the sight of a few masked men.

What had turned Billy Cooper to the wrong side of the law?

Sarah had thought nothing was more important than getting home, but the farther the train moved from the scene of the robbery, the more her thoughts lingered behind. What a fitting welcome back to the Big Bend of Texas. Her heart was hurrying with a stir of emotion for the first time in a long while, and it made her aware of how tame her existence had become.

She'd spent the summer months in Austin, where her

brother, Sidney, was going to school. Under the supervision of her father's sister, she'd gotten her first taste of city life. It had been exciting, the influx of people, the varied entertainments, the clothes . . . the men! Her aunt had scolded her regularly for being such an incorrigible flirt, but after only two weeks within society circles, she'd received no less than five proposals from city beaux. She'd been flattered, but she couldn't picture any of those proper dandies surviving more than a day without wilting in the scorch of the Bend, where she'd grown up. Flirting was fine and fun, but for a life's mate, she wasn't interested in a man who carried a top hat and white gloves and asked permission to kiss her cheek. She wanted the stuff of legends. She wanted to wed a hero.

What good was a man who had to ask if a woman wanted to be kissed?

Besides, after four years, her lips were still shaped to the fit of the first man who'd tasted them.

Homesickness had settled deep and desolate into her heart. She knew her mother was hoping she'd be taken with city life and choose to stay. Rebecca Bass was always harping on her daughter to better herself, but to Sarah, things didn't get much better than what she already had. She had a family who loved and pampered her shamelessly, and she had freedom. Out on the vast plains of West Texas, no one cared if she wore the proper shoes and pinned a silly little hat at just the right tilt. She wanted to wear britches and a good Stetson and ride astraddle across the endless miles stretching from horizon to horizon. And she yearned for the company of folks who were a little shy of being completely civilized.

She missed her Aunt Amanda's cheerful prattle and her Uncle Harmon's stoic smile and endless patience as he taught her how to read signs off the hard-packed earth. She was hungry for the affection filling her brother Jack's house like the warm, inviting scent of just-baked pies and the noise of all her boisterous young relatives. Her hours were empty without the thrill of watching her younger brother break in a mustang or the lean and handsome rangers riding out to serve the sprawling State of Texas. She longed for the simplicity and security of home, and the thought of spending the approaching holidays without them was more pain than she could bear. And finally, her mother agreed to let her return. She was on the first westbound train, her heart and mind filled up with memories and faces, anxious to embrace them all.

Until Billy Cooper had stolen her cash and carried off her dreams with that long, lanky stride of his. She was frowning all over again just thinking of it.

Just wait until she told Jack . . .

Then what? He'd be forced to go after his best friend to see justice done. And Texas justice was not a pretty thing to behold or to wish upon those you knew, even if they had betrayed a precious trust.

Sarah was troubled by her thoughts. No one else could identify Billy as one of the outlaws, but when Jack questioned her, could she tell less than the whole truth? What did she owe the former ranger? Just because he'd kissed a giddy thirteen-year-old and made her pulse race for four entire years with hopes of more, what allegiance did she have to keep his secret safe? If she said nothing, she was as good as an accomplice in the crime. And that notion upset her staunch sense of honor. She couldn't lie for him, not to her own brother.

But if she didn't see Jack, he couldn't ask the questions

and she needn't choose to tell him any falsehoods. At least, until she got her answers from Billy Cooper.

He owed her an explanation.

How dared he eat at her family's table and enjoy her brother's trust and her uncle's rarely given respect, and then do such a thing! How could he kiss her and make her love him madly, then compromise her moral well-being to cover up his misdeeds?

How could he forget her so easily?

The train slowed in a cloud of steam and cinders as it entered the next station stop in Marathon. There, she was close to beginning the southern rail loop home. But as the engine hissed and snorted and the passengers were eagerly telling their views of the robbery to the local law officers who got on board, Sarah made her decision. She said a hasty goodbye and wished a good journey to Herbert Blankenship and got off the Southern Pacific with only her travel case in hand. Purposefully, she walked away from the chaos of the station area and made her way into town. There, she found a merchant willing to take her eastern finery in trade for sturdy boots and a sensible split skirt. With a pang of regret, she bartered the gifts she'd bought for her family to purchase a good horse and saddle.

And then, without considering the consequences, she rode out of Marathon in search of Billy Cooper and the reasons for his defection.

Harmon Bass had taught her well.

No one shy of a full-blooded Apache could run a trail as well as Sarah's Uncle Harm, and he had passed the rudiments along, first to Jack, then to her.

She backtracked along the rails until she crossed the outlaws' path. Seven horses ridden by heavy men, easy to follow in the West Texas dust. She rode at a brisk pace, an eye upon ground that was sandy and flat. She didn't have to guess where they would lead. Once the Indian menace was curbed, the rugged Bend area had filled up with badmen seeking refuge. The Chisos Basin provided a hospitable home and a centralized base for raids on both sides of the border. And it was territory she knew well. Harm and his family lived on the western foothills at Blue Creek. Her own ranch was less than a half day further out.

By nightfall, she had camped in the shelter of the mountains. She slept wrapped in her meager blankets and embraced by the endless heavens. It was cold, but her anticipation as well as the small fire she built held it at bay. She cooked thick sections of rattlesnake for breakfast. She'd learned to like it while camping out with her uncle. He told her a smart man—or woman—would eat anything that didn't eat them first. She took him at his word and enjoyed every bite. Then she was back in the saddle and on the trail again.

It was slower going in the hills. The ground was rocky, and she made several wrong turns and spent time retracing her steps. But she was patient and she was careful. She'd learned that from Harm, too. Unfortunately, she'd never absorbed his canny knack for self-preservation. He always knew when danger was near. It was like a sixth sense gleaned from his Apache relatives. Sarah's senses were dulled by pampered living, and she missed the warnings of trouble to come.

And totally oblivious, she blundered right into the outlaw camp.

The scouts had been watching her approach for some time and the bandits were waiting. They converged upon her horse with guns drawn. Realizing her mistake too late, she simply let go of the reins and elevated her hands. When they saw what they had was a woman, the hostile attitude dropped from her captors. What replaced it was hardly preferable.

They made no move to pull her down from her horse and she rode right into the center of their hideout. It wasn't much; several ramshackle cabins huddling against the canyon wall, a cluster of crude tents hugging a narrow stream, a great store of weaponry and horses. And a number of border whores.

Her common sense was completely knocked askew when the first sight she saw was that of Billy Cooper, relaxing with a bottle and a lap full of harlot. She was off her mount before her guards knew what she was about, and they were too surprised to stop her as she marched across the camp.

Surprise was too mild a word to describe the expression on Billy's face. That look deepened into mortal shock when Sarah jerked out her pistol and directed it with steady purpose, not at him, but at the scantily clad tart reclining in sluttish abandon upon his chest.

And with deadly calm, Sarah Bass growled, "Get up off my fiancé before I blow you straight to Hell!"